I0681801

This story is a product of the author's own imagination. Any similarity to any characters or persons, living or dead, is coincidental. The names of people, places and or things, used in this fictional novel are used for literary purposes only.

J. H. Watrous reserves all rights to this work, for himself and his heirs. Any or all reproductions of this work, must have written consent from J. H. Watrous or his heirs.

Contact at:
jhwatrous@oregonsales.com

Published in the Pacific Northwest by:
Pass Creek Publishing
P.O. Box 1179
Cottage Grove, Oregon 97424

"This story would not have come to print, if not for the loving support and patience of my wife, Betty. With ever present love, I dedicate these pages to her."

J J

A STORY ABOUT LIFE
by J.H. Watrous

Seattle 1941, Jay Samuel Johnson, known to his friends and family by his nickname, J J. Standing six foot one and weighing 180 pounds, a muscular built twenty year old, sits proudly smiling to himself and those he passed, astride his shiny 1937 Harley-Davidson, as he cruises through the cool morning air, on his way to work. As another, potentially beautiful Northwest summer day, unfolds on the road before him, and his magnificent riding machine.

The country was only now recovering from a devastating, decade long, economic depression. J J was lucky, to have a loving grandfather take him under his wing, to teach him an honorable trade. Working as an apprentice machinist. They were both fortunate his grandfather's small company, was a subcontractor for a large airplane manufacture, located in the Seattle, Washington area. Work at times was hard and often tedious, but always challenging. This was a time when life moved at a much slower pace and one could be proud of their accomplishments. J J, was also blessed to have a loving new bride, his Jera Marie, to come home to. Jera, a happy nineteen year old, very much in love with her new husband. Happily living together in their newly completed dream home, with hopes and dreams, of a long and happy life together . . . .

. . . After all, that had become, "The American Dream."

TIME MOVES ON !

Seattle 1984, forty three years later. Jera Marie, now sixty three and in good health, sits in the kitchen of that same dream home, with her 36 year old daughter-in-law, Dorris. The two of them watching Marie's grandson, J J, Dorris's son, shooting hoops in the backyard. Gazing out the window, Marie says. "I wish J J, could have known his grandfather. J J's father Sam, was not like his grandfather J J. My son Sam, was a quiet private man. J J's grampa, was an out going happy go lucky guy, he would talk to anyone, anywhere, anytime. After all these years, I still love thinking and talking about, the only man I ever loved. Even though, we were only married a year, before J J . . . was lost, I still feel the hair on the back of my neck stand up and I tremble all over. . . . Even now, I can sense his presence, as I sit here looking around our home we built together. Dorris, I know you've heard these stories a hundred times, but you'll never know, how much my grandson, reminds me of his grandfather. The way he walks, his mannerisms, his beautiful smile and love of people. Your visits here, mean a lot to me, Dorris. I want to thank you for sharing your son with me. His father Sam, my son, was more like Pop Miller, my Dad. A wonderfully kind and good hearted man, always holding back, putting others first. Dorris, I realize you have not had it easy after Sam's death, raising a boy by yourself in these busy times. I had it much easier raising Sam, in the forties, fifties and sixties. Than you've had raising J J, in the seventies and eighties."

The two women sat comparing memories of events that had taken place in the raising of their sons, as single parents. They proved, not only to themselves, but to many onlookers, they not only had the strength, but were also very capable of the challenges, of raising their sons in tough times.

Dorris smiles, as she sits looking around Marie's cozy kitchen and through it's windows towards a beautiful yard, with it's vegetable and flower gardens, separated by a wonderfully weathered green house. Marie's home had become a friendly place to come, and share feelings and draw strength. After all, they both had lost a husband, and fathers to their sons. Her son J J, was the link that drew the three generations together. The poem, Marie has hanging above her kitchen table says it best, "Let each days strength, sufficient be, to meet the needs, that we shall see."

The poem was composed and signed, by Marie's and J J's personal love phrase: "To love, with love, from love."

Breaking the quiet spell. Marie asks. "Dorris, would you like some hot tea?"

"Yes, I would, thank you."

Marie not showing her age, gets up gracefully from the kitchen table.

"Let me do that, Marie," Dorris says getting up.

"I'll do it, thank you, Dorris," said Marie, putting a hand on Dorris's shoulder. She then turned and walked towards the back door. Opening the door. "J J, would you like a drink?" Marie lovingly asks.

"No, thank you, Gramma, not right now," answered her grandson, as he once more threw the basketball at the netless hoop.

"Ok hon," said Marie, as she closed the door. Walking back through the kitchen, she picked up an old kettle from it's shelf on her way to the sink. "Black tea ok, dear?" asked Marie, as she filled the kettle. She then put the kettle on the stove and lit the burner.

"Yes, that's fine," Dorris replies.

"Dorris, J J is going to be ten. He is becoming quite a young man. Do you have any plans for his birthday?" Marie asks, as she took the hot kettle from the stove and poured the hot water into a tea pot, to be sat on the table.

"My mother would like us to come to her house, for his birthday."

"That would be nice," Marie answers, with a change in her voice.

"Marie, why don't you come with us?"

"That might be fun! I haven't seen your mother and father, for a long time. I will think about it, and let you know. Thank you dear." With a smile back on her face, Marie walked carrying the teapot towards the table.

Bouncing his ball up the back stairs J J stops on the top step. Leaving his basketball there, he turned and opened the door and entered the kitchen. Walking towards the sink, he grabbed a glass from a cupboard, on the way by. He turned the faucet on and stood there at the sink, letting the water run to get cold. With the glass full of cool water, he turned the faucet off and then walked towards the table, to sit with his mother and grandmother. "Whata whe guna do?" asked J J, talking like the vultures in the Disney movie, <u>Jungle Book</u>. Shrugging his shoulders as he rocked in his chair.

"We were just talking and having some tea. Would you like some cookies with your drinks?" Marie asks, getting up from her chair, starting towards the cookie jar, that sits on the counter.

"No thank you." The two replied. J J sprang from his chair at the table, walking quickly to where his grandmother was standing. "Let's go into the living room Gramma. And look at pictures of Grampa J J. You can tell us a story."

Marie looked at Dorris. "Would that be all right with you?"

"That's fine with me, Marie. My son and I, have always enjoyed your stories." Dorris picked up the tea pot. "Here J J, you carry this pot. I will get the cups."

The three of them moved into the living room. Putting the pot on the coffee table, J J turned to help his mother with the cups.

"I have them, thank you," said Dorris, as she bent to put the cups on the table.

J J standing next to the table, looks around the room. Slowly turning, as not to miss anything, remembering, 'this story time, had become very special to both him, and his grandmother.'

The living room of Jera Marie Johnson's home, was a warm and friendly place. Pictures everywhere, on the walls, tables, fireplace mantel, and any other place you could hang or set one. Each picture a story to be told. There were pictures of Marie and J J's wedding. Their honeymoon to Yellowstone, J J in uniform, Sam as a baby, wedding pictures of Sam and Dorris, and of course, pictures of J J, Marie's only grandchild. The room has a large window that faces west, making the room bright and sunny.

J J stopped turning, his eyes focused on one particular picture. He walked slowly over to the table. Bending, he carefully picks up the picture in both hands. He then carries the photograph over to his grandmother sitting on the sofa. The picture was one of his grandfather in uniform, J J's favorite. Handing the picture to her, he goes to sit on the coffee table.

"Don't sit there son. Sit here on the sofa, with your grandmother and I." Dorris moves to make room for her son on the sofa. She then picked up her tea cup and sat back, to relax.

Marie looked down at the photo she held in her hand, smiling even more as she did. She then started telling her attentive audience the story of her husband, 'The Marine.' "Your grandfather was proud to be a Marine, and help his country in time of war. He could have been deferred from service, because of his job at the machine shop. But in 1942, before your father was born, he joined and was shipped to the South Pacific. It was 189 days later, when a Navy officer came to the door with heart wrenching news, a telegram, to inform me, that the only man I ever loved, was missing in action, and presumed dead."

Marie smiling with tears in her eyes, puts her hand into the pocket of her apron and pulls out a hankie, to dry her eyes . . . Marie continued telling J J and his mother, about his grandfather.

"It was about two months after the war ended, in 1945. There was a knock at the door. On the porch stood a man I thought I knew, but wasn't sure. He introduced himself. I knew the name. He was J J's good friend, Robert Robinson. J J had sent me a picture of the two of them together. That's how I recognized him."

Marie laid the picture carefully on the table. She then rose from the sofa and moved to the mantel. There she picked up the picture of the two men and returned to the sofa. Marie began to tell how Robby, that's what J J called him, came into her living room that day, and stood watching, as Sam played with his toy trucks, on the living room floor.

She told Robby, 'Sam was J J's son.' The two sat for awhile, sitting together making light conversation as they watched, as a healthy lively young boy, happily played with his toys. Knowing in their hearts, here was a boy 'deprived of the joys of knowing his father.' Robby and Marie exchanged long looks, until finally, Robby took in a deep breath, in order to gain some composure.

"Why I came Marie, is to tell you that I was with J J, when he was lost."

"Robby's voice shaking, as he started to tell his story."

"J J and I, with two others, were asked to do a night mission. We were to travel by a rubber boat, to a small island. Once there, we were to go ashore and investigate the island's potential, as a possible location for a lookout station. The four of us quickly volunteered. At this point we couldn't wait to see some action. We were so excited! We grabbed our gear and went topside. From the port side of the ship, we went over the rail down a net that hung to the side of the ship, to the rubber raft tide below. Using a hand compass to show the way, we paddled the raft towards the island. It was very dark and extremely hard to see. We could hear the waves breaking and white foam becoming visible, as the waves hit the rocks. We went through heavy surf towards the beach. The four of us pulled the raft out of the water, onto a rocky beach. As soon as possible, we left the beach and moved into a dense jungle. We could hardly move, the jungle was so thick. For thirty to forty minutes, the four of us wrestled our way through the jungle. Then we came upon a well used trail. We followed the trail, moving as quietly as possible. There was light showing on the upper part of the trees. J J suddenly stopped and whispered, "I hear something." We froze in our tracks. The others and I listened. Yes, we could also hear something. But what was it? The two others stayed there in the trail, to watch our backs. J J and I moved closer to the light and sounds. I was so frightened. My heart was pounding so loud, it soon, was all I could hear. I turned to J J, in the dim light I could see he also looked frightened, but determined. We continued moving towards the light and sounds. The sounds we heard, were voices, but it wasn't English we heard. It was Japanese! THE ENEMY! That's what we heard, they were speaking Japanese! We went in for a closer look. We were close enough we could actually see their faces. We watched the camp for what seemed like a life time. There were lots of Japs. I was so scared. J J tapped me on the arm and signaled for us to leave. I turned to move away from the camp. As I started to leave, I felt a slight resistance as I moved. I tried to stop, but it was too late. My boot had caught a booby trap trip wire. The trip wire caused noise in the Jap's camp. J J hollered, "Run!" I jumped up and ran! I could hear J J right behind me, as I ran on the trail towards the others. Run, I told the two guys waiting on the trail. They yelled, "what's wrong?" J J and I turned pointing. We could hear the Japs coming. "JAPS, RUN!" We yelled. The four of us ran leaving the trail, back into the thick jungle towards the beach. The four of us getting separated on the way. I was the third one back to the raft. The Japs were shooting at us! We could hear bullets flying over our heads, hitting the beach and water all around us. J J was missing! Then one of the others was hit. We had to leave! We pushed the raft into the dark sea, bullets flying like mad bees. We paddled into the darkness. That darkness saved our lives. I stopped paddling to check the wounded man. He was hit in the arm. I put a tourniquet above his wound, then went back to paddling. We paddled for a long time."

"Robby stopped talking. Looking over at me, with tears in his eyes, he said. "I'm so sorry, Marie. I wish it was J J here."

"Then putting his head down, Robby began to sob. I put my arm on his shoulder and we cried together."

"Robby, if you had stayed, you wouldn't be here to tell me how my J J was lost. You and the others, also would have been lost, or even killed. You had to leave. Thank you, Robby, for coming here to tell me this story."

Marie turned on the sofa and hugged her grandson. "Robby stayed for dinner that day. That was the last time I saw him. I did get cards for a time, but I haven't heard from him, for many years," said Marie, looking down at the picture she held. . . .

Once again Marie, Dorris and J J, were in Marie's living room. The three of them sitting together on her sofa. Marie telling her daughter-in-law and grandson, another one of J J's favorite stories.

Looking up from the picture she held on her lap, Marie turned to hug her grandson. Abruptly stopping short, she sat staring at him with a startled look on her face.

"What's wrong, Gramma?" asked J J, seeing the surprise on his grandmother's face.

"J J, I can't get over how much you look like your grandfather, especially in that uniform."

J J home on leave, having just graduated from Boot Camp, sat looking smartly, in his new uniform. It was now 1993. J J, now 19, had grown into a handsome young man. He had joined the Marines, as his grandfather before him, some 51 years earlier. J J wanted to be a Marine, for as long as he could remember.

"Gramma, they're sending us to the South Pacific for training," said J J, with a great deal of enthusiasm in his voice.

"I know this is what you've wanted all your life, and for this, I'm very happy for you, and very proud. You know Grampa, Pop Miller, is too. He just wants the best for you, J J. That's why he wants you to go to college. He felt the same way when your grampa joined. He wanted him to go to college too. But your grampa felt as strongly about joining the Marines, as you."

"Gramma, you know I plan on going to college, as soon as I get through with this obligation to myself and the Marine Corps."

"Yes, J J, I know," smiled Marie.

THE ATTACK

Three weeks later on an island
somewhere in the South Pacific.

J J, with three other Marines, were told to explore the island. The
jungle on the island was so thick, even though it was mid morning, under
it's dense canopy it was nearly dark. Trying to lighten their assignment
of trekking through the jungle, the four men were lightheartedly,
laughing and joking, having a good time. Two of the four were rapping,
the other two were trying to rap with the brothers. Rapping and jive
talking, all four were having a great time, joking around, as they
continued on through the everlasting never-ending undergrowth, of the
island's thick jungle.

In an instant, the jungle became a mass of confusion. The four men
were hit and thrown in different directions, as if they were each a small
child's rag doll. . . . All four were down, and the jungle was silent. . . .
J J felt a sharp pain in his chest, opening his eyes . . . in the dim light
descending faintly through the thick jungle, a h u g e knife became visible
over his chest. Held or paralyzed with fear, he couldn't move! The point
of the ominous knife came just above the name on his uniform, (Johnson,
J. S.). He could see a weathered hand holding the foreboding knife. His
eyes followed from the impending knife in-hand, up a sweaty tense arm,
to an absolutely hideous face. A face with an utterly terrifying single
vicious eye. The moment J J's eyes met with that single vicious eye, he
heard in a low voice, "Johnson, J. S.." Then someone shouted, "J J!"
Then the only sound he heard, was the pounding of his own heartbeat.
His mind raced, as his eyes looked up into that single vicious eye, as he
did, the vicious eye softened. J J could see the face was scarred. He heard
a sound, then a groan. In a heartbeat, whoever or whatever, had attacked
the four men, was gone. J J sat up, looking for his rifle. The sounds he
heard, were the others regaining consciousness. He sat there catching
his breath in disbelief, he was still able to breathe. J J was sitting there
thinking. 'Why was he still alive?' And 'very thankful he was.' Laying
down on his belly, he saw his rifle. He reached for and grabbed the rifle,
drawing it close to him. Looking around, he could see two of the three
men. He then saw the third. He got up slowly. More alert than he had ever

been in his life. Making sure they knew it was him, he went to each man, checking to see if any of them had been injured or even killed. To his amazement, they all seemed ok. Very confused, but O K! As they got their wits about them, they prepared for another attack.

"Who were those guys?" whispered one of the others.

"Good question, I don't know. But I do know, it was only one man, and he just beat the shit out of all four of us, why whisper? He knows where we are and could have killed all of us, and didn't," said J J.

"Then who was that masked man?" asked one of the others.

"It wasn't The Lone Ranger! It must have been SUPERMAN! He's probably a hand to hand combat specialist, of some kind. That's why, we're still alive. He had no intention of killing us," said J J.

"One of us could have killed him," said Bo.

"Ya right, with our bare hands. The man knows the area. No live rounds for our rifles. I think he was pretty safe. Obviously, we have been spared," answered, J J.

"Let him come back. We're ready now," said Bo.

"I think that's the point!" said J J.

The four had calmed down and started to compare their thoughts on the attack. As it turned out, J J was the only one of the four, that had seen their attacker's face and could somewhat describe the attacker.

"Now that I've had some time to think about it, his face was badly scarred all right, but not only that, there was something else. And why did he say my name, the way he did? It was like he knew me. He used my nickname, J J! Not my given name, or the name here on my uniform. He used J J."

"It's almost 1230 hours. Let's head back to camp and report the attack to the gunny. We'll see if he knows who attacked us," said corporal Kim.

The four men got slowly to their feet, moaning and groaning, as they did. "It feels like I've been run over by a truck," said Billy.

"I know what you mean," said Tye.

They started through the thick jungle, back towards their camp. They moved slowly, ready for, but not wanting another attack, from their one eyed attacker.

"The gunny! That's who sent the one eyed Superman to attack us," blurted corporal Kim.

"Why?" asked one of the others.

"For training! That's why we're on this island, is for training!" Replied the corporal.

"Ya, but the attack was so real, and so vicious! I thought I was going to die. They got my attention! I've been on the cutting edge ever since the attack. More alert than I've been, in my entire life. It worked for me," answered J J.

Moving slowly with the three others, J J, still thinking about their attacker's face, 'What was it about that face? Was he Black, Asian, White, he wasn't sure, but, that wasn't it. There was something else.'

As they got closer to where their camp was located. They could hear helicopters still bringing in more equipment, for their stay on the island. They had only been on the island part of one day and it had already proven to be an interesting one. Three steps from camp and they couldn't tell, except for the sounds of the equipment, that the camp was even there. That's how thick the jungle was on this island. As the four men walked into camp, they noticed how much it had changed, from earlier that day. Their hearts began to race as they entered camp, looking for the gunny.

"Where is the gunny?" the corporal asked, the first man they came to.

"In the command tent, I think?"

That was news to them. There wasn't a command tent, when they left that morning.

"Command tent?" asked the corporal.

"That one, the one that says command tent, above the door," laughed the marine pointing.

The four men stopped at the door of the command tent.

"You guys, wait here. I'll see if the gunny is here. If he is, I'll report. Then I'll ask, if he sent the one eyed attacker." Corporal Tye Kim, a small Asian man from southern California. Tye, is absolutely petrified, of Gunnery Sergeant Roman. The corporal entered the tent. The gunny was sitting at a desk, facing the door.

"Gunnery Sergeant, Corporal Kim, reporting."

"At ease, Corporal, report."

"Gunnery Sergeant, we were attacked!"

"What do you mean, Corporal, attacked? Attacked by what?"

"Gunnery Sergeant, my men and I, were attacked by . . . by one man."

"What? All four of you?"

"Yes, all of us but Johnson, were knocked out."

"Which Johnson? Where's Johnson now?"

"J J? He's outside with the others."

"Get them in here, Corporal!"

"Yes, Gunnery Sergeant!" The corporal turned and exited the tent.

"Kim, what did he say?" asked the others, as he came out of the tent.

"He wants to talk to all of us." The corporal turned and re-entered the tent. The others followed.

"At ease men. Are you men all right?" asked Gunnery Sergeant Roman, as the men entered the tent.

"Yes, Gunnery Sergeant," they all answered.

"Ok then. Tell me about this attack."

"We thought you may have sent him," said corporal Kim.

"Why would you think that? For what?"

"For training, Gunnery Sergeant," answered the corporal.

"Good point, but I didn't send anyone to attack you men. I just had you men go into the jungle, to see if you could find your way back to camp. And you did! So, tell me what happened, Corporal."

"Gunny, we were all moving east through the jungle. Bo and Billy were ah, were together! J J, was with me. The jungle was so thick, we could just see each other in the dim light. It had been about three hours since we left camp. Then without warning, he attacked. The next thing I knew, I was coming to, with J J asking me, if I was all right."

"And you, Johnson?"

"Gunnery Sergeant, I."

"Not you private! The other Johnson," interrupted the gunny.

The other Johnson, the gunny referred to, was Bo Johnson. Bo a good hearted large Black man, from Detroit.

"Gunnery Sergeant, all I was trying to do was get this big body of mine through that damn jungle. Next thing I knew, I was hit on the back of my neck and everything went black. I couldn't tell you, if he was short or tall, or even what color he was, Gunnery Sergeant. I never even seen the Superman!"

"What did you see, Smith?" asked the gunny.

Billy Smith, another Black man from Sacramento, California.

"Gunnery Sergeant, I didn't see anything before the attack. After I regained consciousness, it felt like I had been run over by a truck. I didn't see anything, Gunny."

"Well, Private Johnson, I hope you can add something! Corporal Kim said, that it was only one man that attacked, all four of you!"

"Gunnery Sergeant, I saw only one man. There could have been more, but that's all I saw, was one, Gunny."

"Can you four explain to me, how one man, could whip four Marines?" asked the gunny, with hostility in his eyes.

"We didn't know we were going to be attacked. We were trying to get through the jungle and at the same time, we didn't have any idea that our lives were in danger. He took us, one at a time, by surprise. Starting with

Bo and Billy, then J J and I. I think, J J was last," answered the corporal.

"Johnson, what did this man look like? Was he a Marine?"

"I don't know, but I don't think so, Gunny. His face was scarred, on the right side, and he had only one eye. I doubt if he is a Marine. I'm sure it's also hard to imagine the impact and force, this one individual had. It's also hard to understand why he didn't kill or seriously harm any of us. Gurrery Sergeant, the attack was so vicious. I'm sure he was going to kill all of us, then something changed his mind. He was about my size and build, and in excellent shape," answered J J.

"How old. . . ?"

"That's it! I'm sorry, for interrupting, Gunny."

"What, Private Johnson?"

"I knew there was something else about that face! The face was scarred, but it was also old. Real old! That's what I saw, when I looked into that single vicious eye. All I remembered, was the eye, and scars. It didn't sink in how old the face was, until now. It's hard to say how old, because of the scars. But old! For as long as I live, I will always be haunted, by that scarred, one eyed face. I'm sure there's a story behind that face."

"Let me get this straight. Four Marines, were attacked, and knocked unconscious, by a one eyed, old man! Give me a break!" said the gunny, with sarcasm in his voice.

"That's what happened, Gunny!" said corporal Kim, in a surprisingly stern manner.

"Ok, if that's your story. I don't want a word of this to leave this tent. Is that understood?"

"Yes, Gunnery Sergeant."

"Is there a mark on any of you men? Something to help show proof of the attack?"

"There has to be a bruise or something on my neck, where he hit me, Gunnery Sergeant," said Bo.

"You're Black, would a bruise show?" asked the gunny.

"Yes! And we sunburn too!" snapped Billy.

"A bruise would be somewhat convincing, but I'd say something more impressive, would be a vital fluid of life. Like blood!"

"I hadn't thought about it, but there may be a mark on my chest, from the point of that huge sharp looking knife."

"You men, take your gear and shirts off. Look for cuts or bruises or something."

"Yes, Gunnery Sergeant."

The four men started to remove their gear, as they did, J J noticed his binoculars were missing. "Gunny, my binoculars are gone. I didn't lose them, because the strap was under my pack's straps. The strap is still here! It's been cut! I must have been knocked unconscious, after all. He must of taken the binoculars, just before I opened my eyes." J J continued to remove his gear, as did the others. As he started to remove his shirt soaked with sweat, he could see it also had been cut. Around the cut was blood. J J stood looking down the front of his blood stained, sweaty undershirt. "Here's your vital fluid of life, Gunnery Sergeant."

"I'll be damned! Are you sure you're all right, Private?" asked the gunny, as he got up from his desk. Walking around to the other side and then sitting on it's front edge. Gunnery Sergeant Roman slowly folded his arms, and stood starring at the undershirt, soaked with the vital fluid of life. Blood!

"Yes, I think so, Gunny," answered J J. Undoing his belt and pulling the undershirt out of his pants, and pulling the shirt off over his head, revealed dried matted blood on his chest. Using the blood soaked shirt, J J brushed off some of the dried blood, revealing a deep cut about an inch long. At this same time, corporal Kim was removing his undershirt.

"Look at the bruise on Kim's chest," said Billy Smith. With his arms still over his head, pulling the undershirt off. The others could easily see a large bruise, on Kim's left side. "A bruise may not show up that well on a brother, but you can see'em. Look here, at the back of Bo's neck, and here at the side of mine," said Billy.

"You four men definitely were in a conflict! It wasn't with each other was it?"

"No, It wasn't!" They all answered.

"Is there anything else, that you can remember, about the attack or the attacker?"

"Yes, Gunny, there is. The way the attacker, said my name. He read the name on my uniform. But he said my name, J J, like he knew me! I know, I didn't know him!"

"That's weird? I better have the medic take a look at you men. Then we'll try to figure out, who it could have been that attacked you." The gunny walked over and opened the door. He stepped outside and ordered the first man he saw. "Private, go find the medic. Tell him, I said, 'to get his kit and report to the command tent, ASAP!"

"Yes, Gunnery Sergeant!"

The gunny re-enter the tent, walking over to and around the end of the desk, he sits back in his chair. "Well men, this island was reportedly, uninhabited. I think you four, might have reason to dispute that report. What do you think?"

"Yes, Gunnery Sergeant!"

Just then the door opened. The medic came in, with his kit in hand. "Gunnery Sergeant, Corporal Hanson, reporting."

"Hanson, I want you to check out these four men."

"Yes, Gunnery Sergeant," said the medic, as he turned to look at the four men. "What happened to you?" asked Hanson.

The four men gazed at Gunnery Sergeant Roman, with a puzzled look on their faces.

"Never mind, Corporal. You just check them out!"

The corporal went right to J J, seeing the blood on his chest. The medic put his kit down. He turned, reaching for the chair at the end of the desk. "May I use this chair, Gunny?"

"Yes, of course, Corporal."

"Here Private, sit here. Let's have a look at that wound," said the medic, as he opened his kit. Removing some sealed packages containing sterile towels and a pair of rubber gloves. He started immediately to clean J J's wound with a towel and some liquid. "If there is too much discomfort, I could give you a shot."

"No, it's not bad," answered J J.

"This wound should have a couple of stitches," said the medic, looking over his shoulder at, the gunny.

"Can you do that, Corporal?"

"Yes, Gunny, but we should have the doctor, do it."

"The doc isn't here, you are! You do it, Corporal Hanson. Is that all right with you, Private Johnson?"

"It's all right with me."

"Is it all right with you, Corporal?" asked the gunny.

"As long as I can make sure the wound is clean, it would be fine with me, Gunny. But what will the Captain, Doc Brown say?"

"I will talk to the doc, he'll understand, Corporal."

"Ok, then. I'll have to give you a shot after all, Private, to help kill the pain." The medic reached into his kit. J J tried to see what the medic was doing, but couldn't. The medic came up with a hypodermic needle filled with a transparent liquid in hand. "This will kill most of the pain."

"Go a head, Hanson, I'm ready."

The medic proceeded getting ready to insert the hypodermic needle. "This will hurt, until the anesthetic works." As the medic inserted the needle, he heard a moan, then a loud thud from behind. He stopped what he was doing, turning to see what happened. There on the floor behind him, was Bo, laid out cold! Billy and corporal Kim, were bending over Bo, to see if they could help. "I'll bet he passed out from the sight of the this needle! It's real common. I shouldn't stop now, I'll check him, as soon as I've finished with this." After finishing with the injection. The medic checked Bo, who by this time, was regaining consciousness. "He'll be alright," said the medic, as returned to stitching up J J's wound. The wound took three stitches, to hold it together. After bandaging up the stitched wound. He checked the others. Bo's neck was bruised, as was Billy's. "Corporal Kim, you may have a couple cracked ribs. I will wrap you up, with this hook loop bandage, it should make you more comfortable. You can tighten or loosen it yourself, for comfort," said the medic, as he took the bandage out of his kit.

"Well, Corporal Hanson, are they all right?"

"Yes, Gunny. Corporal Kim and Private Johnson, the one with the cut, should be put on light duty. The other Johnson and Private Smith, are ok."

"Corporal Hanson, thank you for your help. You are dismissed."

"Yes, Gunnery Sergeant." He picked up his kit and a plastic bag, with the used hypodermic needle and other waste. "I will need to see Private Johnson tomorrow, to check his wound, Gunny. We don't want it to get infected."

Did you hear that Johnson?" asked the gunny.

"Yes, Gunny," answered J J.

The medic turned to leave. "I'll see you tomorrow," said the medic pointing at J J, as he opened the door, to leave.

"Corporal, forget you were here."

"Gunny. . . ? Yes, Gunnery Sergeant," said the medic as he left the tent. With the corporal gone, the four men and the gunny resumed their talk, about the attack.

"Well men, have you had any thought of who it could have been, that attacked you?"

"Gunny, I know when I first opened my eyes and saw that eye, it was full of rage. He was going to kill all of us, in my opinion, and didn't. He had us all down, and about to kill me, with that huge sharp knife. Then he read the name on my uniform and for some reason, his eye softened. He had changed his mind. He wasn't going to kill me. Then he just disappeared! It was like he thought we were someone else. We weren't the ones, he was supposed to kill," said J J, rubbing his wound, 'thinking how close he came to death.'

"We have a one eyed old man, out there in the jungle, who wants to kill someone, but we don't know who! You got me? This island was suppose to be uninhabited."

"Couldn't you have one of the Apache helicopters, fly over the island and use it's infrared sensor, to find the attacker?"

"That's a great idea, Corporal. It's too late today. We'll try that tomorrow. Report back here at 0630. Weather permitting, we'll call for an Apache, to scan the island and find this one eyed old man. You men go report to Sergeant Sanchez. The sergeant will show you what tent you've been assigned and where to stow your gear. Then get cleaned up for chow. You're dismissed."

"Yes, Gunnery Sergeant."

The four men got their gear together. Billy opened the door and then held it, for the others to exit the command tent.

"Well, I think that went pretty well, don't you?" asked Bo, as the four men walked along together.

"Ya right! He thinks we're a bunch of pussies. That's what I think," said J J.

"Who? You think Roman, thinks were pussies?"

"Well, think about it. What would you think? Four Marines, knocked unconscious, by one one-eyed old man?" answered J J.

"Ya! I see what you mean. Let's go find that sucker!"

"I think now, we better leave it up to the gunny," said corporal Kim.

"There's Sergeant Sanchez. Over there by that tent," said J J, as he pointed. The four men walked, in the direction that J J had pointed. They saw Sanchez standing, talking to another Marine. She saw them coming, as they walked towards her. The other Marine turned and walked away. The men had put on their outside shirts, so there wasn't any visible sign of the attack.

"Kim, I'm glad to see you made it back. Looks like you guys had a tough time of it."

Sergeant Maria Sanchez, was a good looking Hispanic woman about thirty years old, from San Diego. One of three women, in their detachment on the island. The other two, being privates.

"Yes, we sure did. You might say that jungle, damn near killed, all four of us," said corporal Kim.

"Come on now, it wasn't that bad, was it, Corporal? What are you guys..?" Sanchez, stopping short with her question.

"No, I guess not," laughed the sergeant.

"Could you show us what tent we're assigned, and where to stow our gear? Sergeant Roman said, to ask. Sanchez, you think we're pussies, don't you?" asked corporal Kim.

"What? Why would I think that? No. Not me," said Sanchez, with a grin.

"Your tent is over there, that one," said Sanchez, as she pointed.

"You're not the only one, Sanchez," whispered the corporal, as he turned to the others, and all three men looked at each other."

"What?"

"Never mind! The gunny told us to stow our gear and clean up for chow. Thank you, Sergeant."

"Ok. You're dismissed."

The four men headed for the tent, Sanchez, had pointed to. One at a time, they entered the tent. Once inside, they stood together a long moment. Throwing their gear aside, they breathed a long sigh of relief. Stacked in the middle, were cots and bed rolls. Their lockers were also there. They walked over and picked up a cot and bed roll each. Quickly, each man set up his own cot and made his bed. They then returned, one at a time, for their lockers, setting a locker at the foot of each bunk. The men then opened their lockers and removed some clean clothes and sat them atop the now closed lockers. Then each man slowly moved to his bunk, as if they were sleep walking, one at a time, they sat down and slowly removed their boots and gradually removed their clothes, and assumed a reclined position, on their cots, clad only in their underwear. In no time at all, it was time, to clean up for chow.

"We should have asked Sanchez, where the showers were? Oh well, we'll find them," said Kim, as he picked up his clean clothes from the lid of his locker. With their uncontaminated clean clothes in hand, they went to leave the tent.

"We'd best go together. Two of us can shower, while the others watch."

"What?"

"Let me rephrase that. Ok?"

"Ya. . . ! I hope to shout."

"What I meant was. While the others act as lookouts or sentries," said corporal Kim, with a bright red face.

"That's better!" said the others laughing.

The night was a long and restless one, for J J and the others. J J dreamed all night about the attack, or attacker, as did the others. Thoughts of the attacker, more than the attack itself, were in J J's dreams. While he was dreaming, for some reason his grandmother's poem, 'Let each days strength, sufficient be, to meet the needs, that we shall see," came into his thoughts. The poem was written by his grandfather, J J. He had made it at work, on a piece of scrap aluminum. The scrap piece, was off a B-17 bomber, made before World War II. Why was this poem in his thoughts? Especially with the thoughts of the attack. It was a puzzle, at the least. He continued to dream.

"J J, wake up. You're grumbling in your sleep. It's time to get up, J J," said corporal Kim. As he shook J J awake. Tye stepped back out of reach, thinking he might wake up swinging. "Are you, still fighting with that one eyed attacker?"

J J heard Tye ask, as he set up in his cot looking around, trying to focus his eyes, as he awoke. "Ya, all night! I've been dreaming, but not fighting. It makes no sense, at all."

The four men got dressed and went to their meeting with the gunny. As they walked through camp, they could see a group in front of the command tent. As they walked up to the group, they asked. "What's happen'n?"

"The gunny is talking to the night sentries. Something happened last night."

"What happened last night?"

"We don't know. The sentries had completed their duty and had gone to their tents. The gunny had them all report back here, at 0610. After they'd gotten off duty. And I heard, he was pissed!"

"I wonder what that's about? Maybe it's our one eyed attacker," whispered J J, in Tye's ear.

Just then the door opened. Three red eyed privates came out and closed the door behind them.

"Whoa! Do you guys have any ass left, or did the gunny chew it off? What was that about?" asked corporal Kim.

"I'm sorry, Tye. I can't say." One of the privates answered, as they walked away, talking to themselves.

The four men looked at each other and thought, 'we're next!'

The door of the tent opened once more. This time, standing in the doorway, was Gunnery Sergeant Roman. The group scattered, leaving the four men and the gunny.

"Good, you're here. I called for the Apache, Corporal Kim. It will start it's scan at 1200 hours. The scan will take about 45 minutes, to complete. Something else happened last night. I know there are seventy five people on this island, or that's all there is supposed to be. So I know any one of those people could be responsible, but I'm asking you? Do you men know anything about this?" The gunny then turned and walked towards his desk, moving to one side, he pointed at something lying on the desk. There on the desk was a big palm leaf. The four men looked at the gunny, as he walked around his desk, to the other side. "Read it!" Ordered the gunny, pointing.

The four men moved to where they could see to read, what was written on the heavy palm leaf.

J J's face went white, as he gasped for breath.

"Johnson you know something. What is it? What do you know?"

"It can't be, it can't be!" said J J, shaking his head, looking down at what was written on the leaf.

"What can't be, Johnson? Johnson. . . ! I'm talking to you, mister!"

Corporal Kim, grabbed J J, and shook him. "The gunny, is asking you a question, J J."

J J looked up at Kim and then over towards the gunny. "I'm sorry!"

"Never mind sorry. Answer the question, Johnson!"

"Gunnery Sergeant?" asked J J. Still looking at the gunny, with a bewildered look on his face and in his eyes.

"It can't be! What can't be?" once again, asked the gunny.

"That's my grandmother's poem!" said J J, looking back down at the writing.

"WHAT? What do you mean, your grandmother's poem?"

"That's a poem written by my grandfather, for my grandmother, over 50 years ago, Gunny!"

"Well then, how did it get here, Johnson?"

"I have no idea."

"Well I know, I didn't put it here," said the gunny, in a disgusted tone.

"How did it get here?"

"Duh! That's what I'm asking!"

"No. Here on your desk, Gunny?" asked J J, pointing.

"Oh. The day sentry, found it inside the camp area, on his way to duty and brought it here to me."

"I dreamt about this poem, last night."

All five men stood and stared at the palm leaf. J J started to read the poem aloud. When he was finished, a strange silence came over the tent, until Gunnery Sergeant Roman spoke.

"Johnson, do you have a history of sleep walking?"

"No."

"Maybe the attack caused you, some unusual emotional problem, or something?"

"That could be, I don't know."

"I was awake most of the night, myself. During that time, J J, Johnson I mean, only left his bunk once. At about 0230 hours, him and I, went to the latrine. To the best of my knowledge, until 0530 hours, that was the only time he left his cot, Gunny," said corporal Kim.

"Damn, this is weird!" said the gunny, with an irritated look on his face.

"This island is weird. First there was the attack! Now this! I know it must be hard for you to believe, but I didn't do this! And the attack, it did happen!" said J J, pointing at the palm leaf.

"Are you saying, they are connected, Johnson?"

"No, I'm not. But it's strange to me, we would have two, not easily explained, bizarre incidents happen, a few hours apart."

"You said this was your grandmother's poem. Is that right Johnson? Word for word, the same poem?"

"As far as I can tell. It is."

"Do you have a copy of it with you, here on the island?"

"No, Gunny, I don't. Except in my head. The only copy of that poem, I knew of, was hanging in my grandmother's kitchen!"

"What I don't understand is. How did it get in camp?" asked the gunny.

"Gunny, I've been listening to what you and the others have been saying. And I've been thinking about what's been said. J J, nor any of the four of us, Bo, Tye, J J, nor myself, could have done this, unless it's been a conspiracy, and then, we're all involved! Think about it. The four of us have never been apart, more than a minute or two, since we came to this island. I know I didn't do this, so that eliminates the others."

The three men and the gunny, stood there looking at Billy, in silence.

"Smith, you don't say much. But when you do, it's profound. What you said, makes some sense. Who do you think, did this?"

"Gunny, I think the attacker did."

"What? How could that be? How could the attacter know Johnson's grandmother's poem?"

"He read J J's mind, Gunny. That's how!"

"What?"

"He read his mind. That's how he knew his name was J J. And that's how he knows, J J's grandmother's poem!"

"Wow! How is that possible?" asked the gunny, as he and the others, stared at Billy.

"I don't know. But that is the best answer I can come up with, given the information I have at his time."

The four men looked at Billy, in disbelief.

"This gets even more weird, by the minute. It won't be long till the Apache flight. Then maybe, we can get some answers. Until then, you men report to Sergeant Sanchez. After the flight, report back here. Somewhere around 1400 hours. You're dismissed."

"Yes, Gunnery Sergeant."

"Gunny, I should go see the medic."

"That's right Johnson, you should. You men go with him. Then find Sanchez."

"Yes, Gunnery Sergeant."

The gunny picked up the palm leaf from his desk, as the four men turned and left the tent, he put it against the tents back wall.

"Thank you, Billy, for what you said in there. Maybe I'm not going crazy."

"If you are Home Boy, then we all are, J J," smiled Billy, as he patted J J on his shoulder, as the four of them walked through camp.

"Do you, actually think that could be the answer? What you said in there?"

"Like I said. At this point, that's what I think."

The men walked slowly through camp. Looking as they walked for the red cross, that would mark the medical tent. It wasn't hard to find. Just outside the tent they stopped.

"I'll see if Hanson is here." J J entered the tent. Hanson was there, but so was the Captain. As J J came into the tent, Hanson saw him.

"Johnson, how are you? Sir, this is the man, Gunnery Sergeant Roman, told you about, Sir," said the medic, as he turned to tell the Captain. "The man I stitched up."

"Johnson was it? My name is Doctor Brown, or Doc is fine. Let's have a look at that stab wound, Hanson stitched up."

"Yes, Sir, my name is Johnson. But they call me, J J, Sir. Sir, the wound seems fine."

"Let's have a look, J J."

"Yes, Sir."

The doctor checked the wound, and then put on a clean bandage. "The wound look's fine. Hanson, you did a good job with the stitches. There is no sign of infection. J J, any complaints with your doctors?"

"No, Sir, I'm fine, Sir."

"What about the man, with the cracked ribs?"

"Sir, he's outside with two other men, Sir."

"Do the two others know about his ribs and your wound, J J? The gunny wanted to keep this as quiet as possible."

"Yes, Sir, they're involved, Sir."

"Call them in, J J."

J J went to the door and opened it. "Hey guys, come in here. The doc want's to see Tye."

The three men came into the tent. J J introduced the men, to Doctor Brown. The doctor checked Tye, and he also checked Bo and Billy. He looked in their eyes, with a flashlight.

"What are you looking for, Doctor? To see if the two brothers, are on drugs?" asked Billy, in a smart-alecky tone.

"No, Billy. I'm looking to see if there is any sign of a concussion, from the blow to the side of your neck and to the back of Bo's. Gunnery Sergeant Roman, told me all four of you were injured and about your injuries. That's why I'm looking. Is that all right with you, mister?" Asked the Captain, with a disgusted tone in his voice.

"Yes, Sir. Thank you, Sir. The guys say I have an attitude. I do have, when it comes to racism, of any kind."

"There hasn't been any racism here, Private! But maybe your attitude, is making you a racist of a kind, Billy. I think, you better think about your attitude and what's been said. That's all I have to say. I think you men will be all right. If you need to talk more, come see me later. You're dismissed."

"Let's go guys. Thank you, Doc. Thanks Hanson, for taking care of us," said corporal Kim, as he opened the door and held it, for the others. Once outside, Tye looked at Billy and said, as they walked along. "Billy, you know, what the doctor said in there is true. You do have a problem. You are so paranoid of racism, you could easily become a racist yourself. I'm sure that's not what you want. Is it Billy?"

Billy turned and looked at J J and Bo, walking a short distance behind him and Tye, both men nodding their heads.

"No! Ok, I'll work on my attitude," said Billy, looking at Bo and J J.

Hearing what Billy said, they gave him two thumbs up. Seeing that, Tye gave Billy his version of hi-five. Which isn't so high, beings Tye is only five foot six. The tension somewhat disappearing, as the four of them walked through camp, laughing and joking, about Tye's hi-five.

It was now 1400 hours. The four men headed for the command tent. It was time to meet with the gunny, as planned. The men entered the tent. The gunny was at his desk.

"Gunnery Sergeant, we're back," said corporal Kim, as the men stood there at attention.

"At ease men. I haven't heard about the flight, as of yet. You men come back, in about 30."

"Yes, Gunnery Sergeant."

The men turned to leave. At that moment a private entered the tent. "Gunnery Sergeant, it's a message from FLEETCOM." The private handed the message, to the gunny.

"That's all, Private. You're dismissed." The private turned and left the tent. The gunny opened the message and read it. "Damn, the flight scan report says there were seventy five people, on the island, at the time of the flight. That's the exact number of people, in our detachment here on the island. What happened to your one eyed attacker and the writer of this poem?" asked the gunny, as he pointed at the palm leaf laying next to the back wall of the tent. The gunny then looked over at the four men standing there with their mouths hung open, in disbelief.

"Gunnery Sergeant, as we all said before. The attack did happen, the way we said. J J, nor any of the rest of us, had anything to do with the writing of that poem," said corporal Kim, in an assertive voice.

Getting up, the gunny walked around to their side of the desk. Sitting on the front edge of the desk, with his arms folded and rubbing his chin with his left hand. "Look guys, what's the answer? Your wounds are real. You believe each other and in each other. But the evidence we have doesn't help your story. We have the palm leaf, found in camp. Suggesting that, only someone in camp, could have left it where it was found. The poem written, actually carved into that palm leaf. A poem known only by one man, on this entire island. An attacker seen, by only one man, that man being one and the same. A scan, by a sophisticated infrared device, and that device showing 75 people, the right number of people present on the island."

Billy holding J J back, steps forward. "Gunnery Sergeant, we stand by what we said. We were attacked by someone. The attack did happen. We didn't have anything to do with the writing of that poem. We believe J J saw the one eyed attacker, inasmuch as we were attacked. And someone, other than J J did it. J J was bringing up the rear. We were attacked head on. J J couldn't have been in two places, at the same time. Gunny, we don't have the answers. We just know, we didn't fake the attack, and we didn't write that poem," said Billy, as he pointed towards the palm leaf still laying against the back wall of the tent.

"Johnson, do you have anything to add, to what Smith has said?"

"Only that, what we have said is true. It did happen, just the way we said. I can't explain how the poem in my head, found it's way onto that palm leaf. All I know is, I didn't put it there!"

"It's obvious, you men believe in your fellow Marine. That's commendable and expected of any Marine. What's our next step, in finding an answer to the question, why and who? We will find the answer to this problem, at some point in time. Until then, we'll take one day at a time."

Just then the door opened. In walked, sergeant Sanchez.

"I'm, sorry, Gunny. I can return later, when you're not busy."

"What is it, Sanchez? These men and I are through."

She hesitated, to answer.

"You, men wait outside. I want to talk to the sergeant," said Gunnery Sergeant Roman.

The four men turned and left the tent.

"Now, what is it, Sanchez?"

"Jack, one of the helicopter pilots told me, there is a small lake or pond, about a mile north of here. I would like your permission, for myself and the other two girls, to go and find this pond. When we're off duty of course. What I need from you, is permission and an order to confine my male counterparts to camp. If we can find it and it's clean and pure, it would be a great asset, to our stay here on the island."

The gunny thought a moment, about the strange things that had happened and then spoke. "Why, the order? Maybe I should have someone go with you, for security?"

"We would like security. But more than that, privacy. From all you horny men," laughed Sanchez.

"I understand. Then I can order you girls confined to camp? To protect the horny men, from you lecherous women. Is that right?" The gunny chuckled, as he spoke.

"Sounds good to me, Jack."

"Ok. But I'm going to send those four men outside with you, to help find that lake. The three of you might walk right past it and get entangled in the thick jungle and get caught by darkness. If you're lucky enough to find the lake, send the four back to camp, marking the trail as they return."

"Ok."

"Just let me know when, I'll make it so."

"1500 to 1900 hours today. Is that all right with you, Jack?"

"That's fine. The order is given, Sanchez. You go out and send those four in. I'll explain, what I want them to do. Ok Sanchez, have fun!"

"Thank you, Jack. I'll let you know what the water's like."

"You, do that, Maria."

Sanchez left the tent. Once outside, she told the men standing there.

The gunny desired their presence.

"Corporal, the gunny, wants to talk to you men, inside."

The five of them, re-entered the tent.

"Gunnery Sergeant."

"Yes, Corporal. I want you four men, to go with Sanchez and two others, into the jungle. North of here, there is a lake. I want you men to help find the lake. Then leave, Sanchez and the others, and return to camp. Marking the trail as you go, for their easy return, and our future use of the lake. Upon your return, tell the night sentry, that all male personnel are confined to camp, until 0600 hours, per my order. Wait outside. You're dismissed."

The men left the tent. "Thanks, Jack," said Sanchez, as she left the tent.

"Sanchez, what is this about?" asked Tye, as she came out.

"I asked Gunnery Sergeant Roman if the other two girls and I, could go for a dip in the lake. We would like some privacy. That's why I asked for the order."

"You three, are going into the jungle, for a swim?" asked J J, when he overheard what she told Tye.

"Ya, what's wrong with that? We're not in a war zone, or going into one," answered Sanchez.

"Oh, he was just thinking about our trip, and what a good time we had, to get ourselves through that thick stuff, back to camp, that's all, Sergeant," said corporal Kim.

"I'm out of here. I'll look you guys up in a few. When we're ready to go." With that, she turned and walked away. The four men watched, as she walked to a tent and went in.

"I hope she and the other two will be all right. They should have been told of the attack. They're Marines, they could take care of themselves, if they knew what to expect. I hope they don't run into, Old One Eye. Maybe Roman warned her, to be on guard against a possible attack," said J J, as he stood there with Tye, Billy and Bo.

"We'd better go get our gear ready. It won't take her and the others long. This time we're going to be prepared," said corporal Kim, as they walked towards their tent.

Sanchez walked up to the men's tent. "Are you guys, in there? Are you ready?"

"Yes, Sergeant, we'll be right out," said someone, from the confines of the tent. With that, the flap of the tent parted. Four of the meanest looking, jungle combat ready Marines you've ever seen, came out of the tent. Sanchez and the other two women, stood there in shock. The white men's faces were covered with blackout and camouflage.

"We're, not going to battle! Would you look at them! You look like, you're going to meet the enemy! We're going for a swim, not to war," said Sanchez, as she looked at the other two women. Then back at the four men, shaking her head.

"Ya, but we're ready for the worst," said corporal Kim.

"Ok, let's go," said Sanchez, still shaking her head as they all walked through camp. As they walked, the people that saw them stared.

"I've got to pass on the gunny's order, to the duty sentry before we leave," said Sanchez, as she walked up to the sentry on duty.

"From now until 0600 hours, all male personnel are confined to camp. Including these four men, upon their return to camp. You will pass this order onto the night duty person. Is that understood, Corporal?"

"Yes, Sergeant."

"Sergeant, the two Johnsons will go first, then you three. Billy and I will bring up the rear. Is that all right with you, Sergeant?"

"Fine, let's go, Corporal!"

The seven of them started through the jungle.

The other women, were Private Sara Conrade and Private Betty Jo Bloom. The two were new to the Marine life, like the four young men. Sara was from up state New York. A big strong girl, with a great sense of humor. Betty Jo was from Arkansas, with a lot of southern ideas.

They were all working their way through the jungle.

"Boy, Tye you weren't kidding, about how thick this jungle is. I'm sure glad you thought to get these machetes, for this little walk, through this damn jungle!" said Sanchez swinging the one, he had gotten for her. With seven of them using machetes, they made a wide swath, through the jungle.

"I hope this is the right way. In this heat, working as hard as I am, this woman is going to be hot, smelly and bitchy. You might say, a bitch in heat," said Sara, as she cut at undergrowth, with her machete.

"I'll climb this tree, and look to see, what I can see. Hey, I'm a poet," said Tye, as he started to climb.

"Well, can you see the lake, Longfellow?" asked Sara, standing at the tree's base looking up at Tye.

The others still laughing, at what Sara and Tye had said, with J J standing guard. The other four, sitting down around the base of the tree resting. Leaving Sara, with her eyes looking skyward, at Tye up a tree.

"What are you doing up there? Do you see anything? If you fall Tye, you won't get hurt. You'll probably just bounce, on the thick undergrowth," said Sara, still looking up at Tye, from the base of the tree.

"With the lay of the land, it looks like a lake could be located, in the direction we've been going," shouted Tye, in a loud voice, from high in the tree. He then started to climb down and out of the tree.

"J J, would you relax! Why are you so on edge? Come over here and sit down and cool off, with the rest of us. Take a break," said Sanchez, as she got up and grabbed his arm. "Come on, Private! You can play war later," she said, pulling him over and down, to sit with the others. They sat there trying to cool off, talking about their trek, through the thick vegetation.

"Once we find the lake, the next trip will be much easier, because of this fine trail we've carved," said Bo, as he looked at what a good job they had done, so far, on the trail. Just then J J jumped to his feet.

"What, J J? Did you see something?" whispered Kim, as he quickly jumped to his feet, as did Bo and Billy. The four men stood in a tight circle, looking into the jungle.

"Damn, you guys are enough, to make anyone paranoid! Why are you so tense, Corporal?" asked Sanchez, getting to her feet as she asked the question.

"It's in our training, Sergeant, you know that! That's why we're on this island, is for the training! On how, to be on the cutting edge at all times!"

"OK, if you say so. Let's go find that lake. So I can send you gung-ho guys back to camp!"

They started back to work on the undergrowth, making their way, hopefully, in the direction of the small lake. Continuing forward, moving steadily through the jungle. Suddenly, breaking out of the thick jungle. They found themselves, standing at the edge of a small clearing, drenched by the light of the late afternoon sun. Next to the clearing, lay the most beautiful, crystal clear lake. All seven, stood in astonishment of the beauty. The sight, was worth all their hard work.

"I've never seen anyplace as beautiful, as this. . . !" said Sanchez. J J, letting his eyes gaze around the parameter of the lake. Taking in not only the wonderment of all the beauty, but more than that, obviously looking for any sign of danger.

"Isn't this place unbelievable. . . ! You guys can rest and freshen up, before starting back to camp," said Sanchez, as she walked slowly to the waters edge with the others.

Once at the waters edge, they stood still overwhelmed, not only by it's beauty, but of the serenity they were now feeling.

"Look at that!" shouted J J, pointing at the waters edge. There in the sand, was a footprint. A print made by a human bare foot! The four men looked at each other.

"Now what? It's a damn footprint. So what!" said Sanchez, as she looked down at the print in the sand and then up at J J.

"Sergeant, this island was reportedly vacant, remember. . . ? Nobody lives here, uninhabited! Right. . . ? Wrong! This footprint says hello, I'm here!"

"So, there's a damn footprint! So what! I'm tired of this paranoia you four have. That someone's out there! I want you men to rest and cool off. Then, I want you to head back to camp. We three women will take care of you until you leave for camp. Then you can play war on your trip back," said Sanchez, as her voice shook, from her frustration with the men's paranoia.

"Ya, boys. If there is anyone out there. The way we three women look, after our journey through that damn jungle. We'll frighten them into submission," said Sara, as she started to take off her gear. Sara then sat down with the others, which had sat down to remove their boots and socks, so they could soak their feet in the cool water. The water had the appearance that it got real deep, just within a few feet of the beach. They got up and took turns, walking back and forth in the water along the beach.

"Be careful, it looks like it drops off and gets deep!" said Sanchez, as she swung her leg back and forth, first one then the other, in the crystal-clear water.

"Boy, it's too bad you guys have to leave and go back to camp. You could stay here and play!"

"Sara!"

"In the water. Is what I meant, Betty Jo!"

"They have their orders."

"I know, Sergeant, but still, we might have had some fun!" said Sara, raising and lowering her eyebrows and looking at the four men, with a smile on her face.

"Do you think there are any snakes in this lake? Back home we would have to be on guard, for snakes," said Betty Jo, as she walked into the clear water.

"I don't think there are any snakes on these islands, at least I hope not," said Tye looking into the clear water, with a nervous look on his face.

"The way it looks, this lake is going to be a great place for our people to come and cool off, when they're off duty. It looks like a picture post card here. It's so beautiful!"

"Boy, you said that right, Tye! I can't wait, until you guys leave! I'm hot!" said Sanchez, as she bent down and cupped her hands in the water, bringing some water up to rinse her face. She then started unbuttoning her shirt and undoing her pants, pulling her clothes off, revealing a swimsuit, she had on underneath her clothes. Throwing her clothes into a pile on the beach, she turned and dove into the lake. The others stood there and watched as she swam beneath the waters surface, then coming up for air. "It's fantastic! Come on in. You guys stay there and get ready to head back to camp."

The other two girls started pealing off clothes, also having suits on under their clothes. Throwing their clothes on the beach, the other two girls turned and quickly dove into the water, to join Sanchez. The four men watched the three girls playing together in the water, as they got ready to return to camp.

"Sanchez, we're ready to head back. I wish we could stay with you three, but we have our orders," hollered corporal Kim.

"That's right, Corporal. You're dismissed. See ya later guys. Have a good hike back to camp. Tell the Gunny, what we found here, when you see him."

The three women waved, as they bobbed in the water. The four men waved, as they turned and started on the trail towards camp. Looking back over their shoulders, as they walked slowly away. "I wish we could have stayed and watched those girls. For their protection, I mean."

"Ya, I know what you mean, J J. Me too, but we have our orders," said corporal Kim.

The men continued towards camp.

"You're right, Bo, it's going to be a lot easier, to get back to the lake next time, with this nice trail we've cut through this damn jungle, to find the lake in the first place," said J J, as they walked slowly along the trail. The four of them not wanting to leave the three unsuspecting Marines, behind at the lake, without telling them about a possible attack, from their one eyed attacker. They continued on their way towards camp, as ordered.

Back at the lake, the girls were giggling and laughing at each other, having a good time. They were really enjoying their new found paradise. "I think Roman, will be well pleased, with our find, don't you?"

"I sure do, Maria. What a great place to stay, especially at, U.S.

Government's expense," laughed Sara, as the three women continued to enjoy the clear water of the indescribable place.

"That's for sure, Sara. That makes this place look even better, than it does. If that's at all possible. And the water, it's not cool at all. It must have felt cool, because we were so hot. The water is actually quite warm," said Maria, as she swam on her back talking to Betty Jo and Sara, about the lake.

OLD ONE EYE

"Have you two noticed how quiet and peaceful it is here?" Everyone agreed, this was a phenomenal place, they had found. Hidden by the thick jungle, except from the bird like view of a helicopter. No sooner, than those words had left Maria's mouth, there was a blood curdling scream!

Betty Jo was hysterically screaming! The other two girls swam to her aid, thinking 'something in the lake had grabbed or bit her.'

"What is it? What's wrong, Betty Jo? Betty Jo! What is it?" yelled Sanchez, swimming up, grabbing Betty Jo and shaking her.

Betty Jo looked over into Maria's eyes, as Maria shook her, Betty Jo stopped screaming. She then turned, looking and pointing towards the beach. Maria and Sara, both quickly looked, in the direction Betty Jo was pointing.

Standing on the small beach was a man. The man stood there, staring right at the three of them, with a pair of binoculars.

"Hey Binocular Man, what are you doing there?" hollered Sanchez, thinking it was one of her fellow Marines from camp. She started swimming in his direction. The other two also swam towards the beach. As they got closer to the beach, Sanchez stopped. He had put the binoculars down to his side, holding them in his right hand. Still standing there staring at them with a big wide smile, on his obscured, shaded face. He also had something in his other hand. It was one of their shirts. He then turned his head, in the direction of the trail. This gave Sanchez, a much better look at him. She could clearly see his face, he wasn't one of her fellow Marines, after all. He was old. Real old! His face was scarred and it appeared, he had only one eye. He then turned back, still smiling at them. Dropping the shirt he held in his hand, in an instant, he was gone!

"Did you see his face?" asked Sanchez, as she spun around in the water, to ask the others. Just then she heard something behind her. She quickly turned, to see what the noise was. The noise she heard, was the four men running from the jungle, out onto the beach.

"Did you guys see him?"

"Are you gu . . . women, all right, Sergeant?"

"We're all right, Corporal. Did you see him?"

"Was he an old ugly guy, with one eye?"

"Yes! Then you saw him?"

"No."

"No! Then how did you know, he was old and had only one eye?"

"We saw him before."

"What?"

"I think we can tell them now, since they saw him too. I don't think the gunny meant that we couldn't talk to someone that had seen or knew about, Old One Eye. Boy I'm sure glad someone else, has seen him. Maybe the gunny, won't think were totally crazy, after all," said J J.

The four concluded it was all right, to talk to the three women, about their one eyed attacker.

"What are you talking about? Where did you guys come from?" asked the sergeant.

"We were on our way to camp as ordered, but we were walking real slow. We were about 200 yards down the trail, when we heard the scream. We got here as quick as we could," answered corporal Kim.

"200 yards! You were walking slow. What were you guys just talking about?" Asked the sergeant, as she came out of the water onto the beach. The other two girls right behind her. Grabbing her shirt and slipping it over her shoulders, as she asked the question.

"We were ordered, by Gunnery Sergeant Roman, not to tell anyone, we were attacked by that one eyed old man! Since you three, have seen Old One Eye, let's hope, the order doesn't apply. That's what we were just talking about, whether or not, we should tell you about the attack. We've obviously decided, to tell you. That's what we meant, when we told you the jungle damn near killed us. It was Old One Eye, that damn near killed us. That's why we've been, so on edge. We thought he might attack again."

"All seven of us?"

"Hey, he knocked all four of us out cold!"

"Is that right? All four of you, at the same time? He must be one tough old man."

"And was going to kill all of us too! But something, changed his mind," said J J.

"Are you serious? Kill you! Why, would he want to kill you? What changed his mind?"

"You bet, we're serious! We don't know why he was going to kill us. He saw the name on my shirt, that had something to do with him changing his mind. This is where his knife, started into my chest," said J J, unbuttoning his shirt and pulling his undershirt from his pants, to show the sergeant, his bandage.

"Wow! Who is, this guy?"

"Nobody knows, Sergeant."

"Well he's gone, for now. You guys go back down the trail, just a bit. We'll get dressed and walk with you back to camp. All of us will report this to, Gunnery Sergeant Roman. You guys go on, we'll be on guard now."

"Let's go find him right now! There's seven of us," said Bo.

"We'll report it to Roman, first. Then we'll see if he'll let us go find him," said Sanchez, as the other two women got out of the water. The four men turned and started back down the trail. The three women got quickly dressed and started down the trail to meet the four men.

"Did you see how old that guy was? I'd say he was in his fifties."

"I didn't see his face that well," said Betty Jo.

"Nor did I, Maria."

The three women, quickly caught up with the four men.

"You guys must, walk slow."

"That way we were close enough, if you needed help. Which is more important, your safety or your modesty? We were far enough away, we didn't see much. But we were close enough to help."

"You're right, thank you guys. Let's get to camp," said Sanchez, as she started walking with the others, double timing it towards camp.

"Sergeant, did you get a good look at his face?" asked J J, as he walked right behind her.

"Yes, I did, J J. He was real old. His face was scarred on the left. No, his right side. Yes, I'm sure it was the right side. There was something unusual though, under the circumstances."

"What was that, Sergeant?"

"I noticed what a warm and friendly smile he had, as he stood there staring at us, holding binoculars in one hand and one of our shirts, in the other."

"Boy, he wasn't warm or friendly, when I saw him! He was about to take my life. When I looked at his one eyed scarred face, I've never seen such anger and rage."

By way of the new trail, they arrived in camp in no time at all, walking right past the sentry, towards the command tent. Sanchez opened the door and went right in. The others following her lead. The gunny looked up from his desk.

"What is it, Sanchez? What's wrong?"

"All seven of us, have seen the one eyed old man. We had found the lake. The guys here, were on there way back to camp, as ordered. When he appeared on the beach, staring at us with a pair of binoculars, while the three of us, were enjoying our swim! The guys heard Betty Jo's scream and came running back, to help."

"So much for the accuracy, of a multi million dollar sophisticated helicopter," said Gunnery Sergeant Roman, his voice low and in a disgusted tone, as he got up from his desk and walked around the end to the other side and leaned on it's front edge.

"What?"

"Never mind, Sanchez."

"The guys told us something about the attack on them. Since we saw, Old One Eye. They hoped your order may not apply."

"Oh ya! Ok, go on."

"He must be an old beachcomber or recluse. We've invaded his island, maybe that's why he attacked you. He was protecting his territory, from invaders!" said Sanchez.

"There was a footprint on the beach by the lake. It must have been his. He probably gets his fresh water from there. That would be a good place to start looking for him, Gunny," said J J, standing in the crowd of seven.

"You think so, Private?"

"Yes, Gunny, I do."

"The water in the lake must come from underground. We didn't see any water running into the lake. It may be the only fresh water, on the island. J J may have something there, Gunny," said Sanchez.

"Tomorrow, the Colonel, is flying in for an inspection of the camp. We'll wait until he leaves, to start our search for, what did you call him, Old One Eye? What about this lake? What was it like?"

"It's fantastic! The water is a beautiful blue green, but it's crystal clear."

"How big is it, Sergeant?"

"Seventy five by a hundred feet, I would guess," she said, looking at the others for input. "There's a good trail to the lake. It's only about a fifteen minute walk. I would like to go back and finish my swim."

"After the Colonel's inspection, and we find Old One Eye. You can finish your swim, Sergeant. For now, you can go and make ready for the inspection, at 1000 hours tomorrow. Sergeant, you stay. You others, are dismissed." The six others, looked at each other, as they turned and left the tent.

"Maria, I'm sure glad you and the other two have seen Old One Eye. I was becoming quite concerned with those four boys. Their story of the attack and their one eyed attacker, was a bit hard to swallow. Especially since this was found in camp, the very next morning."

The gunny walked around the end of his desk, towards the back wall of the tent. Bending over, he picked up the palm leaf, which was laying on the floor next to the tent's back wall. He then returned to his desk, bringing the palm leaf with him and sitting it on top of his desk.

"Read this, Maria."

Sanchez read what was written, on the leaf.

"What's this? It's the poem. Ya, I heard about it?"

"This poem, was Johnson's grandmother's poem. Written for her, by his grandfather, over fifty years ago."

"Who's? Which Johnson's, Jack?"

"The one you call J J."

"So, how did it get here?"

"Now it gets real strange. Nobody knows!"

"What do you mean, nobody knows?"

"The Johnson boy, says the only copies of that poem, that he knew of, is, 'the one in his head and the one in his, gramma's kitchen, back home.' He swears, he knows nothing of how this poem got on this palm leaf or into camp. Here's the best part, Smith thinks, Old One Eye read Johnson's mind, and wrote the poem. Wait! You didn't know about, the J J thing. When the attacker read Johnson's name. The one printed, above the pocket on his uniform! He said, the boy's nick name, J J. That's why Smith thinks, he read his mind. It also made sense, since the poem is here, the attacker wrote it, from reading J J's mind, since Smith, Kim, Johnson and Johnson, have never been apart more then a minute or two, since coming to this island."

"Wow! I see what you mean. I'm glad we saw Old One Eye. It helps give credibility to their story. What was that about a helicopter?"

"Oh. I had an Apache, fly over the island and use it's infrared, to find the attacker. The scan said there were seventy five people, here on this island. There should have been at least one more, if it had scanned him. It didn't find him. Obviously he's out there, since the seven of you have seen him."

"Oh, he's out there all right. I wonder who he is? And where he came from?"

"We'll ask him? When we find him, Maria. How is it, one old man, could knockout four young Marines, and then, could of killed all of them, at will, and didn't? Thank God!"

"I wasn't there, Jack. I can't answer that. The old man I saw, was in good shape. It was his face that was old, not his body. He moved like a young man, when he went into the jungle, when the guys came running down the trail to help us. Like you said Jack, we'll know more when and if, we find him."

"Oh, we'll find him! If we have to go over every inch, of this entire island! We'll find him! You go get the men ready for the inspection tomorrow. Sanchez, thanks again for seeing Old One Eye, it makes me feel a lot better."

The day of the inspection, was beautiful. The sky was so blue! With big white fluffy clouds. There was a slight breeze, which made it even nicer then usual. The people were ready for the Colonel's inspection. His helicopter was on it's way to the island. The gunny was walking through camp, looking things over. He seemed pleased with what he saw. The men were in two groups. One on each side of where the Colonel's helicopter was to land. Just then they could hear the helicopter. They got in formation, for the landing. The gunny was in front of one group, Sanchez the other, as the helicopter came into land.

"Attention!" Ordered, Gunnery Sergeant Roman.

The Colonel's helicopter came to a soft landing, raising some dust as it did. The engine was cut, the rotor came slowly to a stop. The door opened and a white haired Colonel climbed out. The gunny walked to meet him. They saluted each other, then shook hands, as they met. As they walked, it appeared that they knew each other.

The Colonel was third generation Marine. His name was Colonel Robert Robinson. The two men walked around the helicopter, to the group, on the other side.

"Colonel, this is my supply sergeant, Maria Sanchez. Sergeant, this is, Colonel Robinson." The two saluted and shook hands.

"Nice to meet you, Sergeant. You people sure have a beautiful place, to train."

"Colonel Robinson, nice to meet you, Sir. Ya it is beautiful, Sir."

ALONE

Just then, at the far end of the camp.

"Gunnery Sergeant!" yelled one of the sentries, on duty.

The gunny and the Colonel both, looked in that direction. The sentry stood pointing into the jungle. Everyone was looking to see what was going on. There at the edge of camp, appeared a lone man, walking into camp.

"I'll be damned! Would you look at that! It's the old man."

"What Gunny?"

"Colonel, would you excuse me?" asked the gunny, as he signaled for each one of the four men, to come with him to meet their one eyed attacker, face to face.

"Yes, Gunnery Sergeant, what is it?"

"I'll explain, Sir."

The four men ran to meet up, with the gunny.

"Gunny, it's him!" said J J.

"I see it is, Johnson. Calm down."

"Yes, Gunny."

The five men walked in an orderly fashion, to meet the old man. The gunny noticed, he was wearing what once was a uniform.

"I'll be. That's a Marine uniform! World War II style!" whispered the gunny, to himself.

They got with in ten feet or so, of each other, and the old man stopped. The gunny took a few more steps, and stopped. They stood there, the entire camp was silent. Then the old man cleared his throat, and then started to speak, with tears in his eye, he spoke.

"Private Jay Samuel Johnson, reporting Sergeant." His voice clear, as he spoke. The man stood at attention, saluting the gunny, with tears running down his clean shaven face.

The gunny returned the honor, and saluted the old man.

"What did he say his name was?" asked J J, pushing the others aside, coming up next to the gunny, the two now standing face to face, with the old man.

"Jay Samuel Johnson, that's my name, Sergeant." The old man repeated. Looking at the gunny and then at the young man.

J J turned to the gunny and whispered. "That's not only my name, Gunny, it's also my grandfather's! How could that be? He must be using the name, because he read it on my uniform."

"J J. . . ," said the gunny, as he looked at him, trying to calm the young man down.

"Yes, Sergeant."

With J J, still facing the gunny, and his back to the old man. The gunny, looked right past the young man, to the old man. The gunny surprised, at the old man answering to the nick name, J J.

J J's mouth, dropped open and tears filled his eyes, hearing the old man answering, to the name, J J! He stood there looking at the gunny, in silence. Then slowly turning, J J looked at the old man.

"You people are from, the U. S. A.?"

"Who are you?" J J asked, the old man.

The gunny, after seeing the emotion on the young man's face, let J J, ask the question.

The old man looked at the gunny, and then at the young man, asking the question.

"I'm Jay Samuel Johnson, as I told you!"

J J turned back to the gunny.

"He used Jay Samuel! All that's on my uniform is J. S. Johnson, Gunnery Sergeant," whispered J J. He then turned back facing the old man.

"You're the one I saw, in the jungle, with Johson on your shirt," said the old man, pointing to the name on J J's shirt.

"Yes. That's my name. Where are you from?" asked J J, as he looked down to where the old man was pointing, to the name printed on his shirt.

"You're Americans, right?" asked the old man, as he pointed to the American Flag, on J J's uniform.

"Yes, we're U. S. Marines," answered the gunny.

"Seattle Washington. How are we doing?" The old man asked.

"We doing? Doing what?" asked J J.

"The war!" The old man looked at J J, then the gunny, awaiting an answer.

"How long have you been here? Here on this island? Who else is here with you?" asked the gunny.

The gunny grabbing J J, by the arm. Interrupting J J's questioning, of the old man. There was a long silence. Then the old man spoke, as tears filled his eye, and ran down his cheek. With great emotion in his voice. The old man answered the question.

"Over fifty years . . . alone!"

"You've been on this island for fifty years, Alone?" asked the gunny, as he thought to himself, 'that meant the old man must be asking about World War II, if he'd been here that long.'

Everyone that heard what the old man said, stood there in amazement. Astonished at the thought, 'fifty years.'

"Over fifty years, alone! The war against Japan and Germany, ended in 1945. Both countries, are allies, now," said the gunny.

J J, pulling his arm free from the gunny's hold, to ask the old man, some additional questions. The gunny letting J J go, to resume his questioning.

The old man's mood changed.

"1945! That's a long time ago. Allies! You mean they're on our side now! I don't understand. The Japs, attacked Pearl Harbor! They killed thousands of people. Those bloody Japs. You can't trust them! Their sneak attack on Pearl, killed a lot of men and women, protecting our great United States! How can we be on the same side?"

"That's right, they did, and a lot more. Like you said, that was a long time ago. We're on the same side now!" said the gunny.

"I'm not!" Growled the old jungle man. His face and eye showing even more concern than before, as he thought, how appalling, 'such talk, allies!'

"You said, you were from Seattle?" asked J J, as he resumed his questioning of the old man.

The old man stood there, staring at the gunny and the young man asking all the personal questions, and then he saw the two Colored men and then, the Jap! The one that was with the two Colored men and the young man, the one with Johnson printed on his shirt, that he had attacked. The only reason he didn't kill them all, was the name, that was printed on the young man's shirt. His face no longer looked as pleasant, as Sanchez remembered. Could this man be for real? He certainly seemed very serious.

"Yes, that's right, in the state of Washington," answered the old man, short and abrupt, with his answer.

J J, afraid to ask his next question, as they stood in the middle of camp, with everyone watching. "Do you have any family, in Seattle?"

The old man, still feeling uneasy, stood there, as he heard the question being asked, his lower lip starting to quiver and his eye filling with more tears. His mind started to drift, recalling old memories. He often had done this over the years. It was those memories and warm thoughts, that helped him through many tough, unbelievably lonely times. He tried to answer the question. "I'm married, to a wonderful girl. She lives in our house, in Seattle." The old man thought to himself, 'My lovely, Jera Marie.'

J J, swallowed hard, at the old mans answer, but asked the next question. The gunny for some reason, still letting him do so. "What is her name?"

The old man focused on the crowd before him. "Why, are you asking me these questions? These personal, questions?" asked the old man, with concern in his voice. "My number is 36560357. That's all I'm required, to tell you!"

"Calm down, Sir, nothing will happen to you or your family, by answering these questions. Did you write the poem? The one on the palm leaf, that we found?" asked the gunny, interrupting J J's questioning. The old man glared at J J, as he stood there, deciding whether or not, he should answer the gunny's question.

"Yes, Sergeant. I wrote it."

"Where did it come from?" asked the gunny.

"Like I said, I wrote the poem!" said the old man, with frustration in his voice.

"I know, that's what you said, but when did you write the poem?"

"The first time?" asked the old man.

"Yes, the first time."

The old man thought a moment, then answered the question. "It was on June 29, 1941. My wife's birthday."

J J's knees shook, as he heard what the old man said.

"Sir, what is your wife's name?" J J asked the old man, speaking with more respect in his voice. J J's heart was pounding with anticipation, as the old man spoke.

"Her name is, Jera Marie Johnson, my Jera Marie."

J J stood there, looking at the old man. His eyes filled with tears. Could it be! Could what he was thinking be conceivable!

"Gunnery Sergeant, do you know who this man is!"

"No, Johnson. Whom, do you think, he might be?"

Just then the Colonel walked up, with Sanchez. The old man turned and stared, at the white haired Colonel, as he walked up and asked the question. "What is going on here, Gunnery Sergeant?"

"Sir, I'm trying to figure out what's going on myself, Sir."

The old man continued staring at the Colonel.

"Sir, this man attacked these four men and almost killed them.

"What? This old man?" asked the Colonel, as he looked first, at the old man and then at the gunny, in disbelief.

"That's right, Robby. But I didn't . . . thank . . . God," said the old man, with a big smile on his face.

"My name, is Colonel Robert R. Robinson. It's Colonel to you, mister," answered the Colonel, looking at the old man.

"My father . . . went by the name, Robby."

The old man stood there quietly, still staring at the Colonel. "Your father. . . !" said the old man, as he again stood there in silence.

The Colonel looked over at the gunny. The gunny shrugging his shoulders, not knowing why the old man had become silent.

Everyone stood there looking at the now silent old man, waiting patiently, for him to speak.

"Colonel, I know your father! He was with me, here on the island," said the old man, his speech slow and precise.

"My father. . . ? I don't think so mister! My father was killed. He was killed in Korea, in 1952."

"Killed! Robby was killed. . . ? What's korea?"

"What?" asked the Colonel.

"Korea, is a place, near China," said the gunny.

"Robby, was my best friend. The last time I saw him, we were running for our lives, from the Japs, not more than a mile, from this very spot," said the old man, with tears back in his eye.

The Colonel thought a moment. "You're. . . ! The man, my father had to leave, during World War II!

"Robby, didn't leave me!"

"You're J J! This is the island! My father never forgave himself, for leaving you behind."

"Your father didn't leave me! They didn't have any choice. The Japs were going to kill us, if they had their way! Let me tell you, there were lots of them. I always wondered, what happened, to Robby and the other two guys."

"Mister Johnson, J J, all three men made it off the island safely. One was wounded, but not seriously," said the Colonel, as he looked at the old man. His voice filling with emotion, as he spoke. "Roman, dismiss your men. My inspection is over."

"Sir! Yes, Sir. Sanchez, go dismiss the men."

"Yes, Gunnery Sergeant," said Sanchez, as she turned to leave and carry out the order, she saw tears running down J J's face, as he tried to speak. She didn't want to leave, in fear of missing what was about to be said. Just then, the young man spoke.

"Colonel."

"What is it, Private?" asked the Colonel, noticeably upset, by the private's untimely interruption.

"Sir, my name is, Jay Samuel Johnson. My nick name is J J, Sir."
Said J J, his voice shaking with tears running down his cheeks.

The Colonel and everyone else, stared at J J. Then over at the old man.
Hearing that, Sanchez froze in her tracks.

"Sir, I think this man, might be . . . my grandfather, Sir," said J J,
as he walked up closer, to the old man.

Hearing what the young man said. Everyone turned to look at J J.
Then back at the old man. The two men stood, less then an arms length
apart. Looking deep into each other, in silence.

"You're my, grand. . . ?" The old man, tried to speak.

"Yes, Sir. I think you may be my grandfather, Sir. Which makes
me your grandson," said J J, tears still running down his face.

The old man, still stood there looking at J J. "Son, I'm sorry . . .
I can,t be your grandfather . . . I don't have any children."

"Sir, my father was born, two months after Gramma was told, that
the only man she ever loved, was missing. You Grampa."

The old man stood there, in disbelief. He put his hand up to his face,
then he started to fall. J J catching his thought to be grandfather, with
both hands. The old man moved his hand from his eye. Then looking into
the face, of the man that held him. To his surprise, he saw the face he
shaved, some fifty years earlier. All but the eyes. The eyes were different.
They were the eyes, of his Jera Marie, his young wife, the way she looked
the day she said good-bye, so many years ago. Her eyes filled with fear, of
what the future might bring.

The two men, still looking into each others eyes, as a smile slowly
started to appear, on both men's faces. The same big smile, on both faces,
knowing now they were from the same beginning. The two men grabbed
each other. As they hugged, they began to weep. The crowd stood in awe,
to what was, and had taken place, right before their very eyes.

"You're my, grandson? I'm your, grandfather?"

"Looks that way," laughed J J, with tears still in his eyes.

"My wife, Jera Marie. Is she. . . ."

"Gramma. . . ? She's great!"

"Let's move in, and out of this sun. I'm not accustomed to it,
Gunny," said the Colonel.

"Yes, Sir. Let's go to the mess tent, Sir."

"Gunnery Sergeant, I'll go dismiss the men," said Sanchez, with a
mischievous smile, on her face.

"That's a good idea, Sanchez. I wish, I would have thought of that," said Roman, sarcastically, with a smile on his face.

"Thank you, Gunny," said Sanchez, bitting her lower lip, as she walked away. She knew she should have left immediately, after the order was given, instead of delaying.

"After you do, Sanchez, join us in the mess tent."

"That woman, is a sergeant?" asked the old man.

"That's right! She's our supply sergeant, Sergeant Maria Sanchez. You're going to see things have changed in the world of today, it's a much different place, than you may remember, Sir. My name is Jack Roman, Sir, you can call me Jack," said the gunny, holding out his hand, to shake the old man's.

The old man looked down at the gunny's hand. He stood a moment, then he excitedly grabbed the gunny's hand, with both of his, and shook it vigorously, with gaiety in his eye.

"Glad to meet you, Jack! My name is, J J," said the old man. He then looked over at the younger man, his grandson.

"Your name is, J J!"

"You had it first, Grampa, it's yours."

"You're Private Johnson here, J J. We'll call you, Mister Johnson or Sir. Until the Marine Corp, figures out what you are!" said the gunny. Looking first at the younger of the two men, then at the older man.

The two J J's walked towards the mess tent, followed by Bo, Billy, and Tye. The Colonel and the gunny walked together side by side, leading the way. The older J J stopped, as they got close to the tent. Tilting his head back, J J inhaled deeply through his nose, savoring the aroma that was filling the air. It was heavenly.

"That's coffee, I smell."

"It sure is, come in I'll buy you a cup," said the gunny, as he opened the door to the tent. The Colonel entered the tent, with the two J J's behind him, and the gunny following, the others behind the gunny. Once inside, J J stopped, he stood there with his eye closed.

"Are you all right? What's wrong?"

"Nothings wrong, son. To me, these smells, are like an old melody, I haven't heard for years. They bring back, so many memories." Tears filled the old man's eye, as he stood there, enjoying the aromas.

"Here, have a seat." The old man thanked the gunny, and then sat down.

"What language are they speaking, with that music, I hear? It's the same language, you guys were speaking, when I jumped the four of you in the jungle."

"That's Rap, Grampa. It was created by, Black inner-city kids, it's become very popular."

"Son, you shouldn't call Colored people, black," whispered the old man, with disapproval in his voice, and shaking his head. "I know, my Jera Marie, your grandmother, would not approve." Sitting there, the old man thinking about, what he had said, 'his young Jera, a grandmother!'

"You're right. Now they're Afro-American's."

"What, son?"

"Never mind, I'll explain later."

"Son, always learn what you can now, later may be a long time coming."

"So, you guys were Rapping! That's why you were caught, by surprise! Well, I think they have learned a lesson. Am I right?" The gunny grinning, over at the four men, as they all returned the gunny's smile, with a small one of their own.

"Yes, Gunnery Sergeant!" all four men answered.

"Turn down that Rap, crap!" order the Colonel.

"Private, bring us all some coffee," ordered the gunny. They heard the rattling of dishes, as someone turned down the music. A man quickly came with a tray of cups and two pots of coffee. The gunny grabbed a cup, in one hand and a pot, in the other. He filled the cup to the brim, and handed it to J J.

The old man, again savored the aroma. The smell was indescribably pleasing. J J slowly took a sip of the hot coffee, his face changed, as his lips puckered and his eye watered. "This stuff is terrible! I'm so sorry, I can't drink this. It smelled so good, how could it taste so bad?" asked J J, putting the cup down on the table.

The gunny picked up the cup and tasted the coffee. Grinning, he put the cup back down. "Maybe you'd like an ice cold Coke, or Pepsi, J J?"

"Jack, you have Coke-a-Cola, here? I'd sure like to have a cold Coke, Sergeant."

"I'll get it, Gunny." The younger J J, jumped up and went for the Coke. Returning with the Coke. He handed it to his grandfather. "Here, Sir. Here's your Coke."

The old man took the can from J J. Holding the cold can of pop in his hand, he looked up at J J, with a puzzled look on his face. "I see they put Coke, in cans now," said the old man, as he sat staring at the can he held in his hand. "This can is so cold! How do you get it and keep it so cold?" asked the old man. Holding the coldest thing he'd felt, in fifty years.

"We'll show you everything we can, but it will take time, for you to see, and try all the new things, you'll see. Just take one at a time, as they come," said the gunny.

"First one. Show me how, I can open this can, without a can opener?"

"I'll show you." The gunny, holding the man's hand, with the can in it. "You put your finger in this hole and pull up and to the edge, of the can. Then you push the metal tab, back down and drink your pop." As the old man did, what the gunny said. They heard the sound, of the can opening. J J grinned from ear to ear, as he raised the can to his lips. He took a big drink. His eye started to fill with water. "You don't like your Coke either?" asked the gunny, seeing the old man's eye watering.

The old man swallowed hard. It took him some time to clear his throat. "No, it's great!" said the old man, as he took another big drink.

The gunny grinned, a big grin.

"He sure is making that look good. I think I'll have a Coke, instead of this hot coffee, myself," said the Colonel, as he set the cup down.

"Coke's for everyone," ordered the gunny, still grinning.

"Yes, Gunnrey Sergeant." They heard someone say, as they heard the refrigerator door slam. Then a private brought in a tray, filled with Cokes. Each of the men, grabbed a can.

"I can't get over how cold, this can of Coke is. This is the coldest thing I've felt, in fifty years. Oh wow! You know what that means."

"No, Grampa. What?"

The old man sat there in silence, for a time.

"What's wrong?"

"That means, I'm over, seventy years old! That's how old my grandfather was, when I left for the pacific. That also means he, my gramma and many others, have died by now, of old age," said the old man, as he sat there staring at his can of pop. Thinking about all the things that have changed, since he's been on the island.

"What happened to your eye, Grampa?"

The old man sat there still staring at his can of Coke.

"Sir, are you all right, Sir?" asked the gunny.

The man looked up, at the gunny. "Yes, Jack, I'm all right. My eye . . . I fell, when the Japs were chasing Rob. . . , the four of us down the trail through the thick jungle, towards the beach. The four of us got separated in the jungle that night. I had fallen into a crevasse, and never made it to the beach." The old man again became silent, as he sat there holding his Coke. "That crevasse saved my life, in more ways then one, that nite. When I fell, I landed face first, on it's lava floor. I was out for a long time, maybe for days. When I came to and climbed out, everyone was gone. I was alone! From that day until yesterday, alone! I saw ships, but couldn't tell where they were from. So I never signaled them, for help.

The same with airplanes, I couldn't tell! Then I heard and saw those things, you guys came in. They can land and take off, in the same spot. Straight down then straight up, in the same place. What are they called?" Just then the door opened.

Sanchez came in and walked towards the table. J J turned and saw who came in. The old man jumped to his feet. "Here Miss, have a seat."

The rest of the men sat there smiling, at Sanchez and the old man.

"Thank you, Mr. Johnson."

"Just call me J J, Sergeant. Would you like a Coke?"

"Yes, thank you, J J." The old man grabbed a Coke from the tray and smiled. He opened the can and then handed it to her. Sanchez took the Coke from the old man.

"Those things with the big propeller, what are they?" asked the old man, as he sat back down.

"They're helicopters, Grampa. They were developed, during World War II. It was, towards the end of the war, before they were seen much," said the Colonel, as he sat there enjoying the conversation.

"The one you came in Robby, I'm sorry Colonel."

"J J, you can call me, Robby."

"Ok Robby. That hillec . . . thing flew right over my head, as you came in to land today. Do you think you could take me for a ride, later?"

"Most definitely, J J. It would be a privilege," said the Colonel.

"Robby, that would be great."

"J J, what made you realize, we were from the USA?" asked the gunny.

"Oh, when I attacked the four guys, in the jungle. I saw the lettering on their uniforms, was, in what I thought was English. When I read J. S. Johnson, my own initials, and last name, on J J's uniform, and I looked eye to eye with J J, him looking back at me, with a face that looked American. At that time, I thought you may be Americans. I took some binoculars during my attack. I watched everything, to make sure you were Americans. Then at home at night, I carved that poem of mine, on the palm. I brought it into your camp and left it, where it would be immediately found. Why did I do that? For two reasons. To show you I was here, and that I was American, or at least English speaking, anyway. When I saw the seven of you come into the jungle. I thought you were coming for me! Then I saw that three of the seven, were women! And then, the girls took off their clothes. It was then I realized, they were just there for a swim, not after me. The four men left the girls. I was standing there in the sand watching, with the binoculars. I had forgotten, how beautiful a female could be. I really enjoyed watching you girls swim. Then, all of a sudden one of the girl's let out, an earsplitting scream. The men came running back to the pond. I stayed too long on the beach watching, the men almost caught me. You were the one that yelled, Bino Cular Man, weren't you, Sergeant? Was that French, I don't speak French, Sergeant. I know English and . . . then I saw USA, on some of the equipment and the hillec— , or whatever they're called. But when I saw the three beautiful girls! I knew you had to be Americans! I wanted to stay right there on the beach, when you saw me by my pond. I thought you'd probably attack, or might even shoot me, right there on the beach or maybe in the jungle, before I had a chance to tell you who I was. That's why I came into camp, the way I did. I figured, you wouldn't shoot someone, for just walking into camp for lunch. So, here I am. What's for lunch?"

Everyone laughed, at the oldman's funny.

"Private, what's for lunch?" asked the gunny.

A private came out from behind a divider and walked over to the gunny. "The menu today, Gunnery Sergeant, is roast turkey, mashed potatoes and gravy, bread dressing and peas, with cranberry sauce. It will be ready in forty five minutes, Gunny."

"Thank you, Private."

"Is that what we're having for lunch? It sounds like it's Thanksgiving! I will drop in for lunch, more often."

"It is Thanksgiving."

"What! I thought it was June! Not November!" said J J, shaking his head, in disappointment.

"It's June, Grampa. I just meant, we're so thankful you are here."

"Oh, I thought I lost six months. I tried to keep track of the days, weeks, months, and years. I knew, I wasn't right on, but I thought my system, worked better than that."

"What month and year do you think it is, J J?"

"I'm not sure, what day it is, because of being unconscious, after my fall. But it's June 29, 1993, my wife's birthday, I think."

"That's the right year and month, J J. But it's June thirtieth," said the gunny.

"Yes, but at home, it's the twenty ninth. Gramma's birthday! Gunnery Sergeant, can we call her and tell her about, Grampa? What a birthday present that would be!"

"I'm sorry, but I don't think that would be a good idea. What do you think, Colonel?"

"That's right. That would be a tremendous shock, for her. It would be much better if you were there, to help her with this fantastic news."

"You mean, I can go home. How long would that be, Robby?"

"I'm a Colonel in the U S Marine Corp. I'm subject to orders, as you are. We will have to contact, Fleet Command. Let me have your ID number J J. I will see what I can do, to get you sent home, to give your wife, the good news, J J."

"My number is 36560357, Robby."

"I will need yours too, Son. If you're to go with him."

"Me, Sir? Yes Sir, mine is 544-67-7680, Sir."

"There are seventy six or seventy seven people, counting me on this island. Is there enough turkey, for everyone?" J J asked with tears in his eye, from the news that he would soon see his, Jera Marie.

"If there isn't, we'll have more flown in, no problem. So you eat as much as you want, J J. But remember you haven't had this kind of food, for a life time," said the Colonel, as he finished writing their ID numbers down. He then read the numbers back, to the two men. Both men nodding their heads, that the numbers were indeed correct.

"Do you have any medical problems, that need attention, that you know of, J J?" asked the gunny.

"No, Jack."

"The doc should look at you, now that you've been exposed to some of our germs, just as a precaution," said the gunny.

"Gunnery Sergeant, we can serve you and the Colonel and the men that are here now, Gunny."

"Good, bring this fellow some of everything. Also some more Coke, Private," said the Colonel, pointing at J J.

"Yes, Sir."

"Thank you. That would be great. It all smells so good, Robby"

The private brought J J a tray, filled with a Thanksgiving feast. He put the tray down in front of J J.

"I hope this tastes as good as it looks and smells!" said J J, as he picked up a fork from the tray. He held the fork in his hand, looking at it, as he spoke.

"Not like the coffee. It smelled so good but it tasted terrible huh, J J?" laughed the gunny.

The others at the table joined in the laughter.

"Right Sergeant. . . ! Do you know, how long it's been since, I've held a fork in my hand?" asked J J.

"Over fifty years," said everyone aloud, sitting at the table at the same time.

"No, last night! I have forks at home," smiled the old man.

Everyone laughed, together. At the old man's sense of humor. J J took a big fork of mashed potatoes, gravy and dressing, it smelled absolutely delicious. As he took his first bite, everyone sat patiently waiting for his comment. His eye began to water.

"He doesn't like it," said the gunny.

"Yes, I do, it's just a little too spicy and I took too big of bite, that's all," said J J, with food still in his mouth, as he grabbed for his Coke.

"Mikey Like's It!" said Billy.

Everyone, but J J, laughed.

"Whose Mikey?" asked J J.

"It's an old joke," said Billy.

"Hey, I'm the oldest one here. I don't get it," said J J, with smile on his face.

"It's a famous old TV commercial. About a boy, named Mikey, and his two brothers. Mikey's brothers gave him some new breakfast cereal to try, they were leery of trying themselves, not knowing if it was any good or not. Then they saw that, Mikey was eating it, and seemed to like it. That's where the expression 'Mikey Like's It,' came from."

J J sat there, staring at Billy.

"Why are you staring at me, Sir?" asked Billy.

"What's a TV commercial?"

"TV's, the ruination of the American Society!" said Billy, talking like a southern television Evangelist.

"What? What do you mean, ruination of America? Your name is Billy, isn't it?"

"Yes Sir, it is. . . , it's television, Sir."

"Television! I know what television is, I saw a television, at the 1939, New York World's Fair. That's TV, television? Why is TV, the ruination of America, Billy?"

"Sir, the average American, watches five an a half hours of TV a day! Kids watch even more."

"Where do they go, to watch that much TV?"

"Home! Most homes have at least two televisions."

"Like Radio, they have TV in there homes?" asked J J.

"Yes. Some TV's receive as many as a hundred and fifty stations. There's one, on that furthest table." J J, looked to where, Billy, was pointing. There sitting on the table, was a big square box, with a black window, facing them.

"You have one here, and it works, here?"

"Yes, can I show him it works, Gunny?"

"Sure, go a head, turn it on, Johnson." The younger J J, got up and went to the TV. He pushed a button and the sound and picture came on. Then he returned, to his seat.

They all sat there watching the old man, watching the television show, "Good Morning America." The old man still eating his lunch, as he watched. Then putting his fork down he turned to Billy.

"If they're watching that much TV, when do they have time for their school work. There's no time for anything, but TV!"

"That's right! That's why some people think, TV is the ruination, of our society."

The old man sat staring at the TV. He then turned his head. "I heard J J ask, if he could call his gramma. You mean, I could call my Jera Marie, right now, from here? I could talk to her, on a two way radio? I could just pick up the mic and ask the radio operator to get the phone company in Seattle, to ring her number and I could talk to her right now?"

"No, not that way J J," smiled the gunny.

"I, wondered!"

"It's much simpler then that. You would just dial her number, if she was home, she'd answer."

"Then I can, I can call her right now?"

"Yes, J J, you could. I think it would be much better and safer, if you saw her and told her in person," said the Colonel.

"Safer, for her you mean?"

"Yes, much safer for her."

"Yes, but how many months will that take?" asked J J, with concern in his voice.

"If everything goes all right, less than a week, J J."

"Less then a week! How could that be? Oh never mind," said J J, as he sat thinking about 'all the changes he had already seen, in the short time he'd been there.'

"Now, that's up to Fleet Command, not me J J. If it was up to me, you'd be home before you left."

"What do you mean, home before I left?"

"Let me explain, J J. I would put you in that helicopter you saw. We'd fly from here, to the Enterprise. From there, you'd fly to Pearl, where you'd catch a flight to Seattle. It would take less than one day. Being, it is twenty nine hours earlier there, then it is here. You'd be home before you left. We'll see, what FLEETCOM has to say, J J," said the Colonel.

"That's unbelievable! I could be home, with my Jera Marie,

tomorrow or today, oh whatever, soon!"

One at a time, the others were getting up to get their food, as J J was finishing his, still glancing over at the TV.

"After we eat lunch, why don't you show us, where your home is, J J? How far is it, from here?"

"Not very far. The road you made, goes right near where I live. Where I've lived, for how long?" asked J J, as he lifted his arms waving them like a conductor leading an orchestra.

"Over fifty years," said everyone aloud, and then all laughed, including J J.

"I need to find the latrine. I know where it is, I just need to go."

"Go, go a head and go, J J," said the gunny.

Getting up and leaving the table, J J walked out the door. The rest of the camp stared, as he walked to the latrine. On the way, he saw Betty Jo and Sara, standing in front of a tent.

"Good afternoon, ladies. How are you, this beautiful day? Are you ready for another swim?"

"We're fine. A swim would be great, are you going to take us, for a swim?" asked Sara, as she answered, the one eyed old, gentleman.

"Maybe later." J J answered, as his face turned red, at the boldness of the young woman. He continued on his way to the latrine, at a quicker pace. The Cokes were getting to him. He opened the door and entered the bathroom, it was as clean as it could be. There was a fan, circulating fresh air. There were two sinks and above each sink, a mirror. He walked over to be in line with a mirror. He was back some distance so he could see himself, from head to toe. He moved up closer, so he could see his face. When he did, he saw his face clearly. His face, he couldn't believe how old and scarred, his face was. He was, an ugly old man. No wonder the girl screamed, when she saw him at the pond. He stood there looking at his face. How was he to see his, Jera Marie, with a face like this. She would never know he was her, J J. When he left her, he looked like their grandson, not an ugly old man. With a saddened heart, he turned on the water. With the water running into the sink, he put his hands in the water. The water was too warm. He adjusted the two valves, to make the water temperature more comfortable. He washed his hands, while still looking up at himself in the mirror. He went to use the toilet, shaking his hands dry, as he walked towards the stalls. There were three, enclosed areas, one was larger then the other two. He opened the door to each stall. Two were toilets, the larger one, were showers. He went in one stall and used the toilet. While using it, he looked down at the white roll of toilet paper. Unrolling some of the paper, he wiped his eye and nose. The paper was so soft. He flushed the toilet and left the stall. He washed his hands, in the warm water again, as he again looked into the mirror, shaking his head as he did. Rubbing his hands to dry them, he walked towards the door. He opened the door and left the bathroom. On his way back to the mess tent, he nodded to the two girls. He then slowly walked towards the girls.

"I just looked at myself in the bathroom mirror. It's the first time I saw my face clearly, since I was hurt. What a sight! I'm so sorry, I scared you two girls at the pond. This face is enough to scare anyone. It scared me! When I looked in the mirror."

"It was you being at the pond, that scared us, not your face. Of course, if you went boo in the dark, you'd scare the hell out of me, with that face," said Sara.

"Sara, how rude! Sir, my name is Betty Jo. The rude one's name, is Sara."

"Who are you? We know you're the one that attacked the four guy's in the jungle and the one, we saw at the pond. But who are you?" asked Sara, as she held out her hand, to shake his.

"My name is, Jay Samuel Johnson, J J," answered J J, as he held out his hand to Sara, and shook hands with her, then Betty Jo.

"Betty Jo and I, couldn't hear what you and the others were saying, except that, you and Private Johnson, have the same name and nick name."

"Ya, we sure do. Nice to meet you girls. I'd better get back to the mess tent, to finish lunch. Maybe they'll have pumpkin pie. They have had everything else, to go with a Thanksgiving meal."

"Nice to meet you, Sir. I'll bet they do, let's go see."

The two girls walked with J J back to the mess. He opened the door of the tent, the two girls entered and he followed them in.

"I saw these two lovely women, standing talking to each other. I went over and introduced myself. I apologized for scaring them at the pond. I told them what we were having for lunch. We thought we'd see if we were having pumpkin pie for dessert. If so, they'd like to join us."

"I don't know J J, we'll ask." The gunny got up and went to the counter. He talked to someone, then he returned. "J J, how's pumpkin pie, with whip cream on top, sound?"

"That's sounds great, Sergeant. I thought we might just have pumpkin pie, without the whip cream. The whip cream makes this Thanksgiving meal complete," laughed J J.

The two girls went to get their food. After doing so, they returned to a table, near by.

J J's, sad heart was uplifted. He was enjoying the company, at this Thanksgiving meal.

"J J, you said that you were alone from the day you were left on this island. Until you saw us come in the helicopters. What happened to the Japanese?"

"I don't know. All I know, Robby, is when I came to, from my fall, everyone was gone. There have been other people come to the island. But they left, before I saw them, or they were dead."

"Dead! Dead from what?"

"They washed up on shore that way, Robby. When the Japs left, they left in a hurry. They left a lot of their stuff behind. That stuff, kept me alive. Over the years, other stuff has washed ashore." Once again, the old man was silent.

SURVIVE

"Once a sailboat ran a ground. It had been through a severe storm and there was no one on board. Her masts must of been broken off in the storm. She had been a beautiful thing and she had a bounty of stuff onboard. The weather stayed nice for a time, after the storm. It took me that time to bring all the stuff ashore. Then the weather changed. I watched her break up in a storm, as I sat helpless on the beach and cried. That was in the late forties, maybe forty-five years ago. I have her name plaque, hanging on the wall of my home. If that beautiful sailboat, hadn't gone aground, I wouldn't be here today, telling you this story. In the storm that grounded her, my island was destroyed. The storm removed all forms of vegetation. It striped the island clean, but for myself and the stuff I saved, from the wrecked sailboat, nothing else was left. That sailboat was my Vessel Of Life," said J J, with a tear in his eye.

Everyone at the tables sat and listened to J J, answering the Colonel's question. Then telling, a little of what life was like for him, on his island.

"There were no plants left, at all? none?" asked the Colonel.

"No, Sir, none! It took years for them to grow back. They did grow fast, but it still took years."

"What did you live on during that time, J J?"

"The stuff from my Vessel Of Life, Robby. I had canned vegetables, fruits, meats, dried beans, rice and of course fish! I think, I've had fish every way there is! My fresh water comes from the pond you girls swam in. After the storm I thought it would dry up. I really was terrified that it might. It did get a lot smaller. But as the trees grew back, the pond slowly grew, to it's present day size. It's as big as it was or slightly larger."

"J J, it's a pleasure, to listen to someone who can tell a good story. The art of story telling, has all but died out, because of that thing," said the Colonel, as he pointed towards the darkened TV, sitting on the far table.

Everyone applauded, at what the Colonel said.

"J J, have you had enough to eat?"

"Yes, Sir, Robby. I've eaten more in just the last hour, than I would in a week!"

"Let's go see your home, where you've lived . . . over fifty years," said everyone in the entire mess tent, including J J.

"That would be fine with me, Robby. It's not far from here. Let's go."

J J gets up from the table. The younger J J also gets up and goes to open the door.

"You three men come with J J, Johnson, the Colonel and I," said the gunny, pointing to Billy, Bo, and Tye, as he turned to Sanchez. "Sanchez, you're in command."

"Yes, Gunny."

The seven men walked through the camp, talking as they walked. As they got to the edge of camp, they could see the wide trail or the road, as J J called it, going into the jungle. J J lead the way on the trail.

"Sir, why didn't we see any trails, beings you've been here f.. so long, Sir?" adsked Billy.

"That's right, Billy, we didn't see any. Why is that?"

"Because, I did my very best not to leave any trails. That's why! Robby, when your father and I came to this island so long ago, we came through the jungle together and found a trail, we followed it right to the Jap's camp. When I was left here alone, I always remembered that trail. So, I've always been as careful as possible, not to leave any sign. If I saw a trail forming, I would transplant plants and bushes. And within a few days, there wouldn't be any sign of a trail. When the seven of you were cutting this road, I thought for sure, you were coming right to me, at my place. Then when the Jap climbed that tree!" said J J, as he pointed to the tree, Tye had climbed. "I knew I'd been found. Then all of you sat down around the tree and just talked. Then you got up and went right past me, and my home." Soon they had walked the distance to the pond.

"This place is beautiful," said the Colonel, as they walked out onto the beach, near the waters edge.

"Sanchez wasn't kidding, this is a fantastic spot. Colonel, are you ready for a swim?" asked Gunnery Sergeant Roman.

"It sure is inviting, isn't it, Gunny? Maybe later, we can do just that."

"You men will never know, what it was like for me, to stand here and watch those three women swimming in my pond, in their under clothes. Talk about beautiful, that was!"

The six men stood with J J, thinking about what a beautiful spot this truly was.

"Sir, they had their swimsuits on," said the younger J J.

"It looked like underwear to me, J J. The kind a pinup girl would wear, it didn't leave much, to the imagination!" The men thought a moment about what he said, as they gazed smilingly.

"J J, can you see your place from here?"

"No, Robby, not from here. We past it, back a-ways," said J J, pointing in the direction they had come. "Come on, I'll show you where it is."

They started back on the trail towards camp. The seven men walked about a hundred yards, then J J stopped.

"We leave this road at this point and go this way," said J J, pointing into the jungle. With that, J J left the trail and entered the jungle. With the others following close behind, so as not to loose him in the thick jungle. They all noticed, with what ease J J moved through the thick undergrowth, as the six of them struggled to keep up with the jungle man. J J had stopped to wait for the others to catch up. When they had caught up, they noticed where they were standing, the jungle was not so thick, and that the seven of them had climbed out onto the side of a small hill, over looking the lower jungle. J J stood there exhilarated. "My pond is right through there, and your camp is over there. If you look, you can see the flag. I couldn't see it until I got those binoculars of yours," said J J, as he smiled at his grandson. "That tree, is the one the Jap climbed," said J J pointing, as he spoke.

"Gunnery Sergeant, may I say something?"

"What, Corporal Kim? Yes, go a head, Corporal."

"Sir, my name is Tye Kim. You keep referring to me as the Jap. I am not Japanese! My grandparents fought the Japanese, as you did, in World War II. They were and I am, of Vietnamese descent. My parents came to the US, after the Vietnam War was over. I was born in the United States, in the town of Artesia. Artesia is about twenty eight miles southeast of Los Angeles, California, just off the I-5 freeway. Where I lived, until I joined the Marine Corp and came to your island."

J J stood there looking at what he thought was an adversary, was in actuality, a young Marine, like his new found grandson, but with different eyes. "I'm sorry, Tye Kim, I thought you were Japanese. There are a great many things I don't understand. Things that I knew, have no meaning or a different one. Like women in the corp! The Colored, being in a white unit on one hand, but then, being called Black! Has or has not mankind finally, learned to live with each other and that all men are created equal?"

"No, I'm afraid not, J J! Mankind has come a ways, in the last fifty years, but a lot of the old prejudices and some new ones, are still with us, alive and strong," said the Colonel.

"Damn straight, Colonel," said Billy, as he and Bo exchanged a sole-brother hand shake.

The Colonel and Gunnery Sergeant Roman, both turning to see. The two men obviously showing their displeasure, in what was said.

"Where is your home, from here, J J?"

"We're there, this is it, Robby!"

"Where?"

J J smiled, a knowing smile, as he turned and took a step behind a bush. With that one step, he was gone from site. The others went to the bush. On the far side of the bush was an opening into the hill. The gunny went in first, the entrance was small, about four feet high and two wide. He stood there bent over with his head and shoulders in the opening, allowing his eyes to adjust to the darkness. The sunlight from the outside, showed there were steps carved in the rock floor, leading down into the darkness of the cavern. The gunny started down the steps. The others followed him into the darkness. A short ways in, there was enough head room, as to allow them to walk upright. As they walked the cavern became larger. In the light ahead they could see J J standing awaiting their arrival. J J bent at the waist and swung his arm in a welcoming motion. The cavern was quite large at this point. On one side there were openings about two feet wide by one high in size, four of them in all, they let sunlight into the cavern. The walls at the openings, appeared to be quite thick.

"Welcome to my home."

The six men entered the cavern. As the men came in, they all removed their hats, without hesitation. The Colonel and the gunny walked up to J J. The younger four men, stood together looking at the room with their mouths open.

"Wow, this is awesome."

"That it is, Private Smith. You have some place here, J J," said the gunny, as he turned looking around the large room back to J J.

J J stood there beaming proudly, obviously pleased that his first house guest, liked his home. The room was large about twenty five by forty feet. It was oval in shape, with a fourteen foot or higher, dome ceiling. At the other end of the room was a bed. Along the back wall, opposite the one with the openings, were cupboards and shelves. Hung on the wall above one of them, was the name plaque from the wrecked sailboat. The name on the plaque was, The Promise. All the shelves were filled with interesting things. On the same end that they had entered the room, was a kitchen, with pots and pans, hanging on the wall. A stove, ice box and a sink, with dishes in it and cupboards. The wall with the four openings, two of which were about chest high, the other two were lower. The two lower windows had chairs in front of them, one facing in, with the other facing out. The floor was snow white in color. The walls and ceiling were black volcanic rock. With the white floor, the sunlight was enough to light the room, quite adequately. The white floor of the cavern consisted of white beach sand, with runways from the kitchen to the bed, and to the entrance, at the end of the room. The runways appeared to be made of a fine hardwood.

"This place is absolutely beautiful, J J."

"Thank you. I've called it home, ever since the storm, I told you about, Robby. I didn't live here before that. I lived in a palm shack. Not too long before the storm, I started looking for a better place. It looked as though I could be here for a while. I had no idea, it would be this long!" said J J, as he stood there grinning. "I started looking. I remembered the crevasse I fell into. I looked over the entire island for such openings. I found dozens. Most of them were too small or they had water in them. The ones that didn't, were too close to the ocean and at high tide they flood. Then I found this one and two others, that could be used. This one I had to modify. The other two, could be used as is for storage. One is bigger than this one, the other is smaller. Neither of which had anyway to get light into them. I found this one with the help of a bird. She had her nest in one of the holes. I moved the nest, so I could start work on this one immediately. Believe me it didn't look like this. It took me six weeks to clean out the roots, vines, and other things, dead and alive. The floor had big crevasses in it. I had to fill them first with big rocks, then smaller and smaller ones, until it was ready for the sand. I carried sand for weeks. There was a trail from the beach to here then! I was concerned about the trail, but something, kept me working. I wasn't finished with the sand when the storm hit. I came here during the storm, to see if it leaked, within a minute or so, I thought I was going to drown. The water came through those openings like a screen door on a submarine!" said J J, as he pointed at the openings, with tears in his eye. "The water that was coming in, was wind driven rain water. If it wasn't for how this cavern was formed, with it's porous floor, I would have drowned. I was so scared. It was different fear than, when the Japs heard us, at their camp. That was one of frantic! This was one of shear helplessness. I felt helpless and insignificant. I just backed into a corner and waited for my life or the storm to end . . . fortunately for me, it was the storm. When I came out, I couldn't believe it! There was nothing left! As I walked through the devastation I knew, if I hadn't gone to the cavern, when I did, I would have died! Like I said, that fall saved my life, in more ways than one. Saved it, saved it for what, to starve? There was nothing left to eat, no shade from the sun. How was I going to survive under these conditions? It was already so hot!" J J looked around. All six of the men had sat down to listen. "I'm sorry, I've been windjammin again. You probably wonder how I can even talk, after fifty, years of being alone. Let alone, talk so much, and without losing my voice. It's because of all these books you see here, I used to read aloud." J J stood there thinking. . . ,"I also sing and whistle while I work. You know, like the 'Seven Little dwarfs," in the movie 'Snow White." J J stood there a moment in silence with a far away look in his eye. . . , "I saw that movie with Jera, when we were going together."

"How did you survive, J J?" asked the gunny.

"The day after the storm, I went to the far side of the island. I continued to look for something, anything! There was nothing left! I knew as I walked, I would soon be food for the worms. Then on the way back, I saw The Promise. I dropped to my knees and thanked God! At first I was ecstatic! I jumped up and ran to the waters edge. Then I stopped! What was I doing? It could be the enemy! I stood there thinking, looking at the big boat. If it was the enemy, they had me. What was I to do? There was nothing left. . . . In less than a week, I'd be dead. I sat down in the sand and watched. I sat there a long time. I noticed how quiet it was. There seemed to be no movement onboard the boat. Just a slight breeze was blowing. As I sat there in the sand thinking, I noticed the frayed lines dangling from her broken mast, waving in the breeze. There were no footprints on the beach or in the sand. I jumped up, I was still alone! I ran into the water and swam towards the boat. Alone, but still alive! The boat was up right on a small reef. As I swam up to her I couldn't see any holes in her. It looked as though she just ran a ground, at high tide. She must of came ashore, during the high water and wind, of the storm. As I swam up, there was a large line hanging down her starboard side. I grabbed the line, pulling myself up and out of the water, I climbed up the side and looked over the gunwale. The deck was a mass of lines, torn sails and broken rigging parts. I quietly climbed over the gunwale and stood on her deck. There was no one in sight. I started to walk around the deck, as I walked, I noticed that all the hatches were closed, which they would be in a storm. I went to try to open one and couldn't, it was stuck. I continued to try the others. To my surprise they weren't stuck, they were all locked! I didn't understand that at all! It made no sense to me. Why were they locked? I got down on my hands and knees, to look in the port lights, to see below deck. Below, she was an awful mess. I had to get inside, below decks. I started to clear away the lines and rigging, from the main cargo hatch. It was also locked. After it was cleared, I looked for something to break the lock. I found a piece of heavy iron from the mess of rigging and proceeded, to pry the lock off and opened the hatch. There was stuff everywhere. The hold was clear full but what a mess. I thought the boat must of pitchpoled and turned upside down, over and over, to cause such a mess. She was one tough boat to have survived such a storm, nothing else did!"

"You did, Grampa, you survived!" said the younger J J. Bringing the old man back, over fifty years of time, in less then a heartbeat, looking into the eyes of his grandson.

"That I did!" said J J, smiling at his grandson.

"Did you think about sailing her, like you did Grampa's boat, in Puget Sound, when you were a kid?" J J stood there smiling, thinking about what his grandson asked.

"After I opened the hatch and saw all the stuff in the hold, I did just that. I sat down on the edge of the opening to the hold and thought what should I do. How could I get her off the reef? I had no idea how she got where she was, in the first place! It looked as though a large wave just carried her in and sat her gently on the reef. I didn't see anyway for me to get her off the reef. Unless there was dynamite on board. Then I could blast holes in the reef. I could then sail her through those holes, back into open water. If there was. And I could do it! But could I sail her? No sails, mast, or rigging, nothing left on the island, to make new. Even if I could do all that, there was no help, a boat of this size? It was typhoon season. This storm was the first of many. After sitting there thinking about it, for a time. I decided the first thing I should do, was take an inventory of what was onboard, then make my decision on what I found." J J stopped and looked around. "I'm still alive today, in part because of her and the people who stocked her hold. Everything you see here, all that I've learned, all that I've become, from that day, until yesterday, for close to fifty years, came from The Promise. My Vessel Of Life." J J's voice shaking as he spoke, looking up at the plaque on the cavern wall, with tears in his eye.

"J J, didn't you say it was in the late forties when you found The Promise?"

"Yes, I did, Robby. It was on September 29, 1947. I can show you here in my journal," said J J, as he went to a shelf, low on the back wall. Pulling out a stack of books, quickly going to the bottom one in the stack. Pulling out the book, he walked over to the Colonel, holding the book in his hand, he stood there looking at it for a moment. He then handed the journal to the Colonel. "This is the oldest journal, I have left. I had others, but they were swept away by the storm. This one starts the day I found The Promise . . . I would love to read it to you."

"Go ahead, J J. Read it to us," said the Colonel, handing the journal back to J J.

"I can't."

"Why not, J J?"

"I can't see writing that small, anymore," said J J, pushing the book back to the Colonel. "Go ahead. You read it."

"J J, it's odd you didn't find any mention of the war onboard. Some papers, books something, something telling about the war or at least how it ended," said the Colonel, as he looked at J J's journal.

"When did you say the war ended, Robby?"

"They both ended in 1945, J J."

J J turns, and goes to another shelf. He comes back to the Colonel, with another book in hand. "This is, The Promise's Log. The last entries are mine, about how she met her fate," said J J, as he handed the Colonel the ships log.

The Colonel looked through the log. "It says here she was in Valparaiso, Chile," said the Colonel, as he began to read the log. "The Promise is loaded with goods for the south pacific. We are to leave Valparaiso the tomorrow, if this storm ends. The crew has gone ashore. They worked hard and the day went well. I will also stay ashore, this last night in port." It's signed, but I can't read the signature. The date at the top of the page is. . . , it's March 8, 1944! The war wasn't over! That's why there's no mention! The war wasn't over yet! He couldn't write or have any information onboard about the war, because of the possibility that information, may fall into the wrong hands . . . ! That's over three years, before she came here!" said the Colonel, as he looked up from the log.

"The way I see it! She endured three and a half years of open sea and storms, to come to me in one piece. To be here for me, the day after the storm," said J J, as he looked up on the wall, to the plaque from The Promise.

"J J, I take it there wasn't any dynamite onboard."

"No, Sergeant there wasn't. I couldn't think of anyway for me to move her off that reef. So, after doing an inventory, and knowing I couldn't move her from where she was into open water, or even if I could move her, I couldn't sail her alone, I knew that! I couldn't save her, but she could save me. I decided to salvage all I could, before the next storm. I worked as hard, and as quick, as I possibly could. I was in excellent shape after moving all that sand. So I worked around the clock, knowing another storm could hit at anytime. It rained and the wind blew, but it was five weeks, until another major storm hit. This gave me enough time to save the stuff from The Promise. Then a giant storm hit the island with a vengeance! It was as bad as the storm, weeks earlier, but the cavern was more weather tight. I stayed on the beach and watched The Promise, as long as I could. I had tied line together to make a safety line. The line went from the beach, back to the cavern. It was tied to parts of rigging, that I had driven into the volcanic rock, the beach, and tied to roots of trees along the way, left there after the first storm. After I watched The Promise break up. I made it back to the cavern, to wait out the storm. Without the lines to hang onto, I don't think I could have made it back. The wind was so strong, it blew me off my feet. When the storm was over, I saved all I could find of The Promise." J J stood looking up at The Promise's name plaque, with tears running down his cheek, he continued telling his story. "I put what I could of what was left in the caverns. The rest I buried on the beach, as close to the high tide water mark, as there was sand to do so. When I was done with all the hard work. I realized how much I was going to miss her, setting out there in the cove. I would sit on the beach for hours fantasizing sailing her home."

"J J, as much as I enjoy listening to you, I must head back. I have to return to FLEETCOM. It sure will be interesting, what their reaction is, when I tell them what I found, on my inspection tour. I should take you with me, but let's wait until they respond to the news. Why don't you and your grandson spend this afternoon and evening getting to know one another. If I'm right the next few months will be an unbelievable experience. . . ."

"Colonel, I can stay here?"

"Roman, is that all right with you?"

"Yes, It's all right with me. Is it all right with J J?"

"It's great with me, Robby! It's not everyday you find out you have a son and a grandson, you didn't even know you had!"

The younger J J looked at his grandfather, as he spoke of his son, the boy's father, with excitement in his voice. The young man knew, he would soon have to tell his grandfather, his father, the old mans son, had died many years ago.

"You two report to camp, at 0800."

"Yes, Gunnery Sergeant. We'll see you then."

The seven of them began to leave the room. One at a time they went through the tunnel, out into the light of day. Back on the hillside they stood together, over looking the jungle.

"We'll see you two, in the morning."

"Yes, we'll see you then, Gunny. Thank you, Gunny, for letting us have this time, together."

"Yes, thank you, Jack."

"It's ok this time! Don't expect it, everytime, you're alone for fifty years!" said the gunny, as he grinned at J J. He then turned and started down the hill, with the others.

The two J J's watched as the five men disappeared into the heavier jungle. They stood there looking out towards camp and the sea. Each man stood waiting, waiting for the other to speak, not knowing what to say themselves, to start a conversation.

"Sir, I have something, I must tell you."

"What?"

"It's. . . ."

"Go ahead, what is it? After what I've seen and heard today. . . !" said J J, shaking his head.

"It's about your son, my father. . . ."

"Tell me."

Tears came to the young mans eyes, as he started to tell his grandfather, about his father, the old man's son. "I knew my father, as I knew you, by the stories Gramma and my mom, told me."

"What was his name?"

"Sam."

J J thought a moment, as the two men looked at each other. 'If not for the son he never met, his grandson wouldn't be standing there with tears in his eyes, telling him about his son.' J J sensed what his grandson was trying to tell him. Putting his arms out to his grandson. The two men embraced each other.

"What happened to your father?"

"He was killed! Killed by a drunk driver. He died, when I was little. I don't remember him, except like I said, from the stories." The two men separated their embrace and regained their composure. J J's mind filled with questions.

"Jera Marie, your gramma. Gramma, that's still hard for me to say in the same breath, as Jera Marie. . . . She told you stories of me and your father? She thinks I'm dead! She thinks I've been dead over fifty years! Did she. . . ? Did your gramma, remarry?"

"Gramma? No! She said, you were 'the only man she ever loved!' I never heard her say you were dead. She always used words like lost or missing."

"After all these years, I can still remember the look on my Jera

Marie's face, when I left her standing on that dock in Seattle. She said, "I will wait for you, J J. For as long as it takes."

"She's still waiting, Grampa."

"She's waiting for the man she saw go aboard that ship in Seattle, not an ugly old man like me!" said J J, as he walked over to a rock outcropping and sat down.

"She doesn't look the same as she did, either."

"What do you mean! I'll bet she's just as beautiful as ever!" said J J, as he jumped to his feet.

"She is Sir, but she's also fifty years older."

"Fifty years! How could she wait fifty years? That's so long, I didn't have any choice, but she did. How did she do it?"

"Love! That's how, Grampa. I think, she's still waiting to join the only man she ever loved. You, Grampa."

"We were so happy together."

"In a day or two you will be with her, together again."

"The Colonel said that. He said I could be with my Jera Marie that soon!" said J J, as he sat back down on the rocks.

"If the war's over, why are you here and why are you in the Marines?"

"I joined the Marines, because I wanted to be a Marine. I wanted to be like my grampa J J, you, Grampa. Maybe it was to come here to find you! I don't know! If I hadn't joined, I wouldn't be here with you now. You would have attacked Kim and the others, and not seeing the name Johnson, on their shirt, you could have killed all of them! Then you could have been killed, before they knew who you were. Maybe like The Promise, I was brought here to save you! Only this time, save you and take you home!"

J J stood as they both looked towards camp, hearing the helicopter revving up it's engine and taking off. The helicopter became visible in the sky. They watched as it flew in their direction. They could see the Colonel waving, as it flew over. "The Colonel, sure looks like his father, Robby. Did my son look like me? You look a lot like me. Do you look like your father?" He asked as the helicopter flew out of sight.

"Gramma says, I look just like you did, when you were my age. My father looked more like great Grampa Miller."

"Jera's father, Pop Miller? He was always good to me. We worked together at my grandfather's shop. He did get upset with me, when I joined up. He thought I should stay at the machine shop, work nights and go to school during the day"

"Don't feel like The Lone Ranger, he got upset with me too, when I joined! He thought I should stay in school."

"Pop Miller, is still alive? He must be a hundred years old!"

"He was one hundred, his last birthday! How'd you remember that?"

"Who's The Lone Ranger? I heard you and the others call me that, in the jungle."

"What? Oh, The Lone Ranger. He was a TV star."

"You mean like, on the radio?"

"It's like a radio show, but it's on TV. At the end of the show. Someone in the show would ask, who was that masked man?"

"YES! Then him and Tonto, his Indian friend. Would mount their horses and ride away! The Lone Ranger! He always wore a mask, no one ever saw his face! As he road away, he would yell, "Hi Ho Silver!""

"Yes. How. . . ?"

"No, I heard it on the radio!"

"Right. Well nowadays people use that line, 'who was that masked man' or 'don't feel like The Lone Ranger,' to make a point!"

"That's funny, I heard it on the radio and you watched the same show on TV. I first heard "The Lone Ranger" program when I was about ten years old," said J J, as his grandson came over and the two of them sat back on the rocks.

"Does, Pop Miller, still have the cabin up on Spirit lake, near Mt. Saint Helens?" asked J J, as the two men sat together on the rocks.

"No, he doesn't"

"He sold it?"

"No, it's not there anymore, Grampa."

"What happen, did it burn down or something?"

"Or something!"

"What do you mean, or something? If something happened to the cabin, why didn't he rebuild? It was such a pretty spot, near the lake."

"It's not there anymore."

"I know you said that!"

"No! The lake isn't there anymore."

"What do you mean, the lake isn't there?"

"It's gone!"

"What? Did it dry up? What happened to it?"

"Mt. Saint Helens is a volcano. It erupted on May 18, 1980 and destroyed the top of Mt. Saint Helens and Spirit Lake. The eruption also killed something like, sixty five people. When it blew, it destroyed hundreds of square miles of forest, it laid the forest down like straw. It broke huge trees, like they were tooth picks. Like the storm you had here, Grampa, on your island. I heard, when Saint Helens blew, the wind caused by the eruption reached an estimated, twelve hundred miles an hour!"

"Mt. Saint Helens was volcano! I had no idea. I sure didn't know it was an active one. There's so much, so many things have changed, in the last fifty years. How am I ever going to catch up?"

"One thing at a time. Just think of all the things you already know. You know things, I will never know. It's like you're a new born, with seventy years of knowledge and experiences, how exciting! Everyday we're alive, we learn new things. It will be so exciting, from the time you wake up in the morning, until you go to sleep at night. All the changes you'll see, every time you blink, or turn, there will be something new. Almost every thing you see and do, will have a new and or a different twist to it. I'm sure you'll get lots of help from Gramma, Mom and even Pop Miller. Pop Miller! Look at all the changes Pop Miller has seen, in his lifetime. I hope you will let me be a part of that experience, Grampa."

J J thought a moment of what to call his grandson. Grandson! Knowing you've had a son, you never met or even knew had been born, let alone a grandson. J J was now, starting to get used to the idea of being a grandfather. The thought of 'calling his grandson J J' came to mind, after all it's his name too! It wouldn't be any harder for him to learn to call him J J, than it would be to call him son or grandson. J J continued thinking.

"What is it, Sir? What's wrong?"

"Nothings wrong. I was just thinking, you don't have to call me sir. It will be hard for me to get used to being called anything, after all these years. I'm over seventy some years old, and I have to accept that. I'm so lucky to have had a son, to make it possible, to have a grandson, like you."

"Grampa, you can call me anything you'd be comfortable with."

"Why don't I call you J J, ok, J J?"

"Ok, Grampa."

"J J, I want to tell you how happy it makes me, to be here with you. Now that I have had sometime to think. Think about what has taken place here. It's an honor to call you J J! After all, you were named after me, your grampa."

"It has always been an honor, to be called, J J, Grampa. Hearing you, say it, makes it even more of an honor, thank you, Grampa," said J J, as he sat there putting his hand over on his grandfather's shoulder.

"As I get to know you. I will also get to know your father, through you, I will be able to get to know who my son was. I will also get to know other people close to you, people I have never met," said the older man, as he put his hand over on the young man's hand, which was still resting on his shoulder."

The two men sat there together on the rock outcropping.

"How old was Sam, when he was killed? That's it! From now on, I will go by the name, Sam!"

"That's great! My father would be proud, for you to be called Sam. Grampa, he was thirty six, when he was killed."

"Let's go inside, I'm thirsty."

"So am I, Grampa."

The two men got up from where they were sitting and walked towards the bush that concealed the entrance to the tunnel. Once there, J J let his grandfather enter the tunnel first. Through the tunnel they went, back into the cavern. Upon entering the cavern J J stopped again in amazement, at what a awesome place it was.

"Would you like a drink, J J?" asked his grandfather.

"Yes, thanks. I'll have a Diet Pepsi. No, waters fine, Grampa," laughed J J.

"Let me check. No, I'm sorry we're all out of Dieting Pepsi-Cola at this time. But I do have some water left. I'll have it for you PDQ. Have a seat while you wait," said the old man, quick on the comeback with his own sense of humor.

The two men laughing together at their little joke, as J J sat there waiting for his drink.

"Grampa I've been thinking, why don't you keep your name. I would much rather, hear people call you, J J. Hearing it will be music to my ears, now that we have you back. I'll go by my father's name, Sam. If that's not all right with you. I could use my first name, Jay. Don't misunderstand, like I said, it's been an honor to have had the name, J J. But, J J's been your name for seventy some years. Gramma, will have her J J and her grandson, both together, side by side."

J J stood there listening to what his grandson was saying. He then walked over to what was the kitchen area of the cavern.

"Ok, Sam it is, for now. When we get home to Seattle, we'll let my, Jera Marie, decide."

"That's a good idea Ollie," said his grandson, talking like Stan Laurel, of "Laurel And Hardy," fame.

"I know who that was! A . . . give me a minute, I know. . . ! Laurel And Hardy! Right?"

"That's right, Grampa, you got it. We'll let Gramma pick our names, when we get you home, but for now, I'll go by Sam and you're J J."

"Sounds good to me, Sam."

J J still in the kitchen area, walked over to what looked like a port light. The port light appeared to be, just lying on the hardwood part of the cavern floor. He bent down and began to open the porthole.

"What's in there?"

"In here? This is where I keep my drinking water," said J J, as he continued to open the porthole. "It's a cistern."

"What's that? What's a sister?"

"A cistern, not a sister. A cistern is used to store water or drinking water. It's usually a tank made of wood, steel, or concrete. This one happens to be, a small crevasse, that holds water. After the storm I turned it into a cistern."

"Like I said, you know things people my age don't know. I didn't know what a cistern was."

"Well, we'll learn together then, Sam," said J J as he opened the porthole. He then stood up and turned to the wall. There on the wall hung a dipper. He grabbed the dipper turned and bent down and put it in the open port. The dipper had a handle, about two feet long. It looked like the dipper held a quart or more. It appeared to be made of wood. Pulling it out and closing the port he stood up. Turning to a shelf, he got two cups. He filled the cups from the dipper. He then hung the dipper back on the wall. J J picked up the cups and walked towards his grandson with the two cups in hand. "Here's some cool water. It's not cold like the Coke-A-Cola, you gave me." J J handed a cup to his grandson. Sam took the cup from his grandfather and took a drink.

"Thanks. It's cooler than I thought it would be. It's good. How much does the cistern hold?"

"I don't know for sure, I would guess a couple hundred gallons. When I saw that I was being invaded, I carried as much water as I could the night you and the others invaded my island. I didn't do as well carrying the water as I did when I carried the sand for this cavern floor, for some reason it seemed much harder."

"I'm not sorry we invaded your island, Grampa. I'm sorry we scared you."

"Nor am I, sorry. It did make me a bit anxious, for awhile."

"I'll bet it did!"

"I had to be real careful carrying the water that night. Making all those trips in one night. Careful not to leave a trail. I tried to go and come a different way, each trip. It took a lot longer but you didn't see any trails, did you?"

"No, we didn't, Grampa. Grampa you made your shelves, bookcases, cupboards and the runways on the floor from wood you saved from The Promise. It also look's like to me, there must of been quite an assortment of tools."

"There were tools on board and five different size nails, a keg of each size. I became quite a carpenter there for awhile. I still have some wood stored."

"How big a boat was The Promise?"

"She was seventy two feet long and had a beam of eighteen feet. She was a beauty. I'm here to tell you."

"Thanks to her you are."

"That's right, thanks to her!"

"You said you can't read anymore or see to read, I mean."

"No, I can't. Something happened to my eye, oh about twenty years ago. It got where at first I couldn't read in here. I found that I could still read outside, in the daylight. Then a year or so later I couldn't read my books there either. That's why the writing on the palm leaf was so big, so I could see what I wrote."

"You probably just need glasses. Gramma wears glasses to read. She's worn them to read for as long I can remember."

"Do you think that's all it might be, I need glasses?"

"Maybe. Even if it's something more, I'm sure they could put a lens implant or something, to make it better."

J J sat there with a puzzled look on his face. Sitting on a keg he had rolled over from the wall, to where his grandson was sitting drinking the water he had given him. "What do you mean a lens implant?"

"Oh it's a surgery they do, to correct eye problems. Pop Miller had it done on both eyes. That was when I was little, it's been maybe ten or twelve years ago. He said after the surgery, 'he could see better than he could when he was eight years old."

"That's right. At the machine shop, Pop Miller used to take his glasses off, to see to do the really fine close work. It seems like in some ways not much time has past, while in others, a lifetime has. You said, Pop Miller, was upset with you, for leaving school to join the Marines. You didn't drop out, did you, Sam?"

"No, I finished high school. He wanted me to go onto college. I might when I get out. I just knew that I had to become a Marine, now I know why. To come here, to find you, Grampa."

"To go to college. That would be great. I'm glad you came here and found me first, instead Sam."

"It sounds funny, being called by a different name. It will take sometime to get used to."

"I guess at my age, four or five more years might have been too long. Sam, do you have any photographs of your gramma, my Jera Marie? I still find it hard to picture her a grandmother. Do you have some photos with you? When Robby and I volunteered, with the other two guys, for that night mission. We left all our personal stuff aboard ship."

"Yes, I have one with me. It's one of Gramma, with Mom and I. It was taken, the day I left to come here," said Sam, as reached behind, to his back pocket. Pulling his wallet out and opening it, he looked through the wallet for the picture. "Yes, here it is. The last one taken before I went aboard ship. Mother took a lot with her video camera, but this one, was the last one taken with the Polaroid."

J J sat there, with a puzzled look on his face.

Sam handed the picture to his grandfather. Taking the picture carefully from Sam. J J looked at the photograph, he was delicately holding in his hand. After looking down at it for some time, he looked up slowly at his grandson, with a strange smile on his face.

"What's wrong, Grampa?" asked Sam, noticing a change, in his grandfather's mood.

"I can't see well enough," answered the teary eyed old man.

Sam reached out to take the picture back from his grandfather. J J, not wanting to give the photo up, pulled away.

"I can't even tell, which person is, my Jera Marie," said J J, with a tear in his eye and a lump in his throat, as he looked back down at the photograph he held in his hand. Seeing and hearing the disappointment felt by his grandfather, Sam abruptly stood from where he was sitting.

"There must be something," said Sam, as he paced around thinking. "I know! Grampa, do you have a drinking glass? A crystal-clear one, from The Promise?"

J J thought a moment. "Yes. There is one, a beer glass."

"Could you get it for me?"

"Right now?"

"Yes, Grampa. I need it."

"Sure. Do you want more water? Didn't you like the cup?"

"What? The cup! Oh no, the cup's fine. I don't need more water. I just need the glass!"

"I'll get it for you," said J J, as he stood up. Not knowing why his grandson was so excited to have a glass. Going to the cupboard and reaching high onto the top shelf. J J came down with a large heavy beer glass. He then turned to his grandson. "It's not very clean," said J J, as he looked into the glass.

"That's all right," said Sam, as he stood anxiously waiting for the glass.

Then walking towards his grandson, with the beer glass in one hand and the photo in the other. J J handed the glass to Sam.

"I hope this works!" said Sam, as he took his handkerchief out of his rear pocket and proceeded to wipe the glass. First doing the inside and then the out, especially it's bottom. "Grampa, may I have the picture?" asked Sam, holding out his hand, to his grandfather. J J slowly handed the photo to him. Sam took the picture in one hand and the glass in the other. He then walked over to where more light was coming in through one of the holes in the cavern wall. Moving a table from where it was, over into the direct sunlight. He put the picture down on the table. He then put the glass down on top of the photo. "I saw this done in the movie, 'Roger Rabbit!" It was when, Edde Valiant, saw a newspaper photo of Marvin Acme. The photo showed that Acme's so-called missing will, was in his jacket pocket, at the time the photograph was taken, and that it, did indeed exist. This has to work, Grampa," said Sam, as he bent over and looked down into the glass. J J stood there watching his grandson. "Grampa, come over and look into this glass," said Sam, as he looked up from the glass with tears in his eyes and a smile on his face. J J slowly walked over to the table and his grandson. Sam moved out of the way, as to allow him to move in close. With his grandson watching, J J bent and looked into the glass. "The person in the center is Gramma." The old man looked into the glass and said nothing. . . , "You still can't see, Grampa?"

Some more time past. . . , then J J looked up from the glass, with tears in his eye. "Thank you Sam. It's definitely, my Jera Marie! She's as beautiful, as ever. She's older, but it's her," said J J, as he again bent down and continued looking into the glass. . . , "You said this photograph was taken the day you left to come here. How is it you have it with you?"

"It was taken with Gramma's Polaroid. It's an automatic camera. The camera develops the pictures itself. You just take the picture and in about a minute, it's ready."

J J looked up from the glass shaking his head. He then walked over and picked up the keg he had been setting on, and carried it over near the table and sat it down. He then sat down on the keg and looked into the glass.

"Actually the Polaroid Land Camera came out way back in the fifties, if I'm not mistaken. Grampa, here's another picture," said Sam, holding his hand out, to his grandfather. "This picture is one of my father, mother and

I. Gramma, took it when I was little."

J J looked up from the glass into the eyes of his grandson. He then looked to the out stretched hand holding the photo. He reached out and took the photo. He put it down on the table. He picked up the glass and moved it over onto the other photo. He then looked once more into the glass. J J sat there looking at a photograph of the son and daughter in-law he had never met. They were holding the grandson, that only hours before, he met for the first time. The grandson that has told him of some of the things that have come to pass, over the last fifty years.

"Sam do you have anymore photographs, with you?"

"Just of some girls, I know."

"Girls! You know, Sam, I could be a great-grandfather," said J J, as he looked up from the glass, at his grandson and smiled.

"No, way! These girls are just friends."

"Ok then, I'm not a great-grandfather yet. I'm just a grampa, is that right?"

"Right!"

J J laughed, as he looked at his red faced grandson. "You know, Sam, lucky for you, I was married at about your age."

"Lucky! Lucky for you and me both, Grampa! If you hadn't got married, I wouldn't have been born. That being the case, I wouldn't be standing here talking to you."

"My Jera Marie, your grandmother, she's the reason, I'm still somewhat sane. I had my memories of her, and the memories of our short time together. A day's never gone by, without me thinking of my Jera Marie, and our life together . . . I am, aren't I?"

"What?"

"Sane!"

"If I'm any judge of sanity you are, Grampa, but what do I know, I'm no judge or doctor. I think some of those people, sometimes think they're gods! Look at you, Grampa, you haven't seen a doctor, in over fifty years, and I know for a fact, you're in great shape," said Sam, rubbing his chest.

"I'm so sorry, I hurt you, with that knife."

"It's ok. The point just broke the skin, Grampa."

"You know, Sam, I could have killed you and the others. I had so much anger pent-up, for so many years. When I attacked, I intended to kill all of you. I had it all planned. I would knock you all down, then I'd kill the last one down, you, Sam! Then I'd go back to each of the others. There wasn't a doubt in my mind I could kill the enemy. To me, at that time, you were the enemy! It makes me sick, to think how close I came, to doing just that! If I hadn't seen the name!"

"It didn't happen. You didn't kill anyone. Don't think about it anymore, It's over ok, Grampa?"

"It's over. "It's as far as east is to west." I won't bring it up again. Sam, you said you were little when your father was killed. Do you remember him at all?"

"No, not first hand. It's like I said, from stories. Gramma, is as good as you are, at telling stories, maybe even better," smiled Sam.

"So, Jera and I, still have at least one thing in common."

"What do you mean, Grampa?"

"Your, Gramma and I, can both tell good stories."

"Ya, that's right, you can. I'm sure there are many other things you still have in common. I can't wait until I show her what I found on my trip here for training. I think she'll be well pleased, don't you?"

"I know, I am, Grandson!"

"Me too, Grampa!"

"You know, I'm getting used to this grandson, grampa stuff!"

"Ya, me too. Maybe that's what the Colonel had in mind, Grampa."

"Maybe. I'd say he had a good idea, wouldn't you, Sam?" asked J J, as he stood up putting his arms out to his grandson. Sam seeing this, stepped into the open arms of his grandfather and hugged him.

"He sure did, Grampa."

The emotion ran high once again between the two men, as they continued to embrace. Breaking the embrace the two men began wiping their noses and eyes, with the backs of their hands and fingers.

"I've shown more emotion in this one afternoon, than I have in my entire life. I need a handkerchief," said J J, sniveling.

"Since I've been on this island the same goes for me. From one extreme of emotion to another. From the fear of d. . . ! To one of shear jubilation of finding you, Grampa. It has been an emotional roller coaster ride!" said Sam, as he thought about what he almost said, 'death!' He reached into his back pocket for his handkerchief and handed it to his grandfather. "Here, Grampa."

"Thank you," said J J, as he wiped his eye and nose and handed the handkerchief back to his grandson. Sam wiping his own eyes and nose, as he turned and walked around, looking as he did. Regaining some composure, he returned the handkerchief to his pocket, as he walked over and stood in front of the shelves that ran the height and breadth of the back wall. There were things on these shelves, things he had never seen before. As he stood there looking, J J walked up and stood next to him.

"You know, Grampa, this is not a good picture!"

"What? What's not a good picture, Sam?"

"A Marine sniveling. That's what!"

"Don't feel like The Lone Ranger, Sam!"

"Good point! Two Marines standing together sniveling. Not a good picture!" said Sam, shaking his head as he spoke.

"Let's hope there isn't anyone, with one of those Polaroid hand cameras around!"

"Right, Grampa!"

The two men laughed, as they stood there together. As they did, their mood began to change, it became more lighthearted, as they continued to chuckle at their little funnies.

"Grampa, there are some very interesting things on your shelves," said Sam, as he moved along the back wall looking at the many different things.

"A lot of this stuff was on The Promise. Some I found washed up on the beach, while others I made myself, out of different things I found," said J J, as the two men moved along the wall of shelves together, side by side.

"Some of these things are quite interesting. There are some, that are also, quite beautiful. Look at this piece of corral, look at all it's different colors, they're beautiful. Some of this stuff looks like artwork to me, Grampa. You said, you made some of this stuff. Which things did you make?"

"The things on these shelves I made, I made along time ago. I made them, when I could still see to do fine work. I saved a set of fine carving tools, from The Promise. For practice I carved pieces of wood I found, washed up on the beach. I made this sea turtle, you see here," said J J, as he reached to a shelf with a multitude of small carved animals and figures. "This little turtle was one of my first keepers," said J J, as he picked up the turtle and handed it to his grandson.

"Cool!"

"What, what's cool?"

"Cool? Oh, I'm sorry, Grampa. It means good, right on, nice piece of work, it's a positive. It's cool, Grampa."

"If you say so. It's cool, Sam."

"Then you made all these little pieces?"

"Yes, I did," said J J, as he turned and walked to the far end of the cavern. At the far end, the shelves were not as well lit.

VESSEL OF LIFE

"This is the piece I am the most proud of," said J J, as he reached up with both hands, to a shelf hidden in the darkness. The shelf was about shoulder high. His grandson stood back, waiting and watching, to see what he was reaching for in the darkness. The piece his grandfather said, he was the 'most proud.' Bringing his hands down slowly and holding something quite large, he turned and walked towards his grandson, and the afternoon sunlight coming through the holes in the cavern wall.

"That's beautiful!" said Sam, seeing what his grandfather was carrying. "It's The Promise? Isn't it, Grampa?"

J J walked, carefully carrying a large model of the sailboat. "Yes, Sam, it is. It's a model of my, Vessel Of Life," said J J, as he walked towards the table to put the model down. Sam quickly ran and grabbed the glass and pictures from the table, placing the pictures in his shirt pocket, as he held the glass.

J J then, gently sat the model on the table.

"This is unbelievable, Grampa! How did you do this? It must have taken years, for you to make this."

"It took a long time," said J J, smilingly.

"It's amazing! It looks so real! It looks like everything works, too!"

"It does! Everything works."

"You had to do this all from memory."

"Yes, that's right, I did. I also had to make up, what the mast and sails looked like. I had no idea! I had to guess. One of those Polaroid's would have come in handy. It turned out pretty good, I think. I had the time!"

"It's beautiful! It's a piece of artwork, Grampa." The boat was about six feet long and a foot and a half wide. It set in it's own cradle. Sam walked around looking at the model setting on the table. "The detail is unbelievable! All the rigging! Every line and block, it all works! This ought to be in a museum, Grampa!"

"Except for, there isn't any ballast, or glass in the port lights. She's as complete a replica, as my memory and skill would allow me to create."

"All, I can say, Grampa, it's a significant piece of artwork! I see her name is, 'Vessel Of Life."

"Yes, there was only one! Only one that could be called, The Promise," said J J, as he sat down on his haunches.

Sam looked down at his grandfather, looking up proudly at his accomplishment. Sitting there, like a small boy would sit beside a mud puddle, to play with his toy boat in the puddle.

Sam returned the glass to the kitchen. He then walked over and sat down, in the same position as his grandfather. The two men sat there in silence, as they continued to stare at the Vessel Of Life.

"You think it's that good? Good enough to be in a museum?"

"I do! Grampa, it's priceless. It's the only one! Like you said of The Promise. It's the only one, that makes it invaluable. There are people in this world, collectors. Those collectors, would pay lots of money, for a one of a kind item, like the Vessel Of Life."

"Get out a town! I couldn't sell her, at any price. . . . Lots of money, how much, is lots?"

"It could be worth millions."

"Millions! How could it be worth millions? Sam, a million dollars! That's more then a B-17 bomber cost!"

"A B-17. . . ? To some collectors, money wouldn't be a problem, to those type of people, a work of art of this magnitude, would be priceless. And them knowing, it was the only one of it's kind. They'd have to have it! At any cost!"

"Yes, but a million dollars, that's so much money. Maybe, I spoke too soon. I had no idea it could be worth that kind of money."

"It may not be, but it sure could be, Grampa. Especially considering who made it. That would make it even more valuable!"

"What do you mean? Why would that make a difference?"

"A World War II, U. S. Marine, lost for over fifty years, made it! That's why. It'd be worth a bunch!"

"That would be nice, to go home to my Jera Marie, a millionaire. I could buy a real boat, like The Promise and a mansion in Seattle, for us to live in."

"Grampa, a million dollars doesn't go quite as far as it did, in your time. "

"Yes, I'm sure that's true. Prices were going up, even before I left. I'll bet they continued to go up, all during the war."

"Yes, I think they did, Grampa, and long after too."

"You actually think this could be worth lots?"

"You'd never sell her anyway. Besides, Gramma would never sell or move from her little house. She loves it!

"Sam! Never say never! I wouldn't want to sell the Vessel Of Life. But! I'd never say never!"

"Ok," said Sam, as he sat in the same position as his grandfather.

"Grampa, doesn't sitting here like this, hurt your knees?" asked Sam, as he tried to change the subject. Looking at his grandfather, still sitting on his haunches.

"Yes, it does, Sam. I'm not good with time anymore, but if I sit this way more then fifteen minutes or so these days, it does," said J J, as he sat there rubbing his knees with both hands.

"I'm glad you like my Vessel Of Life, Sam," said J J, as they stood. He then picked up the sailboat and walked back towards the shelf, where it had been sitting, all those years. Lifting it high, he returned it to it's shelf. "I put a lot of the stuff I made in storage but I couldn't put this in storage," said J J, as he situated the Vessel Of Life on it's shelf.

"There's more?"

"More! There's lots more. I've been here over fifty years, don't forget."

"That's still hard for me to believe, over fifty years."

"Hard for you to believe?"

"I do of course, Grampa!"

"Don't feel like, The Lone Ranger, Sam. It's hard for me to believe too. Hell, I lived it! Believe it!"

"Right, Grampa."

"Sam, do you want to see one of the most beautiful sights I've seen? I've seen it over and over for years and as many times as I've seen it, it becomes more beautiful each time?" said J J, as he finished situating the Vessel Of Life.

"Sure, let's see it," said Sam, as he walked up next to his grandfather.

"It's not in here. It's outside, Sam. I'm talking about the sunsets here, they are beautiful, Sam."

"Let's go watch the sunset then, Grampa."

"Good idea. Let's go. Follow me," said J J, as he walked towards the exit of the cavern. Sam followed as he did. The two men walked out onto the open hillside.

"This way, Sam," said J J, as he headed down the hill and into the jungle.

"At least you don't have to worry about leaving a trail, Grampa. Every Marine, on this island knows you're here."

"That's right. This is the first time since the storm, I won't have to worry," said J J, as he aggressively pushed the vines and limbs aside, as he went through the jungle. "This makes it a whole lot easier," said J J, as the two men moved through the jungle.

"I sure feel a lot more comfortable doing this, knowing that there isn't someone out here going to attack us."

"Sam, that's one reason you're here, to be trained in how to handle those types of circumstances. Of course, we now know the other reason."

"Right, Grampa."

Just then, J J and Sam broke out of the jungle, onto a beach. They walked to the waters edge, then the two men walked together in the soft sand at the waves high waterline.

"This is the beach where you got the sand for the floor of your cavern, isn't it, Grampa? This sand, it's as white as snow. The sun is so bright. You need sunglasses and a number twenty five sun block, that's for sure. It sure is pretty though."

"We can sit over here, Sam, up on these rocks and watch the sunset. It won't be long. I've missed them the last few nights, because I was invaded," laughed J J, as he climbed up on the rocks and sat down.

"I'm not sorry, about that, Grampa."

"Nor am I, but I did miss two sunsets. I will never know what those two sunsets looked like. I am sorry about that, Sam."

"Me, too," said Sam, when he saw how serious his grandfather was, about missing his sunsets. Sam climbed up on the rocks and sat next to him. The two men sat watching the sun get lower, in the western sky.

"I wish Gramma could be here, to see this, and see how excited you get, about your sunsets. She likes her sunsets, too. See there's another thing you still have in common. Gramma went to Hawaii once, with a friend. She thought it was beautiful but she was glad to get home to her little house, as she calls it."

"You said, my Jera Marie, still lives in our house, in Seattle?"

"Yes, she does."

"You know, Sam, Pop Miller and my father, built that house for my Jera Marie and I, with a little help from the two of us. They worked after work and on weekends, the summer before Jera Marie and I were married. By our wedding day, the house was livable. Jera and I continued to work, after work and with their help on weekends, until the house was completed. My Jera Marie and I, were so lucky to have had fathers that wanted to and could help. Help! They built the house. My grandfather, your great-great-grandfather, Grampa Johnson, he was a grumpy old man, but he had a big heart. He loaned me the money to buy the lot, and money, for materials to build the house. He charged me the same interest, the bank was paying him on his saving, two point four percent. The lot and house cost three thousand seven hundred sixty nine dollars and eighty seven cents. He put it on a ten year contract. He also said, if he died before the contract was paid, the house was ours."

"Is that all the house cost? My Camaro cost more then that! A Camaro, is a car, made by Chevrolet, Grampa."

"You have a car, that cost more then my house?"

"Yes. You have to understand, the dollar doesn't buy what it used to."

"That's amazing. When it was new, your car cost as much as my new house."

"No, Grampa. I bought my Camaro, just over a year ago, it's a '67'."

"It's over twenty five years old! How could it cost, as much as my house?" asked J J, shaking his head in disbelief. . . .

"Sam, you said Pop Miller was still alive. What of my father and mother, and Mother Miller?"

"Grampa, I'm so sorry, but they're no longer living. Great-Grampa Johnson and Great-Gramma Miller, died before I was born. Great-Gramma Johnson died, when I was about eight years old."

J J looked into the setting sun. The two men sat there on the rocks together in silence. Sam looked at his grandfather, wondering what the old man was thinking. . . . The sun sank low on the horizon. As the sun came closer to being parallel with the sea, it seemed to grow in size. It looked as though it was ten times it's size. The sun appeared to touch the sea and the sea embraced it, as the sea changed colors to that of the sun. It appeared the two melted together and became a sea of flame. The two men continued to watch as the sea and sun faded in color, as the sunlight dimmed in the west. They continued sitting there side by side, in silence. J J lowered his head and closed his eye, as if to pray. He then looked up and over at his grandson sitting there next to him.

"Sam, I'm glad I could share this with you. I've watched the sunset, from this spot, thousands of times. This was the best of all, having you here, made it so."

"Thank you. It was beautiful, Grampa."

"I was also thinking about how good my parents and grandparents were to me growing up. How much they cared for my Jera Marie and I. Marie's mother, she was also good to us, in her own way. I'm sure they all mourned, when they thought I had died, as I am mourning their passing. I'm sorry, you didn't get to know my father, your Great-Grampa Johnson. He had the ability to fix or make anything. Your Great-Gramma Johnson, I never saw her unhappy. She always had a smile on her face. No that's not true! I take that back. There was once. December 7, 1941, the day we heard that the Japanese had bombed Pearl. There was surely others but that was the only time, I saw her unhappy. I've thought of that many times, what a way for a person to live out their life, happy!"

Sam felt, he had just witnessed a powerful and highly inspirational sermon. . . . The two men sat there, as it grew darker by the minute. "We best head back, before it gets much darker."

"Good idea, I've seen how dark it is on this island, without street lights."

"Do you want to go to your camp or to my place?"

"Your place, Grampa."

"Let's go. Follow me," said J J, as the two of them jumped down from the rocks onto the sand. They walked through the sand, back into the jungle. As the two men moved through the jungle, in the dim light, Sam got an idea of what it must of been like, for his grandfather, Robby and the other two men, some fifty years earlier.

"Is this the way you came the night you and Robby snuck up on the Japanese camp, Grampa? No! The beach you landed on that night, was real rocky."

"That's right, Sam. How did you know that?"

"What? That you came in from a different beach and it was real rocky?"

"Yes, how did you know that?" asked J J, as they continued through the jungle, growing darker by the minute.

"Gramma, told me that story, many times."

"Your gramma! How did, Jera, know?" asked J J, as they came out of the jungle, back onto the open hillside near the cavern. By the time the two men had arrived at the opening to the cavern, Sam could just see his grandfather, walking in front of him, in the fleeting light of day. "Sam, you wait here. I will go in and light a lamp, so we can see."

"Ok." 'What does he use for light?' Thought Sam, as he stood there waiting outside the entrance to the cavern.

"You can come in now. If there's enough light for you to see."

"Yes, I can see, Grampa."

"You should be able to see to walk."

"I can," said Sam, as he followed his grandfather down into the dimly lit cavern.

"I usually go to bed, when it gets dark. This once, I'll make an exception to the rule, "early to bed, early to rise, makes you healthy, wealthy and wise," and I'll stay up," laughed J J, as the two men entered the large cavern. "Sam, how did my Jera Marie know, of us landing on a rocky beach?"

"Robby, the Colonel's father told her. He went to Gramma's house and told her the story, of how you were lost. She told me the story, many times.

Like I said, she's a good story teller."

"Robby, told my Jera Marie. He went to our house and told her himself? I'm so sorry he blamed himself, for me being left . . . lost. He was a good friend. If Robby and the others would have stayed, they would have been killed. There were lots of Japs. I counted more then fifty that night," said J J, as they walked through the dimly lit cavern, to where they had been sitting that afternoon. "Have a seat, Sam. Are you hungry? I'm not a bit hungry myself, after what I ate for lunch."

"No, I'm fine, Grampa, what do you remember of that night? The night you came ashore and found the camp?"

J J stood there in the dim light, for a moment in silence. "I can remember it! Like it was yesterday!" Sam listened as J J told his recollection, of that night. The story of how he was lost.

"That's the same story, to a point, that Robby told Gramma. His story went onto tell how the Jap's chased them to the beach, shooting at them, as they ran. Of how the one man was shot, as they reached the beach. He told her, "the darkness and the sea saved their lives.""

"I'm so glad the three of them made it safely back to ship that night. I always hoped they did. In my own mind I knew, they may have been killed, that night. I'm so relieved to hear they weren't!" said J J, as he sat down on the keg next to his grandson, who was sitting there by the table listening.

"Sam, what other changes can you tell me about? Things I should know. I know everything has changed some, from a little change, to a great deal. What are some? Tell me, Sam."

"Let me see," said Sam, as he sat there thinking.

"Gasoline cost a dollar thirty a gallon, for regular unleaded. Milk's two dollars a gallon. Breads a dollar and a half a loaf. Neal Armstrong walked on the moon. Uh, let me think."

"Gasoline's over a dollar! I think it was eighteen cents, when I left. Bread was about. Wait! What did you say? Neal walked on the moon! What do you mean? He walked on the moon?"

"Before I was born, Grampa, Neal Armstrong and another man, I don't remember his name. The two of them, walked on the moon," said Sam, as he pointed out the opening in the wall.

J J sat there looking at his grandson.

"Let me understand. You're saying, this Neal fella and the other man, physically walked on the moon!"

"Yes! And the world watched it live, on T.V., as they did!"

J J sat there thinking, about what his grandson just told him, as he looked out the opening, towards the rising moon.

"Sam that's over! What twenty years ago. Are there people living up there now? Living on the moon?"

"No, there isn't. There hasn't been anyone back to the moon or any other planet that I know of, since I've been born. The Shuttle's fly into space, about three times a year. That's the extent of our space program at this time, as far as I know."

"That's amazing! They actually walked on the moon. Like Buck Rogers! They flew to the moon, in a rocket ship? Did they make it home safely?"

"Yes, they made it home safe. They flew in the Apollo. I forget what number it was. The Command Module set on top of a rocket, called the Saturn V. The rocket was like, three hundred feet tall and twenty four feet in diameter. It was huge! It developed over six million pounds of thrust."

"It's hard for me to accept and understand the things you are telling me. Things like men walking on the moon. I'll just have to learn to accept things, whether or not I understand them. I believe and accept that you are my grandson, Sam. That in it's self was hard for me to understand, considering I didn't even know I had a son, in order to make it possible, for me to have a grandson. Tell me some more, Sam. I'll get us some more water."

"Ok, Grampa."

"How much do they pay at the machine shop now?" asked J J, as he got up to get the water.

"Machine shop?"

"Grampa's, I don't know who's it is now! Yours maybe, I don't know."

"Oh Great-Grampa's machine shop. It was gone before I was born. Gramma doesn't talk about it much. I don't know. I'm sorry, Grampa. I'd tell you more, if I knew."

"I wonder what happened to it?"

"Like I said. I don't know. We'll have to ask Gramma. I can guess. A job like that would pay around fourteen dollars an hour."

"Sam, that's over twenty two hundred a month! When I left the machine shop, I was making one hundred thirty six a month and that was good wages! Now that same job pays over twenty six thousand a year. Twenty five year old cars, cost more then my new house and the land it sat on. This is what I meant. I have to learn to accept the unbelievable as believable," said J J, as he walked over and handed Sam a cup of water and then, sat back down on his keg.

"You know, Grampa, your house is worth a great deal more now. I heard Gramma telling Mom, the taxes on her place for a year, were about a third, of what it cost you, to build her little house in the first place, including the land!"

"That would make our taxes, eleven or twelve hundred dollars a year! How can the taxes be that high. . . ? I know, believe it! Wow, how can she pay that much? I see why you have to make so much, because it cost so much more to live. I think the taxes on our house the first year, were thirty three dollars."

"The differences between now and then, are hard for each of us to understand but they are real. It's hard for me to accept that gasoline was only eighteen cents. And at the same time, It's hard for you to accept, that it cost a dollar thirty or more a gallon."

"Yes, it is hard. If we look at it another way, say you and me. It maybe easier to understand."

"How's that, Grampa?"

"Look at the difference between you and me, Sam. You're what, fifty three years younger, then I. Except for those years and my face, we could pass for twins. The difference is time! Time and man, have created these differences between then and now. That, I am going to have to learn to accept, if I'm going to get along in this time."

"Like I said before, Grampa. It's going to be fun. Just anticipate that it has changed and if it hasn't, great!"

"Good idea, Sam."

"Grampa, what do you use for light?" asked Sam, pointing at the small light, on the cavern wall.

"They're candles from The Promise. I also have some kerosene lanterns. Like I said, I normally go to bed when it's dark. So light hasn't been a problem. If I don't go right to bed, I sit outside and watch the night sky. I do, do that, sometimes for hours. Sam, that reminds me. About thirty years ago, I noticed that there were points of light, like stars but they move in the night sky. They moved from east to west. I just saw one at first. Now there's lots of them and they go in many different directions. Do you have any idea, what those lights could be, Sam?"

"They're probably satellites."

"What are satellites?"

"Satellites orbit the earth in space. They're put into space aboard rockets or in the bay of the shuttle. From earth, they send up a signal to the satellite. The satellite boosts the signal and sends it on it's way, back to earth. There are lots of different kinds of satellites. Weather satellites, communication, navigation and even military satellites. The lights you see, moving across the night sky, is the sunlight hitting them and reflecting back to earth. That is how the T V works in the camp. It gets it's signal from a satellite."

"They're relay stations."

"Exactly! Grampa, I have a friend. His dad has a thirty six foot Grand Banks. It's a pleasure boat. He has a GPS onboard. GPS stands for Global Positioning System. The GPS works with satellites. Somehow it can tell him where his boat is, at any given time, within twenty feet of it's actual location. The military has it's own GPS, that cuts that twenty feet, down into inches. I've heard, if they wanted to, they could shoot a missile from say Wyoming, and aim at the Dodgers pitcher's mound, they would hit the stadium."

"I know, believe it! From Wyoming to Brooklyn, that's amazing."

"No, Grampa. Dodgers stadium, is in Los Angeles."

"I say, believe it!" said J J, talking like a preacher man. "Like I said, things I knew," said J J, shaking his head.

"In the Gulf War, they shot missiles at buildings. Those missiles had TV cameras onboard. They showed on TV, how the missile, not only hit the building, it hit the front door, of the building it was fired at. The cameras, looked right down the length of the missile, it showed as it came in, hit and exploded."

"Gulf War! How many different wars has there been, Sam?"

"Well there was World War I, World War II, you knew about those."

"Believe it!"

"Then the Korean War, the Colonel told you about that one. Vietnam War, and the Gulf War. I'm sure there has been others around the world, like Afghanistan. There are a half a dozen going on right now, as we speak. There's a real nasty one, on going in Bosnia. It's on the TV news almost every night. I think Bosnia was called Yugoslavia in years past."

"Yugoslavia, that's where World War I started, if I'm not mistaken."

"I didn't know that, Grampa."

"I might be wrong, but if memory serves me right, it was in that area of the world. Of course, that's a long time to remember, your history."

"Believe it," said Sam, as he reached out and slapped his grandfather on the shoulder.

"Yes! Believe it!" said J J, as he jumped. Startled by the slap on the shoulder.

"I'm sorry, Grampa. I didn't mean to startle you."

"I'm fine, Sam. You must remember, I've been alone for a long time. I'm sorry I jumped. You didn't frighten me, it's just that I haven't been touched, by anything . . . I take that back. I was swimming in the cove once and something touched my foot. It scared me so much, I wanted to jump up on top of the water and run for the beach. Of course, I still hadn't figured out quite how to do that yet. So I swam as fast as I could to shore. I am a good swimmer. I must swim, like I said, I'm not good with time but I swim maybe an hour or two a day. I love to swim."

"Oh, you've figured out how to walk on water?"

"What? Oh, no I still haven't quite figured that out," laughed J J, as he reached over and slapped his grandson on the knee.

"What was it, Grampa?"

"What?"

"What grabbed your foot?"

"You know, I never found out what it was. I've swam in that cove thousands of times, before and since. That was the only time it happened. It felt just like someone reached up from below and grabbed my foot."

"Maybe it was a mermaid."

"Mermaid? Even a merman! As long as it wasn't one of those great white sharks, I read about in The Promise's log. A mermaid may have been ok, as long as we were just acquaintances."

"Friends? A mermaid as a friend. I could dig it. I'm not sure Gramma could. No, that's not true. I think, if she knew you were alone. She would want you to have a companion. No matter who or what it was, rather then be alone, all these years. If I know my Gramma."

"Right. My Jera Marie, is that way. Well, it didn't happen. Not to say there weren't times, when a friend of any kind, would have been greatly appreciated. Like my mother, my Jera Marie was always happy. I only saw her unhappy one time. The day I left to come here."

"Believe it. That was the only time, I saw her unhappy too. Unhappy! The day I left, her and mother were both unhappy."

"You said, you swim a lot. That's why you're in such good shape. Gunnery Sergeant Roman, couldn't understand how, one man could incapacitate, four Marines. Obviously you could, because the four of us were, definitely incapacitated."

"It was a surprise attack. The four of you were, what did you call it, Rapping? I was full of adrenaline, the attack was well planned and you were caught off guard. You just didn't know. Like one of the guys said, I think it was the one named Bo. He said, 'let him come back, we're ready for him.'"

"You were that near, you could hear us talking?"

"Yes, I heard you say. 'He just beat the shit out of all four of us, why whisper," smiled his grandfather.

"Boy, you were close!"

"Yes, I could hear you and the others, I could hear that you were speaking English. I knew I'd made the right decision, to spare your lives. I was thankful that I had done so, hearing that!"

"Believe it. When I say, don't feel like The Lone Ranger."

"Ya know, Sam, the Colonel, really did right by us, letting us have this afternoon and evening, to get to know one another."

"That he did, Grampa."

"How are you doing with your new name, Sam?"

"I think it's good, so far, don't you?"

"Yes, I think it's much better than Jay, don't you, Sam?"

"I sure do."

"What are we going to talk about now, are you going to tell me more?"

"Sure, Grampa. What?"

"Did, my Jera Marie, get my insurance, when I was presumed dead?"

"I can't tell you. I would assume so."

"It must of been hard for her, raising a boy alone."

"I'm sure it would have been much better if you could have been there, to help with my father and with me too, for that matter. I think her and mom, both, did pretty good."

"From what I've seen, Sam, they couldn't have done better."

"Thank you. That's not to say, Grampa, if you and dad could have been there, it wouldn't have been better. There isn't anything that wouldn't have made us happier, than to have the two of you there with us."

"Nor I, Sam."

The two men sat there in silence, in the dimly lit cavern. Fate had given them their own paths, to follow in life. Now fate had given them a new path. A path that the two of them could choose to follow together.

"Sam, you're going to have to excuse me."

"What's a matter, Grampa?"

"Nothings wrong. I have to go use the privy."

"The what?"

"The bathroom. I have to go to the bathroom."

"Good idea, I have to go too. Where is it? Is it outside?"

"No, we're quite modern here. Here on Johnson's Island, we have inside toilets. I'll show you were it is. Come this way," said J J, as he got up and walked over to the light. He picked up another candle and lit it, from the one that was burning. "This way, follow me." Sam got to his feet and followed his grandfather. They walked to the other end of the cavern.

The end where what appeared to be his bedroom was located. On the end wall and where the wall with the openings to the outside met, there was an opening into another room. J J held the light as to allow his grandson to see. "Company first," said J J, as the two men entered the small room. J J reached up with the candle and left it on a shelf, on the wall. "As you're standing, the one on the right, is for number one. The one on the left, is for number two. Unless that's changed in the last fifty years," said J J, as he turned and left the small room. Sam stood there using the facilities. He could see by somehow using water from outside, is how it all worked. Not to keep his grandfather waiting, he finished and left before figuring out, quite how it all worked.

"Your turn. It's still the same, one and two," said Sam, as he moved past his grandfather, back into the larger cavern. Walking back to his seat at the table. 'What a place to live, except for being alone, being really alone. What a wonderful way to live.' Thought Sam, as he sat waiting for his grandfather. "Tomorrow you'll have to show me how that bathroom of yours works," said Sam, as J J entered the room.

"I can do that," said J J, as he walked over and sat back down on the keg.

"I was thinking, while you were using the facilities. I don't have another bed. Obviously, I have never had guests stay over, here at Johnson's Island Resort, before."

"We'll probably stay up all night talking anyway," laughed Sam.

"I don't think I can, Sam. I was up all night, for the last two nights, already. Hauling water and making that poem on the palm leaf. Plus watching all of you, among other things."

"That's right! All that, plus seeing helicopters and thinking your island was being invaded by the enemy. I'm sorry, you're probably exhausted. If I stay, I can sleep anywhere. But maybe I should go back to camp and let you sleep here alone."

"No! I've been alone!" said J J with his voice shaking, as he spoke.

"Right! We'll make do. Ok, Grampa?"

"Thank you," said J J, as the two men sat there in the dim light.

"Grampa, it's so quiet here. Just my breathing, will keep you awake."

"No, I normally sleep like a rock and as tired as I am now, sleeping shouldn't be a problem."

"Anytime you're ready. I can sleep on this sand."

"If my head goes down and I start to snore, then you'll know, I'm ready. That it's time for me to go to bed. Until then, tell me some more."

"It's only seven thirty," said Sam, looking at his watch.

"Like I said. When my head goes down, you'll know."

"Ok, if you say so. That's fine with me. We can sleep on guard duty."

"What!"

"It's a joke."

"After the last couple of days and nights, if they put me on guard duty, it wouldn't be a joke, I'd fall asleep. Believe it"

"Right. I don't think we have to worry about that."

"What, falling asleep?"

"No, being put on guard duty."

"Right." The two men laughed together, at what was said.

"You know, Grampa, I was thinking earlier, what a way to live. Except for being alone. It would be like, living in paradise."

"Except for that one thing. That makes all the difference in the world. If not for that, most of the time it would be paradise here. All things considered, I have had a good life here in paradise. Except for that one thing. Being alone!"

"You're not alone now and you're ready to move on, right?"

"Exactly! I've been in paradise long enough. I'm ready to see what the rest of the world has to offer."

"You might not like what you see, Grampa."

"I'm sure it's not perfect."

"No! Not even close, Grampa!" said Sam, as he shook his head slowly.

"Grampa, I was wondering? Can you see through your bad eye?"

"Yes, I can. If I tilt my head back, I can see just a little. That's originally why I started swimming, was to help keep my eye from getting infected, and help it heal, after the fall. I think the eye is still just as good as the other. As a matter of fact, I can even close the eyelid. If I had a mirror or something like a mirror, after it first happened, I could have cut the skin away, but I didn't have anything, until my Vessel Of Life. Of course, it was too late by then. The skin had long since grown fast. The mirror onboard was cracked in several places, which only let me see a portion of my face, during it's years at sea, the mirror had become discolored. Being cracked and discolored, made it unusable. Do you think in today's world, they could fix my eye? If they can put lenses inside the eye, I would think they could fix my eye!"

"If you can see, I would think a simple surgery could remove the skin and amend the problem."

"I would still have a face, a face like that of 'The Phantom Of The Opera."

"Oh, that's no problem. They can fix your face!"

"They can!"

"If they can make a grown black man, look like a young white girl, they can surely, fix your face."

"Sam, why would a grown black man, want to look like a young white girl?"

"That's a good question, Grampa. I think he's the only one that could answer that."

"I suppose, he's the only one that needs to," said J J, nodding his head.

"I guess."

"Maybe I could get my face fixed, before I see my Jera Marie."

"That might be possible, maybe they'd be able to do it onboard ship, on the way home. The doctor would have to make that decision. It might delay you're getting home, to see Gramma."

"No! I don't want to do that. I can get my face fixed anytime, right?"

"As far as I know, yes. Grampa it's not up to you or me. That's the Marine Corp's call, it's their decision. They might have other plans."

"Yes, I see. They might," said J J, as his mood changed, to one more subdued.

"Don't worry, Grampa, the Colonel will get you home."

"Yes, you're right! He's Robby's boy. He'll do what he can, to get me home, as soon as possible. I shouldn't worry. He'll do what he can. Now that I know it's possible, I want to see her, my Jera Marie, as soon as I can. Do you think I will be able to start for home tomorrow, Sam?"

"I hope so, for both our sakes. I can't wait to see what Gramma does, when she sees who's standing on the porch with me. She won't expect me to be there either. It might take her awhile but I think she'll sense your presence, if I know my Gramma. That's going to be awesome. I just hope I can be there, to experience that with you, Grampa."

"Why wouldn't you?"

"Like I said, that's up to the Corp."

"Right."

"I think the Colonel will come through for both of us, Grampa."

"I think so. A Colonel in the U. S. Marine Corp, he should have some pull. We'll have to wait to see how much."

"Right. I'm sure he'll do what he can, for the both of us."

"It's starting to sink into this hard head of mine. What you told me earlier. About the difference in buying power, our money has. People having to make dollars an hour, rather then nickels and dimes, just so they have money to live, in today's world. You know Sam, back in 1941, a new Chevrolet cost about seven hundred dollars. What would one cost today, by comparison? They still make Chevrolet's don't they?" laughed J J, as he asked the question.

"Yes, they still make Chevys. The cost of a full size Chevrolet?"

"They come in sizes?"

"Yes, six or eight different sizes, I think. The big full size one, I would think twenty, to twenty five thousand."

"Dollars?"

"Yes. Over a years wages."

"Over fifteen years of gross earnings! For a Chevrolet? That's as hard for me to accept, as a man walking on the moon! I know, believe it!"

"You might find this interesting, Grampa. You know that friend, I told you about. The one with the Grand Banks. He's also into old cars. Cars that were new in the twenties, thirties, forties, fifties and even in the sixties, like my car. Some of these cars are worth hundreds of times more than they cost, when they were brand new. A good many of the old car manufactures don't even exist anymore. They went out of business years ago, years before I was even born. Car companies I never even knew existed, were probably household names, in your time, Grampa."

"I know, believe it," said J J, shaking his head in disbelief. . . .

"How do young people get along in the world. If they're watching that T V thing all the time, how do they get enough training, to compete for the higher paying jobs?"

"A lot of them don't. Out of frustration some get hooked on all kinds of different things."

"What things? Hooked, what do you mean hooked?"

"Hooked on things like alcohol and drugs. I don't know the explanation why. I don't think anyone does. I guess to make em feel better, they think. In actuality, it makes it much worse. They drop out of school, they sell the drugs to others, including young kids. They do these things and others, to get the enormous amounts of money, it takes to support a drug habit. I know Billy, he thinks T V is the ruination of this country. I think the drug problem is."

"Aren't drugs illegal?"

"So was alcohol, in the thirties."

"Good point. It's time for The Lone Ranger, right!"

"Believe it! Don't misunderstand me, not all young people are drug addicts. Some get jobs that pay enough. While others get married and they both work to get by. Some, like Tye Kim, are wizards with computers. He joined the Marines, in order to have money to go to college, when he gets out."

"He makes a enough money, being a Marine? Enough so he can save money for college? Either college doesn't cost as much or being a Marine pays a whole lot better, nowadays."

"No, not really. It cost a great deal to go to college. Being a Marine, doesn't pay very much, either."

J J sat there with a puzzled look on his face.

"It's confusing. The military has special programs. They offer these programs, to young men and women, to get them to join. If they join, they get money for college. Some join just for that reason."

"Corporal Kim, he said he was Vietna something, isn't that the same name, as one of those war's you told me about?"

"Yes, he's Vietnamese. The war was in his country, Vietnam. The Vietnamese people were fighting the communists, trying to prevent them from taking over their country. They fought for years. The U. S. got involved in the sixties. Then the U S pulled out, I think in 1973. Leaving the communist to overrun the Vietnamese. Tye's family, like many others, had to leave the country to avoid persecution."

"What do you mean, Sam, the United States pulled out?"

"It was before I was born, so what I know, is what I've been told or what I read in school and have seen on T V and or in the movies. A lot of people were against the war in Vietnam. They felt it was a civil war and that the U S shouldn't be involved. There were many protests against the war, all across America. There was great loss of life in Vietnam, and some at home, in the U S. The war was on T V, almost every night. America watched her young soldiers being killed, right before their eyes, during the dinner hour on T V. Then they would see on the same news report, a protest being covered. There were over fifty seven thousand Americans, both men and women killed, in Vietnam. There were also some people killed here at home, a protest at Kent State, I think there were four students killed, by the National Guard."

"The National Guard, killed four kids?"

"Yes."

The two men sat there in silence.

"Grampa, I'm being as up front with the answers to your questions, as I can. That's the way I would want it, if I was asking the questions."

"Thank you, Sam, I appreciate it. Sometimes, it's just so overwhelming. Believe it, when I say it catches me off guard."

"Telling you this stuff. The differences in people, technology and the cost of things. It has given me a slight insight of just how overwhelming, it all must be for you, Grampa. The things I'm telling you are so incredible and so astounding to you, it must be unbelievably hard for you to accept them as true, and yet you do believe them, because of me. There are so many things, I take for granted."

"Then you understand why! Why, I sit here with my mouth hanging open, most of the time."

"Yes, I do, Grampa."

"Believe it. It's been an education, Sam."

"That's for sure. I've thought more about my education and of what I know, in the last few hours, then I have in my entire life. In fact I've done a lot of things more in the last few days, than I have in my entire life."

"Don't feel like, The Lone Ranger!"

"Believe it!"

"Ya know, Sam, I'm about out of that stuff that costs a dollar thirty a gallon."

"What's that?"

"Gas!"

"You are! Your head is still up."

"Not much longer. I'd better head for bed, while I can still navigate," said J J, as he got up from his keg, with his arms over his head stretching as he did. "I'll get you something to use for a pillow, Sam," said J J, as he walked over to his bed. Reaching high above the bed, to a shelf that had been obscured by the darkness. His hands coming down with what appeared was a pillow and cover. J J turned and walked over to his grandson, handing the pillow and cover to him.

Sam took the bedding from his grandfather.

"I hope you'll be comfortable here tonight, Sam. Sam, thank you for coming here, to save me. I'm so thankful, you're here with me and that you're going to take me home. Home to, my Jera Marie. Sam, may I have your photo, the one of your gramma, my Jera Marie?" smiled J J.

"Of course, Grampa," smiled Sam, as he reached into the pocket of his shirt for the photo. Sam placed the photograph in the out stretched hand of his grandfather. J J looked down to the picture he now held, safe in his hand.

"I'll see you the first thing in the morning!" smiled J J. Sam, with the bedding in one arm, holds out his other arm to his grandfather. J J seeing this, stood there. Then he held his arms out to his grandson and the two men embraced.

"Thank you, Grampa, for staying alive, all these years."

"That wasn't up to me, son. Believe it!"

"Right."

"Thank you, Sam. Tell me you'll be here!" said J J, as they separated their embrace.

"What?"

"Tell me! Tell me this all, hasn't just been a dream!"

"A dream?" asked Sam, hearing the apprehension in his grandfather's voice. "It's been a dream all right, a dream come true! I'm really here with you, Grampa. I'll be here in the morning, believe it."

"If you say so, Sam, I'll see you then," said J J looking into the eyes of his smiling grandson.

"I'll be here when you wake up, Grampa," said Sam, as he patted his shoulder, as his grandfather turned and headed for his bed.

"I may have waited too long. I really am exhausted," said J J, as he sat down on the edge of his bed, and then bent over and started to remove his hand made shoes. After doing so, he slowly laid his head down and was asleep without saying another word.

Sam, stood there in awe, looking at his grandfather laying there, already sound asleep and snoring softly. He was amazed, that anyone could go sound to sleep that quickly. He then sat back down at the table and continued staring at his grandfather as he slept, with his wife's picture still in hand. Sam then started thinking of the events that brought him, to where he was. All that had taken place, over the last two days. He also thought of his grandmother. Of what it was going to be like, to give her this present he'd gotten for her, on his trip to the South Pacific. As Sam watched his grandfather sleeping peacefully. He began to realize how sleepy he was himself. Thinking about how peacefully his grandfather was sleeping and not wanting to disturbed that sleep, Sam slowly stood and gently picked up the pillow and cover, his grandfather had given him. He then quietly walked to the far end of the cavern. As he walked, he noticed the candles that J J had lit, were about to go out. He stood there, at the exit to the cavern, looking around at just how beautiful it really was. He then turned and left the room.

As he stepped out onto the open hillside, he could see the lights from his camp, in the distance. He looked around for a level spot. Finding one, he laid down the cover and pillow. He then laid down on the cover, looking up at the heavens. Which was an indescribably beautiful sight. The stars were so brilliant, there appeared to be thousands more then he had seen the night before. He laid there thinking what a beautiful place to live.

"Sam, Sam, wake up."

"Leave me alone!" said Sam, as he thought 'who's trying to wake me.'

"Sam, it's me." Sam heard as he felt someone shaking him. He then realized he was Sam and opened his eyes, looking into the face of his newly found grandfather.

"Grampa, it's you. I didn't know I'd fallen to sleep. I was just laying here looking up at a beautiful night sky. Then bingo you're here, shaking me awake."

"Leave you alone! I woke up and you weren't there. My heart sank, I thought it was all a dream after all and that I was indeed alone! Then I saw this picture in my hand, and knew it was no dream. So I came out here, and there you were, sleeping like a baby," smiled J J, as he looked down at the picture in his hand.

"I'm sorry, I didn't want to disturb your sleep, so I came out here, to an absolutely magnificent night. I never thought about how it would look to you, I'm sorry, Grampa."

J J held out his hand to his grandson, to help him to his feet.

"Thank you. Boy, did I sleep," said Sam, as he grabbed his hand.

"That's something I do real good," said J J, as he pulled his grandson to his feet.

"What's that?"

"Sleep!"

"Ya, me, too. I wonder what time it is," said Sam, looking at his watch. "It's 0710. We better get ready to go to camp."

"Right."

The two men walked together, towards the entrance to the cavern. J J entered with Sam right behind. J J went right towards the bathroom. "I'll go first."

"Ok," said Sam, as he looked around the room which was much better lit, in the morning light. Much brighter than it had been the day before. Then Sam saw a beautiful sight. A beam of light coming through one of the openings in the cavern's wall, was shinning right on the Vessel Of Life. Sam stood there, looking at the Vessel Of Life. As he did, his mind drifted. He started imagining of how she must have looked in real life.

"Your turn, Sam."

Hearing this, Sam turned and looked to where his grandfather was coming out of his bathroom. He was wearing a clean pair of pants and carrying a shirt in his hand. Sam watched, as his grandfather started to put on the shirt. He was again astonished at what good physical shape his grandfather was in.

"That old uniform didn't smell so good. I didn't want to offend anyone.

I didn't take time the last few nights, to do my laundry, for shame, for shame. These clothes here, were on The Promise," said J J, as he carefully put the picture of his Jera Marie into the pocket of the shirt. "They're the only other clothes I have left. That's why I kept them even though they were little big," said J J, as he look down to see if the picture was safely protected and at the way his clothes fit.

"They look like they fit fine, to me, Grampa."

"Yes, they do, don't they. That's odd. I must have gained a little weight. They fit pretty good now, don't they."

"I'll be right out," said Sam, as he walked past his grandfather, towards the bathroom. As Sam entered the bathroom. J J walked over and sat down on the bed. He then started putting on his shoes.

"Grampa."

J J heard, Sam holler.

"Yes, Sam."

"Maybe, someone in camp will have a. . . . What's a matter with me! I have a spare uniform, you can have. We're about the same size, it should fit."

"That's good. Then I can look like a Marine again."

Sam stood at the sink in the bathroom. The sink appeared to be made of copper. Just above the sink was a small piece of pipe. The pipe was made of bamboo. There was water running out of the pipe, into the copper sink. The small stream of water ran continuously. He started washing his hands and face, in the running water. To his surprise, the water was quite warm. As he washed, he started to notice how the system worked. The water appeared to run from the sink into one toilet. The water would run into one toilet, if the sink stopper was in place and into the other, if the stopper was removed. If the sink stopper was put into place, this sink would fill to it's capacity. The water would then flow, through an overflow pipe, into the other toilet. That toilet being the one for the solid waste. It consisted of a large copper bucket placed under a wood shelf. The shelf had a hole cut into it, in the shape of a conventional toilet seat. Once the bucket was filled, you would remove the stopper and the water would run through the sink drain, into the other toilet. You would then dump the bucket, into the other toilet, at your convenience. This toilet either ran into a very large cavern, or drained out to sea. Most likely it did both, it was hooked to a large cavern, that drained out to sea.

Sam then started looking at some of his grandfather's things. There were small shelves on the walls. The shelves were made of wood and they had been contoured to fit the shape of the cavern walls. The candle J J had lit the night before, was not sitting on one of these shelves, it sat on a small rock ledge that was carved into the wall. Sam then saw his grandfather's razor, it was one of those straight kind. He picked it up and looked it over. He had seen some like it, in the movies but this was the first time he ever saw one in person. "Grampa, do you mind if I use your razor?" asked Sam, as he stepped into the larger cavern to where his grandfather was. "I've never tried a straight one, like this before, Grampa. I should shave," said Sam, looking down at the razor he was holding, in his hand.

"Go a head Sam," said J J, as he got up and entered the bathroom with his grandson. "There's shaving soap, there to use," said J J, as he pointed to a cup, that was setting on a shelf. "You're welcome to use anything, anything I have here, Sam," said J J, as he turned and left the small room.

"Thank you."

Sam picked up the cup, from the shelf. Inside the cup was a brush. He removed the brush and held it in his hand. He thought a moment. He remembered what he had seen in the movies. He held the cup in one hand, as he held the brush in the other. He then put the brush in the running water. After wetting the brush, he put it into the cup. Rubbing the brush in the cup, in no time at all, the cup was full of soap suds. He then took the brush out and rubbed the suds on his face. He took the razor in hand and started to shave. In no time at all he realized, he'd best put that thing down. He knew if he didn't, there was a good chance he would slit his own throat. Sam carefully rinsed the razor off and the cup out and returned them to their appropriate places. After rinsing off his hands and face, he finished by rinsing out the sink. With everything back in it's place. He turned and left the room, rejoining his grandfather, in the main cavern.

"Thank you for the use of your razor, Grampa. I think I best wait. Wait until I get back to camp to shave, with my razor and a mirror. Otherwise I might not make it back at all!" laughed Sam.

"Why?"

"If I used that razor. I would probably slit my throat."

"What?"

"Accidentally, I mean."

"Right."

"Are you ready to go?

"Yes, Sam, I'm ready. Let's go see what amazing things, I'll see, hear and do today! Let's go, follow me, Sam."

"Lead the way, let's go."

The two men walked through the tunnel back out onto the open hillside. Sam looked down at his watch. They had eighteen minutes to get to camp.

"I don't know about you, Grampa. But I'm starved."

"Starved? No. I am hungry though," said J J, as they started walking down the hill towards the jungle. "The smell of that food cooking, is enough to make anyone hungry."

"I'm just hungry, Grampa. I don't smell anything," said Sam, as he tilted his head back and sniffed the air, as they started into the jungle.

"You can't smell that bacon cooking? I sure can. It smells real good."

"I guess I'll have to get a nose job, when you get your face fixed. I don't smell anything," said Sam, as the two men broke out of the jungle, onto Bo's road. As they got closer to the camp, Sam turned to his grandfather. "I smell it now. It does smell like bacon cooking."

"Oh good, then there's hope for that nose of yours, after all."

The two men laughed, as they walked. Ahead they could see the camp in view, at the end of Bo's road.

"There's the camp."

"Right where we left it," said J J, as he saw the guard coming over to meet the two of them. "He won't shoot, will he? Someone's surely told him that the war is over."

"I don't think he'll shoot."

The guard walked towards the two men, as they walked into camp. "Hey, J J. The gunny said you'd be coming into camp this morning and that you'd have your grandfather with you. Did I hear him right, J J? Your grandfather! This man is really your for real, grandfather?"

"That's right, Bob. He's my real Grampa," said Sam, as he put his arm around his grandfather, putting his hand on his shoulder.

"Hello, Bob, my name is, J J," said J J, as he held out his hand and shook Bob's. Bob stood there with his mouth hanging open, as J J shook hands. J J and Sam walked on into camp, leaving Bob standing there, in a daze.

"We better report, to the Gunny."

"That's a good idea, Ollie."

"Right," laughed Sam, as the two of them walked through camp towards the command tent. Walking up to the tent they stopped. "This is it, Grampa."

The two men entered the tent. The gunny was at his desk. "Privates, Johnson and Johnson, reporting, Gunnery Sergeant," snickered Sam, as he and his grandfather, said their names.

"Ok, Band-Aids, at ease," smiled the gunny, catching the humor in what had just been said, as he looked up at the two men. "How'd it go last night, fellas?" asked the gunny, as he got up and walked around and stood in front of the desk, holding out his hand.

"Great!" said J J and Sam, at the same time. J J grabbing the gunny's hand, shaking it vigorously.

"The time together was greatly appreciated. Thanks, Gunny."

"You are welcome, Private," said the gunny, finally getting his hand back from J J.

"Have you heard from, Colonel Robinson, Sergeant?"

"Yes, I have, J J. As a matter of fact, I've heard from him several times."

"Is there anything you can tell us, Gunny?"

"Just that he'll be here shortly, Private."

"Gunny, my Grampa and I, have solved the name problem."

"How's that Private?"

"Grampa's name, will be J J and I will go by my middle name Samuel, Sam for short. Is that all right with you, Gunnery Sergeant?"

"It's fine with me," snickered the gunny, at the question being asked. Thinking, 'why would it make any difference to him.' "Have you men had breakfast?"

"No." The two men answering again, at the same time.

"You two are in sink, aren't you?"

J J and Sam, turned and looked at each other. Then looking back at the gunny, the two shrugging their shoulders at the same time, as they did.

"Yes," laughed, all three men in unison.

"Let's go eat."

"Ok, Sergeant. We haven't eaten since lunch."

"Let's go, you guy's are probably starved."

Sam turned and opened the door and stepped outside, holding the door for the gunny and his grandfather. He then followed, as the two of them lead the way to breakfast. The three of them talking as they walked. As they arrived at the mess tent, two men opened and held the doors, for the three to enter. Everyone in the tent stood, as they saw the three men enter. They all started to gather around J J and Sam, and started asking questions of J J and introducing themselves. He seemed to be enjoying all the attention, as he tried to answer their questions.

"I'll get you a tray of food, while you're meeting the guys, Grampa."

"Ok, Sam, thank you."

Sam and Gunnery Sergeant Roman, walked over to the counter and each grabbed a tray.

"J J looks as though he's enjoying it, doesn't he?"

"Yes, he does, Gunny," said Sam, as the two of them talked, while filling the three trays.

"It's probably a good thing he likes people, as much as he does, because of all the attention he's going to get over the next year or so," said the gunny, as the two men turned and watched J J with the young men around him. "You'd think, all these people, would make him nervous. After being alone all those years."

"Anyone else, it probably would, but not him, not my grampa, Gunny."

"Yes, I see that, Sam."

The two men finished selecting their food. Carrying the now full trays back towards the table. The two stopped and once again stood watching J J with the other Marines.

"We have your food, Grampa."

"Thank you, Sam. I'll be right there," said J J, as he tried to leave the group of men and come over to the table. Which proved to be no easy matter.

"At ease, men. Let, J J, have his breakfast in peace."

The group disbursed hearing the gunny's suggestion. J J walked over and joined Sam and the gunny. Smiling from ear to ear, as he sat down, between the gunny and Sam, he saw Tye, Billy, and Bo coming into the tent.

"Hey, guys, there's room here with us."

"Thank you, Sir," said Tye, hearing J J's invitation. "How are the two Johnson's today?"

"We're great, Tye. Did you three miss me?" asked Sam.

"Ya Home Boy, we missed you," smiled Billy.

"We'll go get our breakfast and join you. Ok, Gunnery Sergeant?"

"That's fine, Kim, go ahead and get your food."

"Thank you, Gunny," said Tye.

The three men walked over and each picked up a tray.

"I wonder why that man is so afraid of me? I don't think I ever did anything different to him, than I do the rest of my men," whispered the gunny, to J J.

"Gunnery Sergeant, I think it's the way he was raised. He want's so much, to please everyone," said Sam, hearing what the gunny said to his grandfather.

The gunny, raising an eyebrow as he and J J both looked over at Sam.

"I'm sorry, Gunny, I didn't mean to eavesdrop, or upset you."

"I'm not upset, Sam. Is that what you think, it's the way Tye was raised?"

"Yes, I do, Gunny," said Sam, as all three men looked over at Tye Kim, getting his breakfast.

"Boy, this food smells good. Is this what I think it is?" asked J J, as he picked up a glass. "What's this?"

"What do you think it is, J J?" asked the gunny.

"I think the stuff inside, is orange juice."

"It is. It's orange juice," said Sam.

"That's what I thought," said J J, as he took a taste. "That's what it is, all right! Orange juice! You have orange juice with breakfast, of course! What's it in?"

"What? What do you mean, what's it in?"

"It's not glass."

"You mean what's the container made of?" asked Sam.

"Yes, it's not glass. It's too light to be glass. It's also flexible. What's it called?" asked J J, as he sat there flexing the container.

"It's plastic."

"Sam, you mean like the stuff, some of the windows, in the B-17 bomber were made of? Plexsee something. I don't remember what it was called."

"I don't know, Grampa," said Sam shrugging his shoulders and looking over at the gunny, for the answer.

"I don't know the answer either, J J. There are literally thousands of products made of the stuff. Some plastics they say, are stronger than steel."

"Stronger than steel!" said J J, as he looked at the plastic container he held in his hand. "I know, believe it."

"Look around this mess tent. I'm sure you'll notice it's every where you look. Like the television, it's almost all plastic. A big part of our hand weapons nowadays are plastic," said the gunny, as they looked around the room. Sam and the gunny pointing out the different things that were probably made of plastic. As they were looking the men came over to sit with them. With their trays clear full of food. They all talked, as they enjoyed their ample and good tasting breakfast.

"Everything is so fresh and good tasting. My compliments to the chef," said J J, as he stood up and toasted the cook with his orange juice glass raised high. Everyone in the tent started clapping after hearing what J J said.

The cook also hearing what J J said, came out from behind the counter. His face red from embarrassment, he took a bow. He then turned to J J and saluted. His lips saying the words thank you, but not out loud, so not to be heard, as he did. He then returned to his work behind the counter. J J sat back down.

"Yes, thank you, J J. Sometimes we forget to say thank you, to a job well done," said Gunnery Sergeant Roman talking to J J and then looking over at Tye Kim, with a hint of a smile on his face, as he did.

"Sergeant, I want you to know something. I told Sam I wouldn't talk about it, but I have to tell you. My attack on these four men, was both, well planned and aggressively executed."

The gunny looked at J J and then at each of the four men and nodded his head slowly as he did. He then looked back at J J and smiled. "That's all that needs to be said about that. Let's say it never happened."

"That's fine with us, Gunnery Sergeant," said Sam, as the four men nodded their heads in agreement.

The men continued enjoying their breakfast talking and asking questions as they did. As they were talking, J J suddenly jumped to his feet.

"What is it? What's wrong?" asked the gunny, seeing the concern on J J's face.

"I hear helicopters."

"You do!" said the gunny.

The men at the table hearing what J J said, all stopped to listen for the helicopters.

"This is amazing to me! All these young men here. All the young people, both men and women. And the very first person to hear the helicopters coming, is J J, a man more then three times their age. This tells me you young people listen to too much loud music," said the gunny, shaking his head as he looked around, at all the young faces. "I suppose it could be, that most of you are fresh from boot camp. And your ears are still ringing. Ringing from your drill instructor's commands."

"That's it, Gunnery Sergeant!" said half the troops aloud as most everyone in the tent laughed. As the laughter died down, the helicopters could easily be heard coming in.

J J had already headed out the door to see the helicopters land. He was in awe, as he watched the helicopters jockey for favorable position to land. There were three of them. There was only room for one to land at a time. There was one coming in to do just that, while the other two waited their turn. He saw what he thought might be the Colonel waving. So he proceeded to wave back, at the person waving. J J got as close as he thought he could, to the landing helicopter. He stood watching as it landed. By the time it did, he could indeed see, that it was, Colonel Robinson doing the waving. As the helicopter touched the ground, the rotors began to slow. The doors opened and the Colonel got out, staying bent over, as he ran out from under the rotating rotors, in J J's direction. He slowed his run to a walk. Then walking upright, the Colonel held out his hand to J J.

J J snapped to attention, as the Colonel and three other men walked up to him.

"Attention!" ordered the gunny. The gunny had walked up just behind J J, facing the Colonel.

Because of all the noise from the three helicopters, only the people close enough to hear the order, came to attention. The first helicopter taking off, after leaving it's cargo. The second one quickly came in, landing in it's place. Unloading it's cargo and getting ready to take off, to make room for the third.

J J stood there with the gunny, the two of them saluting the Colonel. The Colonel returned the salute and walked up next to J J. He then turned to watch, as the second helicopter took off and the third came in and landed. The first two helicopters, flew back in the same direction in which they came. The third helicopter's rotors slowed, as they all stood watching the people exit the helicopter. The noise slowly disappeared, as the two helicopters flew out of sight and the third one's rotors came to a stop.

"J J, how are you today?" asked the Colonel, again holding out his hand to J J.

"I'm great, Colonel! How are you?" asked J J, as he grabbed the Colonel's hand and started shaking it as he spoke. J J then noticed that some of the people around him and the Colonel, had what he thought were cameras. He realized that some of these people were taking their picture as he shook the Colonel's hand. Realizing this J J smiled big and turned his good side to the camera. "Colonel, who are all these people?"

"J J, don't say your name. One is a reporter, for a national news source. We almost always have a civilian news media person with us nowadays, somewhere in Fleet Command. Don't tell them anything, J J," whispered the Colonel in J J's ear. "There are also people here from Fleet Command and reporters from the military news."

"Colonel, who is this man? Is he a solider? I saw him saluting you as you walked up to him. Who is he, Colonel?"

"Now, Jim, I thought we agreed!"

The man asking the Colonel the questions walked closer, looking at J J as he did.

"It looks as though he's been here a long time, by the looks of his clothes, Colonel. Does he know who he is, himself?"

"That I don't know, could be, Jim. We'll let you know, just as soon as we can."

"What's your name?" asked the man that the Colonel had called Jim, in a very loud voice.

"Mister I'm old, not deaf," said J J, looking past the man to the Colonel. The Colonel shaking his head slightly from side to side so J J could see, but not the man asking the question. "Like the Colonel said, Jim. We'll let you know just as soon as we can," said J J, speaking with a heavy southern accent.

"Colonel, what's going on here? Who is this guy?"

The gunny, seeing and hearing what was happening, turned and left, signaling his men to follow, as he did.

The Colonel seeing what the gunny was up to, tried to keep Jim's and the others attention on himself and J J.

"You men go tell everyone in camp, I said not to say anything to anyone, about J J, his name or about who he is. Just go, walk normal but go," said the gunny, to the first couple of men that came up to him. The men walked away, as the gunny walked back to the group, that had gathered around the Colonel and J J.

"Go ahead Jim, you can take all the pictures you want."

"Thanks Colonel, I'll do that. What happened to your face?" asked the reporter.

"I fell on some rocks."

"It must have been a long time ago."

"It's been awhile," said J J.

"How long have you been here?"

"It's been quite awhile. Where are you from?" asked J J.

"Me! What difference does that make?"

"None. I just thought I'd ask," said J J, as he shrugged his shoulders.

The Colonel snickering to himself, at the way J J was handling the reporter.

"What's going on, Gunny?" whispered Sam, as he saw the gunny coming up next to him, out of the corner of his eye.

"The Colonel's trying to keep the reporter from learning who your grandfather is." whispered the gunny.

"I know. Why?" asked Sam, still whispering.

"To protect him and your grandmother. So, he can't put in the news, who he is."

"Right. That's good. He doesn't seem too nice."

"He's a reporter, it's his job to get the news!"

"Right, Gunny. Thanks to you, the Colonel, Grampa and the rest of us. That may prove to be difficult," whispered Sam.

"Let's hope so."

"Colonel, there's more to this story! This man, isn't just some old beachcomber, your men found here on the island. I don't think you would have brought the military press corp for that. If you hadn't brought them, I wouldn't have found out about any of this. Come on, Colonel! I'm going to find out sooner or later!"

"See, Jim, I was thinking of you the whole time."

"That'll be the day."

"There you go, Jim!"

"What?"

"Let's call him, Buddy Holly!" laughed the Colonel and the rest of the people, that were close enough to hear what the Colonel said.

"Ya right! That's very funny, Colonel."

"For now, Jim, why don't you call him, the Jungle Man. That will give you and your readers a name to call him."

"The Jungle Man!" said Jim, as he stepped back and started to take more pictures. "That's probably all I'm going to get out of you about this, isn't it, Bob?" asked the reporter, as he walked up closer to J J and the Colonel.

"Yes, Jim, that's all we're at liberty to tell you, at this time."

"There's more to this old beachcomber than meets the eye. Speaking of eye, what happened to yours?"

"Like I said, Jim. I fell on some rocks," said J J, with a smile on his face.

"Somebody here knows! I'll find someone to talk and tell me! Who this guy is!"

"You be sure to come and tell me if you do, won't you, Jim? Do you have enough pictures, Jim?"

"I think so, Why?"

"Good. It's time for you and the others to go."

"Go! Go where?"

The Colonel moved to one side and twirled his index finger in the air. Jim seeing this, turned to see who the Colonel was signaling. He saw that the Colonel was signaling the pilot. The pilot of the helicopter, to start the engine.

"Oh no! You can't do this, Colonel!" said Jim.

"Have a good flight back, Jim," said the Colonel, as the whine of the helicopter's starting engine could now be heard.

"This is bull shit, Bob!"

The Colonel stood there smiling, as the helicopter's rotors began to rotate.

"This is bull-shit!" said Jim, shaking his head in disgust.

"You said that already, Jim. You'd think a reporter could use the English language more efficiently."

"You'll hear about this, Colonel!"

"I'm sure, I will," said the Colonel, raising his voice, to be heard above the roar of the helicopter's engine. "In a month or so, if he's lucky," smirked the Colonel, just loud enough for J J to hear. The Colonel then turned back to the reporter. "Don't miss your flight, Jim. I would hate for you to be caught in a restricted area. That would violate your agreement with the military. If that were to happen, they would probably revoke your pass. Now we wouldn't want that to happen, now would we?" asked the Colonel, loud enough so the reporter could hear him, even with the roar of the helicopter.

The reporter headed for the helicopter. Bent over as not to be hit by the rotor blades. Jim reluctantly boarded the helicopter, with several other people. Once the people had boarded, the crew closed the door and the rotors began to rotate at a much higher speed. Then the helicopter took off. As soon at it took off, another helicopter appeared on the horizon and came into land. It became obvious the exodus was well planned.

"Boy, I'm glad that's over. I'm sorry about all that, J J. It couldn't be helped."

"What was that all about, Colonel?"

"J J, I had to bring him and the others, but we didn't have to tell him or the others anything. I'd say we handled them pretty well." As the Colonel and J J talked. Sam noticed an officer walking in their direction. The officer was Doc Brown.

"Look, Gunny, there's the doc, Captain Brown. The doc wasn't at the Colonel's inspection yesterday, when Grampa came into camp for lunch."

"Yes, I see him, Private. The Captain left before the Colonel's and J J's visit. He must of been on one of the helicopters. We must not of noticed him, because of the reporter. He said he'd be back this morning."

"That must be it, Gunny. I'm sure I didn't see him," said Sam, as he and the others watched, as the Captain walked in their direction. The doctor walked up and saluted the Colonel. He then put out his hand and the Colonel shook it. Apparently the two men knew each other, quite well.

"Adam, I would like you to meet J J. J J, this is Captain, Doctor Adam Brown," said the Colonel, as he stood next to J J.

"I'm glad to meet you, Doctor Brown."

"You've been here alone, over fifty years! That's amazing!" said the doctor, as they shook each others hand. "I'm sorry, J J, that was rude of me. I'm glad to meet you, J J."

"That's all right, Doc. It's amazed me almost everyday, over the last fifty years or so. Are you the doctor, that took care of my grandson, after I poked a hole in him?" asked J J, turning to look at Sam, as he shook the doctor's hand. The doctor looked from the old man shaking his hand, to a private the old man was looking at. The private, was the young man he had bandage the day before.

"Wait! You mean to tell me! That boy there!" said the doctor, pointing at Sam. "He's your grandson? Let me understand this. This man here, is that man's grandfather? This is unbelievable," said the doctor, looking and pointing from one man to the other.

"You want to hear more, Adam?"

"There's more?"

"There's much more. My father and J J here, were best friends."

"Bob, you're telling me that your father knew this man? He knew him before he came to this island, over fifty years ago?"

"My father and J J, came to this island together. My father, was the one that left J J on this island, fifty years ago."

"Colonel, Robby didn't leave me!" said J J sternly. "Robby and the others, had to leave. I fell into a hole, and couldn't make it back to the boat. They didn't leave me behind!"

"I'm sorry, J J, you told me that already. It's just hard for me, knowing the way my father felt."

"J J, what year were you born?" asked the doctor, trying to change the subject. Seeing the emotion on the Colonel's face and hearing it in J J's voice.

"Doc, I was born on March 6, 1921."

"That means you're what, seventy two or three?"

"I was seventy two, my last birthday."

"How long have you been here, J J?" asked the doctor.

"It was the night of February 7, 1943, when the four of us came ashore."

"You've been here fifty years. That's just unbelievable," said the doctor.

"Believe it! Doc, living on a island alone for fifty years is one thing! Helicopters, men walking on the moon, cars costing almost ten times more then my house. These things are unbelievable! Not that a man could live alone for fifty years! You live! I just happened to live, by no choice of my own, on an island. I also had to live on this island, alone! You think that's hard to believe. When I left home, I could buy a new Chevrolet, for seven hundred dollars. Try believing, a Chevrolet costing over twenty thousand dollars today!"

"Try twenty five thousand, J J. My brother-in-law just bought one. I see your point J J. One thing is just as hard for us to believe, as another is for you," said the doctor.

"J J, did you and your grandson enjoy last night together?"

"We sure did, thanks to you and the sergeant, Colonel. Sam, that's his name now," said J J, pointing at Sam. "Sam and I really want to thank you for that time, Colonel."

"Yes, Colonel, thank you very much," said Sam. "I'm sorry, Colonel. I didn't mean to interrupt."

"That's all right. It was the least I could do, under the circumstances."

"Colonel, Sam showed me a picture of my Jera Marie. I can't wait to see her! When can we leave?"

"Let's get in out of this sun, J J. And we'll talk."

"Colonel, we can use the medical tent. I need to check J J out, at least get a start," said Doctor Brown.

"Lead the way Doc. We're right behind you."

Everyone followed the doctor, as they walked together towards the medical tent. They talked as they walked. It became obvious, the formality of rank was being subdued, for the present time and situation. Everyone had become quite exhilarated with the unbelievable circumstances and of course, J J.

"Doc what are you going to look for, when you check me out."

"I'm going to listen, to your heart and lungs. I want to look at your eye. Just to take a quick look, at your general state of health. That's all right isn't it, J J?"

"It's all right," laughed J J

"Maybe J J would like to go finish his breakfast. He ran out when he heard the helicopters coming. I'll say one thing, Doc, there's nothing wrong with his hearing," chuckled the gunny.

"Would you like to go finish your breakfast, J J?" asked the Colonel.

"Will I still have to see the doc?"

"I'm sure, J J, you'll probably see more doctors, in the next couple of weeks, than most people will see, in a lifetime."

"I never did like going to the doctor, even when I was a little kid. Why will I see so many doctors, Robby?"

"They'll want to see how a man isolated as you, survived."

"Let's get it over with, Robby," said J J, as they got to the medical tent.

"Sam, I should take a look at that wound of yours too."

"Ok, Doc."

They all stopped and stood in front of the medical tent talking.

"Doc, you go ahead and look at J J and Sam. Jack and I, will wait for you either in the command tent or we'll be in the mess tent."

"Yes, Colonel. We'll see you there."

"Ok, Doc."

The doctor, J J and Sam, went to the medical tent. Sam grabbed and opened the door, holding it open as the other two men entered. He then followed them in. The Colonel and the gunny walked away.

"You two relax, have a seat. I'll get ready and be right with you guys," said the doctor, as he walked to the back part of the tent.

"Why is it Sam, that the bathrooms are built so nice and the medical tent, is just a tent?" asked J J, as he looked around.

"It's to protect the environment, Grampa. The latrine or bathroom, as you call it. It's a self-contained unit, that's why. Nowadays people are more aware of protecting our environment."

"Oh," said J J.

"Sam, come over here and take off your shirt. Let's see how that wound of yours is healing."

Sam walked to the doctor, with J J following. Sam unbuttoning his shirt as he walked. Sam took off his outer shirt and laid it on the end of the doctor's examination table.

"Sam, sit up here on the table and let's have a look. How do you think it's doing, Sam?"

"It's fine, Doc. It just itches, that's all," said Sam, as he pulled his undershirt off over his head.

"It itches, does it? Let's have a look," said the doctor, as he started picking at the bandage to get hold of one of its corners. After doing so, he proceeded to peel the bandage off. He then looked at the wound.

"Sam, it looks like its healing quite well. It's early but let's go ahead and take these stitches out. Is that all right, with you?"

"That's fine with me, Doc. Whatever you think."

The doctor turned and picked up an envelope from the counter. He opened the envelope and pulled out a pair of rubber gloves and put them on. He then picked up a pair of forceps off the counter. With the forceps in one hand, he removed the lid of a small tray with his other hand. The tray sat on the back of the counter. With the lid off the tray, he removed a small pair of scissors, that was immersed in a clear liquid. The doctor picked up a smaller envelope from a stack of several. He opened the envelope and removed a small antiseptic wipe.

J J watched as the doctor prepared to remove Sam's stitches. J J crowded in closer to see better.

The doctor proceeded in the removal of the stitches. "There now, that didn't take long, now did it." The doctor then turned and grabbed a small bandage to put over the wound. "When you take this bandage off, Sam, you most likely won't need another," said the doctor, as he put the small bandage over the wound. He then looked up and stared at Sam. With a grin on his face, he stood there staring.

"What is it, Doc?"

"I couldn't help but notice your face, Sam."

"My face! Oh you mean my clean close shave," smirked Sam, as he rubbed his face with both hands.

"Close, I wouldn't call it, close. Except for this one spot," said the doctor, as he pointed at the one spot on Sam's face, that was clean shaven.

"Thanks Doc. It was close, closest I ever came!" said Sam, as he grabbed his shirts and jumped down from the table.

The doctor stood there for a moment, with a puzzled look on his face, trying to figure out what Sam meant. He shook his head, as he looked from Sam to J J. "You're next, J J. If you can remove your shirt and sit here. I'd like to listen to your heart and lungs," said the doctor, as he pointed at the table. The doctor turned and reached up for his stethoscope, which was hanging on the hook of an intravenous bottle rack, that was fastened to the side of the examination table.

J J moved in near the table, were Sam had been sitting. He was removing his shirt as he did, laying his shirt on the end of the table. He then sat up on the table and waited for the doctor.

The doctor had turned and was in the process of changing his rubber gloves. "Well let's see how your heart and lungs sound, J J," said the doctor, as he walked up putting his stethoscope into his ears. "Here's another nice thing about being on a tropical island."

"What's that, Doc?"

"The stethoscope isn't cold," laughed the doctor, as he looked down at the head of the stethoscope he held in his hand.

J J and Sam, looked at each other and shrugged their shoulders, as the doctor laughed.

The doctor started his examination of J J. The three men talked, as the doctor proceeded with the exam. J J at times not talking at the doctor's request, during the exam. As the doctor listened, the room became real quiet. Just at that moment, J J's insides made a deep rumbling sound. "Excuse me! It must be all the food I've eaten over the last two days. I'm not used to eating that much in a week! Let alone in two days! Of course I might also be a little nervous. I haven't had anyone do this, in a very long time!"

"We'll have to wait. Wait until the volcano, either erupts or quiets down," laughed the doctor, pointing at J J's stomach.

"I'm sorry, Doc."

"Do you feel ok, J J?"

"I feel fine, Doc. I feel much better than I sound. That's for sure, Doc."

"I'm glad, J J."

"Me too, Grampa."

The rumbling subsided. The doctor continued with his examination listening to J J's noisy inner workings.

"There now, that didn't take long, now did it? You can put your shirt back on, J J. Except for your digestive system working overtime. Everything else sounds great."

"He's in good shape, isn't he, Doc?"

"Yes, Sam. Your grandfather seems to be in excellent shape."

"Let's go, Sam! Doc, can we go ask the Colonel, when I can go home?" asked J J, as he grabbed his shirt and jumped down off the table, putting on the shirt as he walked towards the door.

"Yes, J J, I'm finished for now," said the doctor, as he picked up the used bandages, gloves and the removed stitches, in his gloved hands. The doctor stepped over to a covered container. He stepped on a lever, on the side of the container and the lid of the container opened, he deposited the used material in the container. He removed his rubber gloves also throwing them in. "After you, J J," said the doctor.

Sam hearing what the doctor said, moved to get the door for his grandfather and the doctor. He opened the door and held it for the two men. The three men left the medical tent and walked through camp towards the command tent, talking as they did.

"J J, what do you do to keep yourself in such good physical condition? What do you do for exercise?"

"I do my calisthenics. I used to do them everyday, but now I do them about three times a week. I also swim everyday. Well I did swim everyday, until you came. I haven't swam since you arrived. And I also like to run on the beach, in the cool of an evening."

"J J, there are very few people your age in as good a condition as you."

"They most likely, had other things to do! Don't forget, I've been at war for over fifty years! I had to be ready for an attack! To be able to fight the enemy. To the death if necessary!"

"That's right, you did," said Sam, as he opened the door of the command tent, for the doctor and his grandfather to enter.

The Colonel and the gunny got up from their seats at the desk, as the three men entered the tent.

"How did it go, Adam?"

"Great, Bob. J J is in excellent shape, as far as I can tell at this point."

"Colonel, when do you think I can leave for home?"

"You're ready, are you?"

"Yes, Sir, I'm ready."

"What about all your things? Don't you want to pack your things?"

"Robby, all I want, is to go home to my Jera Marie! I can go without my things. I want to see my Jera Marie."

Everyone in the tent stood in silence, at what J J said and the way he said it.

"Adam, how much surgery will it take to correct J J's bad eye?"

"I'm not qualified, Bob," said the doctor, shaking his head.

"In your opinion then, Adam?"

"In my opinion. It would be a simple surgery, for a qualified plastic surgeon to perform to correct the problem."

"Wait! You mean to tell me. They'll fix my eye, with that plastic stuff?" said J J, as he stood holding his hand up to his scarred cheek.

"What?"

"That plastic stuff! Like the T V's made of!"

"Oh! No, J J, I'm sorry! It's a form of surgery. It just happens to have the same name, as that plastic stuff, J J."

Everyone in the tent looked at J J and smiled.

"I wondered," said J J, shrugging his shoulders.

"Jack, would you select a couple of people, to pack J J's things."

"You mean we can leave? We can leave right now, Colonel?" asked J J, with tears filling his eye.

"If that's what you want, J J?"

"Yes, Sir, Colonel," said J J, with tears running down his scarred face, as he looked at Sam and the Colonel.

"Roman, after I left here yesterday, I decided what I had to do. I want you to cut new orders for Private, Johnson," said the Colonel, pointing at Sam. "I want him reassigned, as my personal aide."

"Yes, Sir. What of J J, Colonel?"

"I want no mention of J J."

"What? Yes, Sir. May I ask why, Sir?"

"Like I said, I've been thinking about this. I know in my own mind this is going to turn into a media circus. If I can, I'm going to handle as much of this as I can, myself. The fewer people involved the better. I will need some help though, hopefully from you two."

"Name it!"

"Thank you, Jack."

"Yes, name it."

"Thank you, Adam. I will need your help, to keep this as quiet as possible," said the Colonel, as the two men stood nodding their heads in agreement.

"Colonel, this is beginning to sound like it's a conspir..."

"Don't say it, Doc!" said the Colonel, trying to interrupt the doctor, before he could say the word. "I know. If there's any flack. You two, were following my orders, right?"

"Right," answered the two men, at the same time.

"We'll keep all of these people here. I don't think they'll mind staying in paradise, a few extra days," said the Colonel, with a grin.

"What about that nosy reporter?" asked the gunny.

"Ya! J J, it will be up to you to handle him, if he sees you onboard ship. All of us here know what a good story teller, you are. If you could continue pacifying him with contrary answers to his questions. It would sure help."

"What about the old man?"

"What? Oh, you mean the Captain. Adam, I'll have to tell him. I hope he'll be on our side. There's no way I'd do it without him knowing, even if I could."

"You've known him for years, haven't you, Bob?"

"Yes, I have. He's a by the book skipper, Adam. He's also old. I think he's one of the oldest captains, in the Navy. That may be one thing in our favor."

"Do you think he's as old as I am?"

"No, he's not that old! Sorry, J J. . . . I didn't mean that the way it sounded," said the Colonel, seeing the shock on J J's face.

"What I meant, was, he's probably going to be sixty any day now. Sixty, is the age for mandatory retirement. I know, he's very upset about that. Upset, that he's going to have to retire or he'll be forced to retire this year. That's all I meant, when I said he wasn't that old."

"No, Robby, it's not that. It's just that sixty sounds so old, and here I'm, over seventy. It still catches me off guard, that I could be that old! That's all, Robby." The four men stood there looking at J J.

"Gunny, may I say something?"

"Yes, Sam, go ahead."

"I've been thinking. About my grandfather's journals and stuff."

"My journals! I would like to take my journals with me, Robby. The Promise, I don't want anything to happen to The Promise, either."

"What were you going to say, Sam?"

"Colonel, I think Tye, Billy and Bo, would be a good choice, for the gunny to assign, to pack Grampa's stuff. The three of them, are the only one's besides us three, to have seen his stuff and to see where he lives, besides, I think Tye Kim, is the best man for the job. He's a perfectionist, at whatever he does."

"You're right, Sam. I've noticed that about Corporal Kim," said the gunny.

"Good, Gunny. If it's all right with you, make it so."

"It's all right with me, Colonel. It's a good choice."

"Ok then, Gunny, put him in charge of J J's things. Have it all labeled, 'Classified by: Colonel, Robert Robinson. Escorted by: Corporal, Tye Kim.' Cut the orders for me to sign. Orders giving Tye Kim, complete authority to act as me, in regards to this shipment, until it's final destination. Also give him the ability to contact me. Make it as simple as possible, for us to contact each other."

"Yes, Colonel. That's a good idea, Sir," said the gunny.

"If you're going to do all that, Robby, I don't need anything! I'm ready to go!"

"Sam, you go get your gear."

"Yes, Gunnery Sergeant."

"I better use the latrine, Robby, before we leave. I wouldn't want to be like a small child and say I have to go potty, right after we start on a long trip."

"Sounds like the thing to do, J J. I need to drain some of this coffee myself," said the Colonel.

"Sam, you go get your gear. We'll meet you at the helicopter in a few minutes," said the Colonel, as he walked past Sam, holding the door for him and the others.

"Colonel, I don't want to be that small child either."

"Oh, is that right? Well in that case, you're dismissed."

"Thank you, Colonel," said Sam, as he let go of the door.

The others watched outside the tent, as Sam went running off in the direction of the latrine. The four of them started walking in that direction, talking as they walked.

"J J, we'll wait as long as we can, before telling anyone else who you are. It's going to be hard enough keeping a story of a beachcomber being lost for over fifty years, subdued, let alone, one of a W.W.II, U. S. Marine! With the help of the Captain, we can probably do pretty well, until we get to Pearl. Timing is going to be everything. We'll have to hit the different bases or stops with people in command I know! Or at least, a lower ranking officer in command. If we can do that, I should be able to have you home in a couple of days, J J."

"Thank you, Robby," said J J, as he stood there staring at the Colonel. "Robby, I'd like to say thanks again, for allowing me the honor of addressing you, by your father's nick name, 'Robby.'"

"J J, I feel I've known you all my life. In fact! It's been an honor for you to call me, by the name Robby!"

"Yes, it has, for both of us, Robby."

Just then, Sam came running towards the four of them.

, "I'll get my gear and be waiting at the helicopter!"

After visiting the latrine, they returned to the command tent.

"Colonel, I'll go in and type up those orders for Corporal Kim and Private Johnson, for you to sign, Colonel," said the gunny, as he turned and entered the command tent.

"J J, I'll say good-bye here. It's been a pleasure meeting you," said the doctor, as he held out his hand. "I'm glad I could be one of the first, to welcome you back to civilization," said the doctor, as he shook J J's hand.

"Thank you. And thanks again, for taking care of my grandson, Doc," said J J, as he continued shaking the doctor's hand.

"Adam, do you think you could help Roman, instill into these people how important it is to keep this as quiet as possible."

"Bob, if I know Roman, he won't need any help! Of course I'll help, in anyway I can. You know that."

"You're right, Adam. Forget I said anything about it. It's just if this gets out!"

"Bob, we'll do our very best, to see, the only thing to leave this island, is J J himself, until Kim gets J J's belongings ready, and follows him home."

"Thank you, Adam. I'll see you in a couple of weeks," said the Colonel, as he shook the doctor's hand.

"Good-bye," said the doctor, as he turned and walked towards the medical tent.

"Robby, why is it so important, I be kept a secret?"

"In order for me to get you home as soon as possible, J J. I need to be in charge. That way, I don't have to disobey any orders. If the media finds out about you, I would most definitely lose that advantage."

"Oh good! Then it's not because you're ashamed of me, of the way I look, being a Marine and looking the way I do."

"Oh no, J J!"

"Good, Robby, there isn't much I can do about my appearance anyway, without the help of some new clothes and some of that plastic surgery, there isn't much I can do," said J J, as he slapped the Colonel on the back.

"We're not ashamed of you, J J!"

"I was just kidding the Colonel," said J J, as he continued slapping and rubbing, the Colonel's back.

Just then, the door on the tent opened behind them. They turned to see the gunny coming out. "Here, Colonel. Here's the orders for you to sign," said the gunny, as he came out of the command tent and handed papers to the Colonel. The Colonel took the papers. He reached into his shirt pocket and pulled out a pen. The gunny turned half around, with his back to the Colonel. The Colonel put the papers on the gunny's back and proceeded to sign the papers.

"Jack, try to instill in your men, how important it is, to keep this quiet," said the Colonel, as he handed the papers to the gunny.

"Colonel, I will have a little talk with them, about that, just as soon as you are airborne, Sir."

"Thank you, Jack."

As the three men started to talk, they saw Sam running in their direction, carrying something in his hand.

"Colonel, here's a uniform. I think it will fit, Grampa," said Sam, as he saluted the Colonel and the gunny. He then handed the uniform to his grandfather. "I don't have an extra pair of boots, Grampa."

"That's ok, Sam. I probably wouldn't know how to tie them anymore, anyhow," laughed J J.

Sam turned and started to run off, in the same direction in which he came. Then he stopped in his tracks. He slowly turned and saluted, the Colonel and the gunny. After doing so, he turned and quickly ran off. The three men snickered, shaking their heads at his exuberance, as he ran off.

"Robby, can I go inside and put this on?" asked J J, looking down at the uniform he held in his hands.

"Yes, go ahead, J J."

J J turned and went into the command tent. The Colonel and gunny, waited outside.

"How do I look?" They heard J J say, as he opened the door of the tent and came out smiling. The two men snapped to attention and saluted J J, as he stepped out of the doorway. He came to attention and returned the honor.

"You look like one of the few good men, a Marine!" said the Colonel, as the three men finished the salute. "Are you ready, J J?"

"Yes, Robby, I'm ready."

"J J, it's been an honor. Thank you for letting us stay here on your island. It's been a phenomenal experience," said Gunnery Sergeant Roman, as he held out his hand to J J.

"It's been a good place to live this last fifty years, Jack. I'll leave it in your capable hands, Gunnery Sergeant Jack Roman," smiled J J, calling the gunny by his full title, for the first time since they met. J J grabbed the gunny's hand and shook it vigorously.

"J J, do you mind if I keep that poem you carved on the palm leaf?"

"I gave it to the camp, Jack. It's yours."

"J J, your wife still has the original hanging in her kitchen, according to Sam, J J. We'll leave it here, when we leave."

"No! Don't do that! Take it with you. I would like more young people to read it. If it would help just one person, make the right choice in life, it would be a great accomplishment."

"Thank you, J J."

"My pleasure, Jack."

The three men noticed, while they had been talking, most of the people in camp had congregated into three groups, near to where they were. The Colonel seeing this, waved to them to come closer. "Come over and say good-bye to J J," said the Colonel, as him and the gunny moved to make room. They came over and gathered around J J, forming lines and taking turns shaking his hand.

Sergeant Sanchez came up to J J. He reached out and grabbed her hand and started shaking it. "I sure enjoyed watching you and the other two girls. . . , swim. Again let me say how surprised I was, to see three beautiful girls, swimming in my pond," said J J, as he shook her hand.

The shaking of hands went on for sometime. Then Sara grabbed J J, giving him a big kiss and a hug, taking him totally by surprise. "Thanks for putting some excitement into are lives, J J," said Sara, as she broke her embrace.

"Sara! Control yourself," said Betty Jo.

"Lighten up, Betty Jo. You're enjoying this, aren't you, J J?" said Sara, as she once more hugged J J.

"We can end this anytime you are ready, Colonel," said Gunnery Sergeant Roman.

"There's no hurry, Jack. It appears, J J's enjoying himself immensely. It's obvious he really does enjoy people, doesn't he?"

"I'd say he's really enjoying Private Conrade's, form of attention. Wouldn't you, Colonel?"

"I'd say so."

"Who in their right mind wouldn't?" asked the gunny, as the two men stood talking, as they watched the crowd around J J. "I've been thinking. I wonder what J J meant when he said, he "wouldn't want anything to happen to The Promise?" The Promise was destroyed in the storm. What do you think he meant, by that?"

"I don't know, Jack. He did seem quite concerned, didn't he?"

"Yes, I'd say he did. We'll have to ask him."

"This could go on for some time, Gunny. What do you say, we put a lid on it."

"Ok, let's break it up," said the gunny, in a loud enough voice to be heard over the crowd's enthusiasm. No sooner had the words left the gunny's mouth than the crowd started moving away from J J leaving only the Colonel and the gunny, standing with J J.

"J J, we were wondering? What did you mean, when you said, you "didn't want anything to happen to The Promise?" asked the Colonel.

J J stood there a moment. Thinking about the question asked of him. "Oh, I'm sorry, Robby. You and Jack didn't see The Promise."

The two men first looked at each other, then back at J J.

"I should have said, my Vessel Of Life, instead of The Promise. The Promise was the name of the sailboat. My Vessel Of Life, is the name of the scale model of her, I built."

"I'd like to see it, J J."

"Damn! I can't leave yet!" said J J, looking off towards the jungle. "What? What is it, J J? Why can't you leave?" asked the Colonel, as he turned and looked to the jungle, to see what J J was looking at. J J stood there in silence. He then slowly turned and looked into the eyes of his new friend, obviously concerned.

"Robby, I have to show Tye Kim. I have to show him where the other caverns are, before I leave," said J J, as he stood there looking at the Colonel.

"That's right. You told us about them, but you didn't show anyone where they were located. I'm glad you thought of that, before we left, J J. Otherwise they may never have found them."

"Kim was here just a few minutes ago. I saw him, saying good-bye to you, J J," said the gunny.

"Yes, he was."

"Those four men are pretty close. He and the other two, probably went to find Johnson, to ask him more about how your night together, went," said the gunny.

"Where's their tent, Gunny?" asked the Colonel.

"It's over there, Colonel," said the gunny.

"Yes, it's right over here, Robby. Follow me."

The Colonel and the gunny followed as he lead the way to the four men's tent. As they walked, J J explained how he had watched the camp with the binoculars and that is how he knew which tent, was theirs. Just as they walked up in front of the tent, the tent's flap flew open and out came Sam, with his things in hand. He stood there, surprised by their presence.

"Did I misunderstand?" asked Sam, as he stood there. "I was to meet you at the helicopter, wasn't I?" asked Sam, as he looked at the Colonel, the gunny and his grandfather, standing there outside the tent.

"Yes, Sam, that's right," said the Colonel.

"Johnson, is Corporal Kim in there?" asked the gunny.

"Yes, Gunnery Sergeant."

"Johnson, tell him to come out."

"Yes, Gunny," said Sam, as he threw down his things, not hesitating, he turned to re-entered the tent. As he did, he ran right into Tye. Tye, Bo and Billy, were coming out. Sam jumped back as not to squish Tye between himself and Bo.

"Whoa! Tye, you almost became a bow tie," said J J, seeing what almost transpired. Everyone chuckled at what J J said.

Then the three men saw the Colonel standing there outside their tent. Somewhat startled, they stared, then all three men came to attention and saluted the Gunnery Sergeant and the Colonel.

"The Colonel wants to talk to you three," said the gunny, as he and the Colonel, returned the salute.

"At ease, men. I have something special for you three to do. But first. J J has to show you where his other caverns are located. J J, go ahead," said the Colonel.

"Tye, you three can find your way back to my place, can't you?"

"Yes, Sir. I'm sure we can, Sir."

"Good. Then all I have to do, is tell you how to go from there. The other two caverns are not far from there. One is about three hundred feet south on the same ridge. The other, is more like a thousand feet to the north. Just north of a small saddle on the same ridge. The one on the north has two large rocks near it's entrance. The one south has a beautiful orchid plant near it's entrance." The three men stood there listening, as J J described, how to find the caverns.

"Is that it, J J?"

"Yes, Colonel. They shouldn't have any trouble finding them now, as long as they stay near the crown of the ridge."

"You got it, Corporal?"

"Yes, Colonel."

"What I want you three to do is to pack everything in those three caverns. And I do mean everything!"

"Yes, Sir, Colonel. Where are we to pack it to, Sir?"

"Not pack it! Pack it up, Guys. I want you to pack it up, so it can be shipped."

"Yes, Sir, I understand now, Colonel."

"Corporal Kim, there's more I want you to do."

"Yes, Sir. I'm ready, Sir. What is it, Colonel?"

"Good. Gunnery Sergeant Roman, will explain more of what I want you to do, after we leave, Corporal.

"Yes, Sir, thank you, Colonel. I'll do my best, Colonel, Sir."

"I'm sure you will, Kim," said the Colonel.

"Well, J J. Do you think you're ready? Do you think the three of us can leave now? The sergeant will handle the rest."

"Yes, Robby, I'm ready."

"I'm ready, Colonel," said Sam, without being asked.

"Ok. Lets go," said J J.

"You lead the way, J J."

THE TREK BEGINS

"Ok, Robby. Follow me," said J J, as he turned and headed towards the helicopter.

Bo bent down and grabbed Sam's things, that had been dropped outside their tent. "Here I'll get it, Bo," said Sam, as he bent down to help.

"I've got it, Home Boy."

"Thanks, Bo," said Sam, as he stood up.

The six men followed J J, as they walked through camp. The seven of them walked towards the helicopter, talking as they walked along. The Colonel then saw that the pilot and copilot were not at the helicopter.

"It looks as though we're without a pilot. Does anyone here know how to fly one of these things?" laughed the Colonel, as they walked up to the helicopter. All the men either shrugged their shoulders or shook their heads. "I didn't think so," laughed the Colonel. Just then he saw his pilot and copilot running in their direction. "Well, J J, it doesn't look like you'll have to fly this thing, after all," laughed the Colonel, as he slapped J J's back and then pointed at the two men running towards them.

"Sorry, Colonel. We went to use the head and to have a cup of coffee," said the officer that had run up and stopped in front of the men.

"No problem, Lieutenant. How soon can we take off?"

"Two or three minutes, Sir," said the Lieutenant, as he and his copilot stood between the Colonel, the others and the helicopter.

"There's no hurry, Lieutenant. I want you to do something for me."

"Yes, Colonel."

"I want you to take some time and show this man your bird," said the Colonel, pointing at J J. "I also want you to give him a brief explanation of how it works. Can you do that for me, Lieutenant?"

"Yes, Sir, I sure can, Colonel."

While the Lieutenant and Colonel had been talking, J J walked up next to the helicopter. He looked up and inside the cockpit. He then tapped on the side of it with his knuckles.

"Thank you, Lieutenant."

"Who is this man, Colonel?"

"He was left here on this island. He saw us, when we set up our camp. He didn't have any clothes to wear, so my aide gave him one of his uniforms to wear, they happened to be close to the same size."

"What's his name, Colonel?"

"His name? You can call him J J, Lieutenant."

"J J, let me tell you a few things about this fine machine," said the Lieutenant, as he walked up to J J. The Lieutenant's hand held out to shake J J's. J J looked right past the Lieutenant to the Colonel, to see if he should answer to J J or not. The Colonel giving a nod, that it was indeed all right to do so. The two men exchanged hand shakes and the Lieutenant started telling J J about the helicopter and how it flew. This went on for about ten minutes. The Colonel and Sam had said their good-byes and had climbed into the helicopter with the copilot and were ready to take off. Leaving the gunny and the other three standing next to the helicopter, waiting for J J and the pilot, to complete the preflight inspection. The Lieutenant and J J walked up to the others. The pilot turned and climbed aboard the helicopter, he then turned and held out his hand to J J.

"Can I help you get in, J J?" asked the pilot.

"No, I'm fine. Thank you, Lieutenant," said J J, as he jumped aboard the helicopter. The pilot smiled as he watched J J effortlessly board the helicopter. Still smiling he went forward and climbed into his seat.

J J then turned and leaned out of the helicopter in order to get the attention of the others. "I know you three will take care of my things. If you could, take special care in packing the Vessel Of Life. You didn't see it. It's a model I made, of The Promise."

"I saw it! I didn't want to interrupt you telling your story, J J. It was sitting back in the corner, high on a shelf," smiled Tye.

"Yes, that was it."

"J J, we'll do whatever it takes, to pack your things so they'll get home safe."

"Thank you, Tye. You guy's, come and see my Jera Marie and me. Whenever you're on leave in the area or just passing through," said J J, as the pilot started the engine and the helicopter slowly came to life.

"Here, J J, put this on," ordered the Colonel, in a loud enough voice as to be heard over the helicopter's starting engine. The Colonel handed J J a helmet, with a two-way radio headset. J J looked at the helmet he held in his hands. The Colonel signaled him to put it on. J J put the helmet on his head and pulled it down over his ears. "Can you hear me, J J?" asked the Colonel, tapping on the side of J J's helmet with the end of his finger. Slowly nodding, showing the Colonel he did indeed hear him, through the headset in the helmet.

"Sit here, J J. Here, put on one of these seat belts," ordered the Colonel, as he sat in his seat waiting for J J to sit. Grabbing a seat belt the Colonel put on his belt, showing J J where and how to fasten his seat belt. J J sat where the Colonel told him and started putting on the seat belt. He was sitting in the outside seat, next to the door. "J J, are you frightened?" asked the Colonel. Hearing the Colonel asking him, if he was frightened. J J answered the question, by shaking his head. "J J, your helmet has a built-in microphone. Just talk and we can hear you," said the Colonel.

"Yes, I can hear you, Robby. Can you hear me?"

"Yes, everyone with a headset on can hear you, J J."

J J nodded his head yes that he understood. He then looked out the door of the helicopter.

The gunny and the others had moved back, so to be clear of the rotating rotors.

"Lieutenant, this is Colonel Robinson."

"Yes, Colonel."

"How much fuel do you have? Do you have enough to make a few passes over the island, before we have to head for the ship?"

"Yes, Colonel, we do."

"Good. Let's show this man what his island looks like from the air, Lieutenant."

"Yes, Sir, Colonel."

J J holding the sides of his helmet with both hands, heard what the Colonel asked and quickly nodded his head.

The helicopter started to move. Then all at once it was airborne. J J's stomach felt as though it was tied to the ground. It felt like he was leaving it behind, as the helicopter took to the air. It reminded him of when he went to the Pike, in Long Beach California. He had just graduated from boot camp and he and some friends, went to the Pike and rode all the rides. J J had a big smile on his face as the helicopter flew higher and higher.

The Colonel and Sam could see by his smile, that J J wasn't a bit frightened. In fact he appeared to be having a great time.

"Look, Sam, Robby, there's my pond! Look there, there's the lagoon The Promise came into and became my Vessel Of Life, That's where she met her fate," said J J, as he tried to look at everything going by so quickly, beneath the belly of this magnificent flying machine.

"This is like some of the rides, I rode at the Pike and at the World's Fair, when I was a kid."

The pilot flew along the coastline of the island, inland from the waterline, a few hundred feet. He flew around the island and back over the camp. The pilot then flew over what appeared was the middle of the island.

"How's that, Colonel?"

"That's fine, Lieutenant. Head for the ship."

"Yes, Colonel."

The helicopter leaned hard to the starboard side, J J's side of the helicopter. He braced himself against the frame of the open door of the helicopter, as it headed out, over open water. The helicopter gained altitude and assumed a somewhat more level form of flight. J J looked back towards his island. At this point, he could see the entire island. He watched, as his island grew smaller, as they flew farther away. It was like he was leaving his whole world behind. As he sat there watching he thought. 'This is what it must have been like, for the spacemen, that went to the moon. Watching their world get smaller, as they flew towards the moon, leaving their world behind.' J J sat there staring out the open door. He then turned and leaned his head back against the bulkhead.

"What's wrong? Are you getting airsick, Grampa?" asked Sam, as he saw the change in his grandfather's mood. Seeing him sitting there staring. J J looked over at his grandson, as a tear ran down his cheek. "Grampa, did you get something in your eye, during take off?" asked Sam, seeing the tear trickle down.

"Yes, I did, Sam. An island." Sam nodding his head, showing his grandfather, he understood what he meant.

"Lieutenant, how long until we land aboard ship?"

"Colonel, she's been steaming directly away from us, since we took off this morning. Flight time should be about ninety-eight minutes. Give or take a few, Colonel."

"Look, Grampa, there's more islands way out there," pointed Sam, out the door of the helicopter. Looking to where his grandson was pointing, he once again became interested in his ride and the sights to see.

Off in the distance, J J could see the group of islands. It appeared there were four islands, in the group.

"Lieutenant, this is J J. Can you hear me?"

"Yes, I can, J J."

"Could you tell me, Lieutenant, how far those islands are from my island?"

"They look to be eighty to ninety miles off our starboard side. If that be the case, that puts them around a hundred and fifty miles, from your island."

"That's a long ways in open water," said the Colonel.

"Lieutenant, this is me again. Are there any people on those islands?"

"That, I don't know. I doubt it. Your island, is the only island we flew over that showed any potential, of having fresh water."

"Thank you, Lieutenant."

J J leaned as far out the door, as his seat belt would permit. So he could see more out in front, in the direction they were flying. Off in the distance he could see another group of islands. "There's some more islands coming up out in front of us. They're lying in the direction we're flying."

"J J, those aren't islands."

"It's the Lieutenant, isn't it?"

"Yes it's me, J J."

"What do you mean, Lieutenant, those aren't islands?"

"That's our destination. That's the Enterprise and her escort ships, J J."

"You mean, to tell me. Those are ships, I see?"

"That's right."

J J still staring in the direction, of what he thought to be islands, as they flew closer. As he watched, the objects grew larger. He could now tell, what he thought were islands, were indeed ships. He could see trails formed in the sea, by each ship's huge propellers. He continued watching as they flew ever closer.

"Yes, Lieutenant, I can see them. Two small ones and one bigger one. What kind of ships are they? They're not very big."

"J J, the biggest of the three is the aircraft-carrier, Enterprise. One of the smaller ones is a guided missile launching ship. The other is a torpedo launching ship."

"Lieutenant, you said this helicopter could fly a hundred and eighty miles an hour. How fast have we been flying today?"

"About that, J J. One-eighty."

"Then why is it taking us so long to get to those ships? Wait! What's that?" yelled J J, as he excitedly pointed out the door to the horizon.

"What? What is it?" asked the Lieutenant and the Colonel, at the same time.

"That!" said J J, as he pointed.

"It's ok, it's a flight of F-18's Colonel. J J, that flight of F-18's is headed to the same place we are, the Enterprise. They're probably going to get there a little sooner. They're flying two or three hundred miles an hour faster then we are. We might be close enough to see some of them land, before we land," said the Lieutenant.

J J sat looking towards the high speed planes in the distance. He could now see, that the helicopter and the flight of F-18's were flying in the same direction. Still leaning out as far as possible, he looked ahead towards the ships, as they flew ever closer.

"J J, the Enterprise is a nuclear powered aircraft carrier. She's one of the largest ships afloat."

J J moved out of the doorway and sat normal in his seat. He then looked over at Robby.

"I know it doesn't look that big right now, J J. But it soon will," said the Colonel, as he sat there grinning.

"Robby, I've been thinking. When the three helicopters flew into camp this morning, they landed one at a time because there was only room for one. That part I understand. After the third one landed and one flew back to the ship, where did the other one go? There wasn't time for it to fly back from the ship."

"I can answer that, Colonel."

"Go ahead, Lieutenant."

"After the first two landed and unloaded it's people and cargo, one flew back to the ship. The other one landed on the beach, this bird being the one. If you look, you'll see our swimming suits, they're in a plastic bag next to the front bulkhead on the floor. We didn't have a chance to do any swimming. I just barely had time to get my helmet off, when they called for us to come back and pick everyone up. That's why you are with us now, J J."

"How much longer, Lieutenant?"

"We still have some flight time, before we'll be needing our landing instructions, Colonel."

"I can't see the flight of F-18's anymore, they must be to far away. But those ships are sure looking a lot bigger," said J J, as he resumed his position of leaning back out the open door.

"The Lieutenant said that one of those ships, was a missile launching ship. Does that mean it has those missiles onboard, that Sam told me about. The ones that are guided somehow to their targets hundreds or even thousands of miles away?"

"Yes it does, Grampa. It has guided missile onboard. I don't know how many, but lots of them."

"I can see the ships a lot better now. That one, the one you call Enterprise, is beginning to look a lot bigger. It's wake sure shows up now."

"J J, if you look close, you can see one of the AWAX planes, coming into land on the Enterprise."

"Thank you, Lieutenant," said J J, recognizing the Lieutenant's voice.

"Colonel, there's some binoculars in the bulkhead locker. I'll hold her level so you can get them." The Colonel took his belt loose.

"If I start to fall out, you'll grab me, won't you, J J?" laughed the Colonel, as he stood up.

"Yes, Robby! You can count on it."

The Colonel opened the locker door. The binoculars were in the locker, in a cavity molded to their shape. He removed the binoculars from their cavity and closed the locker. The Colonel then sat back down in his seat and refastened his belt. He turned and handed J J the binoculars. J J took the binoculars from the Colonel, and put them up to his eye and looked out the door.

"I can see the ships much better with these."

"J J, look to the stern of the boat. Watch, you'll be able to see the plane coming into land."

"Yes! I can see it." J J watched the plane as it came in low. It looked as though it was flying level with the ships deck. It was going to be landing on the tail or stern end of the ship. The plane landed and only went a short distance before stopping. As the plane came to a stop, J J was just able to make out a crew of men. He could just see the men, as they ran out to meet the plane. They were still some distance from the three ships, but close enough for J J to watch, with the help of the binoculars, the action taking place on the deck's of the Enterprise. As J J watched, he could see there was another plane coming into land. The first plane J J saw land, was immediately moved out of the way and the other plane landed in it's place. All this taking place, right before J J's eyes (eye), in a matter of seconds.

"Lieutenant."

"Yes, Colonel."

"Why don't you see if you can get permission for us to do a flyby of the three ships Lieutenant, per my request?"

"Yes, Sir."

J J continued watching the ships and looking for more planes coming into land.

"Colonel, we can proceed with the flyby, at your discretion or until canceled. Per Flight Command, Commander Walker."

"At your discretion, Lieutenant."

"Yes, Sir."

During this time, J J continued looking through the binoculars, at the three ships, focusing mainly on the busy deck of the Enterprise. They were now close enough, he could put the binoculars down and watch the ships with his naked eye. He could see people on the decks, as they flew by the first of the two smaller ships, J J could see the faces on some of the crew members, as they flew by. The ship was off the starboard side of the Enterprise. They were flying between it and the Enterprise, putting the ship on the helicopter's starboard side. The Lieutenant flew around this ship's bow, keeping it on the starboard side of the helicopter, flying down the other side, putting them starboard to starboard, with the ship. J J could now see the enormous size difference, between this ship and the Enterprise.

"What do you think of the Enterprise now, J J?"

"She's bigger than I could have possibly ever imagined, Robby!" said J J, as they flew around the stern of the ship, just slightly higher then the flight deck of the Enterprise. Then flying even with the stern of the Enterprise J J could see down the entire length and width of the enormous ship. At this point the Lieutenant held the helicopter in one place. J J could see all kinds of different airplanes and helicopters, parked in rows on each side, along the length of the Enterprise's deck showing him just how massive, the Enterprise really was. They flew past the Enterprise and past the stern of the third ship. The Lieutenant then turned the helicopter, flying parallel with the three ships. The helicopter gaining altitude as they flew along the port sides of the ships. J J could see all three ships again at the same time, as he sat looking out the open door of the helicopter.

"J J, are you about ready? Are you ready for us to land this thing?"

"Robby, it's so much to look at, it's gigantic! What a day! Sam, you were right! Each day is going to be an eye opener!" said J J, pointing at his bad eye as he spoke, leaning forward to see his grandson, sitting on the far side of the Colonel. "You're the Colonel. I've already seen more than I could have ever imagined." said J J, as he turned and again leaned back out the open door, of the helicopter.

"Lieutenant, go ahead and land. At your discretion."

"Yes, Sir."

The Lieutenant, flew the helicopter past the port side of the three ships. He then turned and flew at the Enterprise head on, coming in over the bow of the big ship. They were now flying right down the ship's center. J J sat there thinking 'it was as though the helicopter was hanging on a hook in the sky and the Enterprise was passing slowly underneath.' It became obvious they were about to land. It was as though the helicopter was as light as a feather floating in a summer breeze, as it floated closer and closer to the deck of the big ship. All at once the helicopter stopped floating and made contact with the hard surface of the deck. No sooner had the helicopter landed, than there were people at it's open door.

"Go ahead and get out, J J," smiled the Colonel.

J J went to jump out, forgetting about his fastened seat belt, as he did.

"Here, let me get that belt for you, Grampa," said Sam standing in front of him, as he struggled with his seat belt. J J raised his arms up and out of the way, to allow his grandson to release his seat belt.

"J J," said the Colonel, pointing at the helmet he still had on his head. Realizing what the Colonel meant, J J took the helmet off and sat it in the seat next to him. Now free, J J jumped down out of the helicopter. Sam grabbed his gear, and the Colonel and then him, jumped to the flight deck, as J J looked around. The three of them were joined by the Lieutenant and his copilot.

"Thank you, Lieutenant, for a very interesting flight," said J J, as he grabbed the Lieutenant's hand and shook it vigorously. He also shook the copilot's hand and thanked him. Then J J stood and watched the two men going through Navy protocol with the men on deck.

"The Captain is likely on the bridge. J J, let's go introduce you to him, before Jim, that nosy reporter finds out that you're onboard."

"Lead the way, Robby, I'll be right behind you."

The three of them started for the bridge. The Colonel was followed by J J, then Sam.

"It's so big! How many men are there onboard the Enterprise, Robby?"

"In peace time fifty eight hundred or so. During a conflict, it could grow to sixty two hundred or even more."

"I know, believe it," said J J, shaking his head.

They climbed several flights of stairs on their way to the bridge. "This is it, J J. I'll ask the O D if I can show you the bridge. I'll also ask him if we can meet with the Captain. You two wait here. I'll be back as soon as I can."

"Yes, Sir," said the two men, at the same time.

The Colonel opened the door marked, "Restricted Area Authorized Personal Only." He closed the door behind him.

J J and Sam could see the whole flight deck from where they were standing. They stood there watching everything going on, on the deck below. The helicopter they came in was no longer where they had left it. "What did they do with the Lieutenant's helicopter?"

"Grampa, they put them below the flight deck for service and storage. Look over there. That plane there, is on an elevator." Just as J J looked to where Sam was pointing, that part of the deck went down, with the plane sitting on it. "See, I told you, Grampa."

"Believe it." Just then someone tapped J J on the shoulder. He turned to see who it was. "Robby, I'm sorry. I didn't see you come out."

"The Captain is in his quarters, having lunch."

"Do you think we should wait until he has finished his lunch, Robby?"

"No. The sooner we see him, the better."

"Lead the way, Robby."

The Colonel started walking on the catwalk, back in the same direction they came, as J J and Sam followed. They had only gone a short way, when the Colonel went up to another door. He opened the door and entered a hallway, J J and Sam waited for him on the catwalk. There was a Marine in the hall. The Marine was standing guard, at the Captain's door. The Colonel walked up to the Marine.

"Sergeant, I'm Colonel Robert Robinson. I'd like to speak with Captain Paterson, Sergeant."

"Colonel, wait here, Sir. I'll see if the Captain will see you, Sir." The Marine knocked and then entered the Captain's quarters. The door reopened and the Marine came out holding the door open behind him. He was gone less than a minute. "Colonel, the Captain will see you, Sir."

Hearing the sergeant, J J and Sam, quickly joined the Colonel.

"Thank you, Sergeant."

The sergeant held the door for the three men to enter. The cabin door had Captain: P. J. Paterson, written on it.

"Sergeant, you can wait outside."

"Yes, Sir."

The Captain was standing in front of his desk, when the four men entered his cabin. All four of the men saluted each other, as the sergeant left the room, closing the door behind him.

"Colonel Robinson, what can I do for you?" asked the Captain, as he and the Colonel shook hands.

"Pat, I'd like to ask a special favor of you?"

"What is it?"

"Captain, can this be off the record?"

"Yes, of course it can, Bob. What's the favor?"

"I'll take all the risk. I just wanted you to know what I was up to, on your ship. I do need your help, in keeping something quiet, Pat."

"Bob, you know it's hard to do anything on a ship and keep it quiet. It's almost impossible, unless it's marked, 'Top Secret.'"

"Pat, it has nothing to do with the operation of this ship or any other."

"Ok, get to the point."

"Pat, to start with. I'd liked to introduce these two men. Captain Pat Paterson, this is Private J. S. Johnson." The Captain and Sam, shook hands. "Private J. S. Johnson, this is Captain Pat Paterson." J J shook hands with the Captain, as he stood looking at J J's disfigured face. The Captain then turned and stood staring at the Colonel.

"Colonel Robinson, what's this all about? Who are these men?"

"They're who they say they are, Captain. Private's Johnson and Johnson," snickered the Colonel.

The Captain, stood staring at the Colonel, he then turned and looked over at the two men. "You're telling me these two men are both privates and both have the same name. Bob, this man here, is old enough, to be this man's grandfather."

"That's right, Pat, he is."

"What, Bob? He's old enough. Or he's, this man's grandfather?" laughed the Captain.

"Pat, he's both. He's this man's grandfather and a private in the United States Marine Corps." The Captain stood looking, from one man to the other, as the Colonel tried to explain. The Colonel spent the next twenty minutes explaining the situation to the Captain.

"Wow, that's an incredible story, Bob," said the Captain, sitting on the front edge of the top of his desk. The other three men had all sat down in chairs, they had pulled up, in front of the Captain's desk.

"Like you said, Bob. The fewer people that know the better. Who does know?" The Colonel told the Captain, the people who knew of J J's true identity.

"So, no one aboard ship other than us four, knows who he is."

"Except for the pilot and copilot of the helicopter, as far as we know at this time, that's it. Pat, they don't know who he is. They just know his name is J J."

"Well, J J, you may have beat the system."

"How's that, Captain?"

"As far as I know you're the oldest person ever to be on active duty, J J. You may have helped me."

"Captain, what did I do to help you?" asked J J.

"You still being on active duty at your age, even if not by choice. You may have set a precedent, J J. I have been fighting mandatory retirement at sixty, for years. People age at different paces. I'll be sixty in just over two weeks. I don't want to retire, I'm too young. I love what I do, and I'm very good at it. I would like to continue doing this job, long after I turn sixty, if my health stays good, that is. Bob, I'll do what I can to help," said the Captain.

"Colonel, I think I slipped up!"

"How did you slip up, Sam?" asked the Colonel.

"I called him grampa, on the helicopter's intercom, Colonel!"

"That's right. I remember, Sam, you did."

"What was the pilot's name, Bob?"

"Damn, I don't have any idea, Pat."

"Robby, his name was Ted, Ted Anderson. The copilot's name was Tom. I didn't get his last name."

"Great, J J."

The Captain turned and grabbed one of the phones on his desk. He told someone on the other end what he wanted and then hung up.

"Those two men will be here shortly. Maybe they haven't had time to talk to anyone about J J yet. We'll find out soon enough. Sam, I'm sure glad you thought of that."

"I should have thought of it at the time and not called him grampa, on the helicopter's intercom."

"We'll see if we can nip it in the bud, Son."

"Thank you, Captain."

"What's next, Bob?"

"I want to fly J J home, before the news of his existence is released. With your help I can fly him to Pearl, late at night. With any luck at all, it will be a lieutenant or less on duty, at that time of night. If it is, I can probably use my rank and get a flight from there, to Seattle or anywhere on the west coast, for that matter." Just then there was a knock on the door and the sergeant entered the room. Before the sergeant could speak. "Have the two men come in, Sergeant, you can wait outside."

"Yes, Captain," said the sergeant, as he held the door open for the two men. The men entered the Captain's cabin and came right to attention. The sergeant left the room, closing the door behind him.

"At ease, men," said the Captain, as they exchanged salutes. Have you two men talked to anyone about the flight?" asked the Captain, still sitting on the front edge of his desk.

"Just the Colonel, J J and Private Johnson there, Sir."

"Anyone else?"

"No, Captain. We were just getting out of the shower, when we received your order to report here, Sir."

"Good. The Colonel and I would like you two to help us."

"Yes, Captain. How can we help?"

"We would like you to forget any details, you may or may not have learned about J J, on your flight this morning."

"Captain, whatever you and Colonel Robinson say, Sir."

"Lieutenant, are you qualified to fly any of the transports, here onboard the Enterprise?"

"No, Colonel, I'm not. Just helicopters, Colonel."

"Ok, Lieutenant, you two can go. You're dismissed," said the Captain. With J J and Sam, standing off to one side, the four men saluted each other and the two men turned and left the room, closing the door behind.

"Damn, I was hoping we wouldn't have to involve another pilot."

"Bob, everything nowadays is so sophisticated, they have to specialize to become expert enough at a particular skill or craft, in the time they have to learn. There's very few Jack's Of All Trades, nowadays."

"That's right. I know what you mean, Pat."

"Robby, the helicopter the young Lieutenant flies, sure is a sophisticated machine, that's for sure."

"Yes, it is, J J."

"Bob, how soon do you want to fly to Pearl?"

"J J's ready now. The sooner the better."

"It'll be all three of you, right?"

"Yes, all three of us, Pat."

"Maybe I should come with you. This reminds me of when I was in the N I S, during part of my training."

"That's not a bad idea, Pat. We might have a fairly good chance, with two of us pulling rank," laughed the Colonel.

"It also could draw a lot of unwanted attention, Bob."

"That's true, Pat, it would."

"It'd be worth it."

"Thank you, J J. But I have a ship to run. I'll do what I can to help from here, aboard Enterprise."

"Thank you, Sir."

"My pleasure, J J."

"Where do we start? I'd say the first thing is, I need to schedule a flight to Pearl. But before I do that, I'd best get you two some quarters." The Captain turned and again grabbed one of the phones on his desk. The three men talked amongst themselves, as the Captain talked on the phone.

"I got you two a VIP cabin, not far from the Colonel's."

"Thank you, Captain."

"Now for the plane."

"To bad there isn't a plane onboard, that we could fly from the decks of the Enterprise, clear home to Seattle."

"Sam, there probably is. I can justify a flight to Pearl, I'll be damned, if I could justify a flight to Seattle. At the cost of fuel these day's, it'd be real hard to explain. Let's settle for Pearl, for the first leg of the flight home, for you and your grandfather."

"That's great. Thank you, Captain."

"Pat, I made Sam here, my aide. That should explain him, easily enough. Do you have any suggestions for J J?"

"That is a problem. We'll have to think on that awhile." The four men sat thinking of away to explain J J, to the people that would see him on the flight home and there on the Enterprise. As they sat thinking, the Colonel looked over at J J. He was sitting with his face cradled in both hands and his elbows on his thighs. The Colonel thought, as he looked at 'J J,' 'he looked like a representation of The Thinker.' The Colonel then noticed J J's scarred face, as his chin rested cradled in both hands. "I've got it!"

"What?"

"It's perfect."

"What is. What's your idea, Bob?"

"We take J J down to the hospital and have the doctor wrap his head up in bandages. Then as far as anyone knows, he's private J. S. Johnson, on route to Seattle for medical treatment. By the time anyone figures out there's two J. S. Johnson's, we should have him home."

"That just might work, Bob. If you don't see J J's face or hands, the way he walks and stands, he'd pass for a Marine."

"Hey, I am a Marine! According to you, I've been a Marine, longer then anyone else."

"You're right, J J," said the Captain. "J J, what I meant was, you carry yourself like a Marine, much younger than your years."

"Pat, do you think the doctor will help us with this?"

"Robby, if I'm going to wear bandages anyway, maybe the doctor could do some plastic surgery on my eye."

During this entire time, while the Colonel, J J and Sam, informed the Captain of their situation and talked about a solution. Jim, the reporter was watching. He had seen them land in the helicopter and he followed them to the Captain's quarters, being careful not to be seen by the three men. He had no idea what was going on, except his professional nose for news advised him, this man was more then just an old lost beachcomber, they found sitting on the island. He knew in his own mind as he stood watching, that the Captain was far too important of a man to spend over an hour of his valuable time, listening to an old beachcomber telling him his story.

"Pat, what do you think?"

"I think it's a great idea, Bob. Let's go see," said the Captain, as he got up from where he'd been sitting, on the front edge of his desk, grabbing his hat from the desk top, as he stood.

The other three men also stood. Sam quickly moved ahead of the others and opened the door. The Captain exited first, as Sam held the door. The Captain stopped, telling the sergeant where he was off to, in the event he would be needed and where he could be reached. They then moved out of the Captain's quarters, past the sergeant, down the hall to the exit. Sam opening the door to the outside of the ship, stepping out again holding the door, for the others to exit.

As the door opened, Jim saw who was coming out. He moved back to be out of sight, so as not to be seen lurking about. The four men walked right past, without seeing him. Jim followed the four men, as they moved through the ship, keeping out of sight as he did.

"Captain, this is some ship you have."

"Thank you, J J. I've been her captain for sometime. She's always been a good ship and she has a great crew," said the Captain, as they continued through the ship. They then came out onto a lower deck. "Here, we can use this cart to drive to the hospital from here. Sam, you can drive this thing for us, can't you?"

"Yes, Sir, Captain," said Sam, as the four men piled into the cart. "Which way, Captain?"

"Follow the green line, Sam. That way." There were different colored lines, painted on the deck.

"Is everyone ready? Hang on, here we go, ready or not!" said Sam, as the tires of the cart squealed on the hard smooth surface of the deck as it left it's parking place in-a-shot. Sam, following the green line, driving in the direction the Captain had pointed.

Jim watched as the four men drove away in the electric cart.

"Sam, it's up here on the right."

"Yes, Captain. I see it," said Sam.

The cart's tires screeching, the three men's knuckles white from hanging on, as the cart came to an abrupt stop, in a parking space in front of, but off to one side of two large doors, marked with a big red cross. In front of the two doors was a larger space, marked, Emergency Parking. This space was right in front of the double doors. The four of them got out of the cart and walked towards the doors. Sam, pushed open one of the big doors and held it for the others. Just inside these doors were two more doors. The space between the two sets of doors, was about fifteen feet. Sam letting go of the first door, after the three men had entered, ran ahead to open the other two doors.

"Sam, hold up with those doors a minute."

"Yes, Sir, Captain." The four men stopped in the area between the two sets of doors.

"J J, you and Sam, hang back a little, so you won't be seen too clearly. Ok let's go in."

"Yes, Sir," said J J and Sam, at the same time.

Sam pushed open one of the doors. The four men walked into a large receiving area. As soon as the people in the area saw the Captain, someone hollered. "Attention! Captain on deck!"

"I'd like to talk to the doctor in command. The rest of you people take fifteen somewhere, besides here! Unless there's people here that need to be cared for, if so, you shouldn't leave."

"The Lieutenant is in charge. There's no one in the hospital, at this time, Captain. Lieutenant Collins is in the office. I'll get him for you, Captain," said one of the people.

"We'll find him. You, go with the other's."

"Yes, Captain."

Jim saw what he thought might be the cart the four men drove away in. It was parked in the distance. He walked towards the cart along a route marked for foot traffic. He saw several people as they came out the big doors. The doors were marked with a big red cross. Half the cross was painted on each door. When the doors were closed, the cross became complete. As Jim walked up to the area, the people were standing together talking to each other. He walked past the group of people talking, up to one of the large doors.

"I wouldn't go in there unless it's an emergency, if I were you," said one of the sailors, standing there.

Jim hesitated, as he went to push on the big door to enter the hospital. "Why is that, sailor?"

"The Captain is in there. And I don't think he wants any company."

"Is that right? Is he alone?"

"No. There's a Colonel and two other Marines with him."

"Sailor, there's another entrance to the hospital, where is it?" asked Jim, in a demanding voice, as he stood next to the two large doors.

"You go through that door and down the hall, to the first door on the right." Jim turned and walked to the door the sailor pointed to.

"Who's that asshole?" whispered one of the other sailors.

"I don't know who he is. But it's the first and last time he gets any help from me," said the sailor, as the reporter opened the door to the hallway. Jim entered the hall. As he moved along the bulkhead of the hall, listening to hear, if he could hear any people talking, in the hospital.

"You know. That guy was acting a little strange. Come on, let's go see what he's up to," said the sailor that had told Jim about the other hospital door. That sailor and two others, headed for the door. As the sailors opened the door, they saw Jim at the door to the hospital area. It appeared he was listening at the door.

"Hey! What are you doing?" said the sailor, in a very loud voice.

Jim turned. He saw the three sailors coming in the door.

"What's the problem?" asked Jim, as he walked toward the three men. "Why are you yelling?" asked Jim, in a quieting tone, trying to get the three sailors to quiet down.

"Who are you?" asked the sailor in a lower voice.

The four men looked at each other, hearing the yelling coming from outside the door, as they walked through the hospital, still looking for the doctor in command.

"I wonder what that's about?" asked the Colonel.

Just then a lieutenant and a nurse came out of a room, straightening their uniforms, as they did.

"Captain, what can I do for you, Sir?" asked the Lieutenant, in a calm voice seeing his Captain standing there in the hospital.

The Captain and Colonel again looked at each other and snickered.

"I'll, see what's going on out there, Captain," said the Colonel, as he headed for the door.

Jim walked up to the three sailors, grabbing the sailor that was doing the talking by the arm, he opened the door and he and the sailor walked through the door to the deck, the other two sailors followed them as they did, closing the door behind them.

The Colonel walked to the door, where it sounded like the loud voices came from. The Colonel opened the door and looked out into the hall. Stepping into the hall, he looked in both directions. Seeing nothing, he re-entered the hospital, closing the door to the hallway behind. The Captain and the others were not in sight. He then noticed the nurse going into a room. He headed in that direction. Just then he heard someone calling. The Colonel turned and saw Sam. "Colonel, we're in here." The Colonel walked over to Sam. J J and Sam were waiting in a small room. "The Captain asked us to wait in here, while he talked to the doctor and nurse, Colonel," said Sam, as the Colonel joined them in the room.

"Robby, do you think they were, let's say, examining each other?"

"Yes, J J, I'd say they probably were, maybe even a bit more. At least, that part hasn't changed in the last fifty years," laughed the Colonel.

"Good!" said J J, with a big smile on his face.

"My name is Jim. I'm a reporter for the San Francisco Chronicle. I'm doing an article on medical people aboard ship. I thought I could find someone here to help."

"Do you have the Captain's permission?" asked the sailor.

"No!" Snapped the reporter.

"Well, without an order, and with an attitude like that ass-hole, you aren't getting any help from us," said the sailor, in a stern manner. "If you don't like it, the Captain's right inside. I'm sure we can go right in here now and interrupt him to ask," said the sailor, as he grabbed for the door.

"Never mind!" said Jim, as he pushed the sailor's arm down from the door. He then pushed his way between the three men and the door, leaving the three sailors standing there, as he walked off in the direction he came from, grumbling something to himself, as he did.

The Colonel, J J and Sam, stood talking, as they waited for the Captain's return. Just then the Captain came out of the room. The doctor and nurse were behind him. They followed the Captain as he walked in there direction. All three looked to be a bit red faced. Most likely from their little discussion.

"The Lieutenants here, are going to help us. Isn't that right?"

"Yes, Captain, whatever you need, we're here to help," said the doctor with a big smile on his face. The nurse, a bit more red eyed than the doctor, was also smiling nodding her head, showing she totally agreed.

"Doctor, I want you to look at this man's eye," said the Captain, as he pointed towards J J. "Doctor, call him J J."

"Yes, Sir. J J, if you could come this way? I'll take a look at that eye of yours. Sit over here on this table, J J," said the doctor, in a very professional manner, as he lead the way to the table.

"Lieutenant, would you turn on the. . . ." The doctor hesitated, seeing the nurse was already on her way to turn on the large medical light, as she handed him a pair of rubber gloves. The nurse anticipating what the doctor needed for his examination. J J walked over and sat on the exam table, with legs dangling over the edge. Kicking his legs slightly as he sat there, fidgeting like a small boy.

The doctor began his exam. He grabbed and turned the big light, so the brightest part shone right on J J's badly scared face and eye. The nurse, doing her part, handed the doctor a magnify glass, so he could take an even closer look at the eye. The doctor spent the next ten minutes or more looking at J J's eye, with and without the help of the magnify glass.

"J J, I can help you see through that eye, with a little minor surgery. It would take some re-constructive surgery to remove the scars on your cheek, temple, and forehead, which I can do, but it would take longer and be a more extensive surgery."

"Doctor, how long of a minor surgery, are you talking about?" asked the Captain.

"The prep would take longer than the actual surgery, Sir. I would say an hour tops."

"One hour, that's all? Then I could see through this eye?" asked J J, pointing at his scarred eye.

"The surgery would take an hour or so. I haven't any idea how good your sight in that eye will be, J J."

"It will be better than it is now."

"Yes, considerably," said the doctor, still speaking in a dry and to the point professional manner.

"Doctor, you and the Lieutenant step out of the room," said the Captain, standing in the doorway of the small examination room. The nurse and the doctor moved to the doorway. The Captain, Colonel and Sam, moving out of their way so they could exit the room. Once the nurse and doctor were out, the three men entered the room and closed the door.

"You sure have those two right where you want them, Pat. Bad timing for them. Great timing for us!" snickered the Colonel.

"Yes, we sure do. We can get J J's face bandaged. Maybe even a minor surgery done, no questions asked.

"J J, what do you think about the minor surgery?" asked the Captain. J J still sitting on the exam table as the men stood in front of him, crammed together in the small room. The four men talked about what to do next, as J J thought about the Captain's question.

"Captain, I'm going to have to wear bandages anyway, in our scheme to get me home. We have the doctor and the Lieutenant in our corner. I think, I should go ahead with the minor surgery."

"Ok, J J. We'll have the doctor come in and start doing just that. Sam would you get those two to come back in here."

"Yes, Sir, Captain." Sam opened the door and asked the doctor and the nurse to come back in.

"Can the two of you do this minor surgery, by yourselves?"

"Yes, Sir," said the doctor, looking from the Captain to the Lieutenant, and then back to the Captain.

"Doctor, are you qualified?" asked the Captain, as the doctor stood in the doorway of the small room.

"Yes, Sir, I am. I'm obviously qualified to do the minor surgery we talked about. I'm also somewhat qualified to do even the major re-constructive surgery he needs. I would need the additional help of a few more people, for the major re-constructive surgery that is, because of the time involved. The Lieutenant and I can handle the minor surgery, here, ourselves. Captain, you understand, if an emergency occurs, I'll have to leave J J."

"Yes of course, Doctor."

"Of course I'd come back, when the emergency was over," said the doctor, as he re-entered the small room, moving past the Colonel and Sam, to stand next to the Captain and J J.

"Captain, when do you want me to perform this surgery? Which surgery do you want me to perform?" asked the doctor, looking from the Captain, to J J.

"There's two and half hours, until change of duty. Do it now, Doctor. Go ahead and do the minor surgery, now."

"Lieutenant, we can perform the surgery in OR three," said the doctor, as he started taking command of the situation.

"J J, if you'll go with the Lieutenant, we'll get this over and done as quick as possible." J J jumped down from the exam table. The Colonel, Captain, doctor and Sam, moved to allow J J to leave. J J exited the small room and followed the Lieutenant. The Lieutenant lead the way to the operating room.

"Doctor, I also want you to bandage J J's hands. Nothing to clumsy."

"Captain, may I ask what's this all about? Who is this man, J J?"

The Captain raised an eyebrow and just glared at the doctor. "Doctor, under the circumstances, I suggest you do what you can to forget the information you have. If I were you, I wouldn't ask anymore questions," said the Captain, with an irritated tone in his voice. "Doctor, I don't expect a word of this to leave this hospital. Do I make myself clear?"

"As glass, Sir. Excuse me, Colonel," said the doctor, as he moved past the Colonel and Sam, to leave the small room.

"Your name is J J, I heard that much," said the Lieutenant, as she lead J J to the operating room.

"My name is Patty, J J. You can call me Patty, if you wish," said the Lieutenant, as they walked up to a set of doors. The doors were marked: O R # 3 and written under that was OPERATING ROOM NUMBER THREE, in smaller print.

"Nice to meet you, Patty."

The Lieutenant walked right past the double doors.

"I thought the doctor said OR three. Isn't this it?"

"Yes, J J, it is. We have to get you cleaned up first, us too for that matter, before we can go in there. We have to keep the O R as clean as possible." The two of them walked a little further, to a door marked: PREP # 3. The Lieutenant opened the door and held it for J J to enter the room. "J J, if you could take off your shirt. We have a hospital gown, you can put on. I'll get one for you. While I'm getting a gown for you, I would like you to wash your face, hair, oh just wash everything, from the neck up. There's soap in those plastic squeeze bottles on the back of the sink. Go ahead, I'll be right back." As the nurse left the room, J J started removing the shirt of the uniform his grandson had loaned him. Stripped to the waist, he walked up to one of the large sinks. He started washing as the nurse had asked him to do. As J J was washing, the doctor came into the room.

"J J, are you nervous?" J J turned and looked at the doctor.

"Should I be?"

"No, not at all. It will be a piece a cake, J J," said the doctor, as he started unbuttoning his shirt sleeves.

"J J are you allergic to any drugs, that you know of?"

"No, not that I know of," snickered J J.

"Well then, as soon as we get scrubbed, we'll get started." Just then the nurse came in.

"J J, there's a towel and a gown here for you when you are finished scrubbing up," said the nurse, as she sat the folded gown and towel on the counter, behind J J. She then opened a cupboard and pulled out two large plastic bags. She tore the end off the bags and sat the open bags on the counter. When she was out of the room, she had removed the shirt she had been wearing and was now wearing a short sleeve tee shirt. She moved up next to the doctor and they began washing their hands, in order to prepare for surgery.

"Wow that soap is strong! It feels like it's taking my skin off," said J J.

"Be careful not to get any of that soap in your eyes, J J. I've been there, done that. I don't recommend it, at all," said the doctor, as he rinsed the soap from his arms and hands. Holding his arms up, bent at the elbows. The nurse seeing this, hurried and rinsed the soap from her own arms and hands. She then turned and pulled the doctor's clean dressing gown from one of the plastic bags, being careful not to touch the open bag with her hands. She slipped the gown over the doctor's arms. She then turned and pulled a second gown from the other plastic bag, this gown being for herself. J J was putting his gown on at the same time. As the doctor and nurse finished dressing she turned to J J, standing face to face with her. The nurse began to laugh.

During this time the medical people had returned to the area of the hospital. "Do you think we should tell the Captain, about the asshole, that nosy reporter?" asked one sailor of another.

"You can! I'm not going to interrupt him," said the other sailor.

"Here, J J, let me help. The open part of the gown goes in the back. Haven't you ever had one of these gowns on before?"

"No, Patty. I haven't."

"Haven't you ever been in a hospital before?"

"Not since, long before you were born, Miss. Even then, it was just for a physical." The nurse helped J J with his gown and finished tying it in the back.

"It looks like we're ready," said the doctor, as he turned and backed up against the door. This door went directly into O R # 3. Pushing the door with his backside, the door opened and he turned a half turn and went into the operating room. The nurse did the same. J J stood a moment, alone in the room. He then did as he saw the doctor and nurse do and opened the door. As he slowly turned the half turn, he stood in awe at what he saw, as the door slowly closed behind him.

"Colonel, how long has it been?"

"Sam, it's only been forty two minutes and six seconds. Don't worry, he'll be fine. Besides I'm doing enough worrying for the three of us, as it is," said the Colonel, as the three men waited J J's safe return.

The staff of the hospital stayed clear of the three men. As they moved around doing things, trying to look busy for their Captain.

"Here comes the doctor, now. Grampa's not with him!"

"Calm down, son," said the Captain, in a subdued voice. The doctor walked in their direction smiling as he walked. "He's all right. The doctor's got a big smile on his face. I doubt he'd be smiling, if there was anything wrong," said the Captain, as the three men stood waiting for the doctor's report on J J.

"J J's doing fine. Patty is finishing up with the bandages you requested, to be put on his hands, Captain."

"How's his eye?" asked Sam. The doctor looked at Sam, then back towards the Captain, with a puzzled look on his face.

"Go ahead Doctor, answer the private's question," said the Captain, seeing the question in the expression on the doctor's face, 'why was the private asking the question.'

"The eye is very sensitive to light. J J, says he can see, I'm not sure how well. He should probably see, Lieutenant Ross. He's our ophthalmologist onboard."

"Here comes J J now," said the Colonel. The four men watched, as J J came towards them.

"Doctor, I know who, Lieutenant Ross, is. I am the Captain of. . . ."

"Captain, I. . . ."

"Thank you Doctor," said the Captain.

"How do I look, Robby."

"It's hard to tell, with the bandages and sunglasses. Looks fine to me. Are you ok?" asked the Colonel, as he stood staring.

"The doctor gave me four shots with a needle, in and around the eye. The first one made my eyes water a little. I didn't even feel the other three or the surgery itself. Like the doctor said, it was "a piece of cake." Do I look the part?"

"What part is that, J J?" asked the Colonel.

"The part of a young Marine," said J J, as he leaned over and whispered to the Colonel.

"That you do, J J. Take off the sunglasses. Lets see how the doctor, did on your eye," said the Colonel.

J J removed the glasses and stood looking at the four men, with two eyes opened wide, for the first time in over fifty years.

"Captain, I cauterized the incisions around the eye, with a lazer. J J doesn't need those large bandages but he wanted them anyway. He said he needed the larger bandages to feel safe. The two small butterfly bandages would have been adequate. He can remove the large bandages anytime, Captain." J J, winking carefully at the Captain, with his not so new eye.

"Thank you, Doctor, very much. Say good-bye to nurse Patty for me and thank her for the sunglasses."

"J J, I should see you tomorrow. I'll need to take a look at that eye, if that's ok?"

"Thank you for your help. I think we'll be leaving the hospital now. You are dismissed, Doctor," said the Captain.

"Yes, Sir," said the doctor, as he reached out and grabbed J J's hand. After shaking his hand, the doctor turned and walked towards the O R.

TOUR OF THE ENTERPRISE

"Are we ready to leave this place?"

"Yes, Captain. Lead the way," answered all three men. The four men walked through the receiving area of the hospital. As they were about to leave they heard someone say.

"Captain."

"Yes, what is it?" said the Captain, as he turned to see who had called to him.

"Sir, I'm sorry to bother, you. But I thought you should know this."

"Yes, sailor, what is it?"

"Captain, there was a man eavesdropping in the hall earlier."

"What?"

"He said he was a reporter for some newspaper. He didn't want you to know that he was even here, Captain."

"Thank you, sailor. You're dismissed."

"Yes, Captain."

"Damn, that's most likely Jim!" said the Colonel. As the Colonel spoke, Sam moved to push open one of the large doors, for the four of them to leave the receiving area of the ship's hospital. Sam then pushed open the door that opened onto the lower deck. The men walked up to the cart, as the big door closed slowly behind. "Pat, Jim's one of the reporters that saw J J on the island this morning. We didn't tell him anything. He was very suspicious and curious of who, J J was! He didn't think he was just an old beachcomber, that's for sure. He still doesn't know who he is by snooping around, he may find out what his name is. I don't think he's going to find out who J J is from any of us. As far as I know, we're the only ones onboard ship, that know who he is. We're sure not going to tell him," said the Colonel.

"Bob, lets get him to his room. The less people who see him, the better. You drive, Sam."

"Yes, Sir."

"Captain, you've already done so much."

"What is it? What can I do for you, J J? Just name it."

"Captain, can I drive?"

The Captain looked at the Colonel. The two men looked at J J. "Yes, of course, J J," said the Captain.

"You can drive? Can't you?" asked the Colonel.

"Yes! It . . . has been awhile since I've driven. My license expired in March of forty three or forty four, I don't remember which," said J J, as he climbed in the cart behind the steering wheel. The three men stood there looking at J J sitting in the cart. "Come on guys get in. Which way do we go?" Sam jumped into the cart, in the seat directly behind his grandfather. The Captain climbed into the seat next to J J, as the Colonel got in next to Sam.

"J J, go to the left. I'll show you some more of the Enterprise." J J remembered how Sam started the car. He turned on the key. He couldn't go forward because the car was parked in a parking place, with it's nose up against the bulkhead. He sat there looking at the controls for a moment. In no time he had it figured out. Putting the car in reverse, he pushed down on the pedal. Steering a bit the wrong way at first but quick to correct his error, he backed the cart out of it's parking place. Putting the cart in forward, they were off in the direction the Captain had said. Over steering a little but keeping the car under control as he drove. The area they were driving in was enormous, there were helicopters, and planes of all sizes. There were even trucks, tanks and all kinds of other motor vehicles.

"This ship's gigantic, it's like a world unto itself. An Island!" said J J, as he continued driving in the direction the Captain pointed for him to drive. As he drove, some of the people on deck stood and stared as they drove by.

"Why are they staring at us? Is it my driving?"

"No, I don't think so. It's probably the sunglasses and bandages, J J. They probably wonder why the one with the bandages, is doing the driving. Instead of one of us."

"Oh, I thought it might be my driving. Even though from my point of view, I thought I was doing a fair job."

"Your driving looks fine to me, J J," said the Colonel, as he patted J J on his right shoulder.

"Thank you, Robby."

The four men spent the next few minutes riding around in the electric cart. The Captain pointing out different interesting things for J J to drive by.

"J J, drive over there, to that elevator," said the Captain pointing. "We can take the elevator up to the flight deck." J J drove to where the Captain had pointed, to the big area marked: ELEVATOR! USE CAUTION! "Make sure you're all the way on the elevator, J J." The

Captain then waved to someone. A loud horn honked and a siren shrieked, with red lights flashing. As the lights flashed cables began to raise up from the decks surface. The cables marked the perimeter of the opening, left by the elevators departure. The elevator moved and the next thing J J knew, they were back on Enterprise's main flight deck, in the bright light of day.

The Captain looked down at his wristwatch. "All flights have landed by now. Drive towards the bow of the ship."

J J sat there a moment, deciding in which direction the bow of the ship was. Remembering their flyby of the huge ship, he abruptly turned the wheel in that direction. He then pushed down on the pedal and the cart moved off the huge elevator. The cart hummed as they moved along the flight deck in the direction of the ship's bow. They past dozens of sailors, working along both sides of the flight deck, as they drove by in the cart.

"J J, pull up and park on the starboard side. There in that spot will be fine," said the Captain. J J parked the cart in the space the Captain had pointed him to. "Come on, J J. Come out here in the middle of the flight deck," said the Captain, as he got out of the cart. The Captain walked around to the other side of the cart, to meet J J climbing out from behind the steering wheel. J J then followed the Captain, to somewhere near the center line of the Enterprise's immense flight deck. "J J from here you can see the length and beam of this mighty ship." J J stood there with the Captain. He removed the sunglasses as he looked down it's length, at the tremendous scale of it all. "I have one more thing up here on the bow, I want to show you. J J, follow me." The Captain and J J walked back past the cart, with the Colonel and Sam, still sitting in the cart. "Sam, you might want to see this too," said the Captain, as him and J J walked by. Sam jumped out of the cart onto the flight deck and followed the Captain and his grandfather.

"Wait for me. I might as well come too," said the Colonel, as he climbed out of the cart and followed.

The four men walked to a stairway, at the starboard edge of the ship. The stairway had a chain blocking it's entrance. There was a sign hanging on the chain. The sign read, "RESTRICTED AREA." The Captain unfasten the chain and moved to one side of the stairway, holding the chain in one hand he motioned with his other, for the three of them to go down the stairway ahead of him. Re-hooking the chain he proceeded down the stairs. The four men came out onto a small observation platform. The platform, had a open grid type floor. You could see right through the floor to where the bow of the massive ship cut it's way through the ocean below.

"We have what wind there is at our bow. The wind at this point, can reach two hundred knots or more. That's why this area is restricted. I'm glad it's calm today, so I could bring you here and show you this, J J," said the Captain, as the four men stood together on the platform and watched the awesome sight.

"Captain, how far is it from the flight deck, to the waters surface?" asked J J in a loud voice, to be heard over the noise made by the waves hitting the bow of the Enterprise.

"J J, when the ships loaded and ready for a tour of duty and in calm water, it's right at sixty feet."

"I hope this ship doesn't run on that dollar thirty a gallon stuff."

"I didn't hear you, J J. What did you say?"

J J repeated the statement. This time in a much louder voice. "I'm sorry, J J. I don't understand the question?"

"Does she run on gasoline, Captain?"

"The Enterprise?" chuckled the Captain.

"No! The Enterprise doesn't run on gasoline. She's atomic powered. The Enterprise is one of the Navy's nuclear powered vessels. I'll try to explain a little better, when it's not so loud." J J nodded his head that he understood the Captain. A few more minutes past. The Captain then gave a signal to the three men, it was time for them to leave. The four men climbed the stairs, back through the safety chain, up onto the flight deck.

J J jumped into the cart, back behind the steering wheel. "Where to now, Captain?" asked J J, as the others climbed into the cart.

"Back to the elevator, J J," said the Captain. As the cart rolled along the flight deck, the Captain gave J J, a brief explanation of how the ships nuclear power worked.

"So the Enterprise, in actuality, is powered by steam. This nuclear power stuff, just replaces the coal, oil or wood, that you would burn to generate steam. Isn't that all it does?"

"Yes, to the point that's what it does. J J, pull in that parking space over there, the one marked Captain. We'll let someone else take the cart below deck," said the Captain, as he raised and lowered his eyebrows a few times, as he pointed to the space. "Rank has it's privileges," said the Captain, smiling. J J drove the cart into the marked parking place and stopped. "From here, Bob, can take you to your quarters. Like I said they're right near his. But first I'd like to show you the nerve center of this great ship, the bridge."

"That would be great, Captain," said J J.

The four men climbed out of the cart. The Captain leading the way to the bridge. Jim had been watching the four men this whole time. He had been, ever since the four men left for the ship's hospital. Watching as two of the most important people onboard ship, spent three and a half hours of their valuable time, with a young Marine private and an elderly, now bandaged up old beachcomber. And now, the Captain leading the two of them, with the Colonel, to the most important part of the huge ship. The Captain came to the door marked, "Restricted Area Authorized Personnel Only." He opened the door. No sooner had he done so, when someone in a loud voice said. "Attention, Captain on the bridge." The four men walked onto the bridge. J J and Sam started looking around at everything there was to see. It was a bit like what J J had seen on the helicopter, only a hundred times more. The Captain walked along with J J and Sam, explaining what some of the different equipment on the bridge was used for. The Captain continued showing the two men the bridge. As they moved around, the different members of the bridge crew moved out of their way, as the three men got to their area. The Captain spent the next fifteen minutes or so, showing his new friends the bridge of his ship.

"J J, I'd like you and Sam, to meet my Executive Officer, Commander Matt Walker. Commander, this is J J and Sam." The three men shook hands with each other, as the Captain introduced them. "They are here with Colonel Robinson. I wanted J J to see the ship before he, the Colonel, and Sam, have to leave for Pearl. That reminds me, Matt, I was sure there wasn't anything left on the schedule today. When is the next flight scheduled to Pearl?"

"I'll check the flight computer, Captain."

"Matt, would you do me a favor?"

"Yes, Captain. What is it?"

"Would you take J J here, with you?"

"Of course. Come on I'll show you the computer, J J. You can come to if you'd like, Private."

"Thank you, Commander, I would."

The three men left the bridge. The Commander lead the way, as they went through a door in the aft part of the bridge. This doorway, lead them into a room filled with additional sophisticated electronic equipment. "This is our Flight Command Center, personnel, equipment, anything and everything to do with flight, is all handled through here. It's pretty quiet here now. That's because nothing is flying in or out at the moment. This is the computer the Captain spoke of here, J J. It will give us all scheduled in coming and out going flights from the decks of the Enterprise." The Commander poked at the keys on the computer. The images on the monitor changed as he did. He took some time explaining to J J and Sam, what the computer's information meant to him. He also showed how, with the use of computers, this information was right at their fingertips, available whenever they needed it, at a touch of a few keys. With a push of a few of those keys, a printer near the computer started clicking and clattering as it typed out the information the computer had compiled for the Commander. When the printer had quit clattering, the Commander reached over and pulled out some paper from the printer and tore it off. "If you two have seen enough, we should take this information back to the Captain. Or is there something else I can show you?"

"No, thank you, Commander."

The three men left the Flight Command Center and returned to the bridge. The Captain was now sitting in a large seat. This seat sat quite high, putting the seated Captain about eye level, with the more then six foot tall Colonel. The Colonel standing next to the seated Captain, as the two men talked. Sitting in this seat, commanded the Captain a great view through the big windshield of the bridge, to the ship's flight deck below.

"What did you find, Commander?" asked the Captain, seeing the three men returning to the bridge from the Flight Command center.

"Captain, there isn't any flights scheduled from Pearl, until the mail plane comes on Monday at 1100 hours."

"That's four days! Unless something unscheduled comes in," said the Captain, as he looked at J J and Sam. He then turned to the Colonel. "Colonel, you don't want to wait four days? Do you?"

"No, Captain. Not unless we have to."

"Commander, what's the next flight scheduled to leave the Enterprise?" The Commander read over the paper he still had in his hand.

"Captain, the next flight scheduled to leave here is the Experimental returning to Formosa. It flies from there, to northern Japan. From Japan, it flies to Anchorage."

"When Commander?"

"2200, Captain."

The Captain slowly turned and looked at the Colonel, raising and lowering his eyebrows, when he did. "Pat, are you serious?" asked the Colonel, with anxiety in his voice.

"Why not? It's a lot better than waiting the four days, for the flight to Pearl. Sunday's the Fourth. It Would be great to get J J home by the Fourth Of July."

"You're serious! You want us to fly in an Experimental airplane! Halfway around the world!" said the Colonel, as he looked over at J J and Sam, standing with the Commander. "J J, do you understand, what the Captain is saying?" J J stood there a moment thinking.

"Yes, Robby, I do. He wants us to fly home the fastest way we have available to us at this time. That just happens to be a flight that will take us through Japan, in an experimental airplane."

"That doesn't bother you?"

"No, Robby! Not if it will get me home to my Jera Marie a moment sooner, it doesn't. Besides, you've all told me, the Japanese are, what did you call them? Allies!"

"You're sure, J J? What about the plane being experimental?"

"Yes, Captain, I'm sure. They wouldn't fly if it wasn't safe."

The Captain looked at the three men standing there a moment. He then looked at the Commander. "Matt, what are the chances of these three hitching a ride, on the Experimental?"

"I'd say good, Captain. The plane is scheduled to be at the Boeing plant in Seattle. The first part of the month."

"Is that right? When, Matt?"

"I don't know, Captain. I don't have that information here. On this printout it just says, Retrofit: Boeing Plant, Seattle Washington, second week July 1993," said the Commander, as he read the computer readout he held in his hand.

"You mean to tell me, you have a plane onboard, that's flying from the decks of the Enterprise, to the Boeing plant in Seattle?" asked J J, with his voice shaking.

"That's the way it looks to me, Captain. The airplane's not experimental, it's equipment is," said the Commander, as he looked from the Captain to J J, with a puzzled look on his face.

J J removed the sunglasses. The four men could see that J J's eyes had filled with tears. The four men waited, while J J regained his composure.

"Commander, make sure these three have a place on that plane!"

"Yes, Sir, Captain. What should I put on the manifest, Captain?"

"I don't. . . ."

"Put this Commander, Colonel Robert R. Robinson and private J. S. Johnson, with the Colonel's aide, USMC," said the Colonel, interrupting the Captain.

"Yes, Matt, that will be just fine."

"What about J J, Sir?"

"Matt, that gives us three names for the manifest, right? The Colonel, Private J. S. Johnson with the Colonel's aide, right?"

The Commander thought a moment. "Yes it does, Captain. When you hear the 'with.'"

"That's all we need, to get these three on that plane tonight. We'll let the Colonel handle the rest," said the Captain, as he got down from his command chair.

"Colonel, is there anything else you can think of at this time, the Commander and I can do to help?"

"Maybe some additional clothes for, J J."

"We can do that, can't we, Commander?"

"Yes, Captain, I will get a voucher for the ship's store. I'll fill it out, 'as needed,' Captain."

"Thank you, Commander," said J J.

"Yes, thank you, Matt," said the Captain.

"I'll be right back with the voucher, Colonel."

"Well, my schedule is pretty much free the rest of the day. Why don't I show you where your quarters are. Then we can go from there to the ship's store," said the Captain, as the Commander walked up with the voucher in hand. He handed the voucher to J J.

"Commander, I'll either be in the Colonel's quarters, the VIP quarters or between there and the ship's store. Commander, you have the bridge."

"Yes, Captain."

"Matt, I'll tell you about this later, ok?"

"Yes! Thank you, Captain," said the Commander, nodding his head, signaling the Captain, he would like to know more about what was going on.

The Captain and the other three left the bridge. Walking through the ship, on their way to the Colonel's quarters.

"Captain, I left my things on the companionway outside the door of the hallway that leads to your quarters."

"Sam, your bag should still be there. We're going right by there, on our way to your quarters." The four men continued talking as they walked along.

"There's my bag, Sir. Just like you said, right where I left it." As they walked up to the bag, it appeared the bag had been opened. The four men looked down at the bag and then at each other. Sam squatted down to check his bag. After checking his things, he looked up at the three men looking down at him. "Everything seems to be here," said Sam, with a puzzled look, as he looked at the three men. "Why would anyone just go through my things? If they were looking for something of value, instead of sitting out here on the companionway, going through my bag, why wouldn't they just take the whole bag? It doesn't make any sense!"

"Maybe it does, Sam. Did you have anything in your bag, that gave reference to your grandfather? His name? Any letters from home? Anything?" Sam thought a moment about the Colonel's question.

"No, Sir, Colonel. The only thing I have in this bag, is my dirty clothes and some pictures and letters, and my address book. Damn my address book!" Sam picked up the bag and stood with the other three men. "Maybe I just didn't close it. I was in a hurry . . . no! I closed the bag, I'm sure of that."

"Let's see if the sergeant saw anyone," said the Captain, as he started for the door. He opened the door and stepped into the hallway, leaving the door open as he did. The others waited on the companionway for the Captain's return. The Captain came out and closed the door behind him. "The sergeant said "he saw less then twenty sailors, two Marines and one civilian, walk by him in the hallway, since we left to go to the hospital." This door wasn't open, so he couldn't establish who or how many people used the companionway. It's not far to your quarters," said the Captain.

The four men started walking along the companionway, towards their quarters, still talking as they walked.

"This door leads to your rooms. The first door on the left is J J and Sam's room. The second door is the Colonel's. Obviously by no accident, the rooms are side by side."

Sam opened the door to the hallway. He entered the hall and held the door for the others. The Captain opened the door of the first cabin and held it. The other three entered the room and the Captain followed them in and closed the door.

"Boy, it's cool in here!"

"Yes it is, J J. Someone's turned the air-conditioning up to maximum by the feel of it," said the Captain. The Captain walked over and checked the thermostat. "Yes, it's set at sixty five degrees," snickered the Captain, as he reset the thermostat. "How's seventy five sound? You'll only be here a few hours but make yourself at home. Use the head, it's through there. I'm sorry, I just meant it's in there," said the Captain, a bit embarrassed.

"What a beautiful cabin. It's a far cry from what I had when I came to this part of the world. Especially the temperature. I remember how hot it was aboard ship. This is much nicer. Thank you, Captain."

"You're, welcome, J J. Let's head for the ship's store, so you can have some extra clothes for your trip home. You'll probably want to clean up for dinner. This day is going to get away from us, as it is. It will be 2200 hours before we know it. Then I'll have to say good-bye."

Sam went to the door and opened it.

"Lead the way, Captain," said J J.

"I want you three to know, how much I've enjoyed today. I'm so glad, Bob, you elected to include me in this adventure. Being a part of all this, has been a real kick in the ass," said the Captain, as he stood blocking the doorway.

"Pat, I'm just as thankful it was you at the helm, of the Enterprise. If not for your help, we couldn't do any of this. We've made quite a team, haven't we!" said the Colonel, as he held out his hand to the Captain. The Captain shook the Colonel's hand, he then turned and left the doorway of the room, the others followed. Sam closed the door and joined the others.

"For the first time since yesterday noon, the mention of food sounds like a good idea. Sam and I didn't eat much breakfast. I was so involved with the helicopters and all," said J J, as he walked along.

"That's It!"

"What's it, Bob?" asked the Captain, as he abruptly stopped and looked a the Colonel.

"It's that damn reporter!"

"Where?"

"No! What I meant was, it was that damn nosy, meddlesome and of course, ever inquiring reporter. That's who went through Sam's bag!"

"I'll just bet you're right."

"I'm sure I'm right, Pat. Like I said, he doesn't believe J J's just an old beachcomber."

"Nobody on this ship knows his true identity," said the Captain, hitting the Colonel on the shoulder, as he turned and started walking. "Except us four, of course," said the Captain, just turning his head enough to speak to the others, as he walked.

"If he only knew."

"Knew what, Colonel? If who only knew?" asked Sam.

"If Jim only knew, what a big story was going on, right under his very nose."

"He'd most likely have a stroke. You know, It probably could have been, the biggest story of his career," said Sam.

"You know, he is a professional. We forget he's just doing his job. We'd best be on lookout for him."

"Good point, Robby. We'll have to call him, 'The Lone Ranger.'"

"What?" snickered the Colonel.

"I'd say he's more like, The Shadow or The Phantom. Chuckled the Captain. All four of the men laughed together, at the humor of it all, as they continued on their way to the ship's store. More alert to the possibility of their shadow's existence's, and of his potential presence. The Captain and Colonel, saluting the different sailors they met, as they walked.

"Well, has anyone seen our shadow lurking around? The store is just ahead on the right," said the Captain, as he stopped and turned to the others.

"J J, obviously you're the same size as Sam. What about your feet?"

"Captain, I don't have any idea what size shoes I would wear. I've gone barefoot for so many years."

"We should have checked your shoe size, back in your quarters. I just never thought of it," said the Captain.

"No, neither did I," said the Colonel.

"Oh shit. Don't look now."

"What is it, Sam? Is it our shadow?" whispered the Colonel.

"Yes. Our friend the reporter is right over there, just around that corner. I saw him just for a second. Now what do we do?" whispered Sam, as he nodded towards the corner nonchalantly, for the others.

"Nothing! Let him do his own thing. He doesn't know anything," whispered the Captain.

"Let's go get this poor man some new clothes of his own. So he doesn't have to wear yours anymore, Private," said the Colonel, in a normal voice.

"Yes, Sir, Colonel. Maybe we can get the old man some new shoes, as well."

"That's a good idea, Private."

The four men put on quite a charade, for the reporter to catch, as the four walked on towards the ships store.

"What was it like to be on that island for all those years alone Mr. Jones? What was it, eight years? That's a long time to be alone!" said the Colonel, from the end of the line of four, loud enough, so as to be easily heard.

"Yes, it was, Colonel. Colonel, feel free to call me Al, short for Albert," said J J, speaking with the same heavy southern accent he used with Jim, earlier that same day. The four of them barely able to keep from splitting a gut.

"This is the ship's store I told you about Al. We can get some clothes for you to wear for your stay here on the Enterprise. We can check to see if you still wear the same size shoes, after being on the island as long as you were. Eight years, that's so hard for us to believe."

"Believe it! It seemed more like fifty, to me, Captain."

"Oh, we do, Al."

"Captain, I sure want to thank you for your gracious hospitality."

"Al, you're quite welcome. Al, do you still have that voucher, the Commander gave you?"

"Yes, Captain, I do. It's right here in this shirt pocket," said J J, as he reached into his pocket and pulled out the voucher with the picture of his Jera Marie. J J stopped in his tracks and stood, as he looked at the picture he held in his hand. "How about that. That's why people say, 'as handy as a pocket on a shirt," laughed J J, still speaking with his southern drawl, as he put his picture back in his pocket. "It sure was nice of the young private there, to loan me one of his uniforms this morning. My old clothes had about had it."

"Al, you and the private can go into the store and pick out whatever you need."

"Thanks again, Captain," said J J, playing his part too the fullest of his ability.

"On second thought, I think, the Colonel and I, will come along. Come on, Colonel, this might be fun," said the Captain, in a slightly louder then normal voice.

The four men walked into the store. Trying to ignore the presence of their shadow, the reporter. They spent the next forty minutes or so, showing J J, all the different things in the store, as they piled Sam's arms high with clothes and things, the four of them had gathered up for J J.

"We almost forgot shoes."

"You're right, Colonel. Private, sit those things aside for now. We have to get Al here, some shoes."

"Yes Sir, Captain," said Sam, as he sat his arm load down on a nearby counter. The Captain walked over to a sailor.

"Sir."

"If you could, sailor? Get us six pairs or so of shoes. Starting with size ten and go up in size from there. We're not sure what size Al here, might wear."

"Yes, Sir, Captain. I could check his size first, if it's all right with you, Sir?"

"Good idea, sailor! Go ahead, do it your way," laughed the Captain, as he moved back out of the way, waving his hand to one side as he did, making a sign to the sailor, he was giving the sailor the right of way, in this matter. The sailor stood there with a surprised look on his face, amazed at his Captain's unexpected comeback and his lighthearted response.

"Private, if you could come over here. I'll check to see what size shoe you wear," said the sailor, as he grabbed a pair of socks, from a shelf on the way by.

"Thank you," said J J, as he followed the sailor.

While the sailor waited on J J. The others stood talking about how much fun it was showing J J all the new things.

"It's like taking a child to a toy store or maybe to a zoo for the first time. Some of these things he's never seen before. I've really enjoyed it! Like I said, it's been a real kick in the ass! I'll wager that reporter is going bananas. Trying to figure out why a Navy Captain and a Marine Colonel are spending the day with an old beachcomber. Let's hope we've really confused him with our little charade," chuckled the Captain. As the three were talking, J J came walking up with a big grin on his face.

"Look, our boy has a new pair of shoes," said the Colonel, as he and the others watched. J J proudly strutting by in his new shoes.

"I. . . ," said J J, as he hesitated and then cleared his throat. In his excitement almost forgetting his southern drawl. "I still wear the same size after being barefoot for all these years. Pretty good huh? How do they look?"

"Yes, Al, they look great," said the Colonel. "Looks like we're about through with our good old boy's trip to the store. . . . In the words of a great man, "it's been a real kick in the ass," said the Colonel, as he slapped the Captain on the back.

J J went to pick up his hand made shoes and the additional pair of new ones, he had also picked out. He had left the shoes in the back part of the ship's store. Sam again picking up the large stack of clothes, including a new duffel bag, and followed, as J J walked back, still strutting in his new shoes, carrying his other two pair.

"Sailor, I'll sign the paper work, as soon as it's ready."

"Yes, Sir. I'll be just another moment, Captain."

J J, Sam and the Colonel, walked out of the store with J J's new things in hand.

"Here, Sam, I can take some of that."

"Colonel, I didn't quite hear you," said Sam, as he turned and rolled his eyes in the direction of their shadow.

"Sir, that definitely isn't the thing to do," whispered Sam, with his back to the reporter.

"You're right, Private. We'll wait here, for the Captain," said the Colonel, realizing Sam made a very good point. Colonel's don't usually help privates carry things.

"Here comes the Captain now, Private."

"Are we ready?"

"We're ready, Captain. Lead the way."

The four men started on their way back to their room, as they walked, Sam suddenly dropped part of his bundle. J J bent down with Sam, to help pick up the things he dropped. As Sam bent down, he looked under his arm, as he slowly picked up the clothes. It became apparent to the others, why he had dropped his load. He was checking to see what their shadow was up to.

"Tricky, Sam. What's he up to?" asked the Captain.

"He's going into the store," said Sam, as he continued picking up J J's things, as he watched the reporter.

"This is great! I don't think he's going to get any information, from that sailor," said the Captain.

"Except, the sailor might tell the reporter, he thinks his Captain's a bit lackadaisical, or not playing with a full deck. Now we don't want a rumor like that to get started, now do we?" laughed the Colonel.

"I did act a bit nonchalant about it all. Didn't I?"

"That you did, 'My Captain Oh Captain,'" said J J, with a smile on his face, as Sam and him picked up the last of his things.

"Let's get you back to your room and cleaned up for dinner," smiled the Captain. With that the Captain turned his back and started walking. The others had to hustle to catch up. In no time at all they were at the door of their quarters.

"I'll come by to get you three for dinner, in what? Say an hour."

"We'll be here, Captain," said the Colonel.

With that said, the four men went their own way. The Colonel to his room, J J and Sam to their room and the Captain went walking off.

"Let me know soon as you're through with the head. I really have to go."

"Go ahead, Sam, I'm fine."

"Thanks!" said Sam, as he quickly moved past J J to the head. J J started looking through his new clothes. Laying out the ones he was going to wear to dinner. Also unfolding the duffel bag to carry his new clothes home, knowing in his own mind he probably wouldn't have time to change again, before flying out on the big plane. He started packing his other clothes and things into the duffel bag.

"Thank you, Grampa. I really had to go. It's your turn."

"Sam, I don't have to go," said J J, smiling big at being called grampa once again.

"Is that right," said Sam, as he thought a moment and then shrugged his shoulders.

"You want to go first? Get ready I mean."

"No. You can, Sam. I'll just look around here."

"Grampa?"

"Yes, Sam."

"Can I borrow one of your new uniforms, Grampa? As you know, mine are all dirty."

"So they are, Grandson. Here, take one of these so we can both go to dinner looking good, like a Johnson and Johnson should!"

"Right!"

"That will leave us one clean uniform each, to change into when we get close to home. It's nice we wear the same size."

"It sure has simplified things," said Sam, as he picked up one of the uniforms, leaving two for J J to pack into his duffel bag. While Sam was getting ready, J J spent some time looking around the room. On it's back wall was a large picture, of a distinguished looking man in a suit and tie. He removed his sunglasses and sat them on a small table. He then walked over and looked at the picture. Noticing a small brass label mounted in the bottom center part of the picture's frame, he stood reading what was printed on it. The label read, 'President William J. Clinton, Commander and Chief.' Standing in front of the picture of his new Commander and Chief, J J started slowly turning, as not to miss anything, as he looks around the magnificent room. Spotting the T V, he walked over and knelt down looking at it. He didn't see any button to turn it on, or any buttons for that matter. Then he noticed something laying on the T V's top. He picked up the unit and studied it, as he held it in his hand. It had a good many buttons on it. It appeared there was writing near some of the buttons. As he tried to read the writing, he noticed he was just using the one eye. Still relying on the same eye he had used for so many years. Not being able to read the writing with that eye, he covered it with his hand. He then tried the other eye. To his surprise, he could now read some of the printing near the unit's buttons. All of a sudden he looked up, as if he had been shocked. Slowly looking back at the unit he held, he again read the words, Made in Japan. Setting the unit back on top of the T V, he stood shaking his head looking down at the unit. Then abruptly raising his head he stood smiling, reaching into his shirt pocket, he slowly pulled out the picture of his Jera Marie, his grandson had given him. Again covering the one eye he looked at the picture, he held gently in his hand. He stood staring at the picture. He could now make out Sam, Sam's mother and his Jera Marie.

"Grampa, what's a matter?"

J J hearing the word grampa, looked to his grandson's hand pulling at his left elbow. He then looked up into the eyes and face of his grandson, who's picture he held in his hand.

"Are you all right?"

"I'm fine, Sam. I can see better with my new eye close up, then I can with this one," said J J as he pointed to his eye, until just a few short hours earlier was his only eye.

"That's great, Grampa."

"I can see pretty good far way with both eyes and close up with this one," said J J pointing first at the one eye and then the other.

"That reminds me Sam. I forgot about the flag! When I watched your camp on my island, I saw the U S Flag."

"Yes, what about the flag?"

"It looked different. It took me awhile, to figure out what the difference was. Then I saw it! I saw what was different about it."

"What was different, Grampa?"

"It had too many stars!" said J J, with frustration in his voice.

"What?"

"Sam, your flag had too many stars. I had a hell of a time counting them. It was the pattern, the layout of the stars, that first caught my eye." Said J J pointing to his left eye. "I finally got the sun and wind, to cooperate, so I was able to count the stars and stripes. The flag had thirteen stripes, seven red and six white, but it had fifty stars!"

"Isn't that what it's suppose to have, Grampa?"

"No! It only has forty eight."

"You said, it had fifty stars."

"Yes, that's right. No! Wait. That's not what I mean. What I mean is, the flag that flew in your camp had fifty stars. The flag is only suppose to have forty eight. One star for each one of the states, in these United States Of America, forty eight."

"Grampa, I'm sorry, there were only forty eight. Now there's fifty. Fifty stars for fifty states."

"I know, believe it," said J J, standing there smiling. "Wait! Japan isn't one of them, is it?"

"No," laughed Sam, putting his hand on his grandfather's shoulder, as the two of them walked over to where J J had his clean clothes laid out. . . .

"Alaska and Hawaii, became states since you left. Sometime in the late fifties or early sixties, I think. It's your turn. You can use my razor, Grampa. You'll get a real close shave, without much danger of slitting your own throat," said Sam, as he handed his razor to his grandfather, then rubbing his face and neck, with both hands. Sam showing his grandfather what a close shave he had. "There's soap and shampoo in the shower. There's shaving cream by the sink. I have a towel and wash cloth laid out, next to the shower door. Have fun. Take as long as you wish. I'll be here when you get out."

J J walked over and picked up the clothes he had laid out. He then entered the bathroom. Within a few minutes, there was quite a loud melody reverberating from the confines of the bathroom walls. Sam continued getting dressed, as he listened to the different melodies, coming from within the bathroom. He recognized some of the melodies, but most of them, he didn't. This went on for about a half hour. Then all at once the melodies quit and the bathroom door opened. Out came a smartly dressed, but barefooted Marine.

"To bad I didn't get a hair cut today, my hair is so chopped up. If they have a hospital onboard, they surely have a barber shop. I thought it looked pretty good, for my debut in camp yesterday. Boy, was I wrong."

"It doesn't look that bad."

"What's the matter, do you have a bad eye too?" laughed J J, as he walked up to his grandson, patting him on his shoulder.

"No. I can see," laughed Sam.

"It's maybe a little choppy when it's wet and newly combed. As soon as it's dry, it will look fine, Grampa."

"Are you ready, Sam? I'm ready. How's my shave look? You're, right, that razor of yours gives a real close shave. My face is as smooth as ever and no razor nicks either."

"Grampa, your shave looks good," said Sam, as he looked from his grandfather's face, down to his two bare feet. "Aren't you going to wear your new shoes, Grampa?"

J J looked from his grandson's clean shaven face, slowly down to his own two bare feet. . . , slowly wiggling his toes at himself and his grandson, as the two men looked down at his two bare feet. "That way they wouldn't notice my choppy hair cut," said J J, as he tried to raise and lower his eyebrows. "That wasn't such a good idea," said J J, as he looked back into the smiling face of his grandson.

"You've got that right, not just after having eye surgery, it probably wasn't, Grampa. But you're right they probably wouldn't have noticed," snickered Sam, looking back down at the bare feet.

"Do you think these bandages are necessary? What if I just wear the ones on my hands and these sunglasses?" asked J J, as he reached over and grabbed the sunglasses from the table, slipping them on and putting his hands behind his back. "What do you think, Sam?" asked J J, standing there as if he was at parade rest.

"That will work. You don't need the bandages on your face, after all. We'll let the Captain and Colonel decide. It looks good to me, Grampa. You'd better get your shoes on they'll be here any minute."

"Sam, thank you for remembering to get me a toothbrush. I would have never thought of it."

"The Colonel thought of that one, Grampa."

"I'm glad. It was great. That toothpaste was quite an experience, in it's self. So was that shaving stuff, in the can."

"I'm glad you like the toothpaste. It's one of my favorites, of the ones I've tried. Out of the hundreds that are on the market today."

J J walked over and picked up a pair of the shoes and a pair of socks, he had left out of the duffel bag. He carried them with him, as he walked over to a big chair. "It says there, this Clinton fellow is our President," said J J pointing at the tag on the picture frame, as he sat down in the chair and began to put on his socks and shoes.

"Yes, that's right, Grampa. I'll bet he'll. . . ," said Sam, as he paused in what he was about to say.

"Are you about ready, Grampa?" asked Sam, as he tried to change the conversation.

"What were you going to say about the President, Sam?" said J J, as he finished tying his shoes and stood proudly.

"You look great, Grampa," said Sam, as he again tried to change the subject.

"I feel great, Sam. I feel like a new man. From the tips of my toes, to the top of my head. I feel great!"

"Yes, I saw the toes, remember? They looked ready to go all right," laughed Sam, as he walked towards the door of their cabin.

"We can wait with the Colonel, in his cabin," said Sam.

"What about my hands? I'll need help with these bandages," said J J, as he picked up the bandages, which were laying near the duffel bag.

"I'll help you put them on in the Colonel's quarters, Grampa."

"Ok, let's go."

Just as they opened the door and stepped into the hall, they saw the Captain.

"That's perfect timing," said the Captain, as he stopped in the hall, in front of the Colonel's quarters. The Captain knocked on the Colonel's cabin door as Sam and J J walked up next to him. The Colonel quickly opened the door.

"Is everyone ready?" asked the Colonel, as he came out into the hall.

"Robby, I still have to put these bandages on my hands. I thought the sunglasses may be enough for my face. What do you think?"

"Good idea, J J. I have something here, for your hands," said the Colonel, as he held out a pair of white dress gloves. As he handed J J the gloves, he took the bandages and re-entered his room. Quickly returning, as he closed the rooms door behind.

"Good idea, Bob!" said the Captain with a big smile.

"It's all right? The sunglasses with no bandages and the gloves. That's all I need?" asked J J, as he started putting on the gloves.

"It looks good to me, J J. Let's go to dinner," said the Colonel.

The Colonel and Captain started walking. J J and Sam followed along behind, as J J finished putting on the gloves.

"You sure can't tell that mans age by looking at him," whispered the Colonel to the Captain, as they walked side by side.

"That's for damn sure. With those sunglasses and gloves, he looks as young as his grandson. He definitely looks younger than the two of us!" laughed the Captain.

"That's for sure," laughed the Colonel, as he turned to look at the two men walking along behind, talking and laughing with each other.

"Pat, you will never know, how much this opportunity means to me. This chance I have with your help, to pay a fifty year old debt, my father had. I know J J doesn't blame my father at all, for leaving him behind on the island. But my father blamed himself, for J J's loss. When I was four or five years old. I remember my father telling me, with tears in his eyes, how he and two others, left their friend J J, behind on an island. With your help, maybe I can return him and his grandson, safely home to J J's wife, in Seattle," said the Colonel, as he again looked back at J J and Sam, with tears laying on his lower eyelids.

"Like I said. . . ." The Captain stopping short, shaking his head as he put his hand over on the Colonel's shoulder. The two men kept walking with broad smiles on their faces. "We could have eaten in my quarters, but what I've seen of J J. He really enjoys being around people."

"I agree. Back on the island yesterday and this morning, he seemed to do real well with the attention of all the men and of course the women. You would think he'd be nervous around all those people. One thing, he might need help remembering, to use his southern accent."

"Yes, I saw that earlier at the ships store," snickered the Captain.

The four men walked up and stood hesitating before entering the ship's mess hall. As they entered, no one seemed to notice. There was a main corridor that ran between the tables. They walked into the mess, along this main aisle. On both sides of the aisle, sailors one by one saw who they were. Some stood up and came to attention. While others seemed to sit there at their tables, in a state of shock. They continued towards the back of the hall. Then one of the NONCOMS that works in the area, saw the Captain.

"Captain, what can we do for you this evening, Sir?"

"Hi, Mike. We just need a table," said the Captain, as he shook the man's hand.

"No problem, Skipper."

"Mike here, has the same problem I do. He doesn't want to retire until he's ready. He'll be sixty, two days after I am. Isn't that right, Mike?"

"Yes, Sir. I think it is."

"Mike, this is Colonel Robinson, the two private's are with him."

"Hello, Colonel," said the Chief, as he shook hands with the Colonel.

"Sir, do you want a table just for the two of you?"

"No, Chief. A table for four, is just fine."

"Yes, Sir." The Chief lead the four men to a table in the back part of the hall. The table he lead them to, was set for eight. The Chief quickly grabbed up four of the place sittings. "This will give you more room, Sir."

"That's fine, Chief. Thank you."

"Is there anything special you have in mind for dinner, Sir?"

"What do we have to select from, Mike?"

"Let's see. There's pot roast, prime rib, grilled salmon, all different kinds of steaks and lots of casseroles. If you can think of it, we just might have it, Sir."

"Let us think about it for a little while, Mike."

The Chief nodded and then walked away.

The four men took their seats around the table. The Colonel and Captain, on one side. J J and Sam, on the other.

"Wow! Did you hear what we have to choose from?" asked J J, as he sat down and pulled his chair up close to the table.

"It pays to have the Captain's ear," laughed the Colonel.

"Well, enjoy, J J. The next twenty four to forty eight hours, may not be quite so fulfilling," said the Colonel. "I've taken many of these kind of flights, over the years. Sometimes they get you where you're going, in the same clothes you left in, still in pretty good shape. Other times, it looks as though they made you change oil in the airplane's engines, to pay for your flight, your clothes are so dirty."

"Robby, what you're telling me is, it may not be as comfortable, as say a flight aboard 'Pan American.'"

"Yes, J J. You might say that," snickered the Colonel.

"If it will get me home to my Jera Marie. I don't care how comfortable or uncomfortable it is. As long as it's fast!"

"It doesn't look like it will take us long to get to Anchorage. It may take longer from Anchorage to Seattle. If we can't wait for that plane's last leg to Seattle, maybe we can catch another flight. If I have to, I'll rent a car and drive you. If it's within my power, one way or the other. I will get you to Seattle and home!"

"I know that, Robby. It's just that sometimes things are taken out of our hands or not within our power. Life throws us an unexpected curve ball and we have to walk around the bases of life, in a way we hadn't planned. Do you think I planned on being alone for fifty years? Not that it was anyone's fault. That's life!" As the three men sat thinking about what J J said. The Chief came to the table, breaking the spell that J J's profound statement, had put on them. He had a pitcher of water with four glasses, after setting the tray down, he turned and left the table.

Each man talked about what they were going to have for dinner, as they talked the subject changed to other topics and the four men became more relaxed and comfortable for their evening meal.

"I can't get over how high on the hog you guys eat nowadays. Yesterday we had a Thanksgiving feast for lunch. Today I'm going to have a big thick juicy steak and a baked potato. I'm sure glad you boys invited me to join this outfit. . . . Wait, now that I think about it, you guys joined my outfit," said J J, with his chin up. Everyone at the table laughed at J J's point of view.

"Captain, has your party had time to decide what they will have for dinner?" asked the Chief, holding a tray high.

"Yes, Mike. I think we have."

"Boy, that bread smells good," said J J.

"We bake our own bread, here on the Enterprise," said the Chief, as he set two small loaves of bread and two bowls, holding what appeared to be butter in them, on the table. "That bowl, has low fat margarine, made from who knows what! The other bowl has butter, made from the sweet cream of a good old-fashioned dairy cow," said the Chief, as he pointed.

The four men gave their different choices for dinner to the Chief. After he had the men's choices, the Chief turned and walked towards the galley.

"Is there any doubt which bowl the Chief would choose, to get the stuff to spread on his bread?" asked the Captain.

"I don't think so," laughed the Colonel.

The four men sat there enjoying each others company and conversation, as they ate bread and talked. In no time at all. The Chief came with two other sailors, carrying plates with meals on them, fit for a king. J J sat there looking at the food, in awe of the amount of it, set before him.

"Chief, you've been in the Navy since you were eighteen?"

"Yes, Captain, I have."

"Yes, I remember, Chief. You and I talked for quite awhile, during your last evaluation meeting. I also remember you telling me that you also didn't want to retire at the age of sixty. That the Navy had been your whole life and you wanted to stay in, as long as you were physically able to perform your duties."

"Yes, Sir, that's correct. It's amazing to me, one arm of our government is telling you and me, we have to retire at age sixty! While another arm of the government, is telling the public, they may have to wait until seventy, to get their social security retirement. And that same government says no, to all forms of discrimination. Give me a break! If that isn't discrimination, what is? I'm sorry, Sir, you shouldn't have got me started."

"Yes, I can see that now. I'll know better next time. Thank you, Chief."

"You're, welcome, Captain. Thank you for coming down to the hall for dinner, Sir. We enjoyed having you and the Colonel and the Colonel's party, here tonight. Get my attention if you need anything, Sir." With that, the Chief turned and went walking back towards the galley.

"You mean, I've been retired for the last thirteen years, and didn't even know it?"

"Yes, I guess that's what it could mean, J J. You've been retired, living on a beautiful tropical island, for the last thirteen years of your life. For some people that would be an answer to a dream come true. Let's go on the assumption or I should say the reality, that wasn't the case. You were at war with the Japanese Empire! In your world, that's all you knew you were still on duty and at war! That would put you on duty, thirteen years past mandatory retirement. That may give the Chief and I, and others like us, something to fight mandatory retirement, at age sixty. You weren't retired. That thought had never entered your mind, as far as you knew, until two days ago, the U S was still at war, with the Japanese Empire. The day before yesterday, was when you were told, the war with Japan was over.

"Yes, Captain."

"I do agree with Bob, when he says we need to keep your existence quiet. But when your existence is known. You still being on active duty and past the age of sixty, may set the precedent we need, to fight mandatory retirement. Plus we'll have the attention of all the media, once the news of your existence is released."

"What do you mean media, Captain?"

"Media. Radio, T V, newspapers and magazines, to name just a few."

"Do you think I'll be on T V?"

"No doubt about that, J J," said the Captain.

J J looked across at the Colonel and then over at Sam, as they too nodded there heads. That yes it was true, he would be on the T V. "Why would they want to put me on T V?"

"J J, in a few days, you're going to be big news. That's why I want to get you home before that news gets out."

"Thank you, Robby."

"How's that big juicy steak of yours, J J?" asked the Colonel, trying to change the subject. Hearing the concern in J J's voice, about being on T V. "J J, there's nothing difficult or scary, about being on T V. I was on T V, when I was only six years old."

"Is that right? What television show was that, Bob?"

"It was called, The Art Linkletter Show."

"I remember that show. It was on in the fifties."

"That's right, Pat."

"It had to be the summer of fifty four. It was when I first graduated from Annapolis. I remember going to my brother's. I was visiting him and his family in Virginia. This Art Linkletter Show, you're talking about was on T V. It was one of my brother's wife's favorite. So I was polite and sat with her and their two children and watched the show with them. My brother must have been at work. There was this one part of the show, where Art, would ask these little kids questions. The answers he got to some of those questions, were pretty funny," laughed the Captain.

"That's the show. I was one of those little kids! Pat, you didn't see me that day. I was on the show before that. I was only in first grade, when I was on. So it would have been, sometime in fifty two or three."

"Wouldn't that of been cool, if the Captain would have seen the same show you were on, Colonel?"

"Sam, it just shows how small this world really is. Look at the unbelievable fact, you found your grandfather, and yet, there he sits, right beside you. Sometimes in life, the unbelievable happens. I'd say this is the ultimate, of one of those times."

The four men continued enjoying their four star meal.

"My steak is delicious. The potato is great too. I especially like the fresh corn on the cob. It reminds me, of when my Grampa Johnson used to bring us fresh vegetables and beef, he raised on his farm, not far from Seattle. The farm laid along a river. . . . What was that river's name? The name escapes me right now.

"J J, you're trying to remember the name of a river you knew over fifty years ago. That's more years then I've been alive. We understand why, you may not remember it's name," said the Colonel.

"I sure do," said the Captain."

"Me too," said Sam.

"Captain?"

"Yes, J J."

"Is there a barber shop, onboard the Enterprise?"

"There sure is. Why, do you want a haircut?"

"Yes, Captain, I would like to see if someone could do something with this," said J J, pointing at his hair.

"What's wrong with it? It looks as good as half my crew's haircuts, after they come back from leave. J J, the barber shop's closed until morning. If it really bothers you, I could have the barber come to my quarters."

"No. Not if you think it looks all right."

"It's like Pop Miller says, Grampa. "The difference between a good haircut and a bad one, is three days." It's already been what, two days? By tomorrow, it will be a good one." The four men laughed together, at what Sam said. As they were laughing, the Chief came up to their table.

"What would you like for dessert? There are several items to choose from," said the Chief, as he proceeded to name the different choices of desserts available. The four men made their choices. The Chief turned and left the table, with their choices in hand.

"I know, believe it! You know something? It's funny. I remember the different smells, like it was yesterday. But some of the foods taste entirely different then I remember. Maybe I remember them different or maybe I can't remember! I don't know which. I do know, it doesn't taste the same.

It doesn't make any sense. I'm sorry, you guys. I didn't mean to babble."

"No problem, J J. This is all very interesting," said the Captain, as he looked up and saw the Chief coming with their dessert.

"Here comes our dessert. Let's see if these desserts, taste the way they're suppose to, J J," said the Captain, raising and lowering his eyebrows, as he did.

"I'm going to enjoy this. Of course you know, I'm going to have to taste all of these. Just to see if they taste the way I remember."

"I don't know, guys. What do you think? Do you think maybe it's a scheme, for him to get our desserts." asked the Captain.

"That's it! He's been planning this over the last fifty years. Just so he could get our desserts," said the Colonel, with suspicion in his voice.

The three men sat looking harshly at J J.

"Curses, Foiled Again.' That's right! I've been planning this for years," said J J, speaking like the villain, Snidely Whiplash, picking right up on the two men's little joke.

They all laughed, as the Chief sat the dessert tray on the table. He then handed each man his choice of dessert, ranging from a huge piece of chocolate cake, apple pie a la mode and cheesecake.

"If there's anything else, Captain. Just get my attention. Again thank you, Captain, for coming down for dinner. I hope everything was to your liking?"

"Everything was great. Thank you, Chief."

The other three men nodding their heads, as they prepared to partake of the fine looking desserts, that they agreed with the Captain. The Chief said his good-byes, then turned and walked back towards the galley.

"Here, J J, try some of mine. I know you have planned this, all my life," laughed the Colonel, pushing his dessert towards J J.

"My plan worked. But I'm unable to make the final assault. You win. I surrender, this will be enough dessert," said J J holding up his hands, looking down at his plate, with one bite remaining.

"I don't know, guy's, do you think he's eaten enough? Should we let him quit eating or do we make him eat what's left," laughed the Colonel.

"I'll let him off this time and eat mine," said the Captain, taking his last bite of dessert.

"Me too," said Sam.

"Thank you, I couldn't eat another bite," said J J, as he leaned back with his hands on his stomach.

The four men spent the next few minutes laughing and talking.

"Don't look now. Guess who just walked in," said Sam.

"Damn."

"That's right, Colonel."

"Has he seen us, Sam?"

"You'd better believe it, he's coming this way."

"Well, at least we finished dinner. And what a fine dinner it was, especially the company. Thank you, guy's," said J J.

"You're welcome, Al, I'm glad you liked it," said the Captain.

"Do you mind if I join you fellows, for dinner?"

"We've just finished ours. Enjoy your dinner, we sure did. Didn't we, fella's?" asked the Captain, as he stood up.

"We sure did, Captain," said the others, as they too stood up, stepping aside and pushing their chairs into the table, as they did. The four men then walked through the mess hall, back towards the exit. All four men waving to the Chief as they did.

Jim stood there with his mouth hanging open. He then turned and started to pursue the four men. "Captain, wait up." Jim half running after the four men. "Captain!" shouted Jim. The Captain stopped, with the three men. Jim quickly got to where the four men were standing.

The Captain slowly turned to Jim. "Mister, I'm not accustomed to being hollered at!" said the Captain, in a rather loud voice, as he got right into Jim's face. "As long as you're on the Enterprise, I advise you to remember that." With that, the Captain quickly turned and started walking. The others stood there a second looking at Jim, also somewhat surprised by the ferocity of the Captain's response. They then turned and followed the Captain, leaving Jim standing there in a daze.

"Boy, I'll bet he'll walk softly for awhile," whispered Sam, to J J.

"What's he doing?" asked the Colonel.

"He's just standing there, Colonel, watching us. What do you think he'll do now?"

"He'll probably want to go change his shorts. Then he'll be right back at it, on the trail again. He was just caught off guard, as we were, by Pat's unfriendly attitude," laughed the Colonel.

"I don't mind. I'm responsible for everything on this ship. I might as well have some fun along the way. That was fun."

"I'm sure glad he's on my side," snickered J J. The Colonel and Sam, both nodding their heads, that they agreed with J J, as the three of them followed the Captain.

"Captain, what do you think he'll do, after he changes?" asked Sam.

"The reporter? He'll probably go back to the mess hall and ask questions. I don't imagine the Chief will cut him anymore slack there than I. So I don't think he's gained a thing, Sam. We have three and a half hours before your flight. What do you want to do now, J J?" said the Captain turning his head to ask.

"It's up to you guys. I don't have any idea."

"Is there anything special you can think of, you might like to show your grandfather, Sam?" asked the Colonel.

"Is the ship's library still open? The library might be fun."

"I don't know," said the Colonel, shrugging his shoulders.

"Captain, is the ship's library open this late?"

"Yes. It's open until nine. Is that where you'd like to go now? The ship's library?" asked the Captain, as he stopped and turned to the other three men. "It's back on the far side of the mess hall. We can go around and come in from the other side. That way you'll see more of the Enterprise. And maybe we wouldn't see our shadow. In fact, would you like to see the reactor and the engine rooms, J J? They'll be right on our way, if we go around that way to the library."

"That would be great, Captain."

"Well, my doctor's been telling me I needed to get out and walk more. It's this way," said the Captain, as he again took off doing just that, walking.

"If we see the shadow . . . oh never mind. He'll probably be more invisible than ever. Wait, that's kind of redundant. More invisible. That would make him pretty damn hard to see, all right," chuckled the Colonel, as the four of them started walking.

The men walked along talking, about Jim, dinner and other things, on their way to the library.

"This is the way we'd go, to the engine room," said the Captain, as he pointed to a hallway. "Let's go onto the library first. We can go to the engine room and reactor, on the way back. Besides they might ask us to change the oil or something. Then our clothes would be too dirty, to go to the library." The three men looked at each other and then back at the Captain. They caught him turning his head slightly, to see if there was any reaction to his little joke.

"Just great, Captain! I already have to change oil in the airplane. Now you're telling me, I have to change the Enterprise's oil too. Looks like I've got a job. I better get me a pair of coveralls, and get right to work, so I can catch my ride home at 2200." The other two men laughed at J J's quick response, to the Captain's little joke.

"Sam, do you think the library might have some pictures of that rocket ship, you told me about?"

"I would sure think so, Grampa."

The Captain turned, and the Colonel looked over, as the two of them, stared at Sam.

"Rocket ship? What have you been telling your grandfather?"

"Guys, he means the Saturn V. The Apollo space program."

"I'm sure there are lots of pictures in the personal history file of the Enterprise. She was one of the prime recovery ships, for the Apollo program."

They came to the entrance to the ship's library. The Captain opened the door and the four of them entered the library. The four men spent the next hour or so in the library. They then walked on, through the engine room and then to the reactor room. After that, they headed back to their room, to get ready for J J's anxiously awaited flight home.

"Wasn't that amazing? The things the Captain showed us. A person couldn't have dreamed, of most of those things. And yet, someone did because they were all real! I saw them!" said J J, as he walked with the others.

"You'll have about forty five minutes, to use the head and get your stuff together and get to the plane," said the Captain, as they walked up to the door of their cabin. "I'll go see if there's been any changes. If not, I'll meet you at the plane. The Colonel will know how to get you to the plane. I'll see you there." With that, the Captain went walking off.

"I'll meet you two back here, in ten minutes. Ok?"

"Ok, Robby," said J J, as Sam opened the door to their room. Within a few minutes. The three men met back in the hallway, outside their rooms, with their gear in hand.

"You two ready?"

"Yes, Sir! We're ready! Lead the way, Colonel." The Colonel started walking. As they walked, J J continued talking about the wonderful things he had seen his very first day off his island and that day, was far from over.

"You know, fella's. I've never been in an airplane before. At least one that's airborne. That's going to be another interesting thing for me to do tonight, in one unbelievable day and night of things." Just then Jim, the reporter, stepped out into their path.

"Colonel, if you don't mind? I'd like to ask Al there, a few questions?"

"I'm sorry, Jim. I'm afraid I do. We're on our way to meet the Captain. You wouldn't want us to be late, now would you? If we were, we'd have to tell the Captain, why we were late. I don't think you'd want him to hear that," said the Colonel, as the three men kept walking. Walking right past Jim, as Jim moved over slightly, to let the three men walk by.

"Colonel, wait. Colonel! Damn, who is this guy, Colonel?"

"Why Jim, you just called him, Al. Isn't that his name?" asked the Colonel, turning back towards Jim, so Jim could hear what he was saying, as the three of them continued walking.

"I'm sure he's going to follow us. Don't let him see you checking to see if he's following. Let's just ignore him, like the Captain said to do. 'Let him do his own thing and we'll do ours," said the Colonel, as they continued through the ship, not knowing whether or not their shadow was back on their trail. Then the three men stepped out onto the flight deck.

"There's our plane, J J."

"It's so big!"

"J J, it looks big. But there's so much equipment built into it, there probably isn't a whole lot of room onboard," said the Colonel, as the three men stood looking at the big plane. "Maybe there won't be a full crew onboard. That would give us more elbow room."

Just then the Captain walked up. "How's she look, J J?"

"Beautiful, Captain."

"Are you ready?"

"Yes, Sir. I'm ready."

"Pat, we ran into our shadow," said the Colonel.

"That reporters becoming a pain in the ass?" snickered the Captain, shaking his head.

"Yes, he is. He's probably watching us right now," said Sam, as he looked over his shoulder.

"Forget him! J J, we don't have much time. I want to thank you again for letting me be a part of this adventure. Like I said."

"We know."

"It's been a real kick in the ass," said the Captain, the Colonel, Sam and J J, all at the same time, in a loud enough voice, as to be heard over all the noise, on the flight deck. The four men then laughed together, at what was said. As they stood there looking at each other, one waiting for the other to say something, knowing it was now time for them to say farewell.

"Good-bye, J J," said the Captain, as he held out his hand.

J J grabbed the Captain's hand with his and shook it vigorously. Then pulling the Captain in close, J J dropped his gear to the deck, and put his other arm around the Captain's neck and gave him a big long hug. "Thank you, Pat. I'm sure, I'll never know how much your help today, has changed my life, today, and for the future. I do know without it, it wouldn't have been possible and I wouldn't be standing here about to leave for home, on my first plane ride, on the way to my Jera Marie. Thanks again, Captain," said J J, as he broke the embrace. He then stepped back and proudly saluted the Captain. The other two men seeing this, also saluted the Captain. Then the two men stepped forward and shook the Captain's hand.

Just then a sailor came up to the Captain. He was wearing a helmet with ear phones. He said something to the Captain. The Captain nodding, that he understood what the sailor said.

"You guys have to board the plane."

The three men nodded, that they heard and understood the Captain. J J bent down and grabbed his gear. They then started for the plane, the Colonel stopped and turned to the Captain.

"Thank you, Pat," said the Colonel, as he again held out his hand and shook the Captain's.

"Take care of our boy, Robby," said the Captain, calling him Robby, for the first time. The Colonel then ran to join the others. They followed the helmeted sailor, as he lead them towards the awaiting plane. J J turned and waved to the Captain, as he did he could hear that most of the noise on the flight deck, was coming from their airplane's engines. J J turned and looked at a small set of stairs. The stairs lead to the doorway of the airplane. He looked up the stairs to an open door. After hesitating a moment, he started up the stairs. He walked through the opened doorway into the aircraft.

INTO THE NIGHT SKY

The Colonel and Sam climbed the stairs and entered the aircraft. Once the three men were inside the airplane. The door was closed and the stairs were rolled away from the aircraft. At that same time, the Captain turned and left the flight deck.

The big plane began to move, pulled along by a small electric cart, driven by one of the flight deck's crewman. The small cart moved the large plane effortlessly along the flight deck. The crewman continued towards one end of the flight deck, where he slowly maneuvered the plane's nose wheel into position, to be hooked to the catapult boot. Once in position, he stopped the cart and got off and unhooked the cart from the aircraft, seeing the plane's wheel was indeed in the boot. He got back on the cart and drove off. With the cart safely away, the planes engines began to accelerate to a deafening shrill scream. Within a few seconds, the plane was on it's way down the flight deck. Helped along by the Enterprise's tremendously powerful catapulting system. This catapult helped the plane reach airspeed and gain flight. Without it's help, the plane wouldn't reach airspeed and flight wouldn't be possible, from this short of runway.

The plane was airborne, as if it were a kid's toy, made of balsa wood, and shot from a rubber band launcher.

The aircraft rose from the decks of the Enterprise, into the night sky. Disappearing from sight as it did. Only it's navigation lights could be seen slowly blending with the stars of the heavens.

"Wow, this babies really packing the mail. I think my stomach is still on the Enterprise. I see why you wanted us to strap ourselves in, Robby. Robby, how fast does this plane fly?"

"I don't know. When we reach cruising altitude and level off, you can go up to the cockpit and ask the pilot. Until then, I think we'd better stay in our seats, with our belts on," said the Colonel.

"That's a good idea Ollie," said J J, as he nodded his head.

In no time at all the plane started to level off.

"J J, see that green light over there?" asked the Colonel, pointing to a small green light.

"Yes, Sir."

"That means we can unfasten our seat belts. Now you can go up to the cockpit and ask the pilot your questions, J J," said the Colonel, as he removed his seat belt.

J J removed his belt and slowly stood. Much to his surprise, he had virtually no sense the plane was moving at a high rate of speed. For that matter, he couldn't perceive movement of any kind.

"Robby, I don't think we're moving. The engines have slowed."

"J J, you go and ask the pilot," said the Colonel, as he pointed to the front of the airplane, with a big smile on his face. "You go see what he says. While you're there, you can ask him how fast this plane flies and any other questions you might have."

"Ok, if you say so, Robby," said J J, shrugging his shoulders. J J moved into the aisle and started towards the front of the aircraft. He had only taken a few steps and the plane went through a couple of down drafts, changing the plane's altitude abruptly.

"Whoa!"

"Still think were not moving J J?"

"It's moving all right! But, is it moving in the right direction?" asked J J, as he quickly walked back to where the Colonel and Sam, were still sitting in their seats. J J hanging onto whatever he could, to help him keep his balance.

"It's all right, J J. We just hit."

"Robby! We hit something! What'd we hit?"

"Sorry, J J. The airplane's just going through some unstable air, that's all. The pilot will probably go to a higher altitude, to see if he can find some smoother air," said the Colonel. No sooner had the words left the Colonel's mouth, than the plane began to climb. Within a moment or two, the ride started to smooth out and the plane again started to level off. "There you go, J J. Try again," laughed the Colonel. J J looked at the Colonel. He then turned and started slowly towards the front of the plane. Still feeling a little uneasy, he held onto whatever he could, to make himself feel more secure, as he walked.

"Yes, Private. Can I help you?" asked a young Lieutenant, looking up at J J, from his seat in front of a console of some kind.

"The Colonel said, I could come up here and maybe, ask some questions of the pilot. That is if it's all right with him?"

"It seems to be calm enough now. Go ahead and ask," said the Lieutenant, as he turned back to what he was doing at the console, before J J's interruption.

J J entered the cockpit. He stood there just inside the doorway.

"Pete, how's about some coffee?" asked the man in the copilot's seat. He then turned, instead of seeing Pete, he saw J J standing there.

"What do we have here?" asked the man in the copilot's seat. The pilot turned and saw J J.

"What are you doing here, Private?" asked the pilot.

"Sir, the Colonel wanted me to ask you if it would be all right, if I came up here and asked you a few questions?"

"The Colonel asked?" said the pilot, looking over at the copilot. As, J J reached up and slowly removed his sunglasses and stood there looking around the cockpit, holding his sunglasses in his gloved hand.

"Yes, Sir."

"Then it's all right, Private. Go ahead ask your questions," said the pilot. The pilot and copilot sat there looking at each other and then back up at J J. "Man, you're the oldest private I've ever seen," said the pilot.

"That's a big ten four," said the copilot.

"Is there a problem?" asked the Colonel, as he walked up behind J J, and stood in the doorway of the cockpit.

"We were just caught a bit off guard, by your aide's appearance, Sir."

"By him being here, or by his looks, Lieutenant?"

"Both Colonel, by him being here in our cockpit. And of course by his appearance, Sir," said the pilot, looking over at his copilot.

"Yes, most people are a bit at first. . . . J J here, was caught in a mechanical rice picker, when he was a child," smirked the Colonel. Then loosing control, he started to laugh aloud.

The pilot and copilot, looked first at the Colonel, then at J J. They looked back and forth, from one man to the other. Then the two men sat looking at each other, then slowly turnning they stared at the Colonel. J J also turned and stared at the Colonel, with a funny look on his face . . . .

"Sir!" said the pilot, as he looked up at the Colonel.

"All right! Give me a break! I didn't think it through, ok," laughed the Colonel.

"No, Sir, I'd say you didn't," laughed the pilot.

"I heard that one, on an old episode of Star Trek, Colonel," laughed the copilot.

"Yes. . . ! So did I. That's where I heared it. Star Trek! Ok, fella's. All I can tell you, is, this man is being escorted by, me. A Colonel in the United States Marine Corps. And I would appreciate your assistance."

"You've got it, Colonel."

"I would also appreciate you not telling anyone about this after we leave your aircraft, for at least a few days. After that, you have my permission, to have as much fun with this as you wish. The private's name is J J."

"Yes, Sir. You've got it, Sir."

"Thank you," said the Colonel, smiling as he turned and left the plane's cockpit, leaving J J, with the pilot and copilot.

"So, J J, what are your questions?"

"You already know my name, what's yours?"

"My name is, Al Watson," said the pilot, as he held up his right hand to J J. This being very difficult for him, beings he was strapped in his seat with heavy shoulder belts.

"Bill Steward, is mine," said the copilot, as he stood up turning as he did to shake hands with J J.

"Where's the coffee? I can get you guys some coffee."

"The coffee is back by Pete's station. Thanks, J J," said the pilot.

J J turned and walked back to Pete's station. Pete was talking on the telephone, when J J walked up. He quietly stood waiting for Pete to finish with the telephone. Within a minute, he was finished. He hung up the phone and looked up at J J.

"Pete, I'd like to get Al and Bill some coffee. Could you show me where it is?"

"J J, we already know each other's name. That was Al, on the phone, he told me your name," said Pete, as he stood up holding out his hand. J J shook hands with the young Lieutenant. "Let me show you where the coffee is," said Pete, as he moved past J J. "There is a lot of sophisticated, super sensitive, million dollar equipment, on this bird. And there's also a coffee maker, J J. Usually me!" said Pete, as he frowned at J J and raised one eyebrow. "It's built in, right here," said Pete, as he showed J J what they called a coffee maker and where it was located. J J stood and watched Pete, as he showed him the coffee maker and explained to him how it worked. "Space is so important on this bird, our coffee maker, only makes four cups. I'll show you how to make this first pot, then you'll know how to make some for the Colonel and you later. Then if I'm busy with something important, you know, like sleeping," said Pete, as he continued showing J J how the coffee maker worked. The two men talked as they waited for the coffee to brew.

"Is that coffee about ready?"

"Yes, it is, Colonel. Can I bring you a cup when it is? You like yours black right, Colonel?" asked J J.

"Black."

"Yes, Sir. I'll bring it to your seat, Colonel."

"Thank you, J J. That would be just fine," said the Colonel, as he turned and walked down the aisle towards his seat.

"Boy, he talks different than any Marine Colonel, I've ever been around. Of course I haven't been around very many. The Air Force and the Army, they have lots of Colonels. But not the Marine Corp. Here, J J, this first pot's done. Al takes sugar in his coffee. Bill drinks his black. If you need any help, I'll be right over there," said Pete, pointing towards the console.

"Thanks, Pete. Can I get you a cup?"

"No, I don't drink the stuff."

"Neither do I, Pete."

"J J, how old are you?"

"Let's say, I'm old enough to be your grandfather, Pete."

"You mean, my father, not grandfather. I think my grandfather is seventy four."

"Ok, not your grandfather, I'm not that old," laughed J J, as he picked up two cups of coffee and started for the front of the plane, moving past Pete, smiling as he did.

"You're not going to tell me how old you are? Are you J J?"

J J looked back at Pete, as he continued on his way to the plane's cockpit. Within a minute or so, he was back from the cockpit, walking past Pete, who had returned to his seat at the console. J J then poured the Colonel's coffee and headed towards the rear of the plane.

"Robby, here's your coffee."

The Colonel and Sam had traded seats. He was now in the seat next to the aisle.

"Sam fell asleep. He changed seats, when I was talking to you up front. When I returned, he was sound asleep," said the Colonel, as he took the cup from J J's hand. "J J, you must be exhausted. I know I'm tired. I think Sam there, has the right idea. Did you ask the pilot how long our flight to Formosa is?"

"Not yet, Robby," said J J, in a low voice, so as not to wake Sam. "Pete showed me how to make the coffee first. Now I can go back up and they'll help, with my questions, Robby."

"Ok. J J, I might be asleep too, when you get back."

"Ok, Robby. I'll try to be quiet."

"It's not that, J J. What I meant was, if I was asleep I obviously wouldn't be able to visit with you. You'll be left alone."

"Robby, that's not alone! You'd just be asleep. Believe it, when I tell you that's not alone!"

"Right!" said the Colonel, as he looked up at J J.

"Robby, I'll go back up front and ask my questions. I'll talk to you when I come back, if you're asleep, I'll talk to you later." J J turned and headed up the aisle towards the front of the airplane. He waved at Pete, on the way by his station and re-entered the plane's cockpit.

"I'm back."

"J J, what were some of the questions you wanted to ask?" asked Al, as he looked over his shoulder at J J.

J J spent the next hour or so, talking to the pilot and copilot. They told him it would be a four and a half hour flight, from the Enterprise to there refueling stopover in Formosa. It would then be another three hours from there, to their stop in northern Japan. He also learned that the plane would have a layover, in Japan.

"Thanks, you two. For taking the time to answer my questions."

"Having your own personal Colonel, may have helped you some in getting our attention, J J," laughed the pilot.

"Believe it," said J J, as he turned and left the cockpit. Walking past Pete's station, he found Pete sleeping soundly. He walked a bit further and found the Colonel and Sam, also sound asleep. J J moved into his seat quietly as not to wake the Colonel and his grandson.

Again J J sat thinking, about 'all the new things he saw that day.' Sam was most definitely right. Each day was going to be an exciting adventure. His head nodding, he slowly fell to sleep joining the others.

"J J. J J, you have to put your seat belt on."

J J looked up, Pete was telling him to open his eyes, as J J looked up at him, he noticed something different. Then he realized what the difference was. His eye! This was the first morning, in over fifty years he could see through both eyes.

"Hi, Pete. What did you say?"

"J J, you have to put on your seat belt. We'll be landing shortly."

"All right, Pete," said J J, as he looked over and saw the Colonel and Sam, already putting on their seat belts.

"We're, landing? The plane is landing now? We're in Japan?"

"No, J J. We're landing in Formosa."

"That's right, Pete. Formosa, then northern Japan."

"Is everyone strapped in?"

"Everyone but you, Lieutenant," said the Colonel.

"I'm on my way, Colonel," said the Lieutenant, as he headed forward towards his seat.

The plane's nose angled down and it's engines slowed, it became obvious the plane was indeed landing. Then the plane's nose came back up slightly and there was a jolt. They heard the tires squeal, as they made contact with the runway. The nose of the aircraft came back down and the plane was level again. The engines roared up again but they could feel the plane stopping. They felt the plane bouncing, as it rolled along the runway. A short time later the plane came to a stop, and the engines ceased their roar.

"The green light is on Robby. That still means we can take our seat belts off, doesn't it?"

"Yes, J J. It does," said the Colonel, as he removed his belt.

J J removed his belt and stood up. He moved out into the aisle, allowing the Colonel and Sam, to get out.

"Grampa, how are you today?" asked Sam, as the Colonel moved into the aisle.

"I'm ready for another adventurous day, Sam."

"It's still the middle of the night, J J," said the Colonel, as he moved over in the aisle to make room for Sam.

About then Pete walked up behind J J.

"We'll be here for an hour or so, refueling. You'll have plenty of time to get off the plane and walk around," said Pete, as he moved towards the door. Once there, he started to open the door. "You may not want to though," said Pete, as the door opened, to the sound of falling rain. Not just rain, a downpour.

"I think I'll just stay here. I do have to use the head. Does this plane even have a head, Lieutenant?" asked the Colonel.

"You might call it a head. That is if you have a good imagination. In five hours of flight, you didn't see any of us using it, Colonel."

"Lieutenant, right now I have an excellent imagination. Where is it?"

"Right over there, Sir," said the Lieutenant, as he pointed to a small door.

"You're kidding!"

"Like I said, you need an imagination."

"I'd say Lieutenant, that's all that would fit in there with you, is your imagination, that's for sure," said the Colonel.

"The way it's raining out there, we may all be using our imagination, Sir. Five hours plus, is a long time."

"Right Lieutenant, but I'm first," said the Colonel, as he headed for the small head. He opened the door and looked in. He then turned and looked back at the men standing there in the aisle. Shaking his head, he turned and entered the plane's small restroom.

Al and Bill, walked up behind Pete. "Boy, it's really coming down, out there. It started just as we touched down. What are you waiting for? Aren't we going to run for it? What are you guys. . . ?"asked Al, as the door to the small head opened.

"Colonel, what did you think?" asked Pete.

"Think! There wasn't enough room in there to think, Lieutenant. My eight and a half foot camper's bathroom is gigantic, compared to that one. It does seem to work though. Next. J J you're next in line."

"No, I'm fine, Robby."

"Sam, I guess you're next."

"I'm ready, Colonel," said Sam, as he moved past his grandfather and the Colonel, so he could enter the head. "Any port in the storm," said Sam, as he pointed to the open door of the plane, at the raging storm outside. The five men turned and looked through the open door. Then the five turned back to look at Sam. Sam slowly closing the door on his unappreciative captive audience, to his little joke.

"I say, let's throw that smart ass out in the rain, when he comes out," laughed Al.

"I don't think that's a good idea, Al," said J J, as he got right in Al's face.

"Calm down, J J. Gee's I was just joking."

"So was my . . . Sam, Al."

"Let it go, J J," said the Colonel, surprised by J J's reaction.

"Yes, Sir."

"I'm sorry, Sir. I didn't mean to. . . ," said Al.

"That's ok, Lieutenant."

Just then Sam came out of the head. "That wasn't so bad. Like I said. . . ," said Sam stopping short, seeing the expression on the men standing around the door. "What?" asked Sam, as he looked down at the front of himself. "What is it? Why is everyone staring at me?" said Sam, as he moved out of the way, for the next man.

"Nothing, Private. We're just standing here waiting our turn, to use your port in the storm," said Al, as he moved past Sam. "Right guys?"

"That's right, Al," said J J, as he patted Al's shoulder, as Al past him on his way to the head. "It looks like we're all staying onboard the plane. Does anyone want some coffee?"

"Good idea, J J. You get the coffee and I'll get us some of these little cakes I found. I found them when I looked this bird over, when it first came onboard the Enterprise," said Pete.

"That may not be necessary, Lieutenant. The rain's slacking off a bit, it looks like the storm may be over," said the Colonel, as he stood looking out the doorway.

"That's great, now maybe we can get some real food," said Pete.

All five men crowded around the plane's small door and watched the rain slowing to a slight mist.

"Let's make a run for it," said the copilot.

Al came out of the head to find the others all gathered around the plane's door. "What? Has the rain stopped?"

"Yes, it has, Al," said Bill.

"Magnificent! Now we can get off this aircraft and stretch our legs. What are you waiting for?"

"Why, Al. We're waiting for you to lead the way," said Pete. Pete and the others moved out of the doorway. Al walked over to the door and looked out.

As all six men stood, either in the doorway or close enough to it, to at least see out the plane's open door. They saw that some portable stairs were on the way to their airplane.

"Soon as those stairs get here, I'll do just that," said Al.

"The hell with the stairs," said Pete, as he moved past the others and jumped through the plane's doorway onto the tarmac below, on the run as he landed. Turning back as he ran, to see if anyone else, was following his lead.

"I'll wait for the stairs," said Al. The others, nodding their heads yes, that they agreed with Al. They too, would wait for the stairs. The men watched, as a crewman moved the stairs into position next to their plane. Once in position, the five men started, one at a time down the stairs. Once on the tarmac, they waited for the others. All together at the foot of the stairs. They started walking, in the same direction Pete had ran off in, trying to avoid the larger puddles made by the passing storm. Rain still lightly falling as they walked towards a covered walkway leading to one of the building's entrances. Once under the walkway, they slowed their fast walk, to one of a more casual nature, as they walked along talking. The five men walked up to an entrance guarded by a single Marine, who came to attention upon their approach and saluted. All five men returned the salute. The Marine then reached out and opened the door of the building's entry and held it, for the five men to enter the building.

"It's too early for the mess to be open. I think there's a snack bar that's open twenty four hours a day," said Al, as he pointed at a sign with an arrow, that said 'Snack Bar.' The five men walked in the direction the arrow pointed, down a hall around a corner and down another hall. "There it is, and it's open," said Al, as they continued in the snack bar's direction.

"Damn! I don't have any money on me," whispered the Colonel, to Sam and J J. "Lieutenant, ask that fellow in there, if there's an ATM machine around here."

"Yes, Sir," said Al, as he walked on into the snack bar. "Do you know where an ATM machine is located?" asked Al, of an Asian man, standing behind the counter.

"ATM, yes, ATM that way," said the Asian man, as he pointed down the hall.

"We'll be back. Come with me."

"Yes, Sir, Colonel." The three men walked down the hall, in the direction the man had pointed, around another corner they continued walking to yet another corner. Just around that corner, they saw the ATM.

"There it is, Colonel," said Sam.

"Good, I was beginning to get a little tense. J J, you might find this interesting," said the Colonel, as the three men walked up to the machine. The Colonel reached into his back pocket and pulled out his wallet. He opened the billfold and pulled out a couple of cards and shuffled them back and forth in his hands. "I have so many of these things. I think this one might work. Watch this, J J," said the Colonel, as he returned the other cards to his wallet and put the wallet back in his rear pocket. The Colonel then walked up close to the machine, J J right at his side, watching every move the Colonel made. "J J, are you watching?" asked the Colonel, with excitement in his voice, looking over his shoulder to see if J J was watching, acting like a small child showing off his new toy to a playmate. This machine had what looked like a TV in the center of it. The Colonel took the single card he held in his hand and put it into the machine. Just as he did, the three men heard.

"Hello, how may I help you?"

J J looked up at the Colonel and back to his grandson. Then he turned back towards the talking machine, made of steel, glass and oh yes of coarse, that plastic stuff.

"Two hundred dollars," said the Colonel.

"Say or enter your PIN, now."

"One- three- four- nine," said the Colonel.

Some time past, as the three men stood there in front of this machine. Then all at once, out came cash. The cash came out a different slot than the Colonel had pushed his card into. J J slowly reached out and abruptly yanked the money from the machine.

"Thank you, Colonel Robinson. Do not forget to retrieve your card." J J stood there looking at the money he held in his hand and then up at the machine, as he reached out and pulled the Colonel's card from the ATM.

"Grampa, here try my card," said Sam, as he held out one of the small cards to him.

J J handed the card and money he was holding, to the Colonel. He then took the small card from his grandson, looking this one over carefully on both sides. "This card is made of that plastic stuff, isn't it?" asked J J looking up from the card he held, to his grandson and then Colonel.

"Yes, it is, J J."

"Go ahead, Grampa, put the card in the machine."

J J slowly put the card he held into the slot of the machine, as he had seen the Colonel do.

"Hello, how may I help you?"

"Grampa see there on the screen. It asks that same question, in at least two other languages in writing, as it asked you aloud. Ask for fifty dollars Grampa," whispered Sam.

"What's a matter Sam, are you afraid she'll hear you?"

"Grampa, there's nobody here, it's a machine."

"There's a lady on the other side of that one-way glass. She reads the name and that long number printed on your card. You ask her for the money you want and she asks you for your code number. After she gets that number, she bills your account and gives you the money and your plastic card back," snickered J J, in a cavalier manner.

"That's it, J J. But there's nobody here but us. Look here!" said the Colonel, as he pulled J J around to the side of the machine. "This machine is just setting here. It's pushed back tight against this wall. See this here," said the Colonel, as he pointed at the heavy brackets, that held the machine in place. "It's a machine. It's just like that Coke machine over there," said the Colonel, as he pointed to a Coke machine setting just across from where they were standing.

J J turning slightly, stood there a moment, looking at the ATM machine and then over at the Coke machine.

"Hello, how may I help you?"

Standing back in front of the ATM machine. "I'd like to have a fifty dollar bill, please," said J J, in a slow and deliberate manner.

"Repeat your request."

"Grampa, it doesn't understand sentences. You have to stay within the machines parameters. Just say fifty dollars."

"Say or enter your PIN, now."

"See, it heard me say fifty dollars. Watch, Grampa, it will give you fifty dollars."

"Say or enter your PIN, now."

"First you have to give it my PIN number. PIN stands for, Personal Identification Number. Mine's six, two, nine, three. Go ahead Grampa, you do it."

"Six- Two- Nine- Three," said J J into the machine.

In no time at all the machine made a little noise and out came Sam's money and card. "Thank you, Mr. Johnson. Do not forget to retrieve your card."

"Believe it. I should know by now. Believe it, that's all." J J reached out and quickly took the money and Sam's card from the two slots in the machine. He handed Sam, two twenties and a ten dollar bill and his plastic card. "Let's see how this Coke machine works," said J J, as he turned and walked towards the machine. "I don't suppose you can still buy a Coke-a-Cola for a nickel."

"I'm afraid not Grampa. It's likely somewhere between sixty cents and a dollar, Grampa."

"Does that say seventy five cents?" asked J J, as they walked up to the machine.

"That it does, Grampa."

"It's seventy five cents for a Coke-a-Cola! That's amazing. That's all most as much as I made per hour, when I worked at the machine shop, before leaving to come here. I mean there. Oh you know where I mean. The island!"

"Grampa, do you want a Coke?"

"No. Then I would have to use my imagination on the airplane. I did see a sign that said, restroom. That still means bathroom or head in a pubic place, doesn't it?"

"Yes, J J, it does. Let's go back to the snack bar and see what they have," said the Colonel.

"Sounds good, I would like a little something to munch on. Popcorn! That's what I smelled at the snack place," said J J.

The three men started down the hall towards the snack bar.

"There's the sign for the restroom. I think I'll use this one, instead of the one on the airplane," said J J, as he walked towards the rest room's door.

"All right, J J. We'll wait here," said the Colonel, as J J walked away leaving him and Sam, standing together in the hall.

"Sam, It's truly amazing. It's only the middle of J J's first night, of his first day back. And look at all the new things, he has seen."

"What's wrong, J J?" asked the Colonel, seeing him back so quick and the expression on his face.

"That door has a picture of a man and woman on it. What's that mean, it's for both men and women?"

"That's right."

"Believe it," said J J shaking his head as he turned and headed back towards the restroom.

The Colonel and Sam, standing there with broad smiles on their faces, as they watched J J walking back towards the restroom still shaking his head in disbelief.

"It sure is Colonel. Sir, I want to thank you for letting me come along, to be there, when my gramma sees grampa, to be able to see their faces. I'm so thankful, I didn't have to stay there on the island. Standing there watching you fly off with him! That would have been unbelievable! I don't even want to think about it. There's Grampa now. Did you notice, he hasn't been wearing his gloves or sunglasses, since we left the plane?" whispered Sam.

"Wow! You should see what someone wrote on the walls in there. Let me take that back. Nobody should see what's written on the walls in there. It's disgusting! And women and children have to use it too," said J J with a downhearted look on his face.

"Sorry J J, we have some real scum balls, in this assemblage we call mankind."

"Robby, whoever wrote that stuff on those walls, is one sick individual. If he were here right now, I'd give him all the attention he deserves. Knots all over his head. Right now, a paint brush and a can of paint, is what those walls desperately need. Sam told me, I may not like everything I see. Boy, did he hit the nail on the head. Maybe I should have used my imagination after all and used the head on the airplane."

"Right. I'm really sorry you had to see that, J J. And on your very first day back."

"Come on let's go get some of that popcorn I smelled."

The three men started towards the snack bar. As they walked up to the snack bar, they saw that Pete had joined Al and Bill, and all three of them were sitting at a table together. They had already received their food and seemed to be enjoying it, beings they waved, with their mouths apparently full of food. The three waved back as they walked through the snack bar, on their way to the counter. Sam pointed up at the menu on the wall behind the counter. The three of them stopped and stood a moment, as they looked at the menu on the wall.

"Believe me, would you look at those prices!" whispered J J to the others.

"Grampa, these prices aren't bad at all. They're way lower then the prices in Seattle."

"Don't worry about the prices, J J. You know, that Sam and I, have two hundred and fifty dollars between us. I doubt the three of us could spend that much money on food in less than an hour, in a place like this. A fancy place, say like in Anchorage or Seattle, it would be no problem to spend that much and a whole lot more in an hour," said the Colonel.

"What would you like, Grampa?" asked Sam, again pointing at the menu on the back wall.

"I'll have a French dip sandwich. I don't know what it is, but I'll have one anyway and some French fries. I think, I'll go ahead and have a Coke too."

"Ah, you have an imagination after all," laughed the Colonel.

"Boy, at this rate, Grampa. You'll have to start watching your cholesterol before we get to Seattle," snickered Sam.

"My what?"

"Your cholesterol."

"What's that, Sam?"

Sam stood there a moment, thinking. "You know, Grampa, come to think of it. I haven't any idea what cholesterol is. Colonel?"

"I do. I hear about it a lot, from my doctor and my wife. I'm suppose to watch my cholesterol, all the time. The numbers that came back from my last physical were, let's say a little high. Let's go ahead and order. I'll try to explain cholesterol to you two on the plane, J J."

"Can I order for us, guy's?"

"Sure, go ahead, order J J."

The Colonel and Sam, told J J what they wanted. J J stood there a moment and then cleared his throat. Looking right at the Asian man.

"I would like a French dip and fries with a Coke-a-Cola. The Colonel here, wants a hot turkey sandwich and black coffee. My . . . buddy wants a cheeseburger and fries with a Coke-a-Cola."

Robby and Sam, stood there in shock, as they stared at J J, with their mouth's hung open in disbelief. They slowly turned and looked at each other, then turning back to J J, confidently standing there with a big smile on his face, still looking at the Asian man standing behind the counter, who stood there staring back at him. Some time past as the four men stood there, nobody saying anything.

"J J, where did you? No! How did you do that? How do you know? That was Japanese, wasn't it?"

"That's what it was suppose to be, Robby. But he acts like he doesn't understand me," said J J, as he turned to Robby and Sam, still standing there staring at him.

"How did you learn Japanese? No wait. Let's go ahead give him our order and you can tell us while we're on the plane." The three men placed their orders. "I'll take care of this Sam. You guys can go to the table."

"Yes, Sir."

The Colonel pulled out some money and paid for their food.

"I bring food to table when ready. Ok?" said the person behind the counter.

The Colonel nodded, then turned and joined J J and Sam. The two had only moved a short way, as they stood talking about J J's revelation of being able to speak Japanese. "He'll bring our food to the table. Let's go sit with the others." The three men walked over to a table near the other three men. "Here let's move this table here, like this," said the Colonel, as he moved the table to where and how he wanted it. "There now we can visit with you guys." Not mentioning J J's surprising language ability. They sat down with the others, so all six of them could visit. They talked about the weather and other things and in no time, the man brought their food to the table. He put what each man ordered, right down in front of the person that ordered that meal including their drinks.

"You call if me needed, ok?" asked the Asian man, as he bowed respectively several times, as he backed away.

"Ok," said J J, to the polite man. The six men seemed to enjoy their conversation and meal together.

"I best go and check the plane," said Al, as he looked down at his watch. "You guys take your time eating. We're still ahead of schedule and besides, the plane can't leave without me. At least I don't think it can, I'm it's pilot. I've enjoyed the company, so I won't leave without you. I'll see you guys onboard." With that, Al got up from the table and left the others.

The others spent the next few minutes, finishing their meal. "That was surprisingly quite good," said the Colonel, as he finished the last of his meal.

"Yes, so was mine," said Bill.

The others nodded their heads, that they agreed.

"We should join Al. They should be done with the refueling by now. I want to say, it's been a real pleasure having you three onboard this flight. I might be a bit out of line, Colonel, when I say it's been great being with a full bird Colonel and not feel the spurs of those Eagles on your shoulders, Colonel," said Bill.

"That maybe a bit too far, Lieutenant," said the Colonel, in a stern voice.

"Yes, Sir!"

"Just kidding, Lieutenant."

"Thank you, Sir," said Bill, obviously a bit relieved.

The five men got up from the table. The Colonel reached into his pocket and pulled out some money. He counted out some and laid a generous tip on the table. He then turned and walked from the table, towards the back.

The others seeing the generosity of the Colonel's tip, decided to leave a healthy tip of their own.

"Thank you for a meal and a job well done," said the Colonel.

"Thank you, Colonel, Sir, thank you. You come see next time, soon," said the man, as he bowed his head repeatedly.

J J walked up and stood next to the Colonel.

"Thank you. Your meals were superb," said J J speaking in Japanese, to the man behind the counter.

"J J, he's not Japanese," whispered the Colonel.

J J stood there looking at the Colonel.

"He isn't. What is he, Robby?" whispered J J.

"I don't know, J J, ask him."

He stood there thinking. He then turned and looked at the man standing there smiling at him. "May I ask you a question?" asked J J, of the man standing there still smiling at him.

"Yes, Private. You ask."

"What nationality are you?"

"I be, Chinese, Private."

"I'm sorry, I thought you were Japanese."

"I hear you talk Japanese, Private. It ok, Private."

"We'll take a large bag of that fresh popcorn," said the Colonel, as he pointed at the popcorn machine. He then turned and winked at J J.

"Yes, Colonel."

"You forgot, didn't you?"

"Thank you, Robby. It sure smells good doesn't it?" J J and the Colonel stood waiting for their popcorn, as Sam walked up to them.

"What's up?"

"We remembered the popcorn."

"One dollar."

The Colonel paid and thanked the man. He then turned and handed the bag of popcorn to J J and started walking out of the snack bar, J J and Sam followed him out into the hall, where Bill and Pete stood waiting.

"I'm going to use the restroom," said the Colonel.

"J J and I, will wait here, Sir."

"Colonel, Pete and I, will head back to the plane, Sir." With that the two men turned and started down the hall towards the exit.

J J and Sam stood waiting for the Colonel.

"The tip Robby left for that man, was more than I would have made in a day, at a real good job! Sam, how am I going to make enough money to even live? How has my Jera Marie made enough, all these years?"

"I don't know, Grampa. You'll have to ask her, when you see her tomorrow," said Sam, as he quickly tried to change the subject, seeing the concern in his grandfather's eyes and hearing it in his voice.

"Tomorrow?"

"I don't know, Grampa. Maybe even late this afternoon."

"This afternoon? You mean today, this afternoon?"

"Or. Maybe even yesterday."

"Al's right. You can be a smart ass," said J J, grabbing his grandson and holding him, in a Half Nelson.

"What's going on here? Are you boys fighting again?" asked the Colonel, as he stood there in the hallway with his hands on his hips, talking like a mother scolding her two young boys.

"No, Ma'am," said J J, as he released his grandson and immediately came to attention.

"You'd think, I could leave you two in a public place, long enough to use the bathroom!"

"We were just wrestling. We weren't fighting!" said Sam, speaking like a faultless small boy, wrongfully accused, innocently standing there, also at attention. Both men going along with the Colonel's little joke.

"Well, I should hope not."

The three men laughed and clowned around, at what the Colonel said and the way he said it. They started down the hall towards the exit of the building.

"Al, thinks I'm a smart ass?"

"J J how long is the next leg of our flight? The one from here to Japan?" J J stopped walking. He then turned and stared at the Colonel.

"What is it, J J?"

"I don't know, Robby! When I heard you say, what you just said, Japan! It still sent chills up and down my spine. I'm sorry, Robby, I know you explained to me, that they're our allies now. I still felt chills," said J J, as he stood there a moment.

"Why does Al think I'm a smart ass?" asked Sam quietly, not wanting to interrupt.

"Robby, the pilot told me three and a half hours, for the next part of our trip, from here to Japan," said J J, as the three again started walking, talking as they walked towards the exit of the building. The Marine, apparently seeing the three men approaching through the glass in the door, reached out and grabbed the door, pulling the door to him, opening it for the three men to leave the building. He held the door in one hand and saluted the three men, with the other. The three men returned the salute one by one, as they exited the building.

"Having a Colonel around sure helps," said J J, as they walked along the covered walkway towards their airplane. Within a few minutes they were where they could see their plane. They could also hear that the airplane's engines were already running.

At the stairs leading up to the airplane's door, stood a crew person. The person was waiting for the three to board the plane. The three men quickly climbed the stairs, one right after the other. Once they were inside the airplane, the person at the foot of the stairs, rolled them away from the plane. Pete then closed and locked the plane's door.

"Colonel, if I could get you three to take your seats and buckle up. The pilot said, "if we could leave right away, we could save sixteen minutes or more, by leaving early," said Pete, as he checked to see that the door to the plane was definitely locked. He then headed towards the front of the plane to his own seat.

The Colonel, J J and Sam quickly took their seats and buckled their seat belts. As they did, they could feel they were already moving. The plane moved to the end of the runway and stopped. In no time, it started moving again, they were now moving faster and faster down the runway. In just a short time, they no longer felt the vibration of the plane's tires running on the hard surface of the runway. The airplane was once again airborne.

"Boy, I'm sure glad I used the restroom, before we left."

The three men sat there talking, as the airplane continued to climb to it's cruising altitude. The plane's engines slowed and the plane began to slowly level off.

"There's the green light, Colonel."

"J J, we'll be in Japanese airspace, in just a few minutes," said the Colonel.

J J nodded to the Colonel, that he understood. The three men remained in their seats with their belts fastened, talking and laughing, about the different things, J J had seen that day.

"Robby, those people in the restaurant, they weren't Japanese? He said he was Chinese. Were we in China?"

"No, we weren't in China, J J, we were in Taiwan. I think they were Taiwanese or maybe they were Chinese, the two are of the same race, but different people, J J." J J looked over at the Colonel and started to speak.

"Is there anything I can get for you guys?" asked Pete, as he walked up next to J J, who was sitting in the aisle seat.

"No thanks, Pete. We're doing just fine," said J J.

"Al just told me, by us taking advantage of being able to leave that few minutes early. We'll save almost twenty two minutes."

"That's great," said J J.

"If I can do anything for you? Let me know. If you should need more room to stretch out. You guys could sit in any of those empty seats," said Pete, as pointed to the empty seats, in front of the unoccupied workstations. "I will say, it's probably not a good idea, you touch anything on those consoles," said Pete, as he turned and headed for the front of the plane.

The Colonel had taken the window seat, saying something about trying to get some sleep. Sam sitting in the middle seat, leaving J J on the aisle.

"J J, where and how, did you possibly, learn Japanese?"

"Did I surprise you with that?"

"I would say I was somewhat surprised, weren't you Sam?"

"Totally, Colonel," said Sam, as the two men leaned forward and stared at J J, waiting for him to speak.

"This book was on The Promise. It was written by some Professor, somewhere in the US, before the war. I don't remember his name. The Promise must of had it on board, just in case they were ever boarded by the Japanese. That they could at least talk to them in their own language. Thank God, that didn't happen"

"Yes, thank God," said the Colonel.

"To this day, I still don't know, if I'm pronouncing some of the words correctly. But whoever compiled this book, made it possible for one person, to speak and possibly understand the Japanese language. That's if that person had lots of time, and that's something I had a tremendous amount of, was time!"

"It sounded mighty good to me, J J," said The Colonel, as he sat back in his seat.

J J and Sam continued talking. The time seemed to be passing enjoyably, as the two men talked. They hadn't noticed, the Colonel had indeed fallen asleep, while they had been talking.

"He's probably got the right idea, Grampa," said Sam, as he pointed to the Colonel, sleeping soundly. "Maybe you and I should try and get some sleep. Today is going to be a big day."

"It's going to be a great day, Sam," whispered J J, as not to wake the Colonel. "I may get to see my Jera Marie, today. Right now, I'm too excited to sleep."

"So am I, Grampa. So am I! Do you think we should move?"

"Move?"

"Maybe you and I should move back to those two seats," said Sam, as he pointed to the rear of the airplane, also speaking softly, as not to disturb the Colonel. "The ones there at the consoles, Grampa."

Looking towards the rear of the airplane, J J saw the two oversized chairs. The chairs were located in front of some sophisticated looking consoles. J J nodded to his grandson, indicating that he too thought it would be a good idea they move back to the large chairs, thinking perhaps their talking may be disturbing the Colonel's sleep. The two men removed their seat belts and slowly raised out of their seats and moved quietly, one after the other, out into the aisle, and moved towards the consoles, located near the rear of the airplane. Sam swiveled one of the large chairs, as to allow his grandfather to sit. J J still holding his bag of popcorn.

"Thank you Sam. You know? This reminds me of something right out of 'Buck Rogers," said J J, looking at the consoles, as he sat down in the chair his grandson held for him.

"Buck Rogers?"

"For that matter. This whole airplane is like something out of 'Buck Rogers!" said J J, as he turned looking towards the cockpit of this marvel in flight. He then turned back to his grandson, who was standing there looking down at him. Sam rotated the other large black chair, to face his grandfather's. He then sat down and the two men continued talking, as they shared J J's popcorn.

"J J, J J! We'll be landing in Japan, in just a few minutes," said the

Colonel, raising his voice slightly, as he excitedly shook J J's shoulder.

J J opened his eyes.

"What's wrong, J J?" asked the Colonel, seeing the strange look on his face, as he stared up at him.

J J looked up at the man staring down at him. He then slowly turned and looked around, gazing over at the man in the chair next to him. He then looked back up at the Colonel, as a big smile started to form on his face.

"Nothing's wrong, I guess I . . . I thought I was. Thank God I'm not! I'm not alone! I'm not dreaming. Robby, I'm really here with you and my grandson. He's really here and best of all, we're on our way to my Jera Marie." J J reached over and grabbed and shook his grandson's knee. "Sam the airplane is landing. We need to move back to the other seats and put on our seat belts."

"Grampa. I must have fallen asleep. Did I miss anything?"

"I don't know, Sam. I fell asleep too."

"We better move. The fasten your seat belt light is already on," said the Colonel, as he pointed to the red light. The Colonel then turned and walked up the aisle towards the other seats. The other two men got up out of their chairs and followed the Colonel. All three men sat down and quickly fastened their seat belts, just as the airplane started it's descent.

"How long do you think we'll be here in Japan, Robby?"

"I don't know, J J. At least as long as it takes us, either to get a new crew or for these fella's to get some sleep."

"How long will that take, Robby?" asked J J, some concern showing in his voice. "I don't want to sound impatient, but I've waited 50 years . . . Oh, I'm sorry, Robby. I know you'll going to get me there, as soon as you possibly can."

"That, you can count on J J. If we have to, we'll take a commercial flight. I doubt if there's any commercial flights from here though. We'll most likely have a better chance, if we wait until we get to Alaska. Unless by chance there's a flight departing from here. After all, the military has thousands of flights departing from somewhere everyday. Maybe we'll be lucky and there will be one flying from here to Seattle. If not here. There's bound to be one from Anchorage to Seattle."

"That's a great idea. But I don't have any money, Colonel."

"That's ok, Sam. That's what plastic is for."

"I'm nineteen. I only have the one card, and it has a low limit."

"Mine's not," said the Colonel confidently, as he raised and lowered his eye brows, reaching down and unfastening his seat belt, he then reached back to retrieve the wallet from his back pocket. "Let me take that back. They shouldn't be. Unless Ruth went to New York, shopping or something. Oh well, I have more then one card. I don't think she'd max them all out," chuckled the Colonel, as he pulled out his wallet and held it in his hand. He unfolded the billfold and a dozen or more of the colorful plastic cards became visible. "One of these is bound to have some cash available on it," said the Colonel, as he fumbled through the many credit cards.

"Colonel, it would cost a fortune, for three of us to fly, from Japan to Seattle."

"That it would, Sam. It would probably cost four or five thousand."

"You mean to tell me, it would cost that much, just for the three of us to fly to Seattle? That's almost twice what my house and the land it sits on, cost!"

"At least that much, J J. If the truth be known, it would probably cost that much for a military flight. The difference is, we wouldn't have to pay," said the Colonel.

J J was sitting in the middle seat, looking from the Colonel over to his grandson. The two men setting in the adjoining seats, the Colonel was in the window seat and Sam in the aisle seat.

"Colonel, wouldn't it most likely cost that much, just for the fuel?"

"You're probably right, Sam, but if the plane's going that way anyway, it wouldn't cost anymore for us to ride along."

"I say we wait for a military flight. I just hope it doesn't take too long," said J J.

The three men continued talking, as the airplane descended on it's approach. Within minutes, the plane was on the runway. Once on the ground, the airplane's speed seem to increase, as it roared down the rough runway, bouncing as it did. The sensation of the speed began to pass as the airplane slowed. The plane slowly turning one-way and then the other, it then came to a complete stop.

"J J, are you up to this?" asked the Colonel.

J J looked over at his new friend. "Robby, I've come to Japan as a visitor. Not as a warrior. Let's go visit," said J J, as he unfastened his seat belt and stood. J J then looked down at his grandson and then over at the Colonel. The two still in their seats, looking up at him.

"Come on, let's go."

"Looks as though he's ready, Colonel."

"That it does, Sam."

"Come on, Sam," said J J, as he bent and grabbed his grandson's arm. "Come on, Robby," said J J, as he moved towards the aisle, still tugging on his grandson's arm, pulling him into the aisle with him. The Colonel stood and moved behind Sam and J J, until all three men were standing in the aisle. The crew then came from the front of the airplane and stood behind them.

"Colonel, we have to log some rest time. After that we'll be ready to resume our flight to Anchorage."

"How long will that be, Lieutenant?"

"Eight hours minimum, Colonel."

"Is there any chance of finding another crew or another flight to Anchorage, Lieutenant?"

"Another flight? I wouldn't know about that, Sir. You would have to check with the OD, about another flight. For this flight, we're it, until she gets to Anchorage anyway. At that point Sir, there is to be a civilian crew, to take her on from there to the Boeing plant in Seattle, Colonel."

"Thank you, Lieutenant. We may still be here when you have the hours of rest time you need. If not, thank you. Oh, by the way. I would take it as a personal favor, if you three not say anything to anyone about us, for at least a week."

The three men turned and looked at each other, then back at the Colonel. "Yes, Sir, Colonel." At that same time, the six of them heard something outside the airplane. Pete turned and moved towards the door. He unlocked and opened the plane's outside door. As the door opened it revealed a set of stairs a flight crewman had put into place, for them to exit the airplane. Opening the door, also let in a burst of fresh cool air and unveiled what a bright sunny day it was becoming outside the confines of the windowless airplane. The five others moved towards the opened door.

"What a beautiful day."

"Yes it is, J J. Let's go see the OD. We'll just leave our gear onboard for now, if we find another flight we'll have our gear picked up. If not, Lieutenant, we'll be here waiting for your return. Either way, thank you," said the Colonel.

The Colonel moved into the open doorway and then down the stairs, J J and Sam followed. The other three men stayed onboard the airplane.

Once on the tarmac, J J turned and waved towards the airplane and it's crew. Sam and the Colonel had stopped walking and stood waiting, as J J waved. The three men on the plane, had moved out of the airplane's open doorway and missed seeing J J waving to them. He turned and walked quickly to join up with his grandson and the Colonel. The three men started walking, talking as they did about the next leg of their flight. They talked about some of the many different possibilities of that flight.

"Robby, now that we've been delayed, it means I won't be getting home to Seattle, before I left my island?"

"It looks that way, J J. I'm so sorry, I shouldn't have told you that, then you would't be disappointed.

"Robby, how could I possibly be disappointed? You're doing everything you can."

"J J, you'd best put on your gloves and sunglasses," said the Colonel.

The three men continued talking, as J J put the sunglasses on and retrieved the gloves from his back pocket. Just as J J pulled on his gloves, a man pulled up in a small electric cart.

"Sir, can I give you three a ride off the flight line?" asked the man driving the cart, the cart still slowly rolling alongside the three men, as they walked.

"Yes, airman, you sure can," answered the Colonel. With that said the cart came to a stop. "You can also take us to the OD's office," said the Colonel, as he climbed aboard. J J and Sam also jumping onboard the cart. Just as they did, the airman put his foot down on the cart's foot pedal and off down the flight line they zoomed, as the cart hummed up to speed.

"Colonel, the OD's office is coming up here on the right," said the airman, in a loud enough voice as to be heard, over the whine of the cart.

"Airman, what island of Japan, is this?"

"Sir, this is Hokkaido. Hokkaido is Japans northernmost and second largest island, Sir."

The Colonel turned and looked at J J, as the cart slowed and then came to a stop. "What's wrong, Private?" asked the Colonel, seeing J J shaking, as he sat on the rear part of the cart.

"I'm all right, Colonel. It's just much cooler here then I'm used to, Sir," said J J, as he sat there shivering.

"Come on, we'll get you inside," said the Colonel, as he stepped out of the cart and stood waiting on the sidewalk.

"Colonel, the OD's office is through those doors, Sir," said the airman, as he pointed towards the building, looking first at the Colonel and then towards the two men, sitting on the back of his cart.

LIZY

Sam and J J jumped out of the cart and joined the Colonel on the sidewalk. No sooner had they done so, then the cart zoomed away. The three men turned and walked up the sidewalk through the doorway and into the building. Once inside, they saw the door that lead to the OD's office. The Colonel opened the door and entered the office, with J J and Sam right behind. Sitting at a desk, was a young Lieutenant. The Lieutenant looked up. Seeing a Colonel, she jumped to her feet and saluted. "Colonel, what can I do for you, Sir?" asked the Lieutenant, as she stood there at attention.

"At ease, Lieutenant," said the Colonel, as he returned the salute. He then turned and grinned at J J and Sam, as he raised and lowered his eye brows. He seemed very delighted at finding a young Lieutenant in command. "Lieutenant, I'm Colonel Robert Robinson. Lieutenant, I would like you to tell me if there are any flights from here to the mainland, in the next few hours?"

"Sir, I'll check for you, Sir." The Lieutenant sat down and turned to a computer that sat on an adjoining desk, right angles to hers. Pushing a few keys, the Lieutenant then sat staring at the computer screen. "Sir, at this time, the only flight I see from here, is a research plane of some kind. It's returning to Seattle by way of Anchorage. The plane is due to land, in just a few minutes, Sir. It's also scheduled for a ten hour layover, before flying onto Anchorage. I'm not sure why the layover or if there would be room for you, anyway, Sir."

"There's room, Lieutenant."

"Sir?" asked the Lieutenant, as she looked up at the Colonel and then over at the other two men.

"That's the plane we just flew in on, it landed about fifteen minutes ago, Lieutenant. I was hoping to avoid the ten hour delay, on my flight to Seattle. Do you see anything else, Lieutenant?"

"Sir, everything else is going south, Sir. Some of those flights may go east from there, but that information isn't here. There isn't anything else on the screen, Sir," said the young officer, as she looked up at the Colonel. "There may be a non scheduled flight, Colonel. Is there a number where I could reach you, if one comes in? I could call you if something became available, Sir."

"How close is the nearest International Airport, Lieutenant?"

"Colonel, you can't. . . ." Interrupted J J. "I'm sorry, I didn't mean to interrupt, Colonel."

"Colonel, it might take one and a half hours or more, to reach the airport from here, Sir. First you'd have to take a cab or walk, from here to the train depot. From there you would take the train and then a shuttle or cab, from the train depot to the airport," said the Lieutenant, first looking at J J and then towards the Colonel.

"That's out!" said the Colonel in a disgusted tone, as he turned from the Lieutenant. "We might as well wait the ten hours!" said the Colonel shrugging his shoulders, as he stood looking at J J and Sam.

"Sir, I might be able to get a car or maybe even a chopper, to fly you from here to the airport, Sir." The Colonel still looking at J J and Sam, started to smile again, as he raised and lowered his eyebrows, seemingly pleased with the Lieutenant's idea. "I would have to clear it with Major Shoemaker, Colonel."

Hearing that, the Colonel's smile instantly changed to one of a frown. Slowly the Colonel turned to the Lieutenant. "Thank you, Lieutenant. Why don't you wait on that."

"Yes, Sir."

"It would be hard for the three of us to get a commercial flight, all-together on stand-by anyway," said the Colonel, as he looked over his shoulder, towards the two men.

"Colonel, I should inform the Major of your arrival, Sir."

"That won't be necessary, Lieutenant."

"Sir. . . ?"

"Let's not disturb the Major right now, Lieutenant. Maybe the privates and I, will just walk on into town and look around a bit, until later this morning. Until then, let's not interfere with the Major's beauty sleep, ok, Lieutenant?"

"Yes, Sir," smiled the Lieutenant. All three men smiled back, infected by the Lieutenant's delightful smile. "Colonel, I'm off duty in fifteen minutes, Sir. I could give you three a ride into town and show you some of the sights."

The Colonel turned to see Sam smiling from ear to ear, he then saw J J standing there in his white gloves and sunglasses, with a broad smile, the white of his teeth, enhanced by his dark tanned face. "My aide here, seems quite pleased with your generous offer, Lieutenant."

"If we do much driving around, I would need some help with gas money, Colonel. Gas is so expensive here."

"How much does gasoline cost per gallon here, Lieutenant?"

"The equivalent to three sixty five a gallon, Private."

"I can see why you might need some help, Lieutenant," said J J, as he shook his head in disbelief.

"Thank you, Lieutenant. I appreciate your offer. If I could get you to tell your counterpart to watch for a flight to the mainland for me and we could just call this number and check?"

"I'll just have Mike page me, if a flight becomes available, Colonel. Mike and I traded shifts, I generally work day shift, and he works graveyard. But his son had a Karate tournament last night, so he and I traded so he could be there. With the Major's permission, Sir. This way I get three days off for the Fourth of July," smiled the Lieutenant, as she raised and lowered her eyebrows.

All three men quietly snickering at the same time. Seeing the young Lieutenant's eye movement.

"What, Sir?"

"Nothing, Lieutenant," smiled the Colonel.

"I don't know about you, but if this tour is going to be very long, I'm going to need some breakfast," said the Lieutenant, still smiling with her infectious smile.

"Breakfast is on me, Lieutenant."

"I hope to shout, Colonel. I don't have enough money for me, to have breakfast in town, let alone, three hungry Marines."

"Here's Lieutenant Houseman now, Colonel." Just then another Lieutenant entered the office. Seeing the Colonel, he quickly came to attention and saluted the Colonel.

"At ease, Lieutenant," said the Colonel, as he returned the salute.

"This is Colonel Robinson. The Colonel wants to surprise the Major, later this morning. He would appreciate our help on this matter.

"That shouldn't be any problem. The Major was hoping for an uneventful weekend. We won't bother him until you tell us to inform him of your presence, Colonel."

"Thank you, Lieutenant. We're just here on a layover, on our way to Seattle. There's no need to inconvenience the Major this early on the Fourth of July weekend, Lieutenant."

"Mike, I'm going."

"Lieutenant, we'll step out into the hall, while you two talk." Sam turned and opened the door. The Colonel and J J, stepped through the door and Sam followed, closing the door as he left the OD's office.

"I know. Believe it. That young attractive Colored girl, I mean Negro, no, African-American, that's it! She's the officer on duty?"

"That she is, J J," said the Colonel, as the three men moved to the far side of the hall.

"Her uniform sure shows, what a fine figure she has. 'Hubba Hubba Ding Ding." The Colonel and Sam stopped and stood looking at J J, smiling back at them. "What? Guy's, I'm old. I'm not dead, you know," said J J, as he held out hands palms up in a questioning manner. 'Why were they so surprised?

"I agree, Grampa, what a body."

"Ok guy's, we don't need a sexual harassment charge."

"A sexual charge! For what? Just because we said she has a well built body?"

"That's right."

"Robby, I would have thought that, to be a compliment."

"J J, we have to be very careful how we compliment the opposite sex nowadays. Especially, in the work place. Believe it."

Just then the three of them noticed, the door to the OD's office, was open. Within a few seconds, the young Lieutenant appeared in the doorway, smiling, as she headed their way. "Colonel, Mike has my pager number and he'll call if anything becomes available," said the Lieutenant, as she walked up to the three men.

"Thank you, Lieutenant. Lieutenant, what do you say we put aside our military formalities. Inasmuch as the three of us will be your companions for the next few hours. Lieutenant my name is Robert, but call me Robby. This is J J and Sam, my aide," said the Colonel, as he held out one hand as he introduced the others.

"That's great with me, Robby. Hi J J, hi Sam, mine's Lizy May Washington," said the Lieutenant smiling, as she shook hands, first with the Colonel, then J J and then Sam.

"We're with you, Lizy," said the Colonel, as he used his hand and arm, in a leading manner, towards the exit of the building.

The three men followed, as the young Lieutenant headed in the opposite direction, to that of the door they had entered the building and the Colonel had just assumed they would be exiting.

"Come on, I'll show you this beautiful picturesque town, on the way we'll stop and have that breakfast, you promised me, Robby," said Lizy, elbowing the Colonel in the ribs, as they walked.

"I'm starved. It must be because I worked all night. Don't get the wrong idea guy's, I work on day shift too, I just meant. Oh who cares what I meant?"

"I know I don't, Lizy," said Robby rubbing his side, as the four of them walked through the building.

"You would, if I was under your command, Robby."

"I'm sure you're right, Lizy."

They exited the building and entered a parking lot, located to the rear of the building. J J staring at each car and at all the different kinds of cars that he noticed, were all right hand drive, as they walked through the parking lot.

"This is my little beater," said Lizy, as she pointed to a not so shiny but clean and straight, little car. "It doesn't look like much, but it keeps on running. You know like the bunny, on TV. I'm going to paint it pink someday," laughed Lizy.

The three men and Lizy, walked around the small car, two on each side. Sam and Lizy on the drivers side, which in Japan is on the right side, J J and Robby, on the passenger side. "It's open," said Lizy, as she opened the drivers door. The others opened the corresponding three doors of the little faded blue four door and climbed in. The back seat was small, you might say it was a tight fit for J J and Sam. Lizy sat looking into her open purse. After a moment or so, she came up with her keys in hand. "Don't worry, guy's. I found them," she said dangling her keys. She put the key in the ignition. As she turned the key the car's starter cranked a few times and the little car came to life. Just as the car started, this loud music came from all corners of the small car. Lizy quickly reached to turn the music down, to something not so ear splitting. "Sorry, Colonel, I wasn't expecting guests. Is that better?"

"Much! Like you said Lizy, we're your guests. But thank you, for turning it down."

"Robby, I love country and western music. Especially Garth Brooks, he's the greatest."

"I like his music, myself, just not quite so loud," smiled Robby.

"Garth's awesome," blurted Sam, from his cramped seat behind Lizy. J J looked over at his exuberant grandson, as Lizy looked up and into her rearview mirror at Sam and J J.

"Right on Sam. Great minds think alike," said Lizy, as she put the car in reverse and quickly backed out of it's parking place. She then put the car in drive and they were off towards town.

"J J, I understand the sunglasses but why the gloves?" asked Lizy, still looking in the mirror at J J.

"The Private has. . . . Let's say, he has eczema," said Robby trying not to outright lie to their new companion.

"Sounds like a good reason to me, Robby."

"Ya, it does, doesn't it," smiled the Colonel, seemingly quite pleased with himself, with the answer to her question about J J's gloves.

"Here's where I thought we'd eat breakfast," said Lizy, as they drove into the parking lot of a restaurant. "This is one of the only places in town, that serves American style bacon and egg type breakfasts. I didn't think you guys were ready for sushi, at this time of day. Was I wrong?"

"No!" answered Robby and Sam, at the same time.

"What about you? Are you ready, J J?" asked Lizy, seeing J J didn't answer the first question.

"I don't know, Lizy. Sushi this early."

"I think we'll go for the American style breakfast, Lizy."

"Thank you, Colonel. I'm not up to raw fish this early in the morning, myself," said Lizy, as she drove the car into a parking place and stopped. She turned off the ignition, pulled the key out of the ignition, and dropped it into her purse. "I'm ready, let's go eat," said Lizy, as she opened the drivers door and sat looking at the others. The other three doors opened, and all four of them got out of the car and closed the doors. They then headed for the entrance to the restaurant. The four of them talking as they walked, Sam with Lizy and Robby with J J. Sam quickly moved ahead of the others to get the door. He opened the door and held it for the others to enter the restaurant. Once the three had entered, he entered closing the door behind.

"Lieutenant, I'm so glad to see you this beautiful morning," said the Japanese man, as he bowed to Lizy. "May I seat you and the gentlemen in a booth or at a table?" asked the waiter, as he bowed to the three men.

"Either will be just fine, thank you."

The man lead the four to a table that sat in front of a large window. This window provided them a beautiful view of the snow capped mountains in the distance.

"Look, it's snow!" said J J, as he stood looking out the window.

"It's a pretty view isn't it J J," said Lizy, as the waiter pulled a chair from the table for her to sit.

Sam walked up next to his grandfather.

"Isn't it beautiful, Sam?"

"It sure is, Grampa," whispered Sam, as he put his hand over on his grandfather's shoulder, as they stood side by side looking out the large window.

The waiter quickly grabbed another chair and pulled it from the table for the Colonel. "I will be back shortly to take your orders, Lieutenant," said the waiter. The waiter turned and left the table with J J and Sam, still standing at the window.

Lizy and Robby sat talking, as J J and Sam walked up and each took a seat, joining them at the table. As Robby, Sam and Lizy, sat talking with each other, Lizy noticed that J J was sitting there staring intently, at everything and everyone, inside and outside the restaurant, as the four of them sat there at the table.

"Let's see what they have here for breakfast," said Robby, as he picked up a menu, that was laying on the table in front of him, as did the others.

J J sat holding his menu at arms length, as to enable him to read it. To his suprise the menu was written in both English and Japanese. The four of them sat reading their menus. "Colonel, I'm really not that hungry, I just need something to drink. I know, I'll have some toast and jam, with a big tall ice cold glass of milk," beamed J J.

"When the waiter comes back to get our orders J J, you can try your Japanese."

"Thank you, Robby, that's a good idea. Let me have your orders when you're ready." The three of them told J J what they wanted for breakfast and then sat and talked.

"J J, you speak Japanese?"

"I'm not sure, Lizy. I think I do. We'll find out soon enough. Here comes the waiter."

"Are you ready to order?" asked the Japanese waiter. All four sat there, as J J cleared his throat and started to speak. J J spoke to the man standing there with pad in hand, in what he thought to be the man's own language. "You speak Japanses," smiled the waiter. The waiter and J J talked, as the others sat there and listen to the two of them carrying on a conversation in Japanese. The waiter writing on his pad now and again, as the two men continued talking. The waiter then smiled and bowed to the others, as he backed from their table, he then turned and walked away.

"He seemed to understand you," said Sam, his voice showing his excitement for his grandfather's ability not only to speak Japanese but also, understand it.

"Let's wait and see what we get for our breakfast," smiled J J.

"J J, I was noticing what a rubber neck you have. You seem so intense, in the way you look at everything and everybody. It's like you're afraid you might miss something."

"Lizy, I can honestly say, the only thing I know I am truly afraid of, is being alone."

A long silence came over them, as they sat there thinking about what J J had said. "Wow, that's heavy," said Lizy, breaking the spell of silence.

"Lizy, how long have you been stationed here in Japan?" asked Robby, as he quickly tried to change the subject.

"This is my second tour of duty, in northern Japan. I love it here. The people here are so gracious to us Americans, even us Black female ones. I've been here almost three years. Like I said, I love it," smiled Lizy.

"I think I've been here, five different times, but I've never been this far north," said the Colonel.

"This is my first time here," said Sam.

"Mine too. I've wanted to come to Japan, for some time now. The Colonel, gave me this opportunity and I took it," smiled J J.

Just then the waiter came carrying a large tray. "It looks as though you did all right ordering, J J," said the Colonel, as the waiter sat the tray down near their table, on a stand he carried under his arm.

"Colonel, the private here, did a good job ordering. I didn't understand every word, but I knew what he meant by what's on our menu," said the waiter, as he sat J J's order of milk, toast and an assortment of several different kinds of jams, down in front of him. "He just needs a little more practice speaking our language. I'm somewhat sure with more practice, he will be successful in communicating with us, in our own language, Colonel," smiled the waiter, as he continued putting each person's order in front of them. "If I'm needed you call, Colonel, Lieutenant," smiled the waiter, as he backed from their table, bowing as he did.

"J J, where did you learn Japanese?"

J J sat there thinking about Lizy's question. Not wanting to lie to anyone, except Jim the nosy reporter. Especially, to this young girl, sitting there smiling at him with those big beautiful dark eyes. "Lizy, you might say, I took a home study course," said J J, as he spread some blackberry jam on his toast and then took a bite.

"That's incredible. You were able to learn Japanese, from a home study course. It's amazing to me what the home computer has done for us in the last few years. For a person to be able to study and learn something, as complicated as the Japanese language, in the privacy of their own home. That's truly amazing to me." J J just sat there with a bite of toast and jam in his mouth, it hanging open slightly, him staring at Lizy nodding his head, showing her he was in complete agreement.

"It is, I agree," said Robby, also nodding. "I wish I could take some time and learn more about these computers. Like the web and the internet, the amount of all that useful information available at your fingertips, is quite frankly mindboggling."

"This milk is delicious," said J J, as he sat smiling completely unaware of the 'Everybody Needs Milk' mustache, on his upper lip.

Lizy sat staring at J J, as she did her expression change, to one of a more serious nature. "Colonel, who is, J J? I know I'm just a lowly Lieutenant, but give me some credit. A private in the Marines, at his age! I don't think so. I haven't any idea how old he is, but with his obvious intelligence and age, he should be at least a Colonel or maybe even a General," said Lizy, as she turned and looked right into the Colonel's eyes, her jaw set and a determined look in her's, she sat waiting for an answer.

A silence befell the four, as they sat together at the table.

"A General. Yes, I can see myself as a General," smiled J J, as he sat proudly in his seat, the expansion of his chest somewhat exaggerated.

"You can, can you, Private?" said the Colonel, as he raised one eye brow and then turned from Lizy, to staring at J J.

"Can you see me as a General, Sam?"

"Yes, I can," beamed Sam.

The three of them trying to avoid answering the Lieutenant's question. "Can you tell me, or is it some kind of a military secret?"

"Lieutenant, it's a secret all right, it's just not a military one," smiled the Colonel, as he turned back looking her right in the eye.

"Tell me, Robby. I can keep a secret, military or otherwise," said Lizy, as she moved her chair up closer, putting her elbows on the table and cradling her chin in both hands, as she sat staring at the Colonel, waiting for him to tell her the secret. He looked from this girl's determined dark eyes staring at him, towards J J.

"Robby, She said she can keep a secret," said J J, as he shrugged his shoulders. "I think we can trust her, Robby," smiled J J.

"I think so too, Colonel."

"Well, it's your secret, J J," said Robby, as he turned back to looking at Lizy.

"Lizy, what I'm going to tell you, I would appreciate you not repeating, even to the Major for a few days," said the Colonel, as he sat staring at the dark eyed girl. "After that, you can tell whoever you want."

"Deal! What's the secret?" asked Lizy, as her eyes moved from Robby, to J J and Sam, then back to Robby.

"Private J. S. Johnson here, is a World War II veteran, on his way home," said Robby, as he pointed at J J.

Lizy turned and sat staring at J J. He smiled and nodded his head. "That's the secret! A Colonel is escorting a retired private home, with eczema on his hands. What kind of secret is that?" said Lizy, her voice showing some anxiety. "Why not tell the Major, if that's all it is. . . . No, there's more to it than that. His hands, they're radiation burns, aren't they?"

"No, they're not. But you're right Lizy, there's more." The three sat patiently waiting for Robby to continue, as J J slowly removed the gloves, showing no sign of burns or eczema. "Why don't we eat our breakfast, before it gets cold. While we eat, I'll tell Lizy, the true story of the white gloves," said Robby, a bit embarrassed about telling her the eczema hand story.

Over the next twenty minutes or so, Robby told Lizy the story, as they sat eating their breakfast. Lizy at times not eating, as she sat there intensely listening to the inconceivable story. "That's incredible! No wonder you want to keep this quiet. It's probably the biggest goodwill military story, since the War. Colonel, you know this is going to become a media circus. I understand the gloves and the sunglasses, now. I want to help you keep this quiet, until J J gets home to his Jera Marie. The fewer people that know, the easier it's going to be to keep quiet."

"Right now, except for the seventy plus people on J J's island, there's only five people who know, and you're one of them, Lizy." Robby told Lizy, just how Sam and the others had found J J on the island. He had yet to tell her, Sam was also J J's grandson. "Lieutenant, there's more."

"There's more!" said Lizy, as she sat looking at the Colonel.

"I'll tell you more in the car, where there aren't so many people." While the four had been talking and eating their breakfast, people had come into the restaurant and sat at some of the adjacent tables, leaving them a great deal less privacy.

"I'm ready, I've had plenty," said Lizy, as she quickly stood up pushing her chair into the table, obviously anxious to hear more of the inconceivable story. The other three were just standing, as the waiter walked up.

"Thank you, Lieutenant, for coming and bringing the Colonel and the two privates, to our restaurant. You keep practicing your Japanese, Private, next time you'll do much better," said the waiter, as he bowed first to Lizy, then the Colonel, J J and then Sam, as he turned and walked away. The Colonel leaving the money for their breakfast and a tip.

"Where are we headed, Lieutenant?" asked the Colonel, as the four of them walked through the restaurant.

"First, I thought I'd take you to the town's Buddhist Temple, it's beautiful. From there, we can go to this fantastic market place I found, I think it has something for everyone."

Sam moved ahead and opened the door and held it for the others. As Sam held the door for the others to exit the restaurant, a large group of well dressed business men met the three, as they left the building. The two groups forming two lines, as to allow each other to pass on the narrow walkway that lead from the parking lot, to the restaurant's door. Sam stayed holding the door for the men to enter the restaurant, as the other three continued walking towards the parking lot. After holding the door for the business men, Sam quickly ran to catch the others. The three were just opening their doors to the car, as Sam ran up and grabbed his and jumped in. With the four of them back in the small car, Lizy started the car and in short order, they were on their way.

"I'm ready, let's hear more."

"Lizy, after J J walked into camp, and told us how he and three others, had come to this island in 1943. He also told us how he was unable to make it back to the beach, with the other three men. Which is why, he was on this island for over fifty years. This is the best part, Lizy. J J, knew my father," said Robby, looking over at Lizy to see her reaction.

"This man, lost on an island for fifty years, knew your father? How is that possible? Did he know him before he left for the pacific?" asked Lizy, as she looked up at J J in the mirror.

"My father was one of the three men that went to the island that night, with J J. The three men made it back. Unfortunately without J J. Watch where you're going, Lizy," said Robby, seeing her staring.

Lizy quickly turned back to look where she was driving.

"There's more."

Lizy exhaled deeply, surprised by the Colonel's statement, that there was more surprises to come, in this already amazing story.

"Lizy, did you happen to notice that J J nor Sam, have their names on their uniforms?"

"Yes, I did, Robby. I didn't think much of it, because of you, Colonel," said Lizy, as she stared straight ahead, with both hands on the wheel. She then looked slowly in his direction. "You're not going to tell me, they have the same name, are you?" Her voice somewhat sarcastic in tone, as she looked up into the rearview mirror at J J and Sam, and then back over towards Robby. All three men looking at her, with big smiles on their faces. "You are, aren't you!"

"Not only do they have the same name, Lizy."

Lizy's driving becoming somewhat erratic at this point. "There's more?" asked Lizy, regaining her driving alertness.

"Are you ready for this, Lizy?"

"Go ahead, I'm ready," said Lizy focusing more of her attention on her driving, rather than on listening.

"J J is Sam's grandfather."

Some time past as Lizy kept driving not saying anything. Looking now and then, in the car's rearview mirror, at the two men sitting in the back seat, still smiling at her in the mirror.

"Is there more?" asked Lizy, with some concern showing in her voice.

"That's the most of it, Lizy."

She continued driving, not saying anything for a minute or so. During this time, J J was looking out the window at some of the beautiful scenery passing them by, as they drove through the countryside. "This is pretty country. I had this visions of little houses made of paper, so close there would be no room to build more, and the cities crowded with people. I didn't anticipate these beautiful mountains and all this open countryside." Lizy watching J J in the mirror, as he spoke.

"It's quite a story, isn't it Lizy?" asked J J, as he sat there with a big smile.

Some time past, Lizy still not saying anything.

"I'm sorry, J J. I'm seldom one without words. All I want to know, is, when does the movie come out? The story of the white gloves and eczema is one thing. This story is so unbelievable."

"Believe it!" said all three men loudly, at the same time.

"I do! It's just, such an incredible story. It would make a great movie."

"A movie! Who would we get to play my part? Clark Gable, that's who," laughed J J, as he reached up and pulled out on both his ears, exaggerating their size. Everyone laughing together at what he said and did. The others then became somewhat subdued.

"What is it? Don't you think Clark's a good choice?"

No one said anything for a moment.

"I'm sorry, J J, Clark Gable, died some time in the sixty's," said Robby, as a calm again befell the four.

"That means he's been dead over thirty years. You know, come to think of it. Probably the only actors I knew, that are still alive, are The Little Rascals and Shirley Temple."

"J J there's a lot that are still alive," said Robby, hearing the concern in J J's voice.

"Robby, can you think of any?"

Robby sat thinking about J J's question. "George Burns, for one," blurted the Colonel. Lizy and Sam looked at the Colonel. . . . "Cary Grant, Jimmy Stewart, I'm sure there's more, I just can't think of any right now, J J," said Robby, quickly trying to think of some others.

"Clint Eastwood, that's who we'll get to play the part of Grampa!"

"He'd be great! Good choice, Sam," said Lizy, as she looked in the mirror at Sam and his grandfather.

"J J, how old are you?"

"I'm seventy two, Lizy."

"You sure don't look it, J J."

They all sat there once again not speaking, as they drove through the countryside. Realizing J J seemed to be disturbed by the thought of all the years that had past, while he was on that island. Lizy started pointing out some of the sites.

"You can see the Buddhist Temple now. If you look right there, where that bright sunshine is shinning up that valley," said Lizy, as she pointed. In the distance, they could see the sun shinning right on the Temple, as it set high on a grassy noel, the colors were so vivid. "Isn't that beautiful. It looks like a picture on a calendar, doesn't it?" asked Lizy, as they all looked at the beautiful sight in the distance.

"Yes, it does," said Robby. J J and Sam, nodding they agreed.

"I can't get over how astonishingly beautiful everything is. It's so much different here, than I ever expected. That, along with the Japanese people's hospitality of how they treat Americans. I see now, why you love it here so much, Lizy."

"We take this road here, it leads up to the Temple," said Lizy, as she turned at an intersection off the main road, and onto a narrow paved one. In no time they entered the parking lot of the Temple's grounds and Lizy parked the car. For the next hour or so, they walked around and through the Temple and it's spectacular grounds.

"It's amazing how tranquil I feel here. After the way I've felt over the last fifty years, about this place and about the Japanese people."

"J J, I know there isn't anyway for us to be able to understand, how you feel. I was just hoping this might help you with some of those feelings, you justifiably have. Every time I come here, I leave with a more agreeable state of mind, towards my fellow man. And believe me I need all the help I can get in this man's outfit, with my big mouth," said Lizy, as the four of them walked up to her car.

"I've noticed that about you, Lizy. You do have a tendency to speak your mind," said Robby, as they all climbed back into Lizy's car.

"You're right, Colonel. I do have a tendency like you say, to do just that. That's what I really meant, when I said I had a big mouth. Not only is my mouth big, like in large size. It's also big, like in I say things I shouldn't. In other words, I talk way too much and say things I shouldn't, to the wrong people," said Lizy, as she drove back down the narrow road to the intersection, and then turned back onto the main road.

"J J, have you called, Jera yet?"

"My, Jera Marie? No, Lizy. Robby thought it may be too much of a shock for me to call, with that kind of news. He felt Sam could help lessen the shock with his presence," smiled J J, as he looked at Lizy's reflection in the mirror.

"A shock. I'd say that's somewhat of an understatement, Colonel," said Lizy, as she sat driving and quickly looking over at Robby and then back at J J, in the rearview mirror.

Again the four sat not saying anything for a moment. They were now entering a more populated area. Having driven just a short ways further, it had become more like what J J had imagined.

"It's not much farther, to the market place now. J J, does this congestion and all these people, cause you some uneasiness?" asked Lizy, trying to see J J's reactions in the mirror, to what was going on outside the moving vehicle, in what had become fairly heavy traffic.

"I'm fine, Lizy. This is fantastic," smiled J J, as he turned from looking out the car's window, to looking at Lizy in it's rearview mirror. "I don't see any, Geisha Girls or Shoguns. The clothes these people are wearing, look more American to me, rather then Japanese. If you don't see their faces, the men and women both look American, the way they're dressed. I don't see any sarongs or thong or any other type of Japanese clothing."

"The Japanese people have emulated a lot of American customs, both our better ones and also some of our superficial ones. They love, Rock-N-Roll and our country western music. There are some Japanese business men and others, that would just love owning, say something like, a Harley-Davidson motorcycle. Take Levi's, for instance. I heard that a pair of 1950's Levi's, could be worth as much as three thousand dollars over here. Our cars, mine not being one of them," laughed Lizy, as she quickly turned the car's wheel first one way and then abruptly back the other, shaking everyone in the car, the four of them laughing together afterwards. "Take an old car, like a 57 Chevy, it might bring forty or fifty thousand dollars."

"Listen to her, she's calling a 1957 Chevrolet, an old car. Fifty G's, for a forty year old car. Believe it," said J J, as he shook his head. He then turned and looked back out the window, at all the different sites.

"I wonder if my Jera Marie, still has my 37 Harley, I road to work the first summer we were married. . . ? When it wasn't raining."

"That's in, Pop Miller's barn, Grampa," said Sam excitedly. "I tried to convince him and gramma, to let me ride it to school. They said it would be to risky, knowing how valuable it had become. I have ridden it around the farm, but only in the summer, when it wasn't raining."

"It still runs?"

"Perfectly, Pop Miller, has seen to that. He has taken real good care of it, Grampa."

"We're here. Now all we need, is a place to park," said Lizy, turning off the main street, onto a narrow concrete drive that angled down steeply, taking them down and into an underground parking facility. After passing the second level without finding a parking spot, they descended on, to the third.

"There's one, Lizy," said Sam, as he pointed towards the vacant space. She pulled into the space. Once parked, they opened their doors and got out of the car.

"If we get separated. We're parked on level three, space 72. We shouldn't have any trouble remembering that number," laughed Lizy, as she closed her door.

"I shouldn't that's for sure," said J J, as the three men nodded to Lizy, they understood how to find the car, as they closed theirs.

"The elevators are this way, guys." The four of them headed for the elevators, which were located at the far end of the garage. The first two floors of the underground garage were already full of cars. The third was almost full, and yet, it was still quite early in the day. But for as many cars as there were on these lower levels, virtually no people could be seen. The four of them walked through the open doors of an elevator, it's doors then closed. It became a much different situation, when it's doors re-opened. They opened to a mass of humanity moving in many different directions. The four of them departed the elevator and stood together. The three of them watching J J, to see his reaction to the multitude of Japanese. It appeared J J was a bit overwhelmed by it all, beings he turned to re-enter the elevator and was met by it's already closed doors.

"Are you all right?" asked Robby, as he grabbed J J's arm. J J looked down at the hand pulling on his arm. He then looked gradually up and into Robby's eyes, as he heard Robby asking if he was all right. He stood there a moment, as if in a daze.

"I'm all right, Robby. I was just caught a bit off guard. . . . By how many people there are," said J J, as he turned with Robby and again stood with the others.

"Isn't this place awesome? It's a show place, instead of a market place," said Lizy, as she turned towards the others. The three men nodding, in answer to her question. The place was impressive all right. They all stood there as the three newcomers looked around at what was in their field of view.

"Lead the way, Lizy."

"Yes, Sir, Colonel."

With that said, Lizy started walking. Robby and Sam following behind walking amongst the many Japanese. The three of them not even aware J J was not following. Sam taking only a few steps with Lizy and Robby, before realizing his grandfather was not with them. Sam turned to see his grandfather, still standing by the elevator.

"What's wrong, Grampa?" asked Sam, as he ran up to his grandfather.

Some time past, as J J and Sam just stood there together, in front of the elevator's doors. The doors abruptly opened and six people quickly exited the elevator, all of them being Japanese. All six of them walked right around J J and Sam, two on one side and four on the other. The doors to the elevator once again closing, as they stood there.

"I don't know, Sam," said J J, as Lizy and Robby walked up.

"Robby, something's wrong!" said Sam, his voice shaking as he spoke.

"What is it, J J? What's wrong?" asked Robby, as the three of them stood looking at him, as he stood there staring back at them with this strange looked on his face.

"I don't know, Robby. I started to follow you guys, but then I had this funny feeling, like I was going to be sick or something. Not really sick, just light headed or queasy."

"Maybe it was the elevator ride," said Lizy.

"I don't think so. I didn't get sick on the helicopter or the airplane. I've never been seasick. I don't remember ever feeling this way."

The four of them stood there a moment in silence, all of them looking from one to the other and then back again for an answer, to what it might be. In a matter of just a few seconds they were all going to find out, what was bothering J J.

The three started feeling the same strange light headed or

queasiness, that J J was already acutely aware of. A low harmonic rumble began, as the four stood together.

"What's happening. Did you feel that?"

"Feel? Feel what, J J? What did you feel?" asked Robby, as they continued standing there, then their mouth's began dropping open and their eye's began to widen, as they looked at each other. . . . The building's air itself seem to be filling with the strange reverberation, as the unknown rumble's intensity increased.

"It's an earthquake!"

"An earthquake? You're right, Lizy! What should we do?" asked Robby, as the four of them could now hear screaming, through out the market place.

"Let's wait right here, until we see how strong a quake it is. We're away from any glass and I don't see anything that can fall on us. Except for maybe the building itself." Just as those words left Lizy's mouth, the building began to shake. Lizy started pushing the three men back towards the wall.

"Thanks a lot, Lizy. Now the building's going to fall on us," hollered Sam, as he and the others moved back against the wall.

"Standing against this wall, is likely one of the safest places in the building," said Lizy, speaking with authority in her voice.

The building came alive with movement and sound, as the shaking became more powerful. They could now actually see the massive concrete wall moving and twisting, as they stood against it, looking up the wall and then quickly to each side as they stood watching the earthquake's tremendous forces at work, as the quake expended it's energy.

"You don't really think this building's going to fall on us, do you Lizy?"

"I hope not, Sam," said Lizy, her voice quivering.

"I pray, I didn't spend fifty years on that island to come here to. . . ! Maybe the Japanese are going to win after all!" smirked J J, as he and the others looked out towards the people, now moving orderly showing little or no sign of panic, in their actions. The four of them still standing tightly against the wall could now see the market's immense floor was also moving. The floor moved as though it were a huge tapestry, with moving air trapped under it's surface, causing it to undulate, making the gigantic floor appear to ripple.

"The Japanese are very much aware of the destructive power of an earthquake. They live and sometimes die, during the many that occur here each year. J J, this earthquake doesn't know or care, that you're even here," said Lizy, trying hard to grin at J J, as she spoke. The shaking seemed to be lessening in it's intensity.

"Lizy, do you think the worst is over?" asked Robby

"Maybe. We better wait here a little longer, Colonel."

"Lizy, how many of these things have you been through?"

"I think this makes the sixth one, J J. One in southern California, and this makes five here in Japan."

At that very instant another jolt hit the building, instead of being a shaking motion. This time it was a much more violent and sudden jolt. "Forget I asked," said Robby, as the four once again braced themselves for the worst.

THE RESCUE

"It's amazing, this building can stand up to this. Maybe we should head for the exit and leave this place, before it comes down around our ears."

"That may not be a bad idea, J J," said Robby.

"Colonel, this building is probably the safest building in town. It was completed less than a year ago. It has, I would think, the latest in earthquake design built into it's construction."

"Another jolt like that one, may put all those so called built-in designs, to the test. You're the expert here, I've never been in one of these before, Lizy," said Robby, as J J and Sam shook their heads, indicating they too had not been in an earthquake.

"I wish they'd left it out of it's design." All three, quickly looked over at J J. He was still standing up against the wall, as Lizy had told him to do. A slight grin showing on his face, as he looked out from where he had been told to stand.

"J J, you're not enjoying your personal guided tour of Japan?" asked Lizy, causing the three men to turn and look her way.

"Lizy, it's not the tour guide or the tour, I have any complaints with, it's these extra thrills. The extras are a bit too much, for this old man. Lizy, why don't you leave out the extra thrills, on the remainder of my tour," smiled J J, as he and Lizy made some attempt, at helping the four of them cope, with the severity of their situation.

"No need to have them on my account," said Robby, as he too smiled in spite of their predicament, still standing against the wall.

"It's been awhile since that last big jolt. I'll have to agree with Robby and Grampa, you can leave out the thrills for me too, Lizy. Like Grampa said, maybe we should blow this place, while we have a chance."

"Did you guys, notice the electricity is still on? It hasn't gone off during this whole ordeal. That tells me, maybe we are the only ones here, that think the earthquake was a severe one. The only time these people seemed a bit concerned, was when the quake first hit. After that, they seemed to go right back to business as usual," said Lizy, as the four of them stood watching the people once again walking through the market, as if nothing was wrong.

"Looks as though you maybe right, Lizy. Let's continue the guided tour, minus the thrills if you please."

"Are you sure, J J?"

"What? You want to continue these thrills, Lizy?"

"No, J J. I meant the tour. You want the tour to continue, minus the thrills, right?"

"Right. Lead on, tour guide," said J J, as he moved away from the wall, he and the others had been so close too, in more ways then one. He then turned and looked at the other three, as they continued to stand against that same wall, as if they were a mural, that had been painted on the wall, to represent the United States military.

The three moved from the wall, towards J J. The four of them now together, stood cautiously watching the people. They started walking slowly at first, Lizy leading the way. The four of them talking as they walked, about their thoughts on the earthquake. As they walked they started to see visible evidence of some of the damage caused by the earthquake. And yet, no visible damage to the building itself could be seen.

"Wow, look in that store," said Sam, as he pointed through the window of a large store. The store had stuff in all it's aisles, that obviously had either fallen off the store's shelves or off it's walls. The four of them stopping to look at the evidence, showing signs they had definitely been through a major earthquake.

"Look, that store's the same way," said Lizy pointing to another store in the same rummaged condition.

The four of them started walking again, still looking at all the damage that showed in each store, as they walked.

"I'll have to take back what I said."

"What's that, J J?" asked Robby.

"When I said, I wish they would have left the earthquake design out of this building's construction. I'm sure glad now, they didn't. I'm thankful they built the design in, after all. Aren't you guy's?"

"Don't feel like, The Lone Ranger, Grampa," said Sam, as he slapped his grandfather on the shoulder.

"That's a big ten-four, J J," said Robby, as he slapped J J on the other shoulder. Robby and Sam walking along, one on each side of J J, as Lizy lead the way, walking just ahead of the three men.

"Like I said, I think we're in the safest building in town." Lizy stopped and turned to the three men, as to be heard. The three men also stopped, as the four of them once again stood together talking.

"Lizy, this place is a mess. It will take hours for them to clean it up.

We may as well go to the car."

"You're right, Robby, it probably will. There's some stairs to the garage, in the direction we're headed. I wouldn't use them under normal conditions, if I was alone." Lizy looked over at J J. "I'm sorry, J J, poor choice of words. What I meant was, if I wasn't with someone, it may be dangerous for a woman to use the stairs by herself. I think the stairs may be a safer choice under the circumstances."

"I agree, Lizy," said Robby, as they continued on their way through the market place, seeing more damage in each of the many different stores they passed, on their way towards the stairs.

"The door that leads to the stairwell is over there. We'll take the stairs down to. . . ."

"Level three, space seventy two. Right, Lizy?"

"Right on, J J," said Lizy, as they headed towards the door.

Sam opened the door and held it for the others. The four of them entered the stairwell and headed down the stairs to the lower levels, passing the second level and going onto the third. Lizy opened the door leading to the third level garage, hoping to find her small car undamaged by the earthquake. The four of them walked towards space seventy two. They still hadn't seen any visible sign of damage to the building, either in it's stairwell or here on the third level. There still wasn't any people to be seen on this level, or in the stairwell on the way down. All four of them could now see Lizy's car sitting in space seventy two, as she had hoped, undamaged.

"I'm sure happy to see the little beater's all right," said J J, as they walked to the car. "It will be nice to be out in the open and not have all this concrete over my head. If you know what I mean."

"I sure do, Grampa."

All four seemed delighted at being back in Lizy's small car, as she again searched for her keys.

The car once again came to life, as Lizy turned the key. She then quickly backed the car out of it's parking space, it's tires squealing on the garage's smooth concrete floor and they were off, following the arrows painted on the floor, that lead them towards the garage's exit, and to the streets above. The little car's engine roared as it climbed it's way back past the second level on it's way up to the surface and into the light of day. They exited the building's garage and came to a stop at the street's edge. Sitting there in the car at the stop sign, they could see tremendous damage to the building on the opposite side of the street. They sat there a moment at the stop sign, just staring at the extreme damage to the building.

Then looking first one way and then the other, they could see more damage in both directions. As they sat there looking, they began to realize how lucky they were, they chose that building at that particular time. "You know, in a very small way mind you, this is what you feel like, when you come out of a bomb shelter, after a place has been bomb or strafed," said Robby, as he sat looking out the window at the tremendous damage. "Don't misunderstand me. But it does feel a bit like that. I've been there!"

As they sat there, they could here sirens in the distance.

"Lizy, why don't you park over there. I guess it's a loading zone. There may people in some of these buildings that may need help."

"Yes, Sir, Colonel," said Lizy, as she abruptly revved the car's engine up and quickly drove in the direction the Colonel had pointed. Once parked, the four immediately got out of the car. The three stood next to the car with the Colonel, awaiting his orders.

"J J, you and Sam, take that side of the street. Lizy and I will take this side. Don't put yourself in jeopardy, but do what you can to help. These people know a hell of a lot more about what to do, in this situation, than we do!" The four immediately headed, to where they thought they might be need the most. As J J and Sam crossed the street, they could see an elderly woman, as she stood crying on the opposite side of the street. The two of them started running in her direction.

"Are you, all right?" asked J J, as he came up to the woman. The woman speaking in Japanese, said something hysterically to J J.

He quickly turned to Sam, pointing towards the building. "She said her granddaughter is trapped in the building!" He then turned and tried to comfort the woman telling her, in Japanese, that the two of them would go into the building and search for her granddaughter. J J also asked her calmly if she could help in telling him, in what part of the building her granddaughter was last seen. The woman took in a deep breath, as J J stood calmly waiting. She then tried to explain to him, still speaking in Japanese. Where in the building, her granddaughter may be located.

The face of the building had fallen away from it's front. It now laid in a pile, overflowing the sidewalk into the street. The two men left the woman and started to climb over the pile of rubble, in an attempt to enter the building. Once inside the building, the two men stood together as quiet as possible. They could hear debris still falling, as they stood there quietly listening. After standing there just for a moment, they moved still deeper into the damaged building. Repeatedly moving and then stopping, to listen. Hoping to hear something that would lead them to the trapped girl.

Or others, that may have also been trapped by the collapsing building. Progress was painstakingly slow, because of all the rubble. Then they heard something, very faintly at first, but as they moved in the direction of the sound, they thought the sound they heard was a person crying. They continued to move towards the sound, over and under and through entangled debris, the two kept carefully proceeding, directed by the faint sound. It wasn't far now, they were almost there.

"She's right over there, Grampa," said Sam excitedly pointing, as he then moved in the direction he pointed.

"Sam! Here comes another jolt!" At that instance. The building began to shake violently. The two men moved as quickly as possible through the remaining rubble to get to the girl. More of the building came down on top of what was already there. When they were at the place where Sam had pointed. They didn't find what they had hoped. Instead, the two found a small dog, itself snared by fallen debris. The two men released the dog from it's trap and Sam quickly grabbed the dog. The dog proceeded to seize Sam, as the building once again shook.

"Don't let go, Sam," said J J, as he saw the small dog take hold of Sam's hand, in not the friendliest of manner. "The lady said something regarding a dog. I didn't quite understand what she meant. What she obviously meant, was that the girl and her dog, was trapped in the building," said J J, as he stood there shrugging his shoulders and smiling at his grandson, as the dog released his hold on Sam's hand. "She must be close," said J J, as he instantly returned to the severity of the situation. The two men stood quietly listening, as Sam tried to comfort and quiet the dog. They couldn't hear anything, except for debris falling and the building itself creaking. "Put the dog down, Sam. Maybe the dog can find her for us."

Sam bent down and did as his grandfather suggested. The dog stood there a moment on three legs, his fourth leg held up, as he turned and looked up at each of the two men. J J saying something to the dog in Japanese. Sam looked over at his grandfather and smiled shaking his head, as J J stood there still talking to the small dog. The dog started to move through the debris, as the two men did their best to follow. With in a moment or two, the dog had moved out of sight and started to whimper. The two men were close, but the dog had moved in amongst more debris and no longer could be seen. Sam got down on his knees and still couldn't see the dog. He then got down and laid on his belly. "I can see him!"

At that very moment the building shook violently once again and more debris came crashing down on them. The two men covering their heads in defense against the falling debris. As the dust settled, the dog came out and licked Sam's face, causing Sam to re-opened his eyes, staring right into the eyes of the small dog. The dog then turned and went back into the debris pile, as Sam laid there prostrate, watching. The dog once again started to whimper. "I can't see in there, it's to dark. I'd say she's in there though, by the way that dog is whimpering, Grampa."

"I think you're right. Let's move some of this stuff and get in closer." Sam jumped to his feet and the two men immediately began to move rubble, to enable them to move towards the dog and hopefully the trapped girl. Time past, as the two worked together on the heavier pieces and individually on the others.

"There she is! I can see her and the dog both, Grampa. She isn't moving," said Sam, as he stopped and looked at his grandfather, with questions showing in his eyes.

"The dog is just lying by her, whimpering. You don't. . . ?"

"Let's not borrow more trouble than we know, Sam. Remember Gramma's poem," smiled J J, as he put his hand on his grandson's shoulder and looked into his eyes. The two men giving one quick nod to each other, and then worked feverishly to get to the unconscious girl and her dog. Once they had, they dropped to their knees next to the girl. The dog growling as they did.

"It looks as though I'm going to have another bite taken out of me," said Sam, as he reached out and instantly grabbed the dog. "I have him. Well we have each other," said Sam, as he sat back on his lower legs, holding the dog in his arms. The dog released Sam, as it now watched J J moving towards it's master.

J J crawled in close to the girl, putting his hand out, with some hesitation, towards the girl's dusty face, carefully removing the debris and brushing away some of the smaller material from her face, he then slowly and cautiously touched the girl's face. He knelt there a moment. He then lowered his head down next to hers. The dog and Sam watched his grandfather, as Sam sat holding and now petting the small dog. He then turned towards the front of the building, hearing people hollering to them. The dog let out a single bark. The shouts were somewhat muffled by the layers of twisted debris. Sam didn't answer, as not to hinder his grandfather, in their quest to recover the girl. J J raised up and turned to his grandson. "She's breathing."

"Super."

"Let's get her and us out of here," said J J, as he bent down, apparently to pull the girl from the debris.

"No!"

"What?" asked J J, as he quickly turned back to his grandson, showing a puzzled look on his face. Surprised by Sam's attitude. "Why not move her out of danger?"

"It may not be safe to move her. We haven't any idea what's wrong or the extent of her injuries."

"That's true, Sam, we don't. What do you think we should do?" asked J J, as he too sat back on his lower legs.

"I don't know. The rest of this building might come down at anytime, and bury all four of us," said Sam, as he slowly looked from his grandfather, to the structure over their heads. He then looked down at the dog he still held in his arms and then back to his grandfather, who had moved back to the girl. Removing more debris off her legs and away from her.

Just then the dog started to whimper and squirm, as it tried desperately to free itself from Sam's arms. At that same instant, the girl moaned and then started to move. The two men quickly looked at each other and then back to the girl.

"Let the dog go." Sam put the dog at his side and released him. The dog ran quickly to the girl and began licking her face. The girl responded to the dog's obvious affection, by turning her head side to side, as she laid there on her back. The two men quickly looked at each other and smiled.

"Don't move too much, until you see how badly you're hurt." The girl opened her eyes, blinking a few times, as she looked over at J J. Her eyes widen as she stared up at the American soldier, looking down talking to her. She rolled over on her left side and grab for her small dog. The dog seemed excited it's master was conscious and moving again, as it ran from the girl to each of the two men and then back to the girl. Her grabbing the dog as it came to her. The girl looked from J J over to Sam.

"Are you hurt?" asked Sam.

"What happen?" asked the girl, with her and J J both, speaking in Japanese. The girl shook her head and then sat up, tightly holding her dog. "You're Americans," said the young girl, speaking in English, as she looked first at one man and then the other.

"Yes, we're Americans. Are you sure you're all right?" asked Sam, as the two men smiled at the anxious young girl.

"What of my grandmother?" asked the girl, as she looked around.

"Your grandmother is outside. She's not in the building."

"It was an earthquake?" asked the girl holding the dog in her left arm, as she reached to the back of her head with her right hand and rubbed her head.

"Yes. Are you all right?"

"Yes, I think I am all right. Something must of hit me on my head," said the girl, as she pulled her hand back, with blood on her fingers and the palm of her right hand.

J J and Sam both seeing the blood on her hand. "You are hurt! How many fingers do you see?" asked Sam, as he held out his hand.

"Three," said the girl, as she put her dog down and got to her hands and knees, as she looked up towards Sam.

"She has the right idea. Let's get out of here, while we still have a chance," said J J, as he reached out and helped her to her feet, as Sam reached for and caught her dog. Holding the girl under his left arm, J J helped her move the few feet to where Sam waited with her dog. The two of them bending over, to avoid the low hanging debris. "You lead the way Sam, I'll help her," smiled J J, as he moved with the girl.

"I'll carry the dog," snickered Sam.

"Thank you. Scruffy must be so frightened," smiled the girl. Sam smiled pleasantly to the girl. He then turned and lead the three of them back through the rubble, towards the front of the building and hopefully out to safety. Then the three heard someone calling out a name, so they stopped to listen. "That's my name. There calling my name, Toya."

"We're coming out," yelled J J in Japanese to the people calling the girl's name, as they continued carefully moving through the debris. They could now see rescue workers moving through the rubble in their direction. The three stopped again, to wait for J J to say something to the two rescuers, as they came up to them. They nodded to him and then moved past, continuing their search of the building. The three then continued towards the outside.

Outside the building, they were still faced with the pile of rubble, which was much larger than when the two had entered the building. The three successfully met the challenge and made it over the debris pile and back into the street safely. The girl seeing her grandmother, moved from the safety of J J's arm, and ran quickly to her grandmother. Once at her grandmother's side, the two hugged and then proceeded to wipe tears from each others face and eyes, as they told each other how glad they were to be together. The girl then told her grandmother, that the two American soldiers had saved her, as she pointed in their direction. The woman nodding, indicating to Toya, that she knew the soldiers had gone into the building, to try and find her and bring her hopefully out to safety. J J and Sam, walked up to where the girl and her grandmother were standing and smiled.

"My name is, Sam. This is my Grandfather, J J," smiled Sam, as the four of them stood together.

"Grandmother, is known by, Yoko. Toya, as you know, is my name," said Toya, as she and her grandmother bowed to the two men.

"Toya, you should have someone look at what's wrong with your head, a doctor maybe."

"My head?" asked Toya, as she stared at Sam. Toya was a petite young woman, standing less then five feet tall. She had raven black hair and beautiful dark eyes. She could easily pass for any age between the ages of eleven, and say twenty one, no questions asked. "Oh, you mean the blood in my hair."

"Yes!" said Sam, his face turning beet red.

Just then J J saw what he thought was an ambulance, making it's way down the street towards the four of them. He also saw Robby and Lizy in the distance, walking slowly in their direction.

"Toya, I think that's an ambulance coming this way. Maybe there will be someone onboard that could take a look at your injury."

"Thank you, for not speaking in Japanese, J J. That way I don't have to worry grandmother about my injury."

They stood there watching as the ambulance maneuvered it's way around debris and other vehicles, as it slowly continued coming in their direction. The vehicle came to a stop about a hundred feet before reaching their location. It turned out that it was a rescue unit instead of an ambulance. The driver quickly jumped out and ran towards the back of the vehicle, as he did, another man appeared at the back of the vehicle, with a large dog at his side. The dog and both men, were wearing bright colored orange and yellow vests, making them very hard to miss. The two men stood in the street next to the vehicle's left side, the dog standing at there's.

The two men that had been searching the damaged building, appeared standing on the top of the debris pile, yelling something to the men with the dog. They responded by running towards them, with the dog still at their side.

"Rescue people, now use dogs, to help them locate victims that have been trapped, as I was," said Toya, as she turned towards Sam.

At that same instant they felt another after shock, this one not quite as violent as the others. At that same moment a large amount of dust and debris belched out from the confines of the damaged building, covering the four rescue workers and their dog with dust and light debris, as they stood on the large debris pile.

"I'm so glad were not still in there. I hope there isn't anyone else trapped in there," said J J with a worried looked on his face.

"I think I was the only one left in the building. The building was not damaged that bad at first. I went in to get my Scruffy dog. I think that was when it fell on Scruffy and I. Worry not, J J. I don't think there's any people in the building now," said Toya, seeing the concern on J J's face. "This is where I live, in that building," said Toya, as she pointed to the building, that lay in ruins. "Where I did live, before now!" said Toya with tears in her eyes. "Grandmother had come yesterday, to stay with me for the night. We were on our way to the mall, when this all started. I work at the mall nights and go to school during the day. I have school off today. My English teacher is an American. He wanted to have a long weekend, for your Fourth Of July holiday. And guess what? No school for his class today."

"Are you sure you're all right, Toya?" smiled Sam, as he stood there still a little red faced.

"I am fine. I think my head is all right too," smiled Toya.

The four of them stood there together, Sam and Toya talking. Sam then held out Toya's small dog to her. The dog becoming quite excited, as Sam held it out for Toya to take from him. "By the looks of it, your dog is all right too," smiled Sam, as he handed Toya the fidgeting little dog. "Scruffy here, helped us find you. He lead Grampa and I right through that damaged building, right to where you were trapped."

"Thank you, for coming to our rescue," said Toya, as she smiled up at Sam, taking her dog from him, as she did.

"I'm glad we were here to help your grandmother and you, Toya. Where will you stay now, that your apartment has been. . . ?" asked Sam, as he turned from Toya and looked towards the damaged building.

"I will return with grandmother to father's house," said Toya, as she too turned and looked over at the damaged building. "It will take time to find another place. This place was close to my school and work. With help from father with expenses, I could live there on my own," said Toya, as she turned and once again stared up at Sam smiling.

Toya's Grandmother and J J stood together watching, as their two grandchildren talked and smiled, seemingly captivated by each other. The two grandparents turned to each other and smiled. Yoko smiling a knowing smile, maybe there was something wonderful happening right before their eyes. Just then, Robby and Lizy walked up to the four of them.

"Is everyone all right?" asked the Colonel, as he stared at the dust in J J's hair. He then noticed that both Sam's and the girl's hair was also dusty, and that all three of them had soiled clothes.

"Yes, Colonel, we're all right. Toya, and her dog, were trapped in that building," said J J, as he pointed towards the damaged building.

"Wow. Are you sure, you're all ok?"

"We're ok, Robby. Sam and I, found Toya trapped in the rubble," said J J, as he smiled towards the tiny Asian girl. "Scruffy here, helped us find Toya," smiled J J, as he reached out and patted the dog's head that the girl held in her arms. Scruffy licking at his arm as he did.

J J then took a moment and introduced everyone to each other.

"I'm glad Lizy brought us here. That way you two could be here, so you could help."

"Robby, Toya had an apartment in that building. She and her grandmother, were on their way to the market, when the earthquake first struck. Toya went back into the building to get Scruffy. That's when they were trapped by the building's falling debris."

"Toya, I'm sure you have been through a good many of these. Do you think the earthquake is over?"

"Grandmother is the one you need to ask that question. She's been through hundreds of earthquakes. You'll have to ask her that question in Japanese, Robby. Grandmother doesn't speak or understand any English."

"Your, grandmother and I have something in common, Toya."

"What could that be?" asked Toya, as she stared at Robby with a wrinkled brow.

"I don't speak or understand any Japanese," smiled Robby, as he looked from Toya, to her grandmother and then towards J J. "But my friend J J here, speaks Japanese," said Robby, as he held out his right hand palm up in a respective manner, as he proudly smiled towards J J.

"Yes, I know he does. And quite well too. J J, would you like to ask Grandmother Robby's question?" asked Toya, as she turned to J J.

"It would be an honor, Toya. I'll do my very best," said J J smiling, as he turned from Toya to her grandmother. He then proceeded to ask Yoko, about her experience with earthquakes, in her own language. The others stood watching, as J J and Yoko conversed.

"Yoko says, in her opinion. Most of this quake's destructive power, is behind us. At least that's what I think she said. She also said something about her and this building being old and that the both of them had survived a lot of earthquakes, over the many years. And of her being fortunate enough to have survived another, where as the building was not so fortunate," said J J, as he shrugged his shoulders and smiled.

"That's close to what Grandmother said J J," smiled Toya, as she nodded to J J and then smiled to the others.

The six of them stood together talking about what had taken place, and about what they were watching unfold before them, in the aftermath of this potentially devastating earthquake.

"It's like I said, Robby."

"What's that, J J?"

"I know, Grampa! Sorry, Colonel. I didn't mean to interrupt."

"Go ahead, Sam."

"Life throws us a curve ball and we have to walk the bases of life. I mean, around the bases of life! That's it, isn't it, Grampa?" asked Sam ecstatically.

"That's close, Sam. It's closer than I was with my Japanese, I'll bet," smiled J J, as he reached out with one arm and grabbed Sam around his shoulders shaking him, smiling towards the others as he did.

"Sam, you and your grandfather, are very close. You are both very . . . tall, and you have the same warm friendly smile, as your grandfather," smiled Toya, looking directly into Sam's eyes, her face a bit red.

"Yes, I was named after my, Grampa J J," said Sam smiling at her, as he grabbed his grandfather, in the same manner his grandfather had just grabbed him. As he did, Sam smiled proudly and started shaking his grandfather, as his grandfather had just finished shaking him.

"You two aren't going to start wrestling, are you?"

"No, Sir!" said J J and Sam, as they quickly came to attention, both trying to keep from laughing, as they stood there.

"Well I should hope not, after our little talk," said the Colonel, in the same manner he did at the airport earlier that same day. Lizy and Toya, both looking at the three men with a puzzled look on their faces. As the three men stood there looking at them with grins on their's.

"It must be a man thing, Toya," smiled Lizy.

"I think you're right, Lizy. I know it went right over my head. I know that's not hard to do. I'm only one point forty-eight meters high. I'm sorry, I meant tall," said Toya, as she bowed her head. The six of them, including Toya's grandmother stood there laughing together enjoying each others company. Slowly their laughter died down.

"Lizy, what do you suggest, we do now?" asked Robby, bringing all five immediately back to the situation they had been exposed to.

"Robby, maybe we could take Toya and her grandmother to her father's house."

"That's a good idea, Sam. Lizy is that all right with you?"

"It's all right with, me guys. Do you think we can all fit in my little beater?"

"Toya can sit on my lap and hold Scruffy. Grandmother will fit between Grampa and I, no problem."

"There may be a problem."

"What?"

"Sam, we don't know where her father's house is or how far it is from here."

"Right. I didn't even think of that."

"I know," said Lizy, as she raised one eye brow and smiled a knowing smile towards Sam.

Sam smirked, as his face again turned beet red.

"Lizy, father's house is a long way away. It is forty kilometers from this location."

"That's maybe an hour, under normal conditions. After this, who knows," said Lizy, waving her arm towards the damage in the street.

"Toya, is your father's house in the same direction as our base?"

"Yes, it is, Sir."

"Well Lizy, we haven't heard anything from your counterpart, as of yet. We have the time. There's nothing keeping us here, except the damage from the earthquake, itself. I say, if we can, let's go. What do you say, J J? "

"Lizy's the tour guide, Robby. But maybe, someone should ask Toya?" smiled J J, as he looked down at Toya, and then slowly over at his grandson, as Sam stood there smiling, still staring in Toya's direction.

"Good idea, J J," said Lizy, as a mischievous smile formed on her face. "Maybe Toya's boyfriend, lives close by," said Lizy, as she quickly looked over at Toya and then Sam, to catch their reactions.

"Boyfriend!" Blurted Sam, as his mouth dropped open and he abruptly turned towards Lizy. He then slowly turned back, to staring at Toya.

"No! No boyfriends," said Toya, shaking and bowing her head, obviously a bit embarrassed by her reaction, to what Lizy had said. Sam's red face showing a broad smile, as he heard Toya's comment, to Lizy's statement.

"Toya, would you and your grandmother, like a ride to your father's house. That's if we can get there, that is."

"Thank you, Lizy. I will ask Grandmother," smiled Toya, as she then turned to her grandmother and proceeded to ask. "Yes, Grandmother and I would like that. Thank you, Lizy."

"All right then, let's load up. The tour departs shortly."

The six of them started walking towards the car. Lead by J J and Yoko, talking as they walked side by side, as did Toya and Sam and Lizy and Robby. J J explaining to Yoko what the plan was. Yoko giggling slightly, as he told her the part about Toya sitting on Sam's lap. "I'm sure they'll enjoy that," said Yoko, as she turned and smiled towards her granddaughter and Sam, who had walked up alongside of her and J J, as they approached the car. The two of them, not even aware of what the girl's grandmother had been saying to J J as they walked.

J J reached out and opened the car's rear door for him and Yoko. Sam and Toya walked around to the passenger side of the car. Quickly moving ahead of Toya, Sam opened their door and the four of them began to situate themselves, in the small car's rear seat, as Lizy and Robby did the same in the front, Lizy again taking a moment to find the car's key in her purse. In no time at all, they were on their way. Lizy maneuvered her small car around other cars and emergency vehicles, as she drove through the now busy streets. Some additional damage from the earthquake appearing with every turn of the car's small wheels. But nothing nearly as devastating as Toya's building.

"The city looks as though it has come through this quake, in fair shape," said Lizy, as she looked up into her car's mirror at Toya sitting on Sam's lap. The two of them talking and laughing, both outwardly enjoying their ride. Lizy snickering to herself, at the obvious attraction the two seem to have for each other. She thought as she drove, of 'the irony of it all. Of how, Toya's building was virtually destroyed and yet, the rest of the city, was essentially unimpaired by the earthquake's damage.' Then it came to Lizy, 'it must be destiny! Fate must of brought the three men to Japan so J J and Sam would be there that very moment in time, to be able to pull Toya and her dog Scruffy, from the collapsing building.' In Lizy's mind, 'it truly was destiny.'

"What's wrong, Lizy?"

"J J, there's nothing wrong. I guess, I'm just a little tired," smiled Lizy, as she looked in the mirror towards J J. "I've been up since 0530 yesterday, I'll be fine. I'll get my second wind here pretty soon. Then look out!" smiled Lizy, as she continued to look in the mirror, as she drove. Not wanting to say anything to the others, about what she had been thinking to herself. Leaving the city behind, the little car once again moved along the road, that ran it's way through the open countryside. Lizy still continuing to smile to herself, about her personal thoughts as she drove.

"You know that ten hours is going by a lot faster then I thought," said J J, as he leaned forward in his seat and put his left hand on Robby's shoulder.

"Is that right?" asked Robby, as he turned to J J and then looked back down at the wristwatch on his left arm. You're right, J. J. It is passing quickly, it's already been close to five hours. At this rate, it will be time for us to leave before you know it."

"Sam, you have to leave in less then five hours?" asked Toya, as she looked over at J J smiling. She then turned back to Sam, as she sat there on his lap her face only a few inches from his, waiting for him to answer her question.

"Yes, Toya," smiled Sam. "The Colonel and I, are flying Grampa home, as soon as a plane becomes available," said Sam, as he looked into the eyes of the new found friend, he now had sitting on his lap, as she looked at him smiling. "Toya, I can't tell you how much it means to me, to be able to go with the Colonel. For me to be there when Gramma and Grampa, see each other."

"Sam, where do your grandparents live?"

"Gramma lives in Seattle. . . , they live in Seattle. Grampa has been away from her, for a . . . long time," smiled Sam, as he looked over at his grandfather smiling at him. He then turned back towards Toya, as she sat there with a big smile on her face.

"Toya, can I write to you? I haven't any idea if I'll be coming back this way, anytime soon," said Sam in a low voice, as he sat there staring into the girl's eyes. He then noticed how quiet the car had become. Sam turned from Toya to see not only was she staring, everyone in the car was either listening or staring at him, all of them showing a slight smile on their face, as they did. "What?" Blurted Sam, his face again turning beet red. Everyone but Sam laughing at his reaction.

"Sam, I will not be here either."

"Where will you be?" asked Sam, his mood somewhat changed, after hearing what she said.

"After I finish classes this summer. This fall, I'm going to transfer," smiled Toya.

"Where are you going to transfer to?" asked Sam, as he strained a smile. Toya smiled a big smile, as she looked around at everyone still staring at her and Sam, as they all waited to hear her answer to Sam's question. Sam still smiling at her with the strained smile, as he too waited for her to answer.

"Sam, I'm transferring," smiled Toya, hesitating with her answer.

"I know. Where to?"

"To the University Of Washington," smiled Toya proudly.

"That's great, Toya!" said Sam, as a big smile returned to his face. Someone in the small car started to clap. Not knowing who started or why for that matter, at that point, everyone started clapping and laughing. After a moment or so the laughter died down and the two youngster's red faces started to return to a color, closer to that of normal.

"The university is in Seattle."

"I know, Sam," smiled Toya.

"Maybe I can see you, when I come home on leave."

Toya's smile seem to grow even larger, if that could have been possible. "That would be nice."

Lizy's car continued moving it's way through the picturesque countryside. It's load of people, seemingly very much enjoying each other's company, on their ride to Toya's father's house. Which according to her, was located somewhere on the far side of the base, where the men's plane had landed earlier that same morning, and where that plane now sat awaiting it's crew's return. The same base, where Lizy has been stationed over the last three years.

"Here's the road that goes to the base, coming up on the left, Colonel."

"Lizy, there isn't any reason to stop. We haven't heard anything from your counterpart about a flight. I say we keep going, unless we hear something."

"Yes, Sir, Colonel."

"Toya, you'll tell me if and when I turn?"

"Yes, Lizy, I'm watching. We stay to this road for a time," said Toya.

"Ok," smiled Lizy, as she looked up at the girl smiling at her in the car's mirror.

As the car approached the area of the base, it's passengers stared out the windows of the small car. To the amazement of everyone, no visible signs of damage from that mornings earthquake, could be seen. "The base appears to be undamaged," said Lizy, as the car moved along a road that ran parallel to one of the base's many runways. Some of it's buildings, lying within the car's passenger's field of view.

"I'm sure glad to see our planes all right!" said J J, with some excitement showing in his voice, as he pointed to the airplane sitting on the tarmac, somewhat isolated from the other airplanes.

"J J, is that the plane you three flew in on?"

"Yes, it is, Toya," smiled J J.

"It may also be the one we'll be flying out on," said Robby, as he turned from looking out the left side of the car, to looking over his shoulder smiling.

"Look, there's another building damaged by the earthquake," said Sam, as he pointed to a building out the right side of the vehicle.

"That building's been that way forever. At least as long I've been stationed here."

Toya nodded, indicating to the others, that indeed the building had been damaged long before that morning's earthquake. "Grandmother may remember, how and when the building was damaged. I know it has been that way for a long time."

"How much farther is your father's house Toya?"

"It's not far now. I'm quite sure Lizy, and her fine little automobile, will have us there shortly." Lizy snickered, as she looked at Toya smiling, in the mirror of her fine little auto. "I hope this hasn't been too much of an inconvenience for you and your men, Colonel."

"Not at all, Toya. Like I said, I'm glad we were here to help."

"I am sorry, I didn't answer your question, Robby," said Toya, her face turning red, as she bowed her head. "Without any unforeseen delays, we should be at father's in twenty minutes or less," smiled Toya.

Robby trying hard to turn enough in his seat, so as to enable him to look at Toya, as she spoke. "I don't want to appear to be rude. But I can't quite turn far enough in this seat, to be able to look at you while you speak."

"Thank you," said Toya, as she laid her hand softly on Robby's shoulder.

NEW FRIENDS

The car's six passengers continued talking as they road along, looking out the windows at all the different sites, that Lizy and Toya, took turns pointing out to them, as the car moved ever closer to Toya's father's house. As they drove the traffic again became more restrictive. As the car moved from the rural countryside, into a more densely populated urban area.

"Lizy, turn right at the next street." Lizy did as instructed, and the car moved into a residential neighborhood of fine homes. The lawns and yards of these homes were impeccably manicured. The car slowed as they drove in the direction Toya continued to point. Beautiful homes now bordered both sides of the now narrowing streets. Everyone in the car, except Toya and her grandmother, somewhat in awe.

"Is it me, or are these homes as magnificent as I think?"

"They're magnificent all right, J J," said Robby, raising and lowering his eye brows as he spoke, looking over his shoulder at J J, to catch his reaction to the magnificent homes.

Toya sitting on Sam's lap smiling, as she continued pointing directions. "Lizy, turn right, father's house is the house at the end of the street. The street becomes our drive at the gate. You will have to stop, Sason, is not going to recognize us in your automobile. I will have to get out and tell him, that Grandmother and I, are with you, before he will open the gate." Lizy made the turn and the small car moved up to the end of the street and stopped. The car now sat in front of a formidable iron gate. Toya opened the passenger side rear door and with Sam's help stepped out and stood by the car. At about that same time they heard someone say Toya's name. Within a moment, the large gate began to open. As the gate started to open Toya climbed back into the little car and Sam closed the door, as Toya retrieved Scruffy from her grandmother. Lizy revved up the car's engine and zipped through the now partially opened gate, even though the car was through the gate, it continued to open. No one said a word as they left the opened gate behind. The car now moved slowly up the concrete drive through the beautifully landscaped estate. As it rounded a bend in the drive, an incredible house came into view. Slowly the car came to a stop, in front of the spectacular entrance to the enormous home. All of it's passengers sat in silence, as they watched as it's gigantic front door begin to open.

"You, live here? I mean your parents live here?" asked Sam, his voice cracking a bit as he asked the question.

"Yes. Is there a problem?"

"No. There's no problem," smiled Sam, as he opened the car's rear door and again helped Toya out of the car. As he did, the others opened their doors and they all started getting out of the car. J J stood holding the door to help Yoko out of the car's small rear seat. He then held out his left arm bent at the elbow, to help Yoko to her feet. Then holding her by the arm, in an escorting style, they started walking just behind Lizy.

Toya left Sam and ran up the stairs towards a woman coming out of the house, saying something to the woman in Japanese, as she did. The woman and Toya grabbed and hugged each other with Scruffy trapped between. After a moment, they broke their embrace. Still holding hands, Toya turned and her and the woman started down the stairs, talking, as they carefully took each step.

From the drivers side Lizy, then Yoko with J J, walked around the front of the car. The three of them joined by Robby and Sam, walked towards the foot of the stairs.

Toya continued telling the woman on the stairs of the mornings events, as they slowly continued down the stairs, towards the others, which by now, had all gathered at the base of the massive stairs, looking up at them. "Mother, if I may, I would like to introduce these wonderful people to you," said Toya, as her mother and her stood on the last step. "Mother, this is J J, Robby, Sam and Lizy," said Toya, her mother bowing to each person, as Toya introduced her to them individually. "This is my, mother, Toyoko. J J and Sam, are the ones that rescued me from my apartment."

Toya's mother smiled as her and her daughter stood in front of J J and Sam. Being on the step allowed the two a somewhat closer to eye level prospective of the two men. "How may I honor you, for saving Our Special One, from injury or even worse?" asked Toyoko, as she once again bowed to J J. Then looking up, only with her eyes, she cautiously reached out with her dainty elegant hands and took his rugged weathered hands in hers. Slowly bending, she tenderly kissed the back of first one and then the other of the enormous hands she gently held in hers. Toyoko looked up and smiled at J J. Then moving from him to Sam, she gracefully repeated the respectful gesture.

"I'm so grateful, we were there and were able to help, Ma'am," smiled Sam, as he looked first at Toyoko and then over to Toya.

"As am I, Sam," said Toyoko, as she again lowered her head. Then looking up, she looked over to her daughter and smiled. "Toya, ask our friends to come in and have some tea and we will talk. We must first call your father and tell him, Mother Yoko and you, are here and safe," said Toyoko, as she moved off the last step down next to the older woman. With her on one side of Yoko and J J on the other, the three of them started up the immense stairs together, with the others a step or two ahead. All seven now moved up the stairs towards the gigantic door. Toyoko started talking to Yoko in Japanese as they climbed the stairs. J J, hearing what was said smiled a broad smile in their direction. Yoko turned and looked up at him and smiled. She then turned to Toyoko and informed her that J J could understand what she was saying. Toyoko looked up and over to J J, also smiling at him with a big smile. "You understand Japanese?"

"Yes, Ma'am, I do."

"Once again, I am honored," smiled Toyoko, as they climbed the stairs, the three of them taking each step concurrently, talking as they did. As all seven approached the gigantic door, it began to open.

"Miss Toya, I am so happy to see you your Grandmother and Scruffy, are all right," said a man, as he held the large door.

"I am fine, Sason," said Toya, as she walked up and hugged the slight built aging Japanese man. "I do need to shower and wash my hair and a change of clothes," smiled Toya, as she reached up and rubbed her head with her right hand and looking down at her soiled clothes.

"Toya. . . ?" Toya looked at Sam shaking her head slightly. Seeing Toya's reaction, Sam promptly halted his comment.

All seven entered the lavish foyer of the magnificent home. Robby, J J, Sam, and Lizy, all moved to one side of the large entry with it's heavy inlayed natural rock floor and stood politely together in silence, as the Japanese man began closing the ornately carved wood door.

"Sason, if you please. Show our honorable guests to the parlor," said Toyoko to the man bowing to her, as the massive door closed behind him, virtually not making a sound.

"If you, my worthy guests will excuse my rudeness. Sason will escort you to the parlor. We must call my husband at once and inform him, Mother Yoko and Toya are well, and they are here in my presence," said Toyoko, as she too bowed to J J and the others. Toyoko then turned to Yoko and her daughter Toya, still holding Scruffy and all three left the entryway together, as Sason bowed to the others. Then looking up at the four visitors he smiled.

"This way," said Sason, as he lead with his arm and started walking. As the others followed, they couldn't help but notice all the beautiful things they passed on their way to the parlor. There were numerous paintings hanging on the walls, works of art sitting on their own elegant pedestals.

"This place is almost as awesome as yours, Grampa."

"It is magnificent," said J J, as he turned to his grandson and smiled.

"That it is, J J," smiled Robby.

"It reminds me of home," said Lizy in a sarcastic tone they hadn't heard. The three men quickly stopped and turned, to look at Lizy. She continued walking staring up at the different paintings on the wall. The three men stood there staring at her with their mouths hanging open, as Lizy walked into Sam. "What? You guy's can't see me in a house like this?" asked Lizy, as she stood and stared right back at the three men, with her hand on her hip.

"It's not that, Lizy. Lizy, I'm almost fifty years old and I've been all over the world, and I can honestly say, I've only been in a few private homes this elegant."

"Colonel, I was just 'kidding the Colonel.' This place, like Sam already put so elegantly, is awesome," smiled Lizy. The four smiled at each other and then turned and moved quickly to catch up with their escort, Sason.

"If you please, make yourselves comfortable," said Sason, as he held his arm out towards the room, in a welcoming gesture. "I will return shortly with your tea," said Sason, as they all stood at the entrance to the large well appointed room. He bowed to them and then turned and left their attendance.

The four moved slowly into the large room. The room was furnished in several different styles of fine furniture with more artwork becoming visible as they entered the room. There were pieces made of wicker, beautiful woods and many other fine pieces. Amongst the Far East style furniture there were several European pieces and even an older American looking over stuffed leather sofa and chair. The three men headed for the over stuffed furniture. While Lizy moved towards one of the more delicate looking wicker pieces. All four sat in their chosen spot, seemingly quite pleased with their choices. The four sat quietly as they looked around the attractively decorated room, smiling at each other as their eyes met from time to time, waiting calmly for Sason's return and for the others.

"These people know how to live," whispered Lizy quietly.

"They must have a great deal of money. Some of these beautiful

Jade figurines must be priceless and all this beautiful artwork, after what Sam told me, it in itself must be worth a fortune."

"I'm sure you're right, J J. I personally haven't know anyone who lives in a home of this magnitude. Except for maybe the head man, the President of the United States."

"You know the President, William J. Clinton, Robby. . . ?"

"No, not personally, J J. But at present we all work for the guy," laughed Robby, as he sat there in the large leather chair, looking over at J J and Sam, sitting together on the sofa.

"I could live in a place like this," smiled Lizy, as she sat in a high backed wicker chair.

A woman entered the room carrying a tray with what appeared to be small sandwiches on it. She walked towards J J and Sam. Then bending down she put the tray on the low table that sat just in front of the large sofa. Smiling at the two men, she then bowed repeatedly, as she backed away. She then turned and left the room. As she left, Sason entered also carrying a large tray. His tray heavy with several large silver serving containers and cups. "I also have, if you prefer, coffee. May I serve you now?" He asked, looking towards Lizy.

"I'll have coffee, thank you."

"How would you like your coffee, Miss?" asked Sason, as he bowed to Lizy.

"Black," smiled Lizy.

Sason continued serving the four of them, finally getting to J J. "What may I pour you, Sir?"

"I'll have tea. Thank you, Sason."

Sason served J J. He then picked up the tray of sandwiches and carried it around the table to J J. He had just done so when Toyoko appeared at the entrance to the room. Seeing her there, the three men rose to their feet, as she came into the room. "My husband was so thankful to hear his Toya is unharmed. He is leaving his office now, eager to meet the honorable ones that saved Mother Yoko and Our Special One," smiled Toyoko, as she moved gracefully into the room. "You men may take your seats and finish enjoying your tea."

The three men stood smiling, taking their seats, only after Toyoko had sat down. Sason turned to the table and started pouring an additional cup of tea. He then carefully carried the hot tea to Toyoko. Which had taken a seat near Lizy, in a similar wicker chair. Sason stood calmly holding the hot cup of tea. Toyoko looked up at him. He bowed and then cautiously handed her the cup and saucer. She took the tea and then ever so slightly nodded her head, momentarily closing her eyes, as she did. Sason bowed to her and then backed away. He turned and started to leave the room. He was met by Toya, as he did. "Sason, do I look better now?" asked Toya, as she twirled around smiling. Sam jumped up and moved quickly towards Toya. Toyoko obviously startled by Sam's quick response. Her eyes quickly moving to him and then following him as he walked across the room, towards her daughter and Sason.

"Miss Toya. You are always looking beautiful," smiled Sason, as he bowed.

Toya was now dressed in a knee length light weight summer dress. "Thank you, Sason," said Toya, as she stood smiling.

"May I bring you and your friend a glass of orange juice, Miss Toya." "Thank you, Sason."

"That would be great, Sason," said Sam, as he looked from Sason to Toya, still supporting a broad smile. Sason bowed, smiling at her as he did. He then turned and walked away. "Sason's right, when he says you're beautiful," whispered Sam, as he moved closer to her smiling face. Toya stood there, her hair still wet from her shower. Her face crimson, either from the hot shower or from Sam's whispered compliment. He held his arm out to her. Slowly she delicately put her arm in his and they walked into the room arm in arm. "How's your head?" whispered Sam, as they walked. Toya's small delicate arm quickly jerked violently in his, as she looked up at him somewhat glaring, but still unable to inhibit her expression from showing a hint of a smile. "What?" whispered Sam. Toya's face quickly turned away, unable to keep her smile from returning.

"Grandmother will join us shortly, Mother," said Toya, as her and Sam sauntered by. Toyoko smiled nodding to her daughter, as her and Sam moved across the room, as one, towards J J and the sofa. J J and Robby stood politely smiling, Toya's smile once again completely intact, as the two approached. All four then sat down together, as Toya and Sam joined J J on the large sofa and Robby again sat in the large chair. "Did father hear of the earthquake? Was he concerned?"

"He heard and was quite anxious to hear more news of what areas were damaged. We hadn't heard the area near the apartment was so involved. If we had known, I don't know what we could have done to help. You know we were greatly concerned for you and Mother Yoko, Toya. Thanks to our honorable friends," smiled Toyoko, as she bowed her head towards J J and Sam. "Once again, our family has been spared a personal loss, from the earth's violent internal conflict, with our islands," smiled Toyoko. The six of them sat there in silence, obviously thinking about what Toyoko had said.

"Toya, where's Scruffy dog." asked J J, as he made some attempt to change the mood, to one more lighthearted.

"She's in my room asleep, J J."

"Oh. The rescue must have tired her out." Toyoko looked over at J J with a puzzled look on her face. "Ma'am, your daughter's dog, Scruffy, had a great deal to do with her rescue and her safe return home."

"She did Mother! She lead J J and Sam right to me, while I was still unconscious."

"Unconscious! You were unconscious?" asked Toyoko in Japanese, as she sprang from the wicker chair, her tea cup's saucer flying from her lap. "Toya, are you sure you're all right?" With her cup still in hand, she moved instantly towards Toya.

"I'm fine Mother. Let us not be rude to our honored guests," said Toya, also speaking in Japanese, as she jumped to her feet, looking as she did, around to each of their guests, who by this time were all staring at the anxious parent. Toya quickly moved towards her mother, bending and retrieving her mother's landed saucer, on her way to the obviously concerned parent. The two once again embraced.

"I'm sorry, I didn't realize you had been knocked unconscious, Toya. So now, I must remember to thank Scruffy dog, for her part in my daughters safe return," said Toyoko, as the two broke their embrace smiling at each other, as Toyoko took the saucer from her daughter's hand. Turning, they moved from each other, and returned to their seats. All three men standing, as they had been, since Toyoko and Toya abruptly stood. The five then once again sat and all six resumed their conversation.

Sason entered the room carrying a tray with two large glasses. The glasses appeared to be ice cold and filled with orange juice. Sason walked up to Toya, he then bent holding the tray low for her. Toya took a glass from the tray. "Thank you, Sason."

Sason moved and bowed to Sam. "Thank you," said Sam, as he too took a glass. The two took a drink of the orange colored refreshment and smiled up at Sason. Sason stood smiling, holding the empty tray at arms length, flat against the outside of his upper thigh, like a musician would hold a tambourine.

"May I get anything for anyone." asked Sason, as he looked around the room.

"Thank you," said Toyoko. Sason bowed. He then turned and walked out of the room.

"Sason has been with my parents, since before . . . the Special One was born," whispered Toya, as she looked up at Sam and rolled her dark eyes. Her face a bit red, as her and Sam sat together on the sofa next to J J.

"He seems to think a great deal of you, Toya."

"Yes," said Toya softly, as she smiled up at Sam, nodding her head as she did.

The six continued their conversation, it changing to several different topics. As they were talking Lizy's pager beeped. "I'm sorry, Ma'am. It's my pager," said Lizy, as she moved in her seat, to remove the pager from her belt. "Is there a phone I may use, to call my base?" asked Lizy, as she looked down at the unit she held in her hand.

"Lizy, I'll show you to a phone," said Toya, as she rose to her feet. As did Lizy and the three men. The two of them then started to leave the room.

"If you'll excuse me Ma'am, I'll make this call," said Lizy, as she nodded to Toyoko and then turned towards Robby. Robby giving her a sign, in the form of a wink. For her to do just that. Toya and Lizy left the room together. The men looked at each other as they once again took their seats, smiling over towards Toyoko, as they did.

"I'm sorry, Toyoko," smiled Robby. "I must apologize for this discourteous interruption. Those electronic devices can be so intrusive at times. But I must say, the interruption by the beeper, maybe in our own best interest. That could be the call we've been waiting for."

"Robby, I am not offended. If the call is important, I am most pleased by it's timely interruption," smiled Toyoko, as she nodded slightly to the three men. The men returning the gesture, as the room grew quiet, as the four of them sat there in silence, still smiling at one another from time to time, not knowing quite what to say next.

"Toyoko how long will it take your husband to get home?"

"If he takes a train and then a cab, this time a day, I am not sure. His normal commute, is forty five minutes. That's at his usual commuting time of day. At this time of day, it may take more or less time, I really have no idea. He said he may fly, if the company helicopter was available. That being the case, he could arrive any moment, J J."

"His company has one of those helicopter things?"

"Yes it does, J J," smiled Toyoko, as she stared at him obviously with a questions about the way he asked about the companies helicopter. "J J, my husband is the CEO of the company."

J J looked from Toyoko to Robby. Just then Lizy and Toya, came into the room. The two of them stopped and stood, between Toyoko and the three men that had once again rose to their feet. "What did you find out, Lieutenant?"

"Colonel, the page was from Mike all right. He heard the area around the Market was heavily damaged during this mornings earthquake. Knowing me like he does, he knew I would most likely be taking you three there. Knowing that, he was concerned if we were all right. I'm sorry, J J. He didn't have any news of any flights," said Lizy, with a sad expression on her face, as she looked over at him.

"Thank you, Lizy," smiled J J.

"Yes, thank you, Lieutenant."

Just then J J abruptly turned. "I can hear one of those helicopters."

"It must be father. He said if he could, he would fly home. Come, we'll go meet him," said Toya, as she moved towards J J and Sam. "Come on, Sam. He'll be landing in the back. Please come and meet my father, would you please?" asked Toya, as she moved between J J and Sam, putting one arm through J J's arm and the other through Sam's.

"Thank you, Toya, we've been awaiting the privilege," smiled J J.

"Yes, my husband is most anxious to meet you. You boys be careful, as tall as you are, you be careful of those blades," said Toyoko, as she rose from her chair putting one hand above her head making a circular motion, as she did.

"Yes, Ma'am, we'll be careful," smiled Sam

"Come on, guys," said Toya excitedly, as she stepped forward tugging on Sam's and J J's arms, her tiny body trying it's best to get the two men towering over her to move. Once doing so, she started to lead them in the direction in which she wanted them to go. The three of them left the room together arm in arm, with the others not far behind. As they walked through more of the magnificent home, they saw Sason.

"Sason, I think father's helicopter is landing."

"Yes, Miss Toya," said Sason, as he moved out of her way, allowing her and the others to pass, bowing to them as they did. Then they passed an archway. J J turned to see Mother Yoko kneeling in front of a Shrine, as they moved swiftly past, J J apparently the only one to notice the in house Shrine. They exited the house and moved out onto a large observation platform. The platform over looked an absolutely beautiful garden. They could now easily hear the roar of the landing helicopter.

"Follow, me," said Toya, as she let go of Sam and J J. She ran quickly to the stairs at the edge of the platform, going down the stairs into the garden. The two men and the others followed. Once in the garden, they followed a flat stone walkway through the spectacular garden. Moving quickly trying to keep up with their guide.

"Which way did, she go?" asked J J, as they came to a Y in the stone walkway and stopped.

"This way!" yelled Toya excitedly, as she came running back towards the walkway's intersection. She then turned and ran off with Sam quickly running after her. The others followed, quickening their pace. They ran up a small incline and down the other side. Sam catching up with Toya, just as the two of them came out into an open area and stopped. The others came up and stopped right behind Toya and Sam. Hovering there before them, painted the very brightest red imaginable, was a helicopter descending it's last few feet, before making contact with the ground. They all stood together watching, as it touched down.

J J stood quietly thinking, as he watched the helicopter land. 'This brilliantly colored machine was in many ways far different than the dull drab green color, of the Marine helicopter he rode in only a day earlier.' To him, it was like comparing a new Model A truck, to say a Model J Duesenberg or even, a Cord.

"Your fathers waving, Toya," hollered Sam, in a loud enough voice as to be heard over the helicopter's roar. Toya begin happily waving to her father. Her father continuing to wave, through the clear windshield of the fancy helicopter. The helicopter's rotors began to slow, as they all stood there together, at the edge of the helicopter's concrete landing pad. The helicopter's earsplitting sound slowly dissipating. Just then the door of the brilliant red machine opened and a middle aged gentleman, climbed out of his prestigious form of transportation. Bending, he moved quickly from the side of the helicopter, out from under it's now slowly rotating rotors. He quickly moved in the direction of his enthusiastic daughter. Who by now, was bouncing up and down, impatiently awaiting her father's impending embrace. Just before his approach, she stopped bouncing. She smiled and then bowed towards her approaching father. He paused smiling. He then bowed, returning the honor she so graciously bestowed upon him. She then ran quickly towards him. Seeing this, he bent down quickly, putting his briefcase on the cement pad. Standing just in time, to catch her in both arms, the both of them swinging around like a merry-go-round. Then putting her gently on her feet, the two of them hugged. As they hugged, the noise from the helicopter's engine virtually disappeared and it's rotors slowed to a stop. Then moving from their embrace, still holding onto one anothers hand. They walked together towards his smiling wife.

"Toya, were you hurt in anyway?"

"No, Papa. Just a bump to my head, I am fine," said Toya, as she looked at her father and smiled, as they approached the girl's mother.

"Husband, Toya and Mother Yoko, are well. Thanks to our guests," said Toyoko, as she walked up next to her daughter and husband, holding her dainty hand out towards their four guests. Toyoko's husband reached out and gathered his wife in his arm and pulled her close to him. With his daughter in one arm and his wife in the other. They stood smiling towards their guests.

"Father, if I may, I would like to introduce you to my new friends. Father, this is J J, Robby, Sam and Lizy," smiled Toya, as she held out her hand palm up to each one of her new friends, as she introduced them to her father. Her father moving to each person, shaking their hands and introducing himself, as Siako Makido. Bowing to each of them, as he did.

"I am humbly grateful. Toya, Our Special One is. . . ," said Siako, as he turned, carefully placing his hand on Toya's head. "And Mother Yoko, are . . . thank you," said the man bowing before them, his voice shaking, and tears forming in his eyes. "I thank you also for bringing them safely home to my wife," smiled Siako, as he turned from their guests back towards his wife and daughter. "I am so sorry. I can only stay a few hours. I must fly to San Francisco, this evening," said Siako, as he again hugged his wife and daughter. "Come, let us all go to the house, where you will tell me how I may honor you, for your help in my family's good fortune. The three of us will follow you, our guests, to the house," said Siako, as he stood with his family smiling.

J J turned and started back towards the house, with everyone else following his lead. Toya grabbing her father's briefcase, as the others started towards the house on the stone walkway. "Mr. Makido, your home and these gardens are spectacular," said J J, as he turned towards his host, walking as he spoke.

"Thank you, J J. If I may call you J J?" smiled Siako.

"Yes, of course," said J J, as he moved to one side of the walkway and stopped. Robby taking lead as the others moved past J J, as he stood waiting. "J J's, fine," said J J, as he stepped back on the walkway alongside Siako. Holding his hand out to Siako smiling, as the two now walked side by side.

"J J, you may call me Siako," smiled Siako, as he grabbed J J's hand. The two shaking hands as they walked.

With Robby leading the way. The rest of the group slowly paired up. Lizy with Toyoko, J J and Siako. And of course, Toya and Sam, walking just a bit slower then the pace, falling a little behind the rest of the group.

"How do you find time to care for this absolutely magnificent garden?" asked J J, as he walked along looking at all the different kinds of plants and how well cared for they appeared.

"Except for my bonsai."

J J turned and looked towards Siako. Not wanting to interrupt, said nothing.

"The garden is maintained by two gardeners, who work under Toyoko's and Sason's supervision."

"They do a beautiful job, Siako."

"Thank you, J J, it is beautiful. I love walking through the garden in the evening with my family, after a long day of playing the game of corporate chess. I am most fortunate to have the opportunity to regularly walk through such a place of beauty and peace. But more than that, my family living here, relatively safe, is by far the greatest thing about living here. That gives me peace of mind. And with that peace of mind, I have the ability to use that mind, to thrive in the corporate game."

"Siako, by the looks of things, you do that pretty well," smiled J J, as he looked over towards Siako.

"J J, good fortune has bestowed upon me the ability to excel in the corporate world, far beyond my own expectations," said Siako, as he turned and then stared towards J J. The two of them still walking side by side.

J J noticed a change in Siako's mood.

"What's wrong, Siako?"

"Nothing, J J," said Siako, as he then smiled. "J J, I am having trouble understanding this calm and equanimity, I perceive being here with you. Perhaps, it is the realization, if not for you and the young Marine. Our Special One, may never have walked with me and her mother, in this garden again."

"Siako, that's not the case," said J J, as he put his hand on Siako's shoulder and smiled a big friendly smile. "Siako, being there with Sam, so the two of us could be there for Toya this morning. Talk about fortunate! It's like standing here calmly talking to you. In my entire adult life, I couldn't have possibly imagined doing what I'm doing right now!" smiled J J hesitating, as he looked over at the Japanese man scrutinizing him.

"What, J J?"

"Talking to you. And yet, here I am, happily doing just that."

"Why is that, J J?"

"I . . . I didn't think I would ever make it . . . here to Japan."

"I am very grateful you did make it to Japan. And that Sam and you were there this morning and that the two of you are here now, J J."

"No more, than I am," smiled J J, as the two of them started up the stairs, one after the other. J J waiting on the platform for Siako. The others gathering by the rail at the edge of the platform, once again looking at the beautiful garden, as they all stood talking. J J and Siako, joined the others along the platform's rail. Now all five stood together watching, as Toya and Sam came into view. The two of them moving slowly through the garden, walking hand in hand towards the stairs.

"The young Marine and my daughter, seemed to be quite fond of each other," said Siako, as his tone of voice and expression changed to one more serious, as he stood watching his daughter and the young Marine approach the stairs. Toya and Sam started up the stairs together, taking one step at a time. The two of them completely oblivious to Toya's father's stare of concern. Hearing and seeing the change in Siako's demeanor. J J stood quietly watching, not saying anything. Thinking to himself, as he watched. 'What was unfolding right before his and the others eyes. His grandson, known to him only a few days, was seemingly becoming infatuated with this beautiful young Japanese girl, right before him and the girl's obviously concerned father.' Toya and Sam, reached the top of the stairs before they realized they had the undivided attention of everyone on the platform. The two smiling towards the others, as both their faces turned beet red. Toya then focusing her attention on her father, noticing his somber discord.

Toyoko sensing the seriousness of her husband's disposition. "Siako, we are so very privileged to be able to honor our guests. You not being away on business, allowing the two of us to bestow acknowledgment of this honor, together with Our Specail One. Here in our own home," said Toyoko, as she moved up next to her husband, slowly slipping her arm around him. Toya's father's sober expression slowly transformed, to the pleasant smile, that had been there just a short time earlier. Breaking the spell of the shock of seeing his young daughter awestruck over an American Marine, personal hero or not. Toya, seeing her father's smile returning, walked with Sam towards the entrance to the house. Turning as she walked to see her father's continuing reaction to the now obvious situation.

GOOD FORTUNE

"Whata we do now, Ollie?" asked J J in a low voice, as he put his hand on Siako's shoulder, leaning close to be heard, as the door of the house closed behind Toya and Sam. Everyone turned instantly towards J J. The four of them standing there with bewilderment showing on their faces. "I'm sorry, I couldn't help myself," laughed J J, as he tried to make light of their predicament. "It's obvious to all of us, my . . . the boy and your lovely daughter," said J J, as he looked towards Siako and Toyoko. "Are fast becoming, shall we say, close friends." The other four slowly nodding their heads in unison with J J's. Showing that they seem to agree with his interpretation of the situation.

"Well, we all agree. Is there anything you can do. Should you do anything, even if you could? They're not children! I know this sounds crazy, it's like fate, brought these two together. That's my opinion, for what it's worth. It's obvious to me, good fortune has fallen upon all of us, here today."

"Lizy, I feel somewhat the same as you. It must be divine intervention, that brought us here. When you know all the contributing factors, it must have been something of that nature. I'm sorry, Mr. and Mrs. Makido, there is a great deal more to this theory of fate, than your daughter's rescue. Not to take anything away from that special event. In the fate department, J J is most definitely special."

"Thank you, Robby," smiled J J.

Just then the door of the house opened and Toya and Sam came out of the house and stood on the platform. "Father may I speak with you?"

"Yes," said Siako, as he turned to his guests. "Excuse me, for a moment?" asked Siako, as he turned and walked towards his daughter, not waiting for an answer to his question. Toya had moved from Sam's side, and was now standing separated from the others, waiting for her father. The two talked for a few moments. Toya then hugged her father and kissed him on the cheek. She then rejoined Sam and the two of them re-entered the house. Siako stood there alone. Then turning slowly towards the others, he smiled. He then started walking in their direction. The others stood patiently awaiting Siako's return and hopefully information from him, about their conversation. Upon his return to the anxious ensemble, he said nothing.

"My, husband. Will you not tell us what was said between you and your daughter?"

He stood there smiling, not saying a word, as the others stood staring at him. The others turned to each other for help with their obvious dilemma, as Siako smiled.

"She could tell I was concerned by the closeness her and Sam displayed. She said she could understand why I was concerned, but she couldn't understand or explain to me, why she felt the way she did. The attraction she felt for Sam, was different than anything she had ever experienced," said Siako, as he stood facing the others. "She then said, "she nor Sam, would do anything to dishonor me or Sam's grandfather." She looked over toward you four when she said it. What do you suppose she meant by that?" asked Siako, as he looked towards the others for an answer.

J J stood there smiling, holding his hands up, a little over waist high, with his thumbs pointing towards his smiling face.

Siako reacted as though he had just received an electric shock. He then stood staring towards J J. "You're that young Marine's grandfather? I had no idea. For one thing. I didn't realize you were that old. Old enough to be the grandfather of a man that age, I mean."

"Believe it!" said the three guests, all at the same time.

"He's my, Grandson," beamed J J, as he stood proudly.

"That means you have to be at least, in your late fifties or early sixties. Given your physical appearance and the scars on your face, it's hard to tell you're even close to that old," said Siako, as he put his hand on J J's shoulder and smiled.

"You think it's hard for you! It's definitely hard for me, to think of myself, that age and then some."

"How old are you, J J?"

"I am seventy two, Siako."

"I had no idea. We best get this old gentleman in so he can sit down and relax," said Siako, as he tried, as J J had done earlier, to make light, of a somewhat serious situation.

"Yes, these old bones have about had it. You lead the way, you young whip-per-snapper," said J J, talking in the caricature of a frail old man.

Lizy instantly walked over to J J and hit him on the side of his upper arm. "Stop that!" shouted Lizy, sternly.

"Ouch," said J J, as he stood rubbing his arm.

"You, deserved that."

"Oh," said J J, as he stood there thinking about what Lizy said, as he rubbed his arm.

"Come on ancient one," said Siako, as he grabbed J J's arm. The same arm Lizy had just given a commanding blow.

"I think the lady has made her point. There shall be no more distasteful humor of the aged, spouted from these lips. If we live long enough, we'll all be there soon enough as it is," said J J, as he nodded to Lizy smiling. She smiled and moved quickly towards him. Him flinching slightly as she did.

"Come here!" said Lizy, as she grabbed J J and gave him a big hug. Then placing a hand on each side of his face, she gave him a quick kiss.

They all laughed together, as J J stood smiling from ear to ear. Then pulling on his arm, Siako moved him across the platform towards the entrance to the house. The others following their lead. They entered the house, Siako leading them to a part of the house they hadn't seen.

"Siako, your English is better than mine, how is it you speak it so precise. That's not to say, Siako, anything better than mine, is that precise. . . . There's little or no discernible accent, as you speak."

"My mother, would have been pleased to hear that, J J. As I was growing up, she took every opportunity, available, for me to learn your language. It was one of her primary goals for me."

"I take it, Yoko, is not your, mother."

"Yoko, is Toyoko's, mother," smiled Siako, as he looked over at J J, as they walked through the house. "My mother, died a few months ago."

"I'm, sorry."

"Except for the loss of my father and others, that transpired many years ago, she had good fortune in her long life. She was eighty six when she died, apparently peacefully in her sleep."

"What of your father, Siako?"

"J J, I never knew my father. He was killed before I was born."

"How was he killed?"

"He was killed in the war between our two great countries. We have no idea how, when or where, he was killed. Mother said, "after he left her side." She had to believe, "he died as he had lived, in honor." She could never find any record of his plight. It was as though he ceased to exist. Her memories, passed onto me, and others, and of course my presence, are the only things to show he ever existed. I also had two brothers, born long before myself. They were identical twins. They were only sixteen, when they were killed. My mother came to accept the loss of my father. She never accepted the loss of my brothers. She always felt and said, to anyone who would listen. "Her twin boys lives, were sacrificed, in the last desperate days of the war, by our Emperor," said Siako, his voice shaking as he spoke. He then inhaled deeply and smiled. "I am sorry, J J. I haven't spoke of these things for years. Again, I am at a loss, why I feel a need to tell you things."

The two men stopped, as did the others. They were all now standing near the entrance to the Shrine, J J had seen earlier.

"Perhaps, it's just that I'm a good listener, Siako," smiled J J.

"You are, J J, but that is not it. I'm a CEO, I have lots of good listeners around," snickered Siako. "This was my mother's favorite place, her last few years," said Siako, as he held out his hand, in an invitation to his guests to enter their home's Shrine.

"Yes, both Yoko, and my husband's mother, love this place. Ever since it's hard fought conception. We helped the two of them move it here, from their personal homes. Two personal memorials, that were unmistakably individual, merged harmoniously into one Shrine, they could both worship in and feel comfortable doing so."

"J J, the large picture in the center, is of my father. The two smaller ones, on each side, are of my twin brothers. There wasn't any film available in the latter part of the war. The pictures you see here, of the two boys, were taken on their thirteenth birthday. These two pictures, are the only things, that show the two young men, my twin brothers, ever existed. Thanks to my mother's memories passed onto me and my family. They will not be forgotten."

J J stood there in reverence. Some time past as the others also stood in respectful silence. "Thank you for sharing that special heartfelt story with me, Siako," said J J, as he reached out with both arms pulling the shorter Japanese man close, hugging him as tears filled his eyes. Releasing Siako, J J turned to the others. "I know, Sam already pointed that out to me, a Marine shouldn't be seen standing around sniveling." smiled J J, as he saw Lizy and Robby standing there, also a bit red eyed, Lizy more so than Robby. "I take that back. Two Marines and an Air Force Officer, standing together sniveling, not a good picture," said J J, as he put his arm on Siako's shoulder and smiled. "Thank you again for bringing us here and telling us your family's story, Siako. If I may, I would like to tell you a story, of why we may have this connection, we both definitely have. In addition to our good fortune this morning with Toya," smiled J J, as they moved slowly out of the family's Shrine. The five once again moved through the house, again meeting up with Sason.

"Sir, I have your drink prepared and more tea for mistress Toyoko and your guests," said Sason, as he bowed to Siako. "Miss Toya, is showing the young man more of the premises, Sir. Sir, Miss Toya put your briefcase in your office."

"Sason, bring our refreshments there. We can sit in here and you can tell me your story J J," said Siako, as he moved to open his office door for J J and the others. Siako stood holding the door for the others to enter. The door was hinged on the right and opened into the room.

The office was beautifully done all in wood paneling. With floor to ceiling bookshelves on the wall to the right of the entrance. To the left was a wall of windows, including a set of windowed French doors, that lead out into the garden. The room was large. There was room enough for a large leather sofa and a pair of winged back chairs. The sofa was set out from the bookshelves facing the windows. Giving a person sitting there, an excellent view of the garden. The winged back chairs sat at angles to each other, both facing a large desk. Behind the desk sat a large office chair facing more bookshelves that ran from floor to ceiling, along both sides of the room's entrance door, to the adjoining corners, with additional shelves and cabinets behind the large desk and chair.

"Come in and have a seat," said Siako, as he pointed towards the sofa and then the chairs. He then moved around to the back side of a beautiful wood desk. Taking a seat in his high backed chair behind the desk. Lizy and Toyoko were already sitting on the sofa, as J J and Robby stood in front of the two winged chairs. "Have a seat you two. Then you can tell the story you wanted to tell me, J J."

J J and Robby sat in the chairs facing Siako sitting at his desk. With everyone comfortably seated, J J cleared his throat. Just then Sason entered with a tray in hand. He sat the tray on a table that sat near one end of the sofa. He took a large cold looking glass from the tray and carried it to Siako. Then returning to the tray, he poured each of the others tea or coffee, remembering what each person took in their drink.

"Sason, tell Toya and Sam, we're in here, when you see them."

"Yes, Sir," said Sason, as he bowed and then left the room.

"I'm sorry, J J. Go ahead and tell us your story, I am assuming it's for everyone to hear."

"Yes, that's fine. Maybe it would be better if Toya was here too, so she could also hear this."

Siako hearing that, picked up the phone. Within a second or two, was talking to Sason. "Toya and Sam, will be here in a few moments," smiled Siako. In no time at all, there was a knock at the door, as it slowly opened.

"Yes, father," said Toya softly.

"Toya, you and Sam, come in and take a seat." Without saying a word the two came in and quickly took a seat with Lizy and Toyoko on the sofa. "J J has something he wants us all to hear. You have our attention J J. Go ahead with your story."

J J spent part of the next hour, telling Siako and his family, his story. "Now you may see why the story of your father and brothers, affected me so much, Siako."

Sam, not having heard Siako's story, looked over towards Toya, shrugging his shoulders, as they all sat in silence.

"Magnificent story! I knew you were different, J J. Far more patient and compassionate, than any Americans I personally. . . ."

"Fifty years of being alone, may have a similar affect on some of them," smiled J J.

"Fifty years. That means you had never seen Sam, until just a few days ago."

"That's right, Toya. I've known him just a few days longer then you have," smiled J J.

"And your wife! She still hasn't been told you are alive!"

"That's why Robby, is helping us get him home to Gramma."

"Yes, I'm trying to get him home, before news of his existence is known. I will ask a personal favor of you, not to tell anyone about this for a few days."

"Yes, we'll wait until we see it in the press, before we say a word to anyone. It will be quite a story even here in Japan. A World War II American Marine, found after fifty years. It will be on the front page of every newspaper in the world," said Siako, as he sat at his desk looking over towards J J sitting there smiling. "Robby, at this time the three of you are waiting for a flight to Anchorage Alaska?"

"Yes, that's correct. The crew of the flight we're taking, needed to log some rest time. That's why we were with Lizy at the market this morning. We had ten hours, and Lizy, offered to show us some of the beautiful things to see. Your daughter Toya, turned out to be, by far the most beautiful, of all those things," smiled Robby, as he looked over at Toya, sitting next to her mother and Sam, her face turning a bit red, from Robby's compliment. A silence befell the room, as they sat there thinking about what had been said. Siako made the first move. Reaching for his telephone, he quickly dialed a number. Speaking in Japanese, he asked a few questions. Than Siako gave, to the person on the phone, what appeared to the others, as orders. At that point, J J and Toya jumped to their feet, as

Toyoko sat looking up at J J smiling. All three, apparently a bit surprised at what Siako was saying. Siako put down the phone and smiled across his desk towards J J. Sam and Robby, quickly looked from one person, to the other. Then turning towards Siako, the two sat patiently awaiting some clue to what was going on.

"J J, with the Colonel's permission. I have found a way to honor you for your gift to our family, of saving the life of Our Special One."

"Why would you need my permission, Siako?" asked Robby, as he sat there with a puzzled look on his face.

J J took in a deep breath. "Unless I'm mistaken, Robby. Siako has just made arrangements for a flight to San Francisco. With your permission Robby, he's offering the three of us, seats on his company's airplane," said J J, as tears filled his eyes and ran down his cheeks, him wiping away those tears, with the backs of both hands. Being careful of the one side of his face, as he did.

Sam and Robby, jumped to their feet. "That's great," shouted Sam, as he looked over at Robby.

"It's ok, isn't it Colonel?" asked Sam enthusiastically.

"Yes! It's great. When?"

"The plane is scheduled to leave in less then two hours. We could re-schedule, if you need more time, Colonel."

Everyone looked towards Robby, as a silence came over the room. "No! That's great. Thank you, Siako."

"I am most fortunate, there is room on this flight. And I am able to offer this trip. Knowing what I know now, if this flight was not available. I. . . ."

"Thank you, Siako. What should we do now?" asked J J, showing excitement in his voice.

"I say we relax, maybe have some dinner and enjoy each others company, until it's time to leave," smiled Siako.

"Colonel, we best go to the base and gather your things from the other plane. I can go. . . ."

"Lizy, I'll go with you. It will be faster with two of us."

"Colonel, I can call Mike. Under the circumstances, I think I can persuade him to get some grunts to help me load your gear."

"Sir, may I use your telephone?" asked Lizy, as she rose to her feet.

"You sure can, Lizy. What's the number, I'll dial it for you," said Siako, as he grabbed the phone's receiver and held it out to Lizy. Lizy told him the number, as she took the receiver.

"It's ringing. Thank you, Siako."

"This means I could see my Jera Marie even sooner," smiled J J, as he slowly sat back down in the chair.

"J J, I don't remember the scheduled landing time. I can check my notes, here in my briefcase," said Siako, as he pointed to his briefcase.

"No, that's fine."

"Lizy, here let me get something from my case."

Lizy heard Siako. "Hang on a second, Mike," said Lizy, as she watched Siako go through his briefcase.

"Here, Lizy. These are the helicopter's ID numbers. If you can get clearance. You can fly to the base to get their belongings."

"That's fantastic! Thank you."

"You'll need clearance first."

"Ya. Right." Lizy continued her phone conversation with Mike. Writing notes as she spoke. After a few minutes of talking, she handed the receiver to Siako. "Mike has given clearance for the chopper. He said the Major was still not available. We can land next to the Experimental and retrieve your personal gear. He allowed us a one hour window, to get it done."

"Let's go. J J you stay here. Lizy and I will go and get our gear. Siako, Lizy nor I, speak Japanese. Does your pilot speak any English?"

"Father, Sam and I can go along and I can translate for your pilot."

"That will not be necessary Toya, my pilot speaks enough English to understand and communicate with the base's tower. You two can still go if you would like."

"No, thank you. I just wanted to help if I was needed, father." Smiled Toya, as she and Sam sat down together, with Toyoko on the sofa.

"Thank you, for your offer," smiled Siako, as he rose from his chair. "Here's a note for my pilot. He'll do whatever you ask of him. We'll see you back here in a few moments," said Siako, as he handed the note to Robby. Robby took the note and then turned to Lizy.

"J J, you and Sam, visit here with the Makido's. Let's go Lizy."

"I'm with you, Colonel," said Lizy, as she started with Robby towards the door. The two left the office and started through the enormous house.

"When you look at this place, it's obvious, Siako, really has the bucks. And yet, he seems like an o-k-kind-a guy, to me. What do you think, Colonel?"

"An o-k-kind-a guy! Lizy, I don't see how he could do anything more for us, than he's already done! Or offered to do!"

"Ya, you're right, Colonel. J J and Siako, seem to have a bond that can not be easily explained. No, that's not true! All a person has to do is meet J J, and they'll understand!"

"I think you, have it figured, Lizy."

"May I help you?" asked Sason, as he appeared in the hallway.

"Thank you, Sason. We're leaving for a little while. We'll be back."

"Yes, Sir, thank you."

The two came to the door that lead to the platform. They left the house, down the stairs into the garden. In no time at all they were with in sight of the helicopter. The pilot was nowhere in sight. They walked up to the bright red machine's left side. Lizy pointed through the rear door's window. There in the helicopter's rear seat, laid the pilot sound asleep. Robby tapped on the door's window. The pilot quickly sat up and moved to open the door.

"Yes. What I do for you?" asked the pilot, as he climbed out of the helicopter's rear seat and stood with Robby and Lizy. Robby handed the note to the pilot.

"When?"

"Right now."

"Hi. It take four minutes to go."

"Let's go."

"Hi," said the pilot, as he bowed slightly. He then quickly turned and opened the helicopter's door and climbed into the pilot's seat. Once there he motioned to the Colonel and Lieutenant, to climb aboard, as he put on his headset. The Colonel responded by grabbing the rear door handle and opened the door and the two started climbing in on the left side of the helicopter. With the door securely fastened, and them in their seats, the helicopter started to whine. With the helicopter's engine soon warm enough for flight, the two quickly fastened their seat belts and put on their headsets. The pilot reached for and grabbed the microphone of his radio. After a minute or two, they heard the pilot say he had clearance to land and was told where to land. The next thing they knew the bright red helicopter was airborne. In just a matter of minutes they were over the base. The helicopter started it's descend and within a few seconds they were on the ground, right where the tower had told them to land, next to the Experimental. No sooner than they had landed, Lizy saw a vehicle moving in their direction.

"That must be our help," said Lizy, as she pointed to the vehicle, as she removed her headset and unfastened her seat belt. Robby told the pilot to, "leave the engine running, they wouldn't be long." The Colonel, opened the door, and the two of them quickly climbed down and out of the helicopter's rear seat, and ran out from under the slowly rotating rotors, bending over as they did. They had just taken an upright walking posture, when Lizy noticed who was in the vehicle. "Oh, Shit."

The Colonel abruptly looked her way, but didn't say a word. As he too saw who was in the vehicle. The car came to a stop, just a short distance from where the two now stood. The rear door on the right side of the vehicle quickly opened and out climbed Lieutenant Houseman. Mike stood holding the door for a Major to exit the vehicle. Lizy came to attention and stood so, as the Colonel and Major saluted one another and then moved towards each other. The two men introduced themselves and then walked together talking. As they walked away, Lizy walked up to Mike.

"Is the old man upset?"

"Just a tad. He came in while I was on the phone with the tower, telling them our plans. I had to tell him, Lizy, I'm sorry."

"Yes, of course you did, Mike. I know that."

"He wasn't too pleased with me for giving a civilian aircraft permission to land. And when I tried to save my butt, by telling him there was a Marine Colonel involved. He really got pissed."

"Maybe Robby can calm him down. The Major has only been a Major for a short time. I think Robby's been a Colonel, for. . . ."

"Robby! Lizy, you just called a Marine Colonel, by what I would assume is, his first name. Do you two have something going?"

"After what we've been through, no problem. No, we don't have something going on, Mike. At least not the way you mean. I do wonder what's going on with them?" said Lizy, as she looked towards the Colonel and Major.

"Mike, while they're talking, why don't you help me get the guy's gear off the plane? The Colonel, told me where to find it."

"I might as well. The Major looks occupied. I don't see how I can get in too much more trouble doing that. My career is probably already over, as it is. Let's go Lizy." The two promptly headed for the Experimental. Once there they retrieved the three men's gear, from where the Colonel had said it would be. With the gear in hand, they headed back towards the awaiting helicopter. The pilot seeing the load the two were carrying, quickly opened his door and jumped to the ground. Like some kind of, 'Super Hero,' he ran to their aid. The three hastily moved the remaining distance to the helicopter and promptly loaded the gear into a compartment, of the still running machine. With the compartment secure, the pilot moved to his door and quickly climbed back into his seat. Mike and Lizy moved back out from under the still rotating rotators. The two of them then leaned up against the car and waited for the Colonel and Major's return.

"Lizy what's going on. What's this Colonel up to? Did you notice this morning, the two privates uniforms? Their uniforms, didn't have any name tags. Why was that old man wearing a uniform?"

"I can't tell you now, Mike."

"Come on! Lizy, I'll most likely be transferred to Greenland, for what I've done. At least you could tell me, why!"

"Mike, I'll tell you after the Fourth. Ok?"

With the whine of the helicopter's running engine. There was no way for Lizy, to hear what the Colonel and Major were saying to each other.

"I wish, I knew what was going on. The Major is so paranoid about upper command, he's libel to blow it for everyone."

"I can tell you what the Colonel is saying."

"What! How?"

"I'll tell you if you'll tell me," said Mike talking like a spoiled child.

"Mike, I can't."

Mike stood there against the Major's car, folding his arms with a smug look on his face. Lizy saw the look and abruptly elbowed him in the ribs.

"Ok! I can read lips, all right!"

"You can read lips?" asked Lizy, as she stood there shaking her head, looking at Mike with her mouth hung open. "When? Never mind! What's he saying?"

"Lizy, I'm not a hundred percent with this."

Lizy quickly turned and glared at Mike.

"What's he saying, Mike?"

"Your Colonel has been telling the Major he's trying to get home, as quick as possible. He said the Experimental got him and his aides, from the deck's of the Enterprise this far, and now, he has a flight that will take them further towards home." The two men turned and headed back in Mike's and Lizy's direction. "The Major's telling the Colonel they should have the helicopter checked before the Colonel and his aides fly. He's saying something about the possibility of terrorism. Your Colonel's making it clear to the Major, very clear, he doesn't agree, there is anymore danger for himself and his aides on this flight, than there is on any other." As the two men walked up to Mike and Lizy, they stopped and shook hands. The Major then moved quickly from the Colonel towards his awaiting car. Mike moved immediately to open the Major's car door. The Major stopped briefly and glared at Lizy. Mike looked at Lizy, as the

Major bent and entered the rear seat of the car. Mike stood looking towards Lizy and then the Colonel.

"Lieutenant!"

Mike saluted the Colonel and then climbed into the car's rear seat with the Major. No sooner had he done so, than the car drove off.

"What was that all about?" asked Lizy, as she walked up to Robby.

"He's an. . . . Let's just say he's not, 'one of the few good men,' and let it go at that," said Robby, as they stood watching as the car drove away. "I'm sorry, Lizy, I shouldn't have said that about your commanding officer. Enough about that. . . , let's get out of here," said the Colonel, as he spun around and headed for the helicopter. Lizy stood there a second a bit surprised by Robby's actions. She then had to run to catch up, just as Robby opened the left rear door of the beautiful bright red machine. The two climbed in, with Lizy quickly closing the door, and the two of them put on their belts, just as, it's engine began to roar and it abruptly took to the air.

"J J, you can sit here on my right. Toyoko, Toya, and Sam, can sit there on my left. We'll save those two seats next to you J J, for Lizy and Robby," said Siako, as he pointed towards the different chairs sitting around the large table. While Lizy and Robby were off getting their gear. The others had moved into the Makido's dining room for an early supper.

"I hear the helicopter."

"It's amazing, you can do that, at your age, J J," said Siako, as he continued holding out his arm to J J, waiting for him to take his seat.

"It's because I didn't listen to loud music," smiled J J, as he moved towards a splendidly crafted wooden chair, itself a piece of fine furniture. The quality he had only seen since coming to the Makido's home. Sitting carefully, he sat in the chair. The chair was only one of many, sitting around the beautiful dining room table. The table was made of wood. It's top inlaid with many different colored pieces of wood, forming a representation of a beautiful bird. The table was polished to a mirror like finish. J J carefully reached out and lightly touched the table's smooth surface with his finger tips.

"Loud music," smiled Siako, as he nodded looking over towards his daughter and Sam, as the two of them took their seats at the large table, either not hearing or ignoring J J and Siako's, reference to loud music.

Siako and Toyoko, took their seats. Siako at the head of the table and Toyoko, in the vacant seat next to her daughter. Putting Toyoko and J J, across from each other, with her on her husband's left and J J on his right. No sooner had they sat down, than Sason entered the room carrying things for the table. He proceeded placing the paraphernalia needed for dining, including flatware and chopsticks some beautifully woven place mats, in front of each of the five, and the two empty seats for Lizy and Robby.

"Siako, Sam and Robby, told me the tremendous amount of money it cost to fly one of these jet airplanes. How can you justify your company flying the three of us there, costing the way it does?"

"J J, cost is not an issue. The company's flying myself and six others to San Francisco. Five of the six are executives, who just happen to be Americans. We're flying them home for the Fourth Of July. One of the five is retiring. That is the reason the one fellow and I, are going along, so we can be there for his retirement party. It's going to be a surprise party, at our U S facility. J J, the plane has an abundance of room, it's flying there with or without you. It is my good fortune, to be in a position to be able to offer this trip to you. And my pleasure to be a part of it."

"And mine," smiled J J.

"Like Lizy, intuitively recognized, J J. It's destiny," said Siako, as he sat smiling at J J. He then turned and looked over towards his wife and daughter, sitting with the grandson of the man he had come so close to, in such a short amount of time.

"Then all we'll have to do, is get ourselves from San Francisco to Seattle, Sam," smiled J J, as he looked across the table to his grandson.

"J J."

Just then Sason came in with Lizy and Robby. He lead them to the two chairs. Sason pulled out the chairs nearest J J and Lizy sat down, as Robby pulled out the other chair and sat next to Lizy.

"How did it go, Robby?"

"Our gear is stowed in the helicopter. I assumed we were taking it to the airport. Right?"

"Yes, that is fine. We'll leave right after we have something to eat. J J, I started to tell you, we'll fly you to Seattle. We usually fly to San Francisco, by way of Hawaii, for obvious reasons," smiled Siako, as he looked from J J towards his wife. "Let us just say. Our group enjoys the scenery," said Siako, as he sat looking at J J. Toyoko and Toya both giggling slightly, as they held both hands to their mouth's, in an attempt to stifle their reactions to Siako's comment about the scenery. "This time we'll fly by way of Anchorage and Seattle, at virtually no additional expense to my company," said Siako, as he quickly changed the subject. "Does that make you feel more comfortable with this plan, J J?"

"Yes, it does, Siako. Thank you," said J J, as he sat there nodding his head smiling. Indicating to the others, he did indeed feel more comfortable, knowing Siako's company wouldn't incur any subsequent expenditure, because of them flying along with the executives, on their trip to San Francisco, by way of his hometown of Seattle.

Sason entered the room carrying a large bowl, it's contents clearly quite warm, evident by the steam rising from the confines of the bowl. The same woman that had helped Sason earlier, appeared carrying a tray filled with bowls, apparently for what was in the larger one. Moving quickly she laid a pad she was carrying, on the table. Sitting the large bowl carefully on the pad, Sason reached for one of the smaller bowls. With a ladle contained in the large bowl, he proceeded to fill the smaller bowls and served each of the seven, a bowl of hot soup.

J J sat looking at the bowl Sason sat before him.

"J J, is there a problem with your soup?" asked Toyoko, seeing him sitting there staring at his bowl.

"No, the soup smells delightful, Ma'am. I was wondering if I may us the bathroom to wash up?" asked J J, as he rose from his chair.

"Yes, I am so sorry, J J. Let me show you where it's located," said Siako, as he too rose from his chair.

"I'll come too," said Sam.

"I will show you both to a bathroom. If you will follow me." The three men left the room. "J J, there's a bathroom here on the left. I'll show Sam, to another."

"Thank you, Siako. Siako, is there a restroom on the airplane?" Asked J J, as he stood in the hallway holding the knob to the bathroom door.

"Yes, J J. There is a small bathroom onboard," said Siako, as he turned to Sam standing there next to him, as J J closed the door. The two, then walked a few steps down the hall towards the other bathroom.

"Sir, I know you're not happy about the way Toya and I have hit it off. I can't explain it myself. I do know my intentions are honorable. And I wouldn't intentionally do anything to dishonor her or you, Sir," said Sam, as he stopped Siako in the hallway and the two of them stood talking.

"Sam, my daughter is fast becoming a woman. That in itself is what makes me unhappy. Not necessarily her being attracted to you. It's her being old enough, or me having to admit she's old enough. For her to be attracted to any man. Sam, you and your grandfather, have given her the ability to have that opportunity," smiled Siako, as he put his hand on Sam's shoulder.

Just then the door to the bathroom opened and J J stepped out into the hallway. The two men turned and started walking in J J's direction. Sam smiled and moved between J J and the door of the bathroom, opening the door to enter. "You go ahead. I'll be there in just a jiffy," said Sam, as he closed the door.

"The bathroom was so shiny, I didn't want to touch anything. I finally decided the only way I was going to wash, was to turn on the shiny faucet. So I did," smiled J J, as he shrugged his shoulders. "I washed my hands and face. Siako, what do you think of my face?" asked J J, as he reached up with his right hand and rubbed his face.

"Except for your obvious maturity, J J. You look like any other Marine, that may have spent the night in town, running into a fist or two, during the night," laughed Siako, as he looked at J J's face. "J J, what happened?"

"To my face? Yesterday on the Enterprise, the ship's doctor did some surgery on my eye. Until then, I wasn't able to see out of this eye, for over fifty years. I had fallen into a crevasse, landing on the volcanic rock, with my face. In less than an hour, the doctor had it so I could see," smiled J J, as he pointed to his eye. The two men moved slowly down the hall towards the dining room. As they approached the door to the dining room, they were joined by Sam. The three men entered the room, all three quickly returning to their seats, around the beautiful dining room table.

"The soup is delicious guys," said Robby, as he looked across the shiny table towards Sam, and then over to J J, as the two men each took their seats.

Sason entered the room, escorting Mother Yoko, to a seat, at the end of the magnificent table. He pulled out a chair across from Siako. After Mother Yoko was comfortably seated, he ladled a hot bowl of soup and placed it on the table in front of her. He then bowed and backed from the table and left the room. The eight of them sat together enjoying their meal and conversation.

"You must excuse Toyoko and I. We should go and get my things ready for the trip. You may remain here. I will return on the way to the helicopter, when it is time for us to leave. I will be back shortly," said Siako, as he rose from the table. Toyoko also stood, as the three men partially stood. The two, left the room together. The other six continued enjoying each other's company.

"Robby, now that Siako has so graciously invited us to accompany him and the others, on their company's airplane. Now how long do you think it will take to get to Seattle?"

"If we're not held up at the airports, I would guess ten or twelve hours of flight time, should put us landing at Sea-Tac."

J J sat smiling, slightly nodding his head in response to what Robby was telling him. The two men leaning forward slightly in their chairs, as Lizy leaned back in hers, which allowed the two men a better view of each other.

"Grampa, that means we could have you home, as early as tomorrow," smiled Sam, as he sat looking towards his grandfather, from the opposite side of the beautiful table.

"I wish we could be there, Lizy."

"Me too, Toya. It's going to be so cool. When J J and Sam show up at her door. I wish we could be there to see that."

"Maybe, there's room on the airplane for two more, Lizy?" Sam quickly turned to Toya, as his smile widened.

"Toya, that could be. But I don't think the Major is too happy with me right now. I doubt if I could talk him into any leave time, without a real good reason. I know it's a good reason. But I can't tell him that, Toya. Maybe you could go and take a video of the wonderful event and send me a copy."

"No, as much as I would like to be there. That phenomenon is truly a special one. That should be shared by you three and Jera Marie. I'm thankful to have the knowledge that it will soon come to pass. And that the two of you finding me in that collapsed building this morning. May in a very small way have a part in having it come to pass sooner rather then later," smiled Toya.

"You're right, Toya. I'm also thankful to have had a part in this adventure. But I'd still like, to be there," smiled Lizy.

"That would be great, if you could come along, Toya," said Sam, as he sat staring at the beautiful Japanese girl.

Lizy cleared her throat, from the far side of the table.

"You too, Lizy," shouted Sam, as he quickly turned to look in her direction, from his seat next to Toya, his face a bit red.

The five of them continued there conversation. While Mother Yoko sat quietly smiling.

Toya looked in her grandmother's direction. She started speaking to her in Japanese. She explained to here grandmother, what her father was planing on doing for the three Americans. Of how he was going to fly them, on his company's airplane, to Seattle and home. She had no sooner done so, then Siako and Toyoko, entered the dining room, with Sason carrying Siako's briefcase in one hand and a suitcase in the other.

"Siako, is it time for us to leave?"

"Yes, it is, J J. We should leave within the next few minutes."

"I'm ready, Siako," said J J, as he quickly rose from his chair. The others seated at the table smiling, as he stood a moment, staring down at each one of them. "Come on, let's go to the helicopter." J J's voice quivering with excitement, as he carefully pushed his chair into place next to the table. Smiling, the other four rose from their seats, leaving Mother Yoko, the only person still seated. J J moved towards Mother Yoko, bowing he softly spoke to her in her own language. Looking up at him, she held out her hand. Cradling her small hand in both his, he gently shook her hand. They exchanged smiles, as J J moved from her side. The others also saying their good-byes. Everyone but Mother Yoko, started leaving the dining room and once again moved through the Makido's beautiful home. With J J leading the way across the platform towards the head of the stairs. Pausing there briefly to see if the others were indeed coming. From his position on the platform, he could easily hear the helicopter's engine was already running. J J stood there a moment watching, as the others again paired up, Siako and Toyoko, Robby and Lizy, and of course, Toya and Sam, with Sason behind. Seeing this, he quickly ran down the stairs into the garden, on his way to the awaiting helicopter.

In a matter of a few minutes, J J again stood looking at the bright red helicopter, with it's rotors rotating. He once more stood there in awe of this magnificent flying machine.

"J J, thank you from a mothers grateful heart. I will now say good-bye." Toyoko's hands reaching out taking J J's right hand in hers, as she spoke loud enough as to be heard. J J looked down at the hands taking his gently into them. He looked up slightly, into Toyoko's smiling face.

"Thank you, Ma'am, it's been an honor, to be a welcome guest, in your magnificent home, and also, to visit your beautiful country."

"J J, thank you for the privilege and honor to get to know you and your friends. I hope I can see you and meet your Jera Marie in September, when I come to Seattle," smiled Toya.

"It would be an honor for me to introduce you, Toya."

Toya rapped her arms around J J and hugged him tightly, laying her head on his chest. He put his arms around her shoulders and neck, returning the gesture. Breaking the embrace, they moved apart, Toya bowing, as she backed from J J. Then she looked towards Robby. She again bowed and then stood erect, as she held out her hand smiling. Robby smiled, as he took her hand in his.

"Toya, I'm so glad I was able be here and meet you and your family.

It has been a pleasure, thank you, Toya," smiled Robby, as he bent down and kissed her hand. He then stood as she move back.

Putting her hands at her sides, she again bowed to Robby. She then moved to Lizy. Again standing erect, she then held out both arms. The girls hugged for a short time.

"Keep in touch, girl friend. I'll check on you next time I go to the mall."

"Lizy I have your number and you have mine. Call me. Bye for now, girl friend."

Toya then turned to Sam. Standing there just for a second looking at him. She then jumped at him, throwing her arms up and around his neck and rapping her legs around his waist, then planting her lips on his, she kissed him long and hard, as the others watched, their mouths opening, as they watched. Then releasing her hold on him, landing on her feet, she quickly ran off on the path to the garden. Sam's eyes following, watching her disappear. Then standing there his back to the others, his face turning red, as he felt their stares, he slowly turned and faced the others, smiling.

"It's been a gas, being a part of your adventure. Here's my card. Please write me and tell me of your home coming, thank you J J."

"I will, Lizy."

The two then embraced. Then breaking the embrace, Lizy reached up with both hands and patted both sides of J J face.

"J J, I hope you live to be a hundred and get accused of sexual harassment," snickered Lizy, as she winked and then backed away hitting him on his upper arm, as she did. She then turned and hugged Sam, whispering something in his ear. Then breaking her embrace with Sam, she moved towards Robby. Leaving Sam once more, red faced. Stopping, she came to attention and saluted the Colonel. "Colonel Robinson, it's been a pleasure serving with you, Sir. If you ever have another mission like this, please include me. Thank you, Sir." Lizy finished the salute. She then smiled and moved in and gave Robby a big hug.

"Lizy, here's a number you can reach me. I'm glad this Air Force Lieutenant, became, 'one of the few good men.' Here's some gas money for your little beater. Thank you, Lizy," said the Colonel. as he handed her his card and some money. He then stepped back and made a quick salute. Robby, turned and shook hands with Toyoko.

With all the good-byes said. The four moved towards the awaiting helicopter, bending low as they did. Siako reaching out, grabbed J J by the arm. "J J, would you like to ride up front, in the copilot's seat?" J J quickly turned towards Siako and smiled. He then abruptly turned and proceeded quickly around the front of the helicopter, to it's starboard side. He reached up and opened the front door of the shiny red machine, as Sam grabbed a handle, on the bird's opposite side, opening the rear door. With their doors open, they immediately climbed in. This put Sam first in the rear seat, putting him directly behind his grandfather, now sitting proudly in the copilot's seat. Robby reached for Siako's two bags, taking them from Sason, and quickly stowed them in the same compartment he had seen the gear stowed in earlier. With that door once again secure. The two men boarded the helicopter, with Robby quickly closing the door. With all four of them aboard, they hastily buckled their seat belts. Which they had no sooner done, then they were airborne. J J and Sam, quickly turned and looked out the side windows and commenced waving to the others. In a matter of a few seconds the Makido's home was no longer visible. "J J, put your headset on."

"I see it." J J, realizing what Siako meant, reached for the headset hanging on the instrument panel, between him and the bird's pilot.

"We'll be at the airport in about ten minutes, J J." J J turned and nodded to Siako, seated in the center rear seat. As they flew it became obvious, the area below was becoming a great deal more densely populated. The longer they flew the more populated and congested it became. "J J, you see now, how fortunate I am to have a place to distant myself and isolate my family, from this mass of humanity. This fifty kilometers makes a world of difference."

"Siako, fifty of anything, can make a world of difference."

"Yes," said Siako, as the three sitting to the rear of J J and the pilot became silent.

CUSTOMS

"J J, there's the airport in the distance. My colleagues should already be waiting on the plane." They could see in the distance airplanes landing and taking off, on the different runways of the airport.

"Look how big some of those airplanes are. They look much bigger than the one we arrived in. And I thought it was a huge airplane."

"Grampa, that blue one is a 747. So is the white one."

"There are so many. Look, there's two of them in a row coming into land, one right after the other. There's one that just took off. It's amazing! How do they keep from running into one another?"

"It happens, Grampa."

"Those planes are so big! They must hold a hundred people or more."

"They do, J J. A 747, holds over four hundred people."

J J sat there thinking, 'the amount of loss of life, if just one of those big planes went down.'

It became apparent, their pilot was flying a definite flight plan, as they flew ever closer to the airport.

"J J, there's the plane we'll be flying you home on. That red one," said Siako, as he held up his arm between J J and the pilot, pointing an index finger, in the direction of an airplane the same color red, as the helicopter they were presently in. It also became obvious, they were going to land right next to the bright red airplane. Within a few seconds they were doing just that.

"This is great Siako. No baggage check. No airport security. No. . . ." Once again, there was a sudden silence from the rear seat. "Damn! What are we going to do about customs?"

"You're right, Robby. We'll most likely be all right here. This plane goes and comes, several times daily, it's the norm. Unless someone in authority reads our flight plan, there shouldn't be any problem. But it will be a different story in Alaska, Robby."

"You mean, Grampa!" said Sam, as the helicopter gently came to rest on the airport's tarmac, right next to Siako's company's, sleek looking red aircraft.

"Yes, Grampa!" snapped Robby, with anxiety showing in his voice. "I'm sorry, Sam. It's just that I never thought of customs. Sam, your grandfather, doesn't . . . Robby thought a moment of, 'how to put into words what he was thinking.' Your grandfather, hasn't any identification. How are we going to get him into the United States."

"I still have these." J J turned towards the rear seat, smiling, as he dangled his dog tags from a chain which he wore around his neck, towards the three sitting in the rear. The tags and chain concealed by his uniform.

"Yes, Grampa has his dog tags."

"Sam, you have the same name."

"Right. Sorry, Colonel." Sam, a bit embarrassed by his statement.

"These things are so worn, I doubt if anyone could read them anyway," said J J, as he tried to look down at the polished metal tags worn smooth by time, held out from his chest. Straining his eyes enough they crossed, as he did.

The noise from the helicopter slowly ceased to roar.

"Let's not worry about that now. Let's see if we can even leave Japan. If we can, then maybe we'll think of something by the time we arrive in the U.S."

"Yes, Colonel. We best board as quickly as possible, as not to attract to much attention."

"Right."

The four quickly removed their headsets and seat belts. J J and Sam, opened the doors adjacent to them and the four quickly climbed down from the bright red bird, to the tarmac below. Robby immediately proceeded to the compartment to retrieve their gear. The pilot and J J, came from the front of the helicopter to help with the baggage. With them all carrying part of the load, they headed for the aircraft. They could now see the airplane was not only red, it was also gold, not just gold paint. It was trimmed in what looked like real gold, it was so shiny. As they walked towards the awaiting airplane, they saw a small man moving posthaste in their direction. The man bowed to Siako. Then reaching out, he hastily took Siako's two bags. Almost at a run, he headed for the airplane's stairs, climbing them as quick as possible. Then from the far side of the airplane appeared another man. At that same time their helicopter pilot asked the three to follow him with their gear. J J, Sam and Robby, did as asked. He lead the three towards the other man. This man was standing next to an open compartment, in the aircraft. "We will put your gear here, for your flight to America," said the pilot, as he handed the man the gear he had been carrying. The pilot then bowed to the three men, backing away as he did. He then headed for his own aircraft. With their gear left to be stowed away. The three headed for the stairs. They quickly climbed the stairs and entered the aircraft. The airplane was magnificent.

"You three come and take your seats," said Siako, as he pointed towards empty seats. "I have asked the pilot to take the first available slot. You can sit here in these seats, until we're airborne."

The three quickly took their seats, as did Siako. The other six men were already seated. Obviously a bit surprised, by their three unexpected traveling companions, beings the six were just sitting there staring at the three Marines. As they buckled their seat belts, they could tell the airplane was already moving.

"You were right, Siako. It looks as though we may have lucked out, with the Japanese authorities. I hope we can figure something out, by the time we land in Alaska."

The airplane moved along the runway, stopping and turning, then moving and then stopping again. The next time it moved it started, as J J would put it, "packing the mail." In a matter of seconds, the aircraft was airborne. As the airplane climbed to it's cruising altitude, J J, Sam and Robby, sat looking around the beautifully appointed aircraft. In a short matter of time, the aircraft began to level off.

"Now, you three and I, can move back to the lounge. If you gentlemen, will excuse my three guests and I?" The six men nodded slightly towards Siako, as they sat there still staring, obviously still a bit overwhelmed by the presence of the three Marines. Siako and his guests removed their seat belts and rose from their seats. "Where we will be more comfortable and have some privacy," said Siako, as he lead the three men towards the rear of the plane. The entrance to the lounge was along the port side of the aircraft. The lounge had a sofa placed at each end and there was a desk along the opposite wall. In the middle there was a large conference table with ten high back chairs. The room was quite spectacular. There were two other comfortable looking chairs, both placed on the same side as the desk, and there were several paintings affixed to the walls of the aircraft.

"Make yourselves comfortable. Would anyone like a drink?"

"Before I answer that, Siako. Where's the bathroom?"

"Robby, the bathroom's through that door and then the first door on the left. There's also a shower behind the second door," said Siako, as he nodded towards the door at the rear of the lounge.

"What's behind door number three?" snickered Robby.

"The third door?"

"I'm sorry, Siako. I couldn't resist it," said Robby obviously pleased with himself, for the little funny he had come up with.

"I get it, Robby."

"Yes, I also get it, Sam. It is from an American television show. Give me a moment. I've got it! It's 'Let's Make A Deal. Right?'"

"That's right, Siako," beamed Robby.

"Right on. Give me five," smiled Sam, as he held out his right hand, palm up to Siako. The two of them, giving each other, the give me five, hand slap. "I personally didn't watch the TV show. But I do know the phrase, 'What's Behind Door Number Three' and 'Let's Make A Deal.' I've heard those two phrases, over and over, for as long as I can remember."

The three men laughed together, as J J stood smiling.

"Actually." Siako's smile widened. "There is a door number three. And several others, for that matter."

"Well tell us. What's behind door number three, Siako?" Siako looked over at Robby and smiled.

"Sleeping accommodation. Actually, besides door number three. There are three other doors. The four doors lead, to four separate cabins, with two beds in each cabin."

"Now that I know, there is a bathroom close, I'll take you up on that offer of a drink, Siako."

Just then the door at the rear of the lounge opened. The man that had taken Siako's two bags, earlier, walked into the lounge. Speaking in Japanese, he said something to Siako. Siako and the man talked for a time, he then turned to Robby.

"What may I get for you to drink, Sir?"

"Gin, on the rocks. If you got them."

"May I get something for you two gentlemen."

"Nothing for me. Thank you."

"And you, Sir?"

"I think I best pass on the drink. I would, like some hot tea. Do you have any tea?"

"Yes, Sir. I will have it for you shortly. As soon as I prepare this gentlemen's Gin and Mr. Siako's drink. I will prepare your hot tea, Sir."

The man bowed to Siako and then backed away. He turned and left the lounge through the same door he had entered the room. The three men looked over at Siako.

"There's also a kitchen behind door number one. It's located on the side opposite, to that of the bath and shower rooms, before you get to door number three or four," smiled Siako, as he pointed towards the back wall of the lounge. "Why don't we have a seat. It's a long flight to Seattle. J J, sit here in one of these chairs. These two chairs are recliners," said Siako, as he held out his hand towards one of the two chairs sitting near the desk. He then moved to the sofa sitting at the end nearest the one recliner.

The man re-entered the room carrying a small tray with two glasses. He walked up to the now seated Siako and bowed handing him one of the two drinks. He then moved towards Robby, holding out the tray for him to take his, Gin on the rocks.

"Thank you."

The waiter bowed to Robby and then turned to J J sitting in the recliner. "The water for your tea is being heated. As soon as the water is hot, I will bring you your tea, Sir."

"Thank you, there's no hurry." The waiter smiled, as he once more turned and left the room.

"J J, let me show you something about that chair you're sitting in," smiled Siako, as he reached over and grabbed the handle on the side of the chair. By Siako pulling on the handle, he quickly put the chair, J J was sitting in, into a reclined position. J J sat, a bit startled by the movement of the chair underneath him. After the initial shock, he smiled and nestled into the comfortable chair.

"Hey, this chair's all right. I could get used to this."

"J J, most men your age, have gotten, as you say, used to it. They spend most of their waking hours, sitting in a chair like that. Watching television, taking the occasional nap as they do. That's how they spend their day."

"Billy's right about television, Robby. If our youth are spending all their time watching television. And people my age spend all their time sitting in recliners, either watching television or napping. When do they enjoy life? Don't people my age enjoy doing things outside? Things like sailing, fishing, hunting and other things like these? Besides things they can do inside."

"Yes, of course they do, J J."

"Good. I know Grampa Miller was. . . ." J J, stopped what he was saying and sat there thinking, 'Grampa and Gramma Miller had long since taken leave of this earth.' Jera's grandfather was about my age, when I left for the South Pacific. I know for a fact. He didn't sit around on his backside in some fancy chair and let life pass him by. He was always doing something. He had a small farm, where he raised beef and a few sheep. The place had an apple orchard and they always had a big garden. He did all this, after working all day, before he retired. He was a logger and cat skinner. A cat skinner doesn't skin cats. If that's what you're thinking. That's what they call a bulldozer operator in the woods. This man loved his work. When Jera and I, were first married, I can remember having trouble keeping up with him on foot, when we went deer and elk hunting with dad and my two uncles and their kids. If it wasn't hunting, it was fishing. I'm sorry, I'm rambling."

"Not at all, J J. I find this all very interesting."

"I shouldn't be talking about things from the past. Things that happened over fifty years ago. Let's talk about things of today. If we wait more then a heartbeat they'll be the past."

"Siako, Sam tells me our country has a problem with drugs. Does Japan have a similar problem?"

"I'm sorry to say J J, we do. Today's drug problem, is a global one. Until people realize the devastating effect drugs have on both individuals and their families, and of course our society as a whole. There is little hope of abating the spread of drugs. Until such time as the great demand is some how decreased.

"Yes, drug smugglers, smuggle thousands of tons of the stuff into the country, each year. And I can't figure out how, to get one, one hundred and eighty pound Marine, home and into his own country."

"You'll think of something, Robby."

"Yes, I'm quite confident one of us, will think of a solution. By the time we land in Alaska," said Siako.

Just then the waiter came into the room, carrying J J's hot tea. "Sir, all I have onboard to sweeten your tea, is the pink stuff. Next time we land, I must acquire some sugar to have onboard."

"Pink stuff?"

"Grampa, pink stuff is a form of artificial sweetener. We call it pink stuff, because it comes in small pink pouches."

"Is it like that artificial butter the Chief on the Enterprise spoke so highly of?"

"Actually, J J. I find the pink stuff, an acceptable substitute to real sugar," smiled Siako.

"Just think about the words you're using to describe this pink stuff, artificial and substitute. The words themselves make the product sound unappetizing. I'll go ahead and try, the pink stuff," smiled J J. The waiter put J J's tea on the arm rest of the recliner closest to the sofa, which had a cup holder and tray built into it. There were also two small pink pouches sitting on the tray with his hot tea. "Thank you." The waiter backed away. He bowed to J J and then turned to Siako.

"That will be all for now." The man bowed, then turning he quickly left the room.

"J J, Toyoko and Toya, feel the same as you. Toyoko doesn't allow me to use the pink stuff in our home. She says I can learn to use real sugar in moderation, and be happy with that. I obtained a box of the pink envelopes, while on one of these flights to the US. Toyoko, had complained that I was using to much sugar. I had tried the pink stuff in restaurants while in the US. I thought it to be the answer to my problem," smiled Siako, as he sat watching J J preparing the tea, using the small pink envelopes. "I can use it here on the airplane. Everyone aboard uses it, either in their coffee or tea. And Toyoko, is seldom onboard."

"It's white. For some reason, I expected it to be pink," said J J, as he poured the contents of a pink envelope into the cup, looking towards each of the others while stirring the steaming cup, smiling up at his onlookers. Smiles formed on their faces, as he lifted the hot cup of sweetened tea to his lips. "Wow. I'll say one thing for this pink stuff. It's definitely as sweet as sugar. Maybe we best land at the first available airport and get some sugar and lemon?" Everyone laughed at both J J's reaction to his sweetened tea and the suggestion about them landing to pick up some sugar and lemon.

The others quickly noticed, Robby wasn't laughing and quit smiling. "What is it? What's wrong, Robby?" asked J J, with concern showing in his voice, as he looked up at his obviously troubled friend. Robby stood there not saying a word. The others stared at him in silence, waiting for him to answer.

"I have an idea."

"Robby, my tea is fine. I can use this pink stuff. I ran out of sugar for my tea, and the tea, years ago. The pink stuff is just fine."

"What? No. I have an idea, how to get you into the states," said Robby, as he stood there looking down at J J, as a grin started forming on his face and he raised and lowered his eyebrows.

"How?"

"We'll have your pilot think of some reason, to cause him to have to make an emergency landing. We'll pick a military base to use during this fake emergency. Upon landing, the three of us will get off the plane and see who's in command. With any luck at all, it will be a junior officer. If it is and there's a plane or helicopter available, we'll fly to Almendorf. After we fly out, your pilot will miraculously solve the problem and you will resume your flight to Anchorage. Where we'll take a car or a cab from Almendorf and meet up with you at the Anchorage airport." The others each stared at Robby. "What? Don't you think it will work? If it doesn't work, we'll have to think of something else."

"I think, it's a great idea, Colonel," said Sam excitedly.

"Robby, I knew you would come up with a plan," smiled J J.

"I will call the pilot and ask him to come and talk with you, as soon as he feels it is safe for him to do so." With that said, Siako stood and started walking towards the desk. Then reaching, he came up with a phone in hand. The phone was on the opposite side of the desk, hanging on a bracket just out of sight of the others, fastened to the far side of the desk. The others listened, as Siako talked to the plane's pilot. "The pilot will be here shortly, Robby," said Siako, as he bent to return the phone to it's stand-by position. He then returned to the sofa and took his seat. The four men spent the next few moments talking about Robby's plan, until they were interrupted by their pilot entering the lounge.

"Sir, what can I do for you and your guests?"

"The Colonel and I, have a favor to ask of you, Akio."

Siako and Robby, explained to the pilot, exactly what they had in mind for him to do. The pilot told them, he and his copilot had gone over the charts before the plane's departure. He also told them, there were only three airfields along their route, with runways long enough to accommodate their aircraft. He also informed them, that in his opinion, there was only one airfield of the three that would be close enough, to be within range of Almendorf, for a helicopter flight. They all agreed they should give it a try. The pilot shook hands with Robby and then bowed to Siako and the others. He then turned and left the room.

"Have a seat, you two," said Siako, as he looked at Sam and Robby, still standing there looking down at him and J J. Robby moved towards Siako, joining him on the sofa. While Sam moved to and sat in the other recliner. With the two of them now seated, they started talking. They talked about a good many things. About some of the different things that had taken place over the last fifty years, in different parts of the world. The time past swiftly.

"It looks as though Grampa, is just about out of that dollar thirty a gallon stuff," whispered Sam, as he pointed towards his grandfather. J J sat there in the recliner, his eyes slowly opening and closing, as the others sat quietly watching. In a matter of minutes J J was sound asleep, with just a hint of a smile showing on his face.

"I'd say Grampa's second day back, was just as exciting as his first."

"That's for sure. It's going to be interesting to see how the rest of the day unfolds and what tomorrow will bring," said Robby speaking in a low voice, as he raised and lowered his eyebrows towards the others.

"Colonel, I can't say thank you enough. And I say the same to you, Mr. Makido. Thank you. If not for you two, this wouldn't have been possible. Thank you."

All three men sat quietly watching Sam's grandfather, peacefully sleeping soundly. "Grampa told me, that's one thing he could do, was sleep. And I'm here to tell you. Thanks to you," said Sam, as quickly nodded, first towards Robby and then Siako. "I can definitely vouch for that. It amazes me. I've never seen anyone fall asleep, sound to sleep, any faster." Robby and Siako, both shook their heads smiling, indicating to Sam, that they wholeheartedly agreed. Siako then moved forward to the front edge of the sofa and sat erect.

"This is a man, pure of heart and mind. After living alone and relying on himself, for all those years. J J is confident, he has done all he can do. He now trusts, leaving the rest for his grandson and his new friends. For him to fall to sleep so quickly and soundly, demonstrates that unwavering trust and confidence."

Siako slowly stood, as Robby and Sam, did the same. The three men stood a moment looking at J J sleeping soundly. Without saying a word, the three men left the lounge and moved towards the forward cabin, rejoining Siako's original traveling companions. "Sir, if you don't mind. I'd like to stay back there with Grampa. That's if it's all right with you two?"

"Yes, of course, Sam," said Siako, as he sat down in one of the seats.

"It's fine with me, Sam." Sam smiled and then nodded to Siako and Robby. He then turned and nodded towards the others, as he headed for the lounge. Once there, he grabbed a magazine or two, from a rack on the end of the sofa nearest the entrance to the lounge. With magazines in hand, he quietly moved past his grandfather still sleeping soundly, and returned to the recliner. Once seated, he started thumbing through the magazines. To his surprise, both magazines were American.

Five hours had past since the plane's departure from Japan.

"Sir." Siako opened his eyes. "Sir, I have permission to make an emergency landing at the airport, we spoke of early, Sir," whispered the airplane's pilot.

"Very good, Akio, thank you. What do we do now?"

"Have your special passengers ready to disembark. We're still twenty minutes or so from landing. I just wanted to keep you informed, Sir."

"What's wrong? Is there a problem with the airplane?" asked one of the other passengers, with concern showing in his voice.

"No. The airplane's fine. We are landing soon for my three Marine guests, to leave the aircraft. No reason to be concerned."

"I heard the pilot say emergency landing," whispered the passenger, as he looked around at everyone else still sleeping.

"Yes. But there isn't any emergency. It's a ruse to allow. . . . It doesn't pertain to you," said Siako in a low stern voice.

"Yes Sir, Mr. Makido."

"Colonel, Colonel Robby," said Siako, as he tried to wake his friend.

"Yes, what is it?" snapped the Colonel, as he awoke to a Japanese man, staring at him face to face. Taking a moment to associate himself with his surroundings. The Colonel then cleared his throat.

"I'm sorry, Siako. After all these years of being a Marine, you would think I'd be used to being awoke from a sound sleep, in a strange place and different surroundings. As you can plainly see, Siako, I'm not. It still rattles my cage, now and again."

"Robby, the pilot has informed me, he has been given authorization, to make your emergency landing. He said this will take place in approximately twenty minutes."

"That's great, Siako. We best go tell J J and Sam." Robby rose from his seat, stretching his arms, shoulders and neck, in several different ways, as he stood. The two men then quickly headed for the plane's lounge. Upon entering the lounge, they found J J, as they had left him, sleeping soundly in the recliner. His grandson was sleeping just as soundly in the other recliner. "Siako, you best let me be the one to wake J J. Don't forget, until just a few days ago. . . ," said Robby, as he looked towards Siako, with one eyebrow slightly raised.

"I concur, Robby. Your assessment of the situation, is obviously correct. You wake J J. I'll wake the boy," said Siako, as he raised and lowered his eyebrows. With a knowing smile appearing on his face.

"Right," smiled Robby, as he and Siako moved quietly towards the two men, sleeping with their recliners reclined to the maximum position.

"J J."

"Sam."

"J J, we'll be landing in a few minutes," said Robby, as he reached for and shook J J's right foot.

"We're landing?" asked J J, as he quickly started climbing out of the recliner. The chair still in a fully reclined position. Before Robby, could reach the handle and up right the chair, J J was on his feet. Sam's chair went to an upright position and he also stood.

"We should move to the forward cabin, Robby."

"Right. Let's go." The four men quickly moved from the lounge, to the forward cabin. Each man returning to the seats they had occupied during take off. Once seated, everyone quickly fastened their seat belts. The plane already starting it's descent, as it's occupants grew silent. In a matter of minutes they felt the airplane's tires make contact with the surface of the runway. Immediately on landing they could feel the plane slowing. In no time at all it came to a complete stop.

"Colonel, it's your show," said Siako, as he unfastened his seat belt and rose from his seat. The three others also stood. At this same time, the man that had waited on the four of them earlier, appeared from the rear of the airplane. He quickly moved past them to the planes door. Once there, he began to unlock and open the plane's exit door. With the door swung open, the plane's occupants could see it was still light outside, even though it was now late evening.

"J J, it's the first of July here. We've crossed the International Date Line, and it's now hours earlier than when we left the airport in Japan. I'm not sure what time it really is myself. But as you can see, we're now in the land of the midnight sun," said Robby, as the four of them moved towards the open door.

"Sir, the tower informed me that the airport is a little short handed. It could be a few moments before there are stairs to disembark the aircraft." The pilot had no sooner told them about the stairs, than they saw a vehicle coming in their direction. The vehicle itself was a set of stairs. The stairs went from the rear of the vehicle up and over the driving compartment. As it approached the aircraft the operator adjusted the height of the stairs to match that of the plane's open door. The operator moved the stairs within an inch or so of the side of the aircraft and stopped.

"Siako, if everything goes as planned. We'll see you in Anchorage. Speaking of seeing. J J, your glasses and gloves." With that said, the three Marines started quickly down the stairs. By the time they reached the bottom of the stairs, the vehicle's operator was there to greet them. Seeing the Colonel, the airmen immediately came to attention.

"Colonel, we had no idea you were onboard, Sir. Colonel, I can see if I can get someone on the radio, to come get you, Colonel."

"Thank you, airmen. I would appreciate not having to walk."

"Yes, Colonel." The airmen grabbed a radio hanging from his belt and proceeded to make the call. As the Colonel and his two aides stepped from the stairs onto the tarmac. "Colonel, the Lieutenant, will be here shortly with a car for you, Sir."

"Airmen, who's in command here?"

"Major Mckenzie, is base commander, Colonel. Lieutenant Baker, is in command at the present time, Colonel."

"Lieutenant Baker," said Robby under his breath, as he turned to J J and Sam, a 'Cheshire Cat' grin forming on his face.

"Here comes the Lieutenant now, Colonel." The Colonel abruptly turned to see a car coming towards them at a fairly high rate of speed. In no time the car pulled up and stopped nearby. The drivers door swung open and out climbed a young Lieutenant.

"Colonel, what can I do for you, Colonel?" asked the Lieutenant, as he came to attention saluting the Colonel.

"Lieutenant, I'm Colonel Robert Robinson and these two are my aides," said the Colonel, as he returned the Lieutenant's salute.

"What I want you to do for me, Lieutenant, is get me a flight to Almendorf, as soon as possible, Lieutenant!"

"Colonel, I was not informed of your impending arrival, Colonel. Especially not on a private jet from Japan, Colonel."

"Well, now you know, Lieutenant. The CEO of the company that owns this aircraft, is a dear friend of mine. He was gracious enough to offer myself and my two aides, a ride home for the holiday weekend. Now the plane has a problem of some kind and I'm afraid we may miss our connecting flights. Lieutenant, is there anyway you can help?"

"Colonel, there's a shuttle leaving for Almendorf shortly. What I don't know is if there's any room for you and your aides, Colonel."

The Colonel's left eyebrow raised, as he glared intently in the Lieutenant's direction. "Lieutenant, my advice to you is, that myself and these two aides, are comfortably seated on that flight to Almendorf, Lieutenant," said the Colonel in a stern manner, as he pointed towards J J and Sam. The Lieutenant stood there a second, his mouth hung open staring back at the Colonel. "Lieutenant!"

"Yes, Sir, Colonel. Consider it done, Colonel."

"Thank you, Lieutenant."

"Colonel, does the Colonel and his aides have any gear? The airmen and I can help, Colonel."

"Yes, Lieutenant."

From the plane's open door, the man that had earlier been their waiter, heard the Lieutenant's question and came quickly down the stairs. "Colonel, I will help. Please follow me, if you please," said the man, as he moved past them.

The Lieutenant, airmen and the Colonel's two aides, followed the man as he lead them to the other side of the aircraft. By the time they caught up with him, he had a compartment door on the airplane open and was in the process of unloading the gear. With their gear in hand and the compartment door secure, they returned to the stairs.

"Let's move out, Lieutenant."

"Yes, Sir, Colonel," answered the Lieutenant, as he set the stuff he was carrying down and opened the car's drivers door. "I'll get the keys, Colonel. We'll put your gear in the trunk, Colonel." J J and Sam stood with the airmen holding their gear. The Colonel and the others watched the Lieutenant get the keys and quickly pick up the stuff and headed around to the rear of the car. With everything in the trunk. The Lieutenant opened the rear door on the drivers side and held it for the Colonel. Once all four men were in the car the Lieutenant drove off. Grabbing the car's radio as they moved down the runway. Because of the emergency aspect of their landing, their pilot had obviously been told to land clear of all buildings and other aircraft. It took sometime to get to the main part of the airport complex. "Colonel, the shuttle leaves in ten minutes. I have reserved a place for each of you, Colonel," said the Lieutenant, as he smiled putting the car's radio receiver back into place.

"Well done, Lieutenant. Thank you," said the Colonel with some excitement showing in his voice.

"You're welcome, Colonel. Colonel, there's your shuttle," said the Lieutenant pointing, caught a bit off guard by the Colonel's friendly response. Sitting off in the direction the Lieutenant had pointed. They could see parked in the distance, a large double bladed helicopter. "Your timing is perfect, Colonel. That's the last flight scheduled to leave here tonight. There's one tomorrow at this same time. That's it, until after the holiday weekend. I hope there is nothing seriously wrong with your friends plane. It would be the pits for them to be stranded in this place all weekend. Believe me, I know!"

"Where would you like to be stationed, Lieutenant?" The lieutenant quickly looked over and stared at the Colonel. "Watch where your driving."

"Yes, Sir," said the Lieutenant, as he quickly looked back to where he was driving. His eyes looking up into the car's rearview mirror, at the two privates in the rear seat, as they sat there smiling.

"Well, Lieutenant?"

"San Diego! Colonel." Blurted the Lieutenant, as he slowly looked over, to catch the Colonel's reaction. The Colonel sat there looking straight ahead. Not saying a word, as the car pulled up near the large helicopter and stopped. The Lieutenant grabbed the keys. "I'll get the trunk, Colonel."

The car's doors opened and all four men quickly got out of the vehicle. The others moved to the rear of the vehicle to retrieve the baggage from the car's trunk, while the Colonel stood next to the car waiting. The Lieutenant and Colonel's aides gathered their things and then walked up to the Colonel with gear in hand.

"Thank you, Lieutenant. I greatly appreciate your help, Lieutenant. I'll see if I can show my appreciation in some sunny way," smiled the Colonel, as he turned and headed for the helicopter. Leaving the Lieutenant once again standing with his mouth hung open. "Are you going to keep my things, Lieutenant?" asked the Colonel, as he turned to see the Lieutenant standing there, as if in a stupor, still holding the Colonel's bag, as the Colonel and his two aides continued towards the helicopter.

"Colonel? No, Colonel," said the Lieutenant, as he then ran to catch the three men.

"Good, Lieutenant, I might need my ditty bag."

"Yes, Sir, Colonel."

The four men continued walking towards the helicopter. There was a line of ten or so people waiting to board the large helicopter. The men moved to a place near the rear of the line. No sooner than they did, the people at the head of the line, began to board.

"You weren't kidding, Lieutenant. Our timing is perfect."

In no time, it was the Colonel's turn to board the helicopter. As he started to board an airmen asked. "Colonel, may I have your boarding pass, Sir.?" Without hesitating, the Colonel raised his left hand and pointed with his thumb over his left shoulder towards the rear of the now short line.

"Airmen, the Lieutenant, will handle the paper work, for myself and my two aides," said the Colonel, as they continued boarding the helicopter.

"Colonel?"

"Is there a problem?" asked the Colonel, as he waited for J J and Sam, to finish boarding and then leaned out the open door of the helicopter. First glaring at the airmen and then towards the Lieutenant.

"Yes, Colonel. . . . Airmen, I'll take full responsibility for the Colonel and his aides. Colonel, I have your name, Sir. What are the names of your aides, Colonel?"

Just as the Lieutenant asked the question, the helicopter's engines began to roar. The Colonel hesitated a moment, thinking of what to say. While he hesitated, the engine's roar increased. "Lieutenant, their names are, J. S. Johnson Jay Samuel Johnson," answered the Colonel quickly. Purposely running the two names together, in hopes to cause some confusion, as he abruptly pointed first towards Sam and then J J.

"Privates, J. S. Johnson and Jay Samuelson?" asked the Lieutenant in a loud enough voice to be heard, as he took a pen and tablet from his shirt pocket and proceeded to write the two names.

"Thanks again, Lieutenant," said the Colonel, as he held out his hand, his thumb pointing skyward, with a big smile showing on his face. With that said, the Colonel turned and joined the others seated on the far side of the helicopter. With their gear safely stored just under their seats and everyone's seat belts fastened. The fifteen or so passengers sat together, ready for takeoff. The Lieutenant and airmen moved back a safe distance from the now roaring helicopter. An onboard crewmen began closing the large single door on the helicopter's starboard side. With it's door now closed, the helicopter's engines began to accelerate. The awkward looking machine started to take on a much different appearance, as it began to float, breaking temporarily free of the earth's hold over it. The three sat amongst the other passengers not saying a word, it appeared they were all safely on the way, headed for Almendorf. The Colonel looked discreetly to the right and winked at J J and Sam. He then slowly looked down to his hands, one resting on each thigh with the first two fingers on both hands crossed.

"Corporal, how long a flight is it to Almendorf?" asked the Colonel, of the crewmen sitting by the door, in a loud enough voice, as to be heard over the helicopter's engines.

"Colonel, we land first in Anchorage. I think today's flight time to Anchorage was sixty five minutes. Then we fly onto Almendorf. It only takes a few minutes longer for us to get to Almendorf, Colonel."

"Myself and my two aides, will be disembarking at the Anchorage airport, Corporal."

"Yes, Sir, Colonel."

The airmen that had met the jet with the portable stairs, still stood at the bottom of the stairs leading up to Siako's jet. Posted there earlier by the Lieutenant, for not only their guest assistance, but also for the airport's own security. He had been standing there for about forty minutes, when he received a call on his radio that informed him that the Jet was soon going to resume it's flight and he should remove the stairs as soon as possible and upon it's departure, return to his prior duties. While still talking on the radio, he started around the vehicle and climbed into the driver's compartment. In no time, he was ready to back away from the aircraft. He honked the vehicle's horn, to get the attention of someone on board. After seeing someone in the open doorway waving to him, knowing that they saw and were aware the stairs were departing the aircraft. He slowly backed away from the bright red and gold aircraft, now glistening in the late night Alaskan sunshine. He watched as whoever had waved, started to close the aircraft's door. He then drove to within a short distance of the aircraft's wing and stopped.

"Colonel, we'll be landing in ten minutes or so, Colonel." The Colonel nodded towards the corporal, indicating to him he understood. The helicopter had windows but from their seated position, they were useless. They sat there virtually blind to their present location, as they flew ever closer to Anchorage.

The airmen had removed a large fire extinguisher from a rack on the vehicle and had put on ear protection and stood near each engine, as the airplane's pilot started that particular engine. With the aircraft's engines all running safely. He returned to the vehicle, remounted the large fire extinguisher and in a matter of seconds he drove away, waving to the plane's pilot as he did.

The three felt the helicopter touch the ground, as did the others. The helicopter's engines came to an idle and soon ceased to roar. The corporal unfastened his seat belt and headed for the door. He quickly opened the door and turned to the Colonel. "Colonel, the main part of the airport is to the left, Colonel."

The Colonel and his two aides, unfastened their seat belts. The aides quickly grabbed up the gear and the three men stood and moved towards the open door. Climbing down out of the helicopter they headed in the direction the corporal had said the main part of the airport was located.

"Robby, wasn't it fortunate the helicopter started it's engines, just as the young Lieutenant asked you for our names."

"That's a big ten-four, J J."

The jet's engines accelerated and it began moving down the runway. Moments later the jet was again airborne and headed for Anchorage.

The three men entered the airport complex. The Colonel, seeing a sign saying, 'Information Booth,' headed in the direction the sign pointed. Arriving at the booth, they found it unoccupied. A phone marked 'For Information,' sat on the counter. The Colonel grabbed the phone and stood waiting for someone to answer. In a matter of a few second, someone came on the line to help. Within a few moments, the Colonel had the information he requested.

"Customs is this way. J J, you best, keep your sunglasses on," said the Colonel, as he started walking.

"Colonel, I need to use the restroom, Sir."

"Good idea, Sam."

"It's up here on the right."

"Yes, I see it, Sam. After we use the bathroom, we'll get to a window where we can watch the in coming planes. By chance we may see Siako's plane land."

The three men walked into the restroom. They appeared to be the only ones there. Sam took a moment and glanced under the door of each stall. "Colonel, we're the only ones here," said Sam, as he opened the door and entered a stall.

"Good. When we see Siako's plane land. We'll wait until customs has completed their inspection, before we go anywhere near that area. If our luck continues, we'll be on our way to Seattle in no time."

They walked out of the restroom onto the concourse. "There's a good spot. I think we'll be able to see the runways from there." The three men headed for a bank of windows with a row of seats adjacent to the large windows. They walked over and stood looking out the windows. After a short time of standing there. The Colonel, went to a seat and sat down. "It may be awhile, before Siako's plane lands. We have no idea, how it went after we left."

J J stood watching the different events taking place, as he continued looking out the windows, as Sam joined Robby. "Anchorage must be a huge city, to require an airport this extensive.

"It must be close to three hundred thousand, by now."

"Wow," said J J, as he continued to watch, as if hypnotized by the great deal of action taking place on the opposite side of the large plate glass. Breaking the spell now and then, to glance over at Robby and Sam, as they now sat side by side, also watching. "Look, here's Siako's airplane now," said J J, as he pointed to the airplane shimmering in the evening sky. Robby and Sam jumped to there feet and joined J J at the windows. The three of them stood and watched as the brightly colored airplane came in and landed.

"According to the person I spoke to on the phone, customs was located at the far end of this building." They stood there and watched as the red and gold airplane taxied around. Going first one way then another, until finely parking at the far end of the building, as the Colonel had been told. "Even if it goes successfully, it will be awhile." All three men sat down to wait. About twenty minutes went by. Then thirty. J J had half turned in the seat to be able to watch the concourse.

"Robby, here comes, Siako," said J J, as he quickly stood, excitedly waving like a small child, waving to a friend. His white gloved hand, held waist high at his side, rapidly waving.

Siako walked up to the three men, now standing together to greet him. "With our presence here, Colonel. I presuppose your plan was a success."

"It's like Lizy said, Siako, it must be fate. I keep waiting for the other shoe. . . , never mind. How long before we can leave?"

"The pilot is obtaining additional fuel. As soon as that is accomplished. I would assume we can leave immediately. Is there anything I can get you to eat or drink? I would imagine we have twenty minutes or more. J J, would you like a Seattle newspaper to read, on the remainder of your trip home?"

J J stood there in silence, still wearing the sunglasses.

"What's wrong, Grampa?"

"Nothing's wrong, Sam. I was just thinking how wonderful that sounded . . . home. . . . I've waited so long, and now I may be home with my Jera Marie, by this time tomorrow." His voice cracking with emotion, as he spoke. Then reaching up he removed his sunglasses.

"I know, Grandson, not a good picture," smiled J J, as he wiped some tears from his eyes.

"Yes, Siako, I would like to read, if I was able, that is."

"One of these stores along here, might have a pair of those dollar reading glasses."

"That is a marvelous idea, Robby." The three men gathered up their gear and the four of them moved back onto the concourse.

"There's a place with newspapers and books. And look, they have a rack of reading glasses, Colonel. This is great!" said Sam, as he quickly moved ahead of the others. Sam was already at the rack looking at the glasses, when the others arrived. "Here, Grampa, try these. Stand here and see if you can read the writing," said Sam, as he handed the glasses to his grandfather pointing to a sign mounted on the rack. He then moved back as to allow him room. J J put on the reading glasses. Standing there quietly he slowly reached into his left shirt pocket. Carefully, he pulled out the picture of his, Jera Marie. Still standing there, he looked down at the picture he held gently in his white gloved hand. Then looking up from the photograph, he smiled.

"These are perfect. How do I look?" asked J J, as he stood proudly smiling from ear to ear, as he carefully returned the picture to the safety of his shirt pocket.

"I'd say our boy, looks to be a happy camper," smiled Robby.

"May I help you, gentlemen?" asked a young woman.

"Yes, miss, I would like to purchase the glasses the private has on and a Seattle newspaper. Do you require the glasses?" asked Siako.

"No, Sir, I can use another pair off the rack and scan them, Sir. Is there anything else I can help you find?"

"I think we'll just look around briefly, if we may?"

"Yes, of course you can, Sir. Just get my attention when you're ready."

"Thank you, Jennifer," said Siako seeing the girl's name tag.

"The displays in here are so colorful and shiny. But did you notice, there isn't any prices posted on anything."

"Grampa, I'll bet things are expensive. That's probably why they're not priced. If they were, people would get sticker shock. I would think in a place like this people would only buy what they needed for there trip, or maybe a gift."

"There's so many pretty things to look at here. If I had some money, I might be tempted."

"J J, like I mentioned before, money is not a problem. If you see something you require or want, tell me. If it's within my ability, it's yours."

"You and Robby have already done so much for Sam and I. I'm sure these glasses are the only thing I need from here.

"Are we about ready to go?" asked Robby, as he moved with the others through the store.

"Jennifer, we're ready," said Siako, as the four of them walked past the girl, on their way towards the checkout counter. Siako stood at the counter as the others stood back. He laid his credit card on the counter. Jennifer, took the card and returned shortly with the sales slip for him to sign. Siako signed the slip.

"Thank you. Please stop by on your next flight to Anchorage. Here's your paper," said Jennifer, as she handed Siako his credit card and the newspaper, she had laid aside earlier. The four men smiled and nodded to Jennifer, as they walked out of the store back onto the concourse headed for Siako's plane, located at the far end of the building.

"After refueling, my pilot said the plane would be standing by, at gate B8."

They moved quickly until they got to security.

"J J, put your sunglasses back on."

"Yes, Robby. What's all this about?"

"They have to check our bags for guns or explosive devices. That conveyor runs through an x-ray machine. The arch is a metal detector. We have to remove anything metallic from our pockets and walk through the arch. Even my watch may set off the alarm. J J, put anything metal you have in your pockets into that tray." J J looked at Robby and smiled. Sam, as usual had arrived first, placing the bags he carried on the conveyor to the x-ray machine, as did the others. J J watched, and did the same as they did.

"Right, J J. Just go ahead and walk through the archway," said Robby, as he pointed. J J stood erect . . . . He then walked proudly threw the archway. Immediately a loud buzzer sounded. J J stopped in his tracks and stood with his mouth open in shock! The others stood on the lee side of the arch, watching the scene taking place on the far side of the detectors.

"Here, let me scan you," said a man, as he came towards J J, with a hand held scanner. J J, quickly held up his hands, as if he were being robbed, by a man with a gun. The man waved the thing he held in his hand, up and then down both sides and back, of the entire length of J J's body. He moved to his front and started at J J's feet. The man bent and moved the hand held device up and then down both legs. He stood directly in front and did the same to both his arms. Then the man moved the device over J J's chest. As he did, the device made a buzzing sound. The man quickly looked up into J J's face and frowned. J J smiled. "What do you . . . , your dog tags, Private!" said the man, as he continued to scan. J J smiled towards his two friends and grandson, as they stood smiling in his direction. "Thank you, Sir. Enjoy your flight."

In no time the four were through security and headed to the far end of the conveyor to pick up their gear. Which by now, was in one big heap, at the very end of the conveyor. "There's gate B8 right there, Sir," said Sam, as he again moved ahead carrying the majority of the gear since leaving security. Through the window he could see the bright red and gold airplane already waiting for the four of them to board. Sam went to the door marked B8. Putting one bag down, he opened the door, it opened to a ramp that lead right to the aircraft. Sam held the door with his foot, while he bent down and picked up the bag. Then backing against the open door, he held it open for the others. With the other three through the door Sam followed. All four men moved down the ramp towards the aircraft.

"I see you made it, Colonel. Just keep your bags with you, Sir. We can store them in one of the cabins in the rear later. We can taxi in about eleven minutes, Sir," said the pilot to Siako, as they came aboard. The four men quickly moved to their seats. The others were already seated. Everyone again nodded to each other. The three put their gear in a couple of empty seats and then quickly took their seats and fastened their seat belts.

"J J, there's only one more stop, Seattle. If everything goes ok, we'll have you home in about six hours," smiled Robby, as he pulled once more on the lose end of his seat belt.

J J sat there a moment smiling, as he removed first one and then the other, of the two white gloves, placing them on the seat's armrest. He then reached up and removed his sunglasses, replacing them with his new reading glasses, he had, in the right pocket of his shirt. With glasses now switched, he reached up to the left breast pocket of his shirt, once again carefully retrieving the photograph of his Jera Marie. He sat there for awhile, staring at the photograph, not saying a thing. He then looked up smiling.

"These glasses really help. They work almost as good as the beer glass, Sam," snickered J J, as he reached up and adjusted his new glasses.

"That's great, Grampa."

Just then they heard the engines starting to whine. Within a few moments, the airplane began to move. In no time at all they were once again airborne and on their way to Seattle. The plane climbed quickly to it's cruising altitude and then leveled off.

"When you're ready we can return to the lounge, J J."

J J removed his seat belt and rose to his feet. "It looks as though he's ready, Siako," smiled Robby, as he released his belt and also stood. Sam and Siako quickly joined him and J J, all four moving from their seats into the aisle. Sam and J J gathered up the gear and the four of them started towards the lounge. No sooner had they started, than their waiter appeared once again.

"May I help you store your baggage?" asked the man, as he reached for the bags. Relinquishing the bags to him, J J quickly moved ahead to the lounge. Followed by the waiter and then the others.

"I will return for the rest of your things shortly." With that the waiter left through the rear door of the lounge.

"Let me put these gloves in Robby's bag. Robby, may I?"

"Here, J J, I can do that," smiled Robby.

"J J, here's the newspaper for you to read," smiled Siako, as he handed him the newspaper.

"Thank you, Siako."

J J took the newspaper from Siako and moved towards the recliner, looking at the paper as he did. He sat down in the recliner without taking his eyes off the paper.

"I think we may have lost his attention for awhile."

"Not at all, Robby. I can read this anytime," smiled J J, as he quickly put down the paper.

"I would rather . . . I would much rather visit, than read a lifeless piece of paper. I am happy to see, I can still see to read. These glasses Siako purchased for me, really do the trick."

The other three took their seats and the four of them, once again visited. As they talked, the waiter came and retrieved the remaining gear. The topic changed several times. The hours past swiftly. Sam was the first to fall asleep. A short time later, Robby did the same.

"J J, you must be exhausted. I will move to the forward cabin, to be with my associates. I have utterly neglected my colleagues, for an excellent reason. With me occupied with them, I would not be here, keeping you from joining Sam and Robby in joyful sleep."

"Siako, with all you've done for me, and here I am, wasting your valuable time, bending your ear. You need to be with your coworkers, discussing important company business."

"J J, I know how important tomorrow will be for you. What I assumed was, you may need a little rest, to be superlative for your home coming, in just a few short hours."

J J smiled a knowing smile. "Thank you, Siako."

"J J, I'm quite sure, the way Our Special One and your Sam, said sayonara, we are going to have sometime together to visit, in the near future," smiled Siako, as he stood and bowed closing his eyes as he did.

"Believe it," said J J, as he quickly reached for the handle on the recliner, instantly putting the chair in an upright position he rose from the chair. Standing he slowly bowed to Siako. The two men then bowed to one another. Standing erect looking directly into each others eyes, they stood there smiling. J J slowly held out his right hand to Siako. Siako reached out taking J J's hand in both his. The two men stood there as if frozen in time. Siako still holding J J's hand in his. He then shook J J's hand one time pausing for a moment, before shaking it one additional time. Siako bowed once again, putting both hands to his thighs, as he backed away bowing. Siako then stood erect. The two men smiling to one another. Siako turned and left the lounge. J J returned to the recliner, pulling the handle he quickly reclined the chair. With his new glasses in place he started to read the newspaper. Within a matter of minutes he joined Sam and Robby in blissful sleep.

"Grampa, wake up." J J awoke to the smiling face of this grandson. "We're almost there, Grampa."

"Seattle?"

"Yes, J J," said Robby and Siako primarily at the same time. J J looked to see his two friends were also standing there with Sam.

"We have forty five minutes before we land. J J, if you would like to take a quick shower and shave. You have time to do so, before we land. What I meant by quick, is our water supply is limited. Robby and Sam have already taken showers. Four or five showers, is usually tops for our resources. My colleagues and I will shower at our hotel."

"You mean I slept through you two taking a shower?"

"J J, the shower is located in the rear of the airplane. I doubt even with your excellent hearing, you could hear the shower," snickered Robby.

"Grampa, I laid out your clean clothes, razor, toothbrush and alike. They're in the first cabin. . . ."

"Behind door number three. Right?" J J went to get out of the recliner, momentarily forgetting the handle. Then quickly remembering, he grabbed the handle and uprighted the recliner. "I'll be quick."

"Grampa, I'll come with you." The two men headed towards the rear of the airplane, as Robby and Siako sat down to visit. The two re-entered the lounge with both arms laden with gear.

"You look great, J J. Are you ready?"

"There are no words on earth, to tell you how ready I am," said J J with a serious look on his face. His expression quickly changing back to his usual warm and friendly smile, as he continued through the lounge towards the forward cabin, still carrying the arm load of gear. Siako and Robby rose from their seats. Sam pausing a moment to allow the two men to move between himself and his grandfather. J J again put the gear he was carrying in the empty seat and quickly took his seat. Sam doing the same with the gear he carried. With everyone safely buckled in their seats, they waited patiently for the airplane to land. J J sat looking out the windows, watching for the lights of the city. It was fifteen minutes or more before he saw any lights. Within a few minutes of seeing the lights he felt the airplane's tires touch the runway. Another ten minutes went by before the plane ultimately came to a stop and it's engines came to rest.

"J J, I will say good-bye here. My colleagues and I will stay on board, long enough for the three of you to leave the area. It will be much less conspicuous, then having this entourage following along. The pilot informed me earlier, he would be docking the airplane on concourse C and that the main part of the terminal would be located to the left," said Siako, as everyone removed their seat belts and the four of them stood.

J J and Siako embraced one another. Then breaking their embrace, Siako turned and shook hands with Robby and Sam. Then moving into the aisle, each of the three men grabbing an arm load of gear. The waiter at this time was already in the process of unlocking and opening the plane's door.

"The words, thank you, don't even come close, Siako."

Then turning, J J quickly headed for the open door, with Sam and Robby following close behind. The three nodded to the pilot, seeing him through the open cockpit door, on their way. They exited the airplane on a ramp hooked directly to the building. Upon entering the building, Sam quickly took the lead. "I know the quickest way from here, guys."

"Lead the way, Sam."

The three men entered the concourse walking at a much faster pace then the people already walking there. J J looking at as much as he could take in, at the speed they were walking. They were in the main lobby in a matter of minutes. "Sam, hold up a minute. Instead of taking a cab this time of morning. Let's rent a car," said Robby, as he quickly turned leaving J J and Sam standing in the lobby. Sam stood watching, as his grandfather surveyed the magnitude of the main lobby. J J slowly turning as not to miss anything from his position, located approximately in the center of the huge lobby.

PROMISES KEPT

"Come on, Grampa."

In no time they caught up with Robby standing at the escalators. "This way we'll have a car, if and when we need it," said Robby, as he looked towards them raising and lowering his eyebrows as he did.

Sam and Robby stood there a moment with J J. The two of them watching J J, as he watched the escalators. Then the two of them moved onto the escalators quickly turning to watch J J. He hastily stepped onto the moving stairs and all three rode them down to the baggage level. This level had an area dedicated to the different car rental companies. They stood there a moment looking. All the car rental booths were unoccupied.

"Great. You would think, they would have at least one booth open, in an airport this size." No sooner had the Colonel said those words, than a woman appeared in the Avis booth. The three men quickly headed in her direction.

"How may I help you gentlemen, this beautiful morning?"

"We need a car."

"We have whatever you need, Sir. From compacts through full-size, including minivans and convertibles, are available for your comfort, Sir."

"We'll take a minivan, Miss."

"I'll need your drivers license and a major credit card, Sir. No pun intended, Sir," smiled the woman.

"Right." snickered Robby.

The Colonel and the Avis agent finished their paper work, as the other two stood back. J J continuing not only to watch them, but also trying to observe everything within his field of view. In the short time since their arrival, the airport had become busier. "Here's your keys, Colonel. You'll find your minivan in the parking garage across from the terminal. To get there, you take the escalators to the fourth floor, then take the sky-walk across to the parking garage, your van is located on the second floor. Thank you, Colonel, for choosing, Avis "we try harder."

"Thank you, Miss," smiled Robby, as he took the keys. The Colonel turned and rejoined Sam and J J. Holding out his right hand, dangling the keys between his thumb and fore finger. "Let's hit the road, guys."

The three men headed back through the lobby towards the escalators, they proceeded to ascend to the next level. Once on the fourth floor, the three quickly moved across the sky-walk. As the three approached the large doors they automatically opened. J J stopped, then backing a few steps he stood, as Robby and Sam continued on through the open doors. The doors then closed with Robby and Sam on one side and J J still standing on the other just out of range of the sensor that operated the automatic doors. Once outside, Sam quickly realized his grandfather, didn't come through the open doors. He promptly turned to see him still standing in the terminal. "Grampa, just walk forward a little," said Sam, as he waved to his grandfather, in a come-to-me motion. As Robby stood watching, J J walked forward as instructed and the automatic doors abruptly opened and J J slowly exited the terminal. He walked up to Robby and Sam, quickly turning to watch the doors as he did. In a matter of seconds the doors closed. This time with all three men outside the terminal. J J turned to Robby and Sam shaking his head.

"I know, believe it."

"Believe it, wait until you hear this, Guys." J J and Sam stood looking at Robby. "The van is located on the second floor in a space marked, 'J' seventy two." The three men looked at one another, smiling and shaking their heads, at the signs of fate shown to them once again. They turned and all three headed for the escalator, in search of space 'J' seventy two. "That must be it up there, it's the only van." The three men stood looking up at the big green J, painted on the cement support column, and then down to the 72 painted on the concert floor at the van's parking space. All three men stood there in silence. Robby quickly unlocked the back door of the van and all three men abruptly threw the gear they had been carrying into the rear of the van. Robby went to the driver's door. Opening the door, he immediately pushed the power door lock button. J J and Sam were on the passenger side. Hearing the power door locks, Sam opened the front door for his grandfather. J J quickly climbed into the van and Sam closed the door. Opening the van's sliding side door, Sam jumped in the rear seat and closed the door. "Put your seat belt on, Grampa. It's by you're right shoulder. Just pull it out and fasten it down on the left side of your seat," said Sam, as he fastened his own seat belt. Robby started the van's engine and backed out of space 'J' seventy two. Driving out of the parking garage the three were welcomed by the dawning of another potentialy beautiful Northwest summer day, unfolding on the road before them.

"J J how far is your house from here?"

"Robby, I don't have any idea, where here is. This doesn't look anything like Boeing Field to me."

"Robby, stay in the left lane. Grampa, this is Sea-Tac airport."

"Sea-Tac. That's good," said J J, as he exhaled deeply wiping his forehead with the back of his right hand. "I thought maybe my cheese had slipped off my cracker."

"No, Grampa," snickered Sam, as he and Robby both stared at his grandfather.

In the eastern sky they could now see the rising sun. Just to the south of the brilliant sun rising in the morning sky, they could also see Mt. Rainier. "Look! Isn't that beautiful. We're near Seattle all right, there's no mistaking that sight, Robby," said J J, as he reached to his right shirt pocket and pulled out his sunglasses. Putting them on he continued to watch out the van's windows.

"Grampa, Sea-Tac is located about halfway between Seattle and Tacoma, three or four miles west of Kent."

"I was hoping my memory was better than that. In that case Robby, I would guess maybe fifteen miles to the northwest of here. Our house is located near Greenwood over looking Shilshole Bay."

"What time is it, Robby?"

"I set my watch in Anchorage, J J. It's just after six."

"The van's clock says the same, Colonel," said Sam, as he held his arm up between the two front seats, pointing to the digital clock.

"This vehicle is really something. It has seats for what, seven or eight people? It's so quiet, even with my excellent hearing, I can hardly hear that it is even running. What make of vehicle is this?"

"I have no idea, J J," said Robby, as he looked up into the mirror, for some assistance from Sam.

"It's a Dodge Caravan, Grampa."

"It's amazing. Except for the mountain, I don't recognize anything. Is it my memory, or have things really changed that much?"

"You definitely won't recognize the next part of our journey, Grampa. We'll be on I-5 going north."

Watching the road while looking directly into the bright morning sunshine, still trying to catch J J's reaction to it all. Just then the traffic abruptly stopped. Catching Robby a bit by surprise he slammed on the brakes. The van quickly came to a stop without sliding. "I'd say, the brakes work."

"That's for sure, Robby. I must have a different perception of speed. I was sure you wouldn't get stopped without sliding into that car. This belt also works pretty good," said J J, as he pulled out on the belt across his chest and then released it.

"This thing must have anti-lock brakes, otherwise we would have just done a number on that guy," said Robby, as he pointed to the car just ahead. They started moving once again headed for Interstate 5 northbound. The van moved down the hill and onto the I-5 freeway headed north. It was already quite busy with Friday morning commuters.

"Didn't, Tye Kim, use an I-5 reference, in respect to where he lived?"

"Yes, he did, Grampa. It's the same Interstate. It runs from, Canada to Mexico, Grampa."

"Believe it."

J J sat there watching all the different kinds of cars, trying hard to see the faces on some of the people they passed and on the ones that went speeding past them.

"There's so much to watch. This highway's so big and yet look how busy. . . . There's Boeing Field!" said J J, as he pointed out the left side of the fast moving van. He quickly turned and looked out the rear window of the van. "I know where we're at now!" smiled J J, as he sat turned enough in his seat to look out the rear of the van. "Mt. Rainier is right in line when you look south along Boeing's runway," said J J, as he turned once again looking out the van's windshield. "Look! Look at the size of those buildings. They must be as tall as the 'Empire State Building."

"Not quite, Grampa. The freeway goes right near those big buildings. You'll get a close look at them. Grampa, we call these highways freeways. I-5 is just one of the many freeways in the Seattle area."

A minute or so later, the traffic began to slow. In a matter of just a few seconds, they were moving about the speed of a fast walk.

"Look at all these people. And all these cars!"

"Yes, J J. And a large percentage of these cars, are Japanese."

J J quickly turned towards Robby. "Japanese?"

"That's right, Grampa. One of the most popular cars in America, right now, is the Honda. And it's Japanese. There's a Honda plant somewhere on the east coast, I don't know where. So now some of them are being made in the United States. Right now I can see. . . ," said Sam, as he quickly turned looking out the windows of the vehicle. "I can see at least ten Hondas, right now. And that's just the Hondas. That doesn't even begin to count the Toyota, pick-ups and other makes. Grampa, I would guess over half the vehicles we can see from here right now, are Japanese."

"I thought you said we won!"

A silence came over them as they sat there in the van, amongst the multitude of vehicles. The traffic started moving a little faster and before long they were once again speeding along with the other traffic.

"How fast are we going, Robby.?"

"About seventy, J J."

"Seventy miles an hour! Most of the cars passing us, must be doing seventy five or eighty. Isn't there any speed limits anymore?"

"Yes, there are, Grampa. I think it's sixty through here."

"The speed limit is sixty. And yet we're doing seventy and most everyone else is driving seventy five and eighty. So much for speed limits."

"Watch what happens if any one of them spot a highway patrol car. If their caught on radar going eighty, they may have to sell the farm to pay the ticket."

"How much?"

"Three hundred and fifty dollars or more. Half the price of a new Chevy, in nineteen forty one."

J J sat there thinking about what Sam said. "I'll bet that slows them down. I have another question? Just a few short minutes ago, we were almost at a stand still, and now we're moving faster then before. What happened that slowed us to nearly a stop, in the first place?"

"That is one of the unanswered mysteries of modern times, J J."

They continued towards the tall buildings. The traffic once again slowing as they approached the city's center.

"What's that over there?" asked J J, as he pointed through the van's windshield.

"That's the Seattle Kingdome, Grampa. That's where the Seattle Mariners, play baseball, and the Seattle Seahawks play football."

"They play baseball and football, inside a building? I know, Sam, believe it. . . . Not at the same time, right."

"No, not at the same time. They change the field layout inside, first."

"There's Interstate 90. We would take that freeway if we wanted to go to Mercer Island, Issaquah or even Spokane, Grampa."

Still traveling at near the speed limit. The van past near the bases of the towering buildings. The freeway then almost becoming a tunnel, as it ribboned it's way through city center.

"What's that?"

"That's the Space Needle."

"What's it for?"

"Beats me, Grampa. All I know is there's a restaurant in the dish thing on top," said Sam, as him and J J both looked towards Robby.

"The Space Needle, was part of the original exhibit at the 1964 Seattle, Worlds Fair. After the fair was over, it became a permanent part of Seattle's skyline."

"That's right, Colonel, I had forgotten. See, Grampa, we're all going to learn from showing you things."

"I've recognized some of the names, printed on those big green signs, I've seen along this freeway. They're names of streets. I can't see the streets from here but that's what they are?"

"That's right, Grampa, they are. Those big green signs tell the driver's what's coming in advance, so they can plan ahead to be in the proper lane, if they need to take the next off ramp to a particular street."

"Sam, couldn't we have taken Columbia street to highway 99?"

"Yes, Grampa, we could. I just thought the freeway would be faster."

"I'm sure your right, Sam, as long as this freeway doesn't stop."

"Right, J J. You can see that possibly happening. Can you?"

"Robby, what I've seen of these freeways, all it would take is one stalled car or even a flat tire and this so called freeway, would be better known as a parking lot."

"Right," snickered Robby.

No sooner than those words had left J J's mouth, there was a river of flickering red tail lights appearing ahead by the thousands. A red ribbon running to infinity. Traffic immediately slowed.

"J J, you may have, in a very short time, seen both the advantages and disadvantages of freeways," smiled Robby, as the van moved along at a much slower pace.

"How fast are we going now, Robby?" asked J J, as he leaned in Robby's direction trying to see what he thought, 'may be the van's speedometer.'

"J J, we're still going thirty five."

"After going as fast as we were, it seems now, we're barely moving."

"As slow as we're moving, Grampa, it's still usually faster to take the freeway, than the surface streets."

"I'm sure you know the best way, Sam."

With that said, J J grew silent. He sat there staring through the van's windshield, thinking, 'it was as though the van had some how become Jules Verne's, "Time Machine," and he was it's passenger moving through time. The city he had been raised in, could have just as easily been a city on some distant planet. The only thing he could say for sure, that was still the same, was the city's name, Seattle, and some of the names he had seen going by on those big green signs.'

Robby was driving along also thinking, 'this was one mission he was very happy to be apart of. A mission to bring a man home to his family. A man, his own father felt, his last few years of life, responsible for leaving behind on an island, possibly being killed or captured by the enemy. He now knew, even though his father felt in heart and mind it to be true, it was never the case.'

The van continued north along Interstate 5. J J again looked out the driver's side as they moved past Lake Union. Bringing him back to reality.

"Look at the hills, look how they're covered with houses, everywhere you look, in all directions, as far as the eye can see, since we drove by Boeing Field, it's been that way. This city is enormous. It must be that way on the Bellevue side of Lake Washington, too."

"It is, Grampa. Robby, take the next exit and go west."

The van left the freeway and then headed west on a two lane road. J J again sat quietly watching. The van moved down a hill into the small community of Greenwood. That was obviously the town's name, beings the name Greenwood was posted on a good many signs and buildings on both sides of the street. Even though the two lane road was quite busy with commuters, Greenwood itself was just starting to come to life, on this beautiful July day. "There's so many people, even the small town of Greenwood is huge. Everything is so close together." The light turned red and the van came to a stop at the crosswalk. J J sat looking in both directions as they sat waiting for the light. "You're right about the cars, Sam. I've been watching and I haven't seen any names of cars I recognize. I have seen some trucks with Chevrolet and Ford on their tailgates. I've also seen the name Toyota a lot. Sam, I see why the freeway's faster."

"Why is that, Grampa?"

"All these traffic signals, they're at every major intersection. You spend half your time waiting for a green light."

"Right," snickered Robby.

"I recognize some of the buildings here in Greenwood. It's not very far now."

The light turned green and the van continued through the intersection and on through the town of Greenwood. Within just a few short minutes they were approaching the three way intersections of 85th and Loyal Way and NW. 32nd.

"We turn left here and go south to 77th."

"Which way, Sam."

"I'm sorry, Colonel. That way," said Sam, as he pointed straight south on 32nd. "You turn right on 77th. and then left onto 34th. and our house is . . . was the third house on the left facing west."

The van turned onto 77th. and moved to the corner slowly making the turn onto 34th. J J tried to move to the front edge of his seat, but he was held in place by the van's set belt. They all sat watching the left side of the street. Sam sat not saying a word, of course knowing, it was no longer the third house, on the east side of 34th street.

"Robby," whispered J J softly, as he slowly raised his left hand pointing, as he removed his sunglasses with his right.

Robby parked the van on the west side of the street. Sitting there a moment, before putting the van into park and turning off the engine. All three men just sat there in silence watching the house, in the morning calm, it casting long shadows in the rising sunshine, of this bright July morning.

J J sat listening to the silence. Time came to a stand still, as he sat there remembering. Staring at the home, until a few short days ago, he thought, 'he was never going to see again.'

"What do we do now?" asked Sam, breaking the silence. J J quickly turned, looking at his grandson a bit wide-eyed. "What's wrong, Grampa?" J J not saying a word, just sat slowly shaking his head.

"Sam, it's only 0645, I would think your grandmother may still be in bed. Why don't you go and wake her. Tell her you have some friends arriving shortly, you want her to meet. Then at least, she'll be up and dressed, when you bring the two of us in, Sam."

"Good idea, Colonel," said Sam, as he unfastened his seat belt and opened the van's sliding door and quickly stepped out of the van onto the sidewalk, closing the sliding door quietly. Sam then moved to the front of the van, pausing a second, he stood looking through the windshield at his grandfather. Smiling he gave him a thumbs up and then continued towards the house.

The only sound J J could hear, was the pounding of his own heartbeat. His mind raced, as he watched his grandson move up the concrete walk, that he poured so many years before and onto the porch. J J sat there holding his breath as Sam reached for the doorbell. Releasing his breath as he saw Sam release the doorbell. In a matter of moments the door slowly opened a crack.

"J J, J J, how?" asked Marie, with a obvious look of surprise, quickly changing to one of shear joy, as she opened the door wide.

"Hi, Gramma."

J J sat straining his eyes, trying to see into the morning shadows to no avail, he couldn't see the person who had opened the door for his grandson.

"J J, come in my boy. What are you doing here?" asked Marie, as she stood there in the doorway, in the flowered housecoat, his mother had given her that Christmas, with a big smile on her face. Sam entered the house, closing the door behind, as he did. Sam and his grandmother walked through the house towards the kitchen. Upon entering the kitchen the aroma of fresh baked cookies, still lingered from the previous evenings bake-a-thon. "J J, I was under the impression you would be gone much longer than this."

"Gramma, I have someone I want you to meet."

"You have someone, J J?"

"Yes, Gramma. Why don't you go finish getting dressed and I'll introduce you."

"They're here now?" asked Marie with excitement showing in her voice, as she quickly glanced over her grandson's shoulder.

"They'll be here shortly, Gramma."

"Does your mother know?"

"No, Gramma, you're the first."

"I'm so excited for you, J J," smiled Marie, as she quickly hugged the grandson towering over her.

"Thank you, for coming and sharing this with me, J J. I'll hurry and make myself presentable for your friend. You make some tea and coffee and promise me, you won't disappear."

"I promise, Gramma."

"Help yourself to some cookies. They're fresh, I just made them last night. I won't be long."

"I wonder what's taking, Sam, so long?" asked J J, still sitting on the edge of his seat, somewhat restrained by his loosened seat belt.

The door opened and Sam came running out of the house and off the porch towards the driver's side window.

"Gramma's getting herself presentable, she'll be just a few minutes. She thinks I have a friend, wait . . . she thinks I'm bringing my girl. . . !" snickered Sam. "She thinks it's my girlfriend!" said Sam, as he quickly turned back and looked towards the house.

"What kind of cookie is. . . ? Never mind, I can smell it, it's oatmeal. I'll have one, Sam." Sam reached over to his Grandfather, handing him a cookie. J J carefully took the cookie and held it near his nose. He sat there a moment with his eyes closed taking in the aroma of the cookie, as if he were a fine wine taster, and he was the master at approving a rare vintage wine.

"Hey, Private."

"Sorry, Colonel, here," said Sam, as he handed Robby a cookie. The three men smiled at one another, as they enjoyed their cookies.

"What do you think we should do now?"

"Go back inside and be there. So when she is ready you can signal us to come in. Sam, how is your grandmothers physical condition? She doesn't have any heart problems?"

"No, not that I know of," said Sam, pausing a moment, as he looked over at his grandfather. "She's . . . in great shape."

"Signal us when you think she's ready."

Sam nodded as he quickly turned and ran towards the house, back up the walk missing all the steps but one as he leaped onto the porch. Having left the door ajar he re-entered the house and moved quickly back to the kitchen, as to be there upon her return.

"J J, are your friends here?" asked Marie, anxiously.

"They'll be here shortly," smiled Sam, as he prepared the tea and coffee, as requested.

"You have a seat and I'll check and see if they're here," said Sam, as he pulled a chair from the table for her. Marie sat, as her grandson held the chair. "You sit here and I'll go check. All right?"

"Yes, of course, J J," smiled Marie, as she sat thinking as he walked away, 'how excited he was for her to meet his young lady friend.' Sam moved back through the house to the front door. Opening the door he stepped out onto the porch. Marie sat there straightening her summer dress, so as to look as good as possible for J J's new friends.

"There's Sam, Robby."

"Are you ready, J J?"

'Was he ready? So many times he had rehearsed this moment in his mind. The things he would say if he ever again had the chance to see his lovely bride and now his chance was at hand.' He abruptly turned to open the door. Taking a second to figure out just how the door opened. Once doing so, he quickly opened the door and started to step out of the van, forgetting his seat belt. Realizing his error, he quickly tried frustratingly to unfastened the belt. Robby, noticing his predicament, immediately reached over and hit the button that released the seat belt. Free at last, J J quickly stepped out of the van, closing the door he stood there a moment on the sidewalk. Using the van's side window's reflection, he straighten his tie, also checking his uniform, including a quick check of his fly. Then walking around the front of the van he met up with Robby, and the two of them headed for the house. They crossed the street and started up the walk.

J J's feet felt heavier then he could ever remember. All the years his energy had gone into survival, not dealing with emotion. The material changes he had seen were nothing, compared with the emotional changes that were taking place. "I told Lizy, the only thing I was afraid of, was being alone . . . I was wrong."

"I have no idea what your going through, J J. All I can say to you is, Sam and myself and now your Jera Marie, are here to help," said Robby, as he moved up onto the porch. Robby turned to see J J still standing at the base of the steps.

Sam stood just inside holding the door open, for J J and Robby to enter. J J slowly climbed the steps observantly rubbing the hand rails that were worn smooth, also looking down at the worn weathered steps. 'He thought of the similarities, of himself and of the old house, when he left to fight for his country, the house was all new, and he was a young man.' J J moved up on the porch and stood next to Robby.

"Come in. Gramma's, waiting in the kitchen."

J J and Robby entered the living room. Sam closed the door and headed for the kitchen. Robby followed Sam, while J J moved into the main part of the living room. Standing next to a table, he looked around the room. Slowly turning, as not to miss anything. The two men re-entered the living room and stood quietly waiting. J J turned to them and smiled. The three once again headed for the kitchen. Upon entering the kitchen they found Marie sitting at the kitchen table waiting patiently for her grandson's return. Hearing them enter, she stood to greet her grandson's friends. Seeing the three men, she smiled and moved to one side to look past the men. The morning sun shining brightly through the kitchen window, illuminated the area behind her grandson and his two friends.

Marie stood smiling, looking directly at her grandson. Not wanting to show any disappointment to him, of 'not seeing a young lady present, to be introduced.' Her warm smile slowly changed, to a look of concentration, as she looked over towards the two men standing with her grandson, one man standing slightly behind and in the shadow of the other.

"Do . . . I know you?" asked Marie, as she stood staring intently.

"No. Marie, you knew my father."

"Yes . . . J J's friend, Robby," said Marie, as the warm smile returned.

"That's right, Marie. Marie, would you mind calling me, Robby."

"It would be my pleasure, Robby."

J J stood there seeing his Jera Marie, for the first time. Not as he had remembered, but as she was, an elderly woman with beautiful silver gray hair. All those years, he had only thought of her as memory dictated. A flood of emotions came rushing forth. The realization of just how much had gone by. The many years that were gone, never to be recaptured. The birth of their son, a lifetime of sunsets, they could have shared together. Not only the years of enjoyment but also the many trials and tribulations couples often share, growing old together. With each rapid beat of his heart his mind raced with thoughts like these.

"Robby, all these years I've wonder what happened to your father. Robby, your father came here to our home, to share with me, just how my J J was lost and how he may never be coming home. After Robby did that for his friend J J, his son and his new young wife. I never saw him again. I did receive cards for a time and then, nothing. I've never heard from him again."

"Marie, my father was killed in Korea."

"I was afraid . . . I'm terribly sorry, Robby."

"Thank you, Marie."

A silence came over them as they stood together, each not knowing quite what to say.

"Marie, that was a long time ago."

"Yes, Robby it was. But I'll never forget how your father and I felt the day he came. To tell me how 'the only man I ever loved, was gone.' He blamed himself for J J's disappearance. I did everything, I could, to try and change that notion. But when your father left that evening, I knew I had failed."

"Marie, your grandson and I have brought you someone, that will help you and perhaps help my father rest more comfortably." Marie stood there a bit puzzled by what Robby was saying.

With his right hand out stretched, J J moved slowly forward. Marie looked at the out stretched closed hand, as the hand slowly opened, Marie leaned forward to look into the open hand. She slowly reached out and carefully picked up the object, the open hand was holding.

"It's beautiful. . . . It's a ring!" said Marie, as she stood there a moment holding up the ring between her thumb and forefinger for everyone to clearly see. Robby and Sam quickly looked at one another, both shrugging their shoulders, wondering to themselves. 'Where did that come from?'

"Jera Marie, I promised you a pearl . . . I've always tried to keep the promises, I make . . . I'm so sorry it took me so long to keep this one, and my promise, to return home. Now, those promises have been fulfilled." J J's lower lip quivered, as the emotions of many years filled his eyes with tears and his voice shook as he began to sob uncontrollably. Inhaling deeply he tried hard to calm himself, enough to continue. "Jera Marie, our grandson, Robby and many others, with help from Our Heavenly Father, have brought me home to you," smiled J J, as he stood looking at his Jera Marie. . . .

"J J, how is this . . . possible. . . ?" asked Marie, her voice shaking, as she looked up from the ring, into her grandson's eyes, for answers.

Sam moved over next to his grandfather. "Gramma, this is . . . 'the only man you ever loved," smiled Sam. Carefully reaching out, Sam gently took her hand in his. The hand still holding the ring. Sam slowly turned to his grandfather and delicately placed her hand in his. Holding her hand, J J carefully took the ring from her hand. Still looking up at her grandson, Marie slowly turned, to look into the eyes of the man that stood before her holding her hand. Her eyes began to fill with tears as she stood there totally overwhelmed by what was happening. Carefully placing the ring he held, on the ring finger of her left hand, J J noticed a ring worn thin by time encircling that domain. Speechlessly Marie watched what was taking place. "Gramma, he is everything you always said he was and more," whispered Sam smiling, as tears ran down both sides of his face.

Marie and J J, closed their eyes, as J J held her hand in his. The two of them slowly weaving back and forth, as Sam and Robby heard them say. "Let each days strength, sufficient be, to meet the needs, that we shall see," whispered the two, simultaneously.

"To love, with love, from love. Jera Marie, I am home."

The four stood there in silence, not a dry eye amongst them.

"Gramma, are you all right?" asked Sam, as he stood there unable to wait any longer. Seeing the two of them together for the first time in his life, except for old photographs taken over half a century earlier.

"I can hear you, J J. I just don't want this dream I'm having to come to an end. Right now, I can not only hear your voice and feel your presence. I can also feel and hear your grampa is here with us, J J."

"It's not a dream," said all three men softly, at the same time. Marie slowly opening and closing her eyes, repeatedly in disbelief. Once again looking into the eyes of the man she now knew was her, J J.

"Jera, may I. . . ." J J pulled her close, then carefully taking her in his arms they became one. Marie's sobbing slowly disapated, as J J held her in his arms. Then moving slightly apart, they again looked into each others eyes, and smiles formed on their faces. "Jera, I love you. Like I said, Sam, she's as beautiful as ever." Marie stood there trying to speak.

"J J. . . I . . . I told you, 'I would wait for you, for as long as it takes.' J J, by the looks of you and I . . . it almost, took too long," smiled Marie, as she looked up at the elderly man standing before her. Smiling at her with the same smile and eyes, that lovingly said good-bye to her, on that pier so many years earlier.

"If I thought for a moment, it would have been possible, I would have swam home, to you, my Jera Marie. Impossible as it may . . . I'm home and I feel the need to say this with every beat of my heart, I love you, Jera Marie," smiled J J, as he held his Jera Marie in his arms. Then looking over her head, J J saw the poem still hanging above the kitchen window, where he had hung it some fifty years earlier. Robby and Sam looked to where J J was staring and also saw the poem.

"I don't know about you Sam, but I feel, I have just witnessed the completion of an amazing miracle."

"Me too, Robby," smiled Sam, as the two of them moved past J J and Marie still hugging, as they walked over to the kitchen table. "Robby, would you like a cup of coffee?"

"Yes, I would. I'd also like a few more of those marvelous cookies."

"No problem, Colonel."

J J and Jera broke their embrace and now stood side by side, arm and arm watching their grandson. "Sam's a wonderful young man. I'm so proud of what you and his mother have accomplished," whispered J J into Marie's left ear, as she looked from the poem, over towards her grandson.

"J J, we must call your mother. . . . We can't tell her on the phone," said Marie, as she looked from her grandson, back up to J J standing next to her.

"Gramma, just call mom and ask her to stop by this morning and have breakfast with you, on her way to work."

"Good idea, J J. She'll think I'm a little touched. But what's new, she thinks I lose it now and then, as it is. If I told her you two were here, she'd most definitely have the men in the white coats with her, when she came," chuckled Marie with tears still lingering.

"Gramma, Grampa and I, thought . . . we thought I could go by the name Sam. That's, if it's all right with you, Gramma?" Marie stood there with J J, the two of them looking over towards their grandson. Then turning she again looked up at J J and smiled.

"That's a wonderful idea, J J. I'm sure your father, our son would be pleased."

Sam took three cups and sat them on the table. He then turned and picked up the coffee pot and walked over and filled the three cups to the brim. "Grampa, I'll see if Gramma has anything good in here for you to drink," said Sam, as he raised and lowered his eyebrows as he returned the coffee pot and then walked towards the refrigerator.

"There's some fresh buttermilk, I brought home yesterday."

"Yuck!"

"J J love . . . loves buttermilk."

"I used to drink coffee, too. I'll try the buttermilk, Sam," smiled J J, as he looked down at Jera Marie.

"If you say so, Grampa," said Sam shaking his head, as his upper body quivered, as he walked towards the table carrying the buttermilk, grabbing a glass from the cupboard on the way.

"I'll call, Dorris." Marie moved from J J's side, holding his hand until the last possible second. Releasing his hand she went to call Dorris. Gone less than a minute, she returned with a cordless phone held to her right ear. "It's ringing. Dorris, It's me . . . I'm sorry, did I wake you. . . ? Good, I . . . I'm fine. I was wondering if you could stop by this morning and have breakfast with me. . . ? No, here at my little house. What. . . ? Ok, I'll see you shortly, dear." Marie stood there a moment a bit mystified. She then walked over to the table and laid the phone down. "That's odd."

"What is, Gramma?"

"Your mother said there were two calls on her answering machine. One from some reporter. She said he wanted to talk to her about her son. The other was from a friend of yours, named Tye. She said she'd tell me more, when she got here," smiled Marie, as she turned and walked back to J J.

All three men quickly looked at one another.

"She was already up and dressed. She said for some reason she couldn't sleep. We all know now why her and I, couldn't sleep. It was worth it," smiled Marie, as she put her arms around J J, and once again hugged him tightly.

"I have your coffee Gramma, and Grampa's buttermilk," said Sam, as his body once again shuttered at the thought of 'anyone drinking that stuff.'

Marie and J J walked over to the table and joined Sam and Robby. The four of them sat there in silence, smiling at one another, as they sat drinking and enjoying their cookies.

"How did this possibly come to pass? How is it possible you are sitting here with me, J J?"

"Jera, our grandson and three of his friends found me, on this island.

The island where I've lived, these last fifty years."

"What kind of people. . . ?"

"Just one . . . kind, Jera."

"What kind of people wouldn't help someone get home to their family, after all these years?" asked Marie with hostility showing in her voice.

The three men all sat smiling at Marie.

"Gramma, until five days ago, Grampa, was on that island alone."

Marie's eyes filled with tears, as she gripped J J's hand tightly, as both his right and her left hand laid together intertwined on the table just in front of where they were sitting.

"It's obvious, it's true, because you're here with me, J J. But, how could it be possible? The odds must be absolutely astronomical."

All three men just smiled and shrugged their shoulders, as they softly said. "Believe it."

"Marie, there's only one explanation that makes any sense at all."

"What could that possibly be, Robby?"

"It's like Lizy . . . it's fate," smiled Robby.

A silence once again befell the four as they sat there together.

"It's unanswered prayers, finally answered," smiled J J.
TIME MOVES ON!

First, I would like to thank you, for taking time to read J J.

THANK YOU.....

If you found the story enjoyable, I personally invite you to give a gift wrapped copy of J J, to a friend or family. Please E-mail me at:

jhwatrous@oergonsales.com

or send $19.95 for each copy. Include $4.05 for shipping and handling for each copy in check or money order, and the address for each copy. If you wish, include a personal note to each of your friends, to be received with their gift wrapped copy.

Pass Creek Publishing
P.O. Box 1179
Cottage Grove,
Oregon 97424